BABY'S BREATH

ALSO BY LYNNE HUGO

A Progress of Miracles
The Time Change

ALSO BY ANNA TUTTLE VILLEGAS

All We Know of Heaven

ALSO BY LYNNE HUGO AND
ANNA TUTTLE VILLEGAS

Swimming Lessons

Baby's Breath

Lynne Hugo

A N D

Anna Tuttle Villegas

Synergistic Press   San Francisco

Copyright © 2000 by Lynne Hugo and Anna Tuttle Villegas

All rights reserved.
No part of this book may be reproduced or used in any form
without permission in writing from the Publisher.

Library of Congress Cataloging-in-Publication Data
Hugo, Lynne.
Baby's breath : a novel / Lynne Hugo and
Anna Tuttle Villegas. — 1st ed.
p.   cm.
ISBN 0-912184-13-2
1. Mothers and daughters—Fiction.
2. Infanticide—Fiction.
I. Villegas, Anna Tuttle.   II. Title.
PS3558.U395 B3   2000
813'.54—dc21   00-027663

Design and composition by Wilsted & Taylor

Printed in the United States of America on acid-free paper

FIRST EDITION

1   2   3   4   5   6   7   8   9   10

SYNERGISTIC PRESS
3965 SACRAMENTO STREET
SAN FRANCISCO, CALIFORNIA 94118
WWW.SYNERGISTICBOOKS.COM

Belief is the lifeblood of love.

This book is for the women who gave us theirs:
ANNA FUNDULAKIS TUTTLE
(1914–1953)
and
EVELYN MEYER HUGO,
our mothers

And for our children,
DAVID, BROOKE, AND ADRIA,
to whom we give ours

And she went, and sat her down . . .
a good way off, as it were a bowshot:
for she said, Let me not see the death
of the child. And she sat over against
him, and lifted up her voice, and wept.

GENESIS 21.16

And there is hope in thine end . . .
that thy children shall come again
to their own border.

JEREMIAH 31.17

CHAPTER

1

A single eye peeped back at her, glassy and peaceful. *Abandoned but resigned,* Leah thought. *I could take a lesson.*

She lifted the panda out of the box she'd dragged from the back of her daughter's closet. The longest-lived, the favorite—if a mother could guess a favorite based on which stuffed animal her introverted daughter slept with—Lazzie had been the last of the menagerie to be boxed when Allie packed for college. She'd been adamant they were *all* going with her, matted, worn, dirty as they were, ignoring Leah's protests about allowing space for her roommate. Only her grandmother's long dying and the decision that she'd have to fly to school instead of driving cross-country with her mother changed her mind. But when she came home the Christmas of her freshman year, Allie never mentioned taking the zoo back to Berkeley with her. And now *she* wasn't even coming home for the summer. So much for childhood, for childhood's friends, so much for seeing her mother. Some days, some weeks, Allie's absence was still like the aftermath of a punch to the stomach. Just *live with it,* she'd learned, and let something else live alongside the empty place.

Leah's nose tingled while she fought a sneeze long enough to whip a hand around to brace the small of her back. Fifty years and five months old. Still, her pesky lower back was really the only sign of it. People always thought her much younger, her hair long and darkly, wildly, wavy as ever. There was still time for a life. Nineteen ninety-seven had taken her mother to the grave next to her father's, and her daughter to college; Leah had become an expert mourner. But there was still time to have a life, wholly, instead of in dribs and drabs, stolen or broken, and to have it without guilt.

"Allie got an apartment in Berkeley, and a summer job, waitressing . . . so I'm making her room into a studio!" Leah sang out to Dave Allen, the flirty, sloe-eyed bartender whose house adjoined hers. The two-bedroom rowhouse had been perfect for a single mother and her child. Under an oak canopy, the cobbled one-way street was intense with color splashing from window boxes and planters by wrought-iron gates, a charming, almost European atmosphere as Leah knew Europe: from slides in art school classes.

She was carrying a load of Allie's high school notebooks to the trash and absorbing the sunny-cool splendor of a May day, the sort of day that makes people witlessly happy.

"Need a hand?" Dave called back, inspecting the polish on his baby, a Nissan sports coupe, before heading toward his door. He was probably twenty-five years younger than Leah, but turned his charm on her like a sprinkler. Last year Leah had gone so far as to wish he'd try to date Allie. She'd have refused permission, of course, but Allie needed the attention of someone like Dave, drop-dead handsome and outgoing, to boost her confidence. But Dave was either attracted to older women or just didn't care for Allie's look. Leah had seen the tall, slender model-type he was dating now, bouncy and vivacious, nothing like Allie, whom some of her teachers had described as sullen. Leah thought she just looked like a girl who needed to be drawn out of herself, to have her prettiness proven by the attention of a boyfriend. Not that Leah hadn't told her a million times how pretty she was, at which Allie rolled her eyes in disgust.

"You know, actually, I might need a little help," she answered. "Not yet, though. I'm not that far along. But I want to dismantle the painting table in the basement and set it up in the studio. It's big and it's heavy—I'll never be able to carry it."

"No problem. Just yell," he waved. And she would. By tomorrow she should have the closet emptied. If Allie was making a life elsewhere on her own, without Leah, then surely she didn't need her own room in her mother's house anymore. Leah would never have taken it away, especially not from the teenage Allie, who'd been more likely to shun company than accept Leah's invitation to watch a video and share a bowl of popcorn on Saturday nights after fatigue drove Leah away from her canvas. Not even when the first stroke had disabled Esther to speechlessness and baby food, not when Leah's only choices for her mother had been a nursing home or hers; even then she hadn't flinched, just moved Esther into her own bedroom, rather than switch Allie's. The rowhouse that was perfect for two was impossibly cramped for three, especially when one of them required medical equipment and a parade of therapists and caregivers, but Leah was determined the sacrifice would be hers, not her daughter's.

But this wasn't taking the room away. Allie was gone by her own choice. Three galleries carried Leah's work now. She might have been able to make it anyway, but her mother's insurance, her father's annuity, and the sale of their house in March made it a moot point. There was enough—enough to pay Allie's tuition no matter what, thanks to the college trust fund with which Dennis had bought his freedom. Leah had enough, had done enough, been through enough. Maybe she'd even mourned enough. Now she was claiming the best room in the house, the airy front bedroom that hoarded the natural light painters crave, and she was claiming the time to use it. Her letter of resignation was already signed, sealed against second thoughts, and tucked into the wide side pocket of her purse ready for tomorrow. She tried to name what she felt and couldn't until she saw the word in her mind, a stick figure come to life, dancing. Joy.

*

Baby's Breath

"Of course, I'll stay until you find a replacement," Leah said to Corinne, who'd been her boss at Atherton Real Estate for over ten years.

"What'll I do?" Cory moaned, and Leah gave her credit for not faking the distress.

"Cory, it'll be okay. You think there's more to it than there is. Anyone with good taste could do what I do." Leah prepared all the agency's advertising, from taking the pictures to laying it out on a light table, but that wasn't what had Cory so upset. What Leah did unofficially took more of her time, and every agent at Atherton admitted outright that it made their sales consistently tops in the city. Leah was a genius at redoing houses. She'd walk through a new listing and pinpoint exactly what new shade of paint, what rearrangement of furniture, what framed prints or potted ficus and mantle arrangement would—for almost no money—make the house into a must-have. She warmed places, gave them personality, hid their flaws.

"But you know more than design. . . . You know *art.* I just can't replace you. Nobody could *teach* someone to see the way you do. *I* can't do it myself." Cory had a point. Leah had been practical and finished a major in design instead of in painting when she moved herself and Allie into her mother's house after the divorce and went back to the University of Pennsylvania at thirty-two. She'd seen how the agency kept finding new ways to use her talent, and making a living as a painter . . . well, she couldn't count on it. But Cory was right: it was her painter's eye redoing the houses, and that she'd been born with.

Leah glanced at her hands. Her short nails were ringed with a nondescript paint that never entirely came off anymore, and she tucked her fingers into hiding. She was dressed casually, for a day at the light table, in black and beige striped slacks and a long-sleeved black top. She'd known it would be the hard part, telling Cory. The women were friends, confidantes at least about their teenage daughters.

"Why now? I mean, I'd have understood if you'd left when your mother was so bad, or while Allie was still home, but . . ."

6

Chapter One

"I know it must sound ass-backward."

"You're going to paint full-time, aren't you?" From Cory, it sounded like an accusation.

"Yes." Leah met her eyes, though she wasn't able to stifle the little gesture that could have been interpreted as either defensive or defiant, tossing her loose hair from in front of her shoulder to behind it.

Cory sighed. She was fifty-seven, plain, smart, kind, owner of the franchised agency, the sort of woman who'd closed more than her share of deals because she simply knew her stuff better than the competition. And she had Leah. She shook her straight gray bob and gave Leah her smile, which always curved up higher into the natural rouge of her left cheek than her right. "If you ever want to come back ... even for a while. When Allie's home and driving you insane, maybe...."

Leah relaxed. "Oh, Cory, that's it, see? She's not coming home for the summer. When she told me, I was just upset, well, hurt really. She's so ... distant."

"And so far away."

Leah smiled. "That too. And, oh god, don't call her Allie. Not if she can hear you. It's *Alyssa*. Since she left...." She paused, the smile tapering into a sigh. "And you know what she said? 'I'll *never* come back there.' The way she said it made Philadelphia sound like a nuclear waste site."

"And you the project director, doubtless."

"Doubtless."

"You know, she *will* come back."

"I know how she meant it, but ... it felt like such a blow. Last summer was so awful with my mother—and, you know, I'd thought Allie and I could spend some time together this summer. I said that to her and she did this flash freeze silent thing she does to shut me right out. I swear I can feel it through the phone." Leah shrugged, turning her palms up in Cory's direction. "And then after a few days—I mean, I guess you can only cry just so much per year—it came to me: well, I can

7

make a studio in her room and have all that light. Three windows! I'm so sick of the basement, god, it's ugly and dank . . . and the best I could do was fluorescent lighting. Anyway, so I started cleaning her room out." Leah stopped to smile, rolling her eyes to suggest her own foolishness. "At first I was still crying—over her stuffed animals and junk she doesn't care about at all, like Girl Scout badges, but then . . . I started to feel free. You know?"

"Not yet, but I'm a-waitin' for that glory day." Cory laughed. Her fourth child was in the ninth grade, and Cory made cracks about a nursing home attendant pushing her wheelchair to that son's high school graduation, what a damn shame it was she'd be too senile to know which kid was hers. She had a daughter Allie's age, and two in their twenties; Leah had always been able to talk to her, especially the morning after a bad night.

"I feel guilty, though," Leah said.

"For what?"

From where she sat, Leah could glance at her own desk where Allie's high school graduation picture sulked at her, though Cory had told her no, Allie didn't look sulky, really, only extremely serious. (She'd put up her waves of shining near-black hair, her one physical resemblance to Leah, inexplicably hiding it like whatever thought had produced that deadpan gaze head-on into the camera.) "I think I'm . . . a little bit happy that she's not coming home, underneath how terrible it makes me feel. Honestly, Cory, sometimes I think she can't stand me."

"Honey, they're all like that, especially girls. It's your punishment."

"For what?"

Cory grinned and tilted her chair back. "No mother of a daughter actually knows the answer to that one. It's the only evidence God might not be female after all. Don't worry about it. The daughter holds all the strings—she'll reel you in when she wants you and toss you back the minute she doesn't. Enjoy it while she doesn't. How'd she take it when you told her about her room?"

Chapter One

Leah looked at the ceiling.

"You chickenshit," Cory snorted her laugh. "They all think their rooms should be preserved as permanent shrines, so brace yourself for a major fit. If you're lucky, she just won't talk to you for six months."

"She's good, though, Cory, even if she doesn't like me." It was a statement, but Leah let her voice inflect a question. *Right?*

"Of course she is. Come on, they all hate us all sometimes. And they need to get out on their own, test their wings. Look, you've done a good job, a fine job. Have some faith in yourself, will you?"

"It's just that . . . I don't know . . . sometimes I have this feeling, like she's not even *mine*, you know? Like I don't know her . . . but I *want* to."

Cory stood, came around her desk, bent and gave Leah a hug. "It kills me to lose you, but god, woman, quit worrying about Allie. You go for it. It's your turn."

Leah's eyes watered. "Thanks, Cory. I'll miss you."

Cory pulled back enough so Leah could see her face. "And just to show there's no hard feeling, you can call me the next time you want to kill her, if I can call you for the same reason. Or just call me for lunch, whichever is the strongest need at the moment. And I want an engraved invite for the opening of your first one-woman show."

"Deal."

Leah sighed. She was going to have to repaint the room after all. Despite Leah's entreaties, Allie used tape to put up the posters of the bands whose music she'd played over and over and over while she sat or lay in the dark—Leah's guess, anyway, from the wrong side of a locked door.

Leah tried not to tear the Deftones poster. Allie'd tried dreadlocks too, but Leah wouldn't pay for her to get them done at a beauty parlor, and after several months, Allie had given them up. A poster for The Bends was more disquieting: a computer-generated picture of a man whose lips were peeled back in throes of agony, like an Edvard Munch Scream picture, disturbed her from a distance of six inches. Another

Baby's Breath

(Radiohead again, the Pablo Honey album, Allie had informed Leah, disdainful of her mother's ignorance) was a giant yellow daisy whose petals were built with phallic-looking pistils, its center a photograph of a worried-looking infant's head.

Allie had taken to singing the chorus to one mournful melody—Leah thought it was on the daisy album—playing it over and over, etching grooves into Leah's brain.

> I wish I was special
> So fucking special.
> But I'm a creep.
> I don't belong here
> I want to have control
> I want a perfect body
> I want a perfect soul
> I want you to notice
> When I'm not around.

One afternoon, Leah stopped loading grapefruit into the refrigerator and went upstairs to where Allie was cleaning the bathroom. She'd come up behind her, caressed Allie's hair, and said softly, "You're *not* fat. You're fine the way you are, and I do notice when you're not around." Allie twisted away.

"God. Don't you have something to paint in the basement?"

The baby head poster did tear several inches in, but Leah wasn't sorry. She contemplated throwing it away, but instead sighed again and rolled it up, fastening the top and bottom with paper clips, distracted by what its removal had revealed.

Eight scarred yellow thumbtacks pinioned a strip of instant photos from a booth in the mall. Allie and her best friend, well, once-best friend, Sharon in four silly poses. From Sharon's hairstyle—she'd let it grow long after their sophomore year—Leah guessed the picture to be several years old. Sharon's fair, cherubic face twinkled in each picture.

Chapter One

Even one in which her lips were smooched up as if kissing the camera lens, had a grin in her eyes. Next to her, Allie smoldered or leered. For one shot, she'd curtained her hair so as to entirely cover her face. Still, they'd been having fun. It was understandable, natural as the turning earth that Sharon cooled the friendship when she finally captured a long-pursued boyfriend during the girls' senior year, but Allie had taken it hard. Sometimes Leah could see through the indifference her daughter wore like a baggy sweatshirt.

Leah had saved sorting Allie's books for last because with them were her best memories of her daughter: curled in Leah's lap or beneath the wing of her arm, chewing the end of one of her braids. Boxed sets of Lewis' Witch and Wardrobe series, Tolkien, Piers Anthony, beautifully, expensively bound. Dennis had been good about giving Allie books, which was about all—except the trust for college—he'd contributed after that single willful sperm. Here was a whole collection of biographies, famous and less famous women from history. When Leah got to the bottom of the pile where only three early childhood books had survived the successive winnowings of the collection, she let her legs fold beneath her and read *Little Bear* for the comfort of the wise mother and her errant cub. In the end, she culled only a couple of bedraggled paperback mysteries and lurid true crime stories, books Leah found revolting, for the give-away box.

Creating the studio was such luxury that Leah actually had to adjust. She was used to happiness in closed circles of time, confined and defined by when she'd have to stop, ready or not, clean her brushes, shut down the progress of the work inside herself and on the canvas. Once she was past the first stage, emptying Allie's room, the whole feeling had changed, and she let the process extend, unhurried as a cat stretching out in the sun.

She pulled up and dragged out the dark navy wall-to-wall carpet Allie had chosen for her room when they moved in. None of Leah's nudgings had inched Allie toward a more pacific blue; Leah had finally capitulated and bought her a good plush. With the furniture removed—a downtown homeless center was quick to send two men in a defeated pickup to get the donation of bed, bureau, and never-used desk, though she kept the night stand and bookcase to put in her own room for Allie—Leah discerned how little care Allie had taken with the carpet. What looked like chemical stains discolored several spots, and other areas were bristly from spills.

Leah shrugged off irritation at Allie's disregard because beneath the carpet waited the marred hardwood floor, perfect. Maybe she'd put down some plastic, but, she decided, probably not. She'd always had to before, but it inevitably rumpled into an annoyance under her feet. Let the paint that would land on this floor start her new history. An amazement: she could do whatever she wanted.

It was an expanding notion, too, a spreading patch of blue sky in her mind, like the view from Allie's—Leah's!—studio windows, that attracted her each time she carried another armload up the two flights from the basement into the generous light.

"You know," Dave Allen suggested when, good to his word, he came over to help her get her painting table up the stairs, "if you're so big on windows, you could put in a skylight. It's not that big a deal, even through plaster. Some houses just like yours and mine, built way back I mean, have them. Do you want this carpet in the dumpster? You could, y'know, just lay it down in the basement. . . ."

"No, I'm done with underground work," Leah said. "It's like a cave down there. Well, *you* know. Do you really think—a skylight?" Their houses had been constructed in the 1850's, and gave them similar pleasures and headaches. "Okay, let's set this up here. I want this whole area for painting, where the light's best. What a great idea. I would love a skylight. My ex-husband—he's a painter too—had one . . . but of course, *he* had *everything*." She grunted as she pulled out an errant nail with the claw of her hammer. "There, out, be gone, you pain in the ass," she muttered.

Dave glanced at her and started to say something, but decided against it. Leah saw and appreciated the restraint.

A few minutes later, as she and Dave hammered the base of the work table back together, an idea came to Leah. "Do you know anything about plumbing? Is there a chance I could put a darkroom in the basement?"

Dave pulled a nail out of his mouth. "Could," he said, leaning back onto his haunches. "I think, yeah. For what?"

"I have an idea for a series of paintings, this street, maybe sometimes a figure in it. . . . There's such . . . well, life, when you watch for it. I've never had the time to be out and about, you know? Observing. To take pictures and then use them as the basis for paintings." Leah didn't want to say more about the notions taking shape in the amniotic sac of her freedom, as if wording them might be a jinx. "But that skylight, do you really think so? That would give me the longest natural light, wouldn't it? Yeah, good idea. . . . Would you mind helping me get the carpet to the basement?" She shook her head. "*Why* would she have picked *this* color? I never figured that one out. I'll hang onto it. Maybe. . . ." She left it unfinished, and used the hammer jutting out of her back jeans pocket to claw out a nail. She wanted a high shelf near the door for her CD player and the stack of Mozart and Vivaldi and Bach that floated around her working.

Later that afternoon, intoxicated with the possibility of a wider spectrum of light she could use, Leah called a construction company.

"Sure it's possible. Lotsa yuppies put 'em in when they rehab. Plaster ceiling's more though. Dark room depends on how the pipes're run," the contractor said when he returned her call the next morning.

"That's okay. When can you come take a look?"

*

13

Baby's Breath

While she waited for the contractor, Leah began rearranging her own bedroom to make room for her daughter. Allie had a roommate at school; it wouldn't be so different to room with her mother when she was home for breaks. And she'd love a real darkroom, not the make-shift job they'd sometimes set up in the half-bath under the living room stairs, smothering the outline of light around the door with dishtowels and duct tape. It would give Allie something special when she did come home. She had to know that she wasn't just a guest who could sleep on the blue pull-out couch in the living room, temporary as weather that blew in and out. Maybe they would get closer. Maybe Allie would talk to her when the lights were hushed and they lay dreamy and defense-less, protected by dark. Sometimes Leah wondered what secrets Allie and her roommate shared and was jealous of Cindy, whom she knew only as a chipper and friendly voice that usually answered the phone.

Leah left the rolled up posters in her walk-in closet. She could put those up when Allie did come home rather than look at them every day until then. Too bad Allie'd taken the only one Leah would have happily gone ahead and put up, maybe even spent the money to frame as a sur-prise for Allie: a Mary Cassatt titled "Mother Playing with Her Child" that Leah bought her, a souvenir of their first trip to the Metropolitan Museum of Art. Still, it was comforting that Allie had it with her, something Leah could take to mean maybe Allie liked her mother bet-ter than she let on.

The few items of clothing Allie hadn't taken with her fit into one side of one bureau drawer, though Leah had emptied two. She left the second with nothing in it, so it was really *Allie's*. A Hummel figurine stood on the cleared side of the bureau. A little girl with downcast eyes, it was a gift from Dennis one of the years he'd managed to remember Allie's birthday on the right day. Leah arranged her brush, perfume, framed pictures, and idle clutter all to the left of center. Really, though, when she'd subtracted the obviously disposable—old notebooks, an-cient paperbacks, half-remaining rolls of lifesavers, a blue bra with broken fastener languishing under Allie's bureau—there had been surprisingly few personal objects to move. For a while she'd had a wrenching knowledge of loss, as though the daughter who'd been so hard to hold had escaped her completely now, having deliberately erased every fingerprint of her soul, leaving just detritus and debris in final rebuke. The childhood books hardly counted; they'd been Leah's and Dennis' choices, gifts. Leah remembered what Cory had told her, how teenage girls are all that way, tried to imagine her feeling was no more than an outdated outfit, one she could take off and discard.

It'll be all right. Leah echoed Cory. Allie's place was made. Leah could keep that safe and let herself go on.

Once the skylight was installed, she took a whole day to set up the studio, not because it had to take that long, but because she reveled in the pure pleasure. Glass jars of upright brushes lined the wall like sentries, the brush handles smeared with Leah's favored colors. Turpenoid to clean the filbert tipped brushes she liked best. Linseed oil. Paper towel, razor blades for her scraper. And, neatly lining the front of the table, arranged from warm to cool, Titanium White, Cadmium Orange, Cadmium Yellow, Burnt Sienna, Raw Sienna, Dioxazine Violet, Ultramarine Blue, her precious tubes of the expensive Winsor & Newton's oils she'd allowed herself since linking up with George George.

George was the owner of the ninth gallery to which she'd applied in the Olde City section of Philly, back when Leah and Allie were still living with Leah's mother, and the first to represent her. A troll-like man with Einstein hair whose card said "George George, Proprietor, George Gallery" propped her paintings against the wall, scrutinized them from every angle, and then simply said, "Yes. I have room for you." One piece sold—a cityscape that featured a lone tree—then George took another. When the second sold, George asked what else she had. Not nearly as many as either of them wished, but the sale of a painting here, a painting there, had seeded the money for a home of her own.

Baby's Breath

Leah's easel went up next, and then her palette, the clear glass one she'd treated herself to five years earlier, white cardboard taped to the underside for a neutral white surface to mix paint on. Drops of color on the wooden easel stand remembered long-sold paintings.

What didn't go on the table holding her brushes and paints she put on another table, with her sketch pads and charcoal. Coffee pot and mug. No point in running up and down stairs every half hour for a re-fill. A good-sized corkboard and push pins for photographs, a few extra clean rags, her dog-eared copy of Gray's anatomy: this was her *stuff* table. The closet got wood, two rolls of canvas, stapler, hammer, saw, ruler, triangle. Tools for stretching her canvases hung on small nails hammered into the plaster of the back wall.

Leah hung a variegated wandering jew from the ceiling near one front window, and a spectacular trailing ivy by the window to the side of her house partly detached from Dave's, above her flowered walkway. Her violets squatted like Buddhist monks on the windowsills. She propped the two paintings she'd completed but not yet taken to George between the floor and walls, took the new painting she'd begun and set it on the easel.

She was ready.

CHAPTER

2

Even in sunlight, after the bay fog rolled up tight into the Berkeley hills, even with the Campanile's carillon tolling the noon hour, she had trained herself to cling to the lure of sleep. Beneath two pillows, a corner of the down comforter hooding her face, she could slip inside a dark trance for twelve, fourteen hours on end. The trick was covering her head, letting her heavy hair cape her face, thinking only darkroom thoughts: negatives under safelight. In her mind, close to sleep, she could see the shadows turning, the images reversed and fixed on clean, wet paper, slick with newness.

Sleep would be easier to reach if Cindy wouldn't leave the window open, if the chatter from Telegraph weren't a constant backdrop twenty-four hours a day. She could find it at this very moment if only Cindy's giddy laughter weren't singing in the hall, broken first by Marc's low voice, then the distracting silence that meant they were kissing.

"You guys, I'm awake." She threw one of her pillows against the door. "I'm awake." She sat up, pulling her hair back and her T-shirt down.

They tumbled into the room, red-cheeked and steamy. Marc tossed her the pillow, then leaned over her, eyes wide.

"Hibernate no more, oh goddess of nepenthe," he said, half-falling back onto Cindy's bed, then pulling Cindy down into his lap. "Don't you ever get up before the soaps, Alyssa?"

Alyssa wanted to say, straight in his face the way she'd seen red-haired Linnie from across the hall do it, "Fuck off, asshole." She stood, instead, and picked up her towel and took the near-empty bottle of Finesse shampoo from the medicine cabinet in the alcove between the built-in desks. At the door, she turned and said, looking at Cindy, "I thought he dropped mythology. I thought he was *failing*."

At least the showers were empty. In the stall furthest from the door, she turned the knob to hot and set the spigot so it shot fierce bullets instead of a soft jet like the water that pulsed from the shower head at home, the one her mother had wrestled into place with a pipe wrench after Gran had come to stay for good and home had been changed forever. Fall semester, with the other girls on her floor, she'd used the showers in the evening or the morning, when the whole room filled with steam and a highpitched melodic babble. But after she'd found her name on the list of the girls who qualified as Freshman Fatties—Linnie's roommate Tricia had posted the final cut on the bulletin board by the pay phone—she'd started taking her showers midday on Tuesdays and Thursdays when she could sleep in without missing a class. The rest of the week she showered in the break between her advanced comp section and Professor Miller's freshman honors seminar, when hardly anybody was on the floor.

Alone in the empty shower room, she didn't have to struggle to keep her towel wrapped around her as she pulled her sweatpants on and off. She could bypass the long mirrors on either side of the sinks and brush her teeth without being sabotaged by her own reflection. Usually, when Cindy was off somewhere with Marc Raymond, she'd turban her waist-length hair and comb it out in the narrow dormitory bedroom, where the only mounted mirror was the face-sized one on the medicine cabinet. Now, with Cindy and Marc in her room, she brushed her wet hair in the shower stall, taking so long that the water on her skin had nearly dried before she towelled. A lock at a time, she worked her nubby comb through the tangled strands. Once, when they were eating delivered pizza and watching Letterman, Tricia had tugged at a strand of Alyssa's hair and asked if she were trying for dreadlocks. Linnie said something sharp back, but since then Alyssa was careful to comb it out, every snarl and tangle, even though sometimes after she'd shampooed and conditioned and rinsed, it took all her energy to lift the brush in her hand.

She didn't mind seeing her hair reflected; it was her naked self, softer and heavier than when she'd arrived in September, that she wanted to keep safe in hiding. First-year fats. A lot of girls got them, she'd heard in orientation. Homesickness and cafeteria food were to blame. Still, it was seeing her name on the list—Alyssa Pacey Staton, Tricia even spelled it right—that made her shift her schedule so she could shampoo her hair and rinse it out without hearing another girl's voice complaining, clear and high above the din: Alyssa has been in the shower for more than half an hour, didn't they all know California was suffering a drought, when are we calling in the search and rescue team.

She told Leah to stop sending the care packages, not because she didn't hunger for the soft homemade brownies and the Tollhouse cookies and the thought of her mother's hands stirring the batter in the eggshell blue mixing bowl, but because she didn't want to share anymore with Linnie's roommate. She couldn't figure out how she could share with Linnie without sharing with Tricia, who would make a big phony deal about taking two or three of the cookies. Alyssa would see them in Linnie's room, untouched and petrified, like castoff jewelry on Tricia's desk. Cindy said she thought Tricia was anorexic or bulimic or both. After the list was posted, Alyssa thought she was just evil.

This was her second reason to be glad about the little apartment she'd found on Dwight Way: no more shared bathroom. The first reason, the big one, was that she'd never have to see Cindy Cheung or Marc Raymond or Mrs. Cheung sitting around in *her* room, on *her* unmade bed, gaping at her as if she were a lab specimen, the way they were when, after her shower and back in her sweats, she pushed open the cracked door and found them sitting, a family circle, a classical tableau of chitchat. Their conversation stopped, as if a guest of dubious character had said something indelicate at a tea party, and each turned to her, expectant. Marc had helped himself to her tan scrunchie and pulled his sleek blond hair into a ponytail low on his thick neck, like that somehow made him a more acceptable candidate for Cindy's affections. Cindy smiled—she spent three-quarters of her life practicing her smile, though Alyssa tried hard not to hold it against her—and Mrs. Cheung was the first to speak.

"There you are, Alyssa," she said, her voice plumped by the same breathy exultation with which she had invited Alyssa across the bay to the Cheung house in Pacific Heights. "Since your family's all the way across the country," she would repeat until Alyssa gave up and found herself riding across the Bay Bridge in Cindy's Mustang like some hitchhiker hijacked by a persistent charity.

"Hi, Mrs. Cheung." Alyssa lifted a rope of her hair and pushed it back over her shoulder. It fell, wet, fragrant, and weighty, dampening the Deftones T-shirt against her back. "Are you getting Cindy's things?"

"Just some. Just the dirty clothes," she laughed. She crossed her tan legs. A thin gold ankle bracelet, the sister to the one Cindy wore, shimmered above her tennis sock. "That's a carload by itself," she said, patting Cindy on the knee. With their matched height and their bobbed hair and their coordinated jewelry, they looked like twins. Twice, walking to the Berkeley Blood Bank to give blood (they needed Type B, and she was faithful to give once a month), Alyssa had seen them on the courts at the Cal Rec Club, playing their weekly Saturday match for which Mrs. Cheung drove gladly from San Francisco. As they ran to the net and back, rackets swinging forehand to backhand, she couldn't tell which perky player was mother, which daughter.

Chapter Two

"Mama," Cindy said, rolling her eyes at Marc. "Alyssa, we're going to lunch at Chez Panisse. Mama wants you to come. Our treat."

Alyssa folded her towel neatly in thirds, the way her own mother liked, and slipped it through the rack beneath the medicine cabinet. "I've got one more final," she said, bending her head so her wet hair veiled her face. "Anthro. It's a take-home essay."

"It's just lunch, honey," Mrs. Cheung said, standing and pulling Cindy to her feet. "A reward for you kids, for a good first year."

"Thanks, but no. . . . I need to work on my paper. Really, thanks."

"We could bring you take-out," Mrs. Cheung said, looking back.

"No, thanks. . . . I'm eating in the cafeteria, with Linnie. From across the hall." It was easy to lie, to make up one of those simple untruths that didn't really count because they never hurt anybody. To get her out of a scrape, to save her from the unbearable prospect of watching the muscles in Marc Raymond's jaws flex when he chewed, a small lie was allowable. Mrs. Cheung believed her. Alyssa's sacrifice of lunch to her Anthro exam nicely complemented her role as the studious roommate, the no-nonsense honors student who—Alyssa sensed Mrs. Cheung's pity—unfortunately lacked her own daughter's vivacity.

Cindy heard the lie, though, and gave her the same expression she had when Alyssa said no, she didn't think they would be roommates their sophomore year. Maybe Cindy knew that Linnie was, at that moment, in her one o'clock final, and maybe she didn't. Alyssa figured Cindy's opinion didn't matter so much now, not with only two more days until the semester's close. If she needed to, she could lie from here to kingdom come. With the apartment on Dwight Way waiting for her, nothing Cindy or Marc or the perfectly cute Mrs. Cheung could say or do would make her suffer her own lies. The apartment was hers, the first and last month's rent paid two weeks ago with her own money from the account at the Bank of America on Telegraph. First and last. She liked the sound of that, the boundaries the words put on time, which seemed otherwise to stretch out like one long desert highway in a direction she couldn't name to a destination she couldn't determine. She liked the obligations of the word "lease," the ownership it ensured. She liked her name and address spelled out on the books of imprinted checks she'd found last night, squeezed into her mailbox, crumpling a pink package pick-up notice into an unevenly crimped paper accordion.

"Okay then," Mrs. Cheung said. "Do a good job, honey."

"Sayonara," Marc called, slinging his arm around Cindy's bare shoulders and pulling her into the hall. Alyssa waved, waited a heartbeat, then pushed the door shut with her foot and locked it with a twist of the deadbolt.

It was dorm policy, after all, to lock your door when you were alone.

She did dilute the lie by walking to the food service building for lunch. She was late. In fact, the checker was closing up shop just as Alyssa reached an empty table with her loaded tray. She'd heard the older dining halls at the Ivy Leagues—Harvard and Yale and Stanford—were medieval, cavernous, but the cafeteria that served Griffiths Hall and the other three dorms one block from campus was just plain dismal, institutional and bright, so noisy during dinner that you had to yell to make your friends hear you, if you happened to be eating with friends. Lately Alyssa preferred not to. All the girls on her floor were talking about summer break, about going home and getting jobs and eating their moms' food, and the few times she'd told people she was staying, they'd said, after one offbeat pause, "That's cool." Then they'd assumed she was taking summer classes, and she had to explain no, she was volunteering for the Library Literacy Program and she'd gotten a job at Alfredo's Pizza on Shattuck. She always stopped before telling them about the apartment on Dwight. That was hers, and she didn't want them to think, well, if they came back in September and tried to find her, she didn't want them to know she'd still be there in the apartment, instead of with them in campus housing.

Chapter Two

She ate a plate of gluey spaghetti and the whipping cream hat off a
bowl of chocolate pudding, then rolled four peanut butter cookies into
her napkin to take back to her room. She debated leaving her tray on
the table or bussing it, the way they were supposed to. Bussing it meant
she might run into Tony Messina, who'd been working in the food service kitchen all spring. It hadn't been so awful earlier when they were
dating, if you could call it that, because he'd smile at her and say something so the other girls would know Alyssa was going out with him.
They all wanted to, he was so drop-dead cute, and many before Alyssa
had their turns, too, which made Alyssa feel like she'd achieved membership in an elite sorority. Until her name made another one of Tricia's
lists, this one unpublished: the Tony Messina Deflowered Virgin Honor
Roll. Linnie said to Alyssa, "She's just jealous," and Alyssa let herself
believe Linnie because Tony did have a sincere thing about her breasts,
and Tricia didn't have any to speak of.

"Sexy, sexy, sexy," Cindy said when Alyssa first grumped about the
obligatory double-date with Marc's best friend, his old pal, the stud of
Fresno High.

"Your only criterion," Alyssa came back with a cruelty she regretted,
but Cindy didn't rile easily. Instead, she took Alyssa to the city to pick
out black pants and a silvery jacket to wear to the Alpha Kappa
Lambda spring house party. Neither Marc nor Tony belonged yet, so it
was some kind of status blessing inherited from Marc's grandfather, a
legendary Cal football player, that allowed them to go as freshman
house members, bringing dorm dates no less. Cindy said her hair
looked really striking pulled back into the low coil on her neck; she said
Alyssa was prettier when she pulled her hair back off her face, why
didn't she cut all that hair, it was so *sixties*. In the silver jacket and the
strappy sandals she'd borrowed from Linnie, armed with Cindy's
praise, Alyssa surprised herself with her coyness toward Tony.

Maybe it was the silver jacket, or the three beers she drank on the
fraternity porch, or the way Tony's brown curls turned to baby down

23

on the nape of his neck, it could have been any one of these which made her sleep with him that night. Maybe it was what Professor Miller had said to her that very afternoon in March, standing outside the seminar room in Wheeler Hall before she returned Alyssa's midterm essay. "Seeing writing like this submitted by a freshman is a joy, Ms. Staton. I find your interest in the repression of Wharton's characters refreshing, indeed." Miller went on, her stout fingers extended to hold her point for emphasis as she did in lecture, to say that Alyssa was to register for her sophomore honors seminar, just let the department secretary know that Miller had already admitted her. Was Alyssa certain her talents were best applied to a history major?

Smart girl though she knew herself to be, maybe it was just that she liked thinking there was something special about her, about Alyssa Staton from Room 412 in Griffiths Hall, which caused Tony to lift the coil of shining hair off the back of her neck so he could kiss her there even before he'd ever kissed her lips.

Probably it was the ease with which it happened, their quick and fumbling sex act, the way no bells chimed, no doves flew overhead, no earth moved, that made it happen again, and again, until the beginning of May. It was the very ordinariness of it, the casual way Tony would slip on a condom when he was "warmed up" as he liked to say, as if he were positioned at the starting line for a fifty-meter sprint, a feat which, Alyssa was forced to admit after the newness had worn off, he performed with the same single-minded concentration he displayed when making love. The finish line was everything to Tony.

But she had nothing, no other lover, to whom she might compare him. On that count, Tricia's virgin list had been accurate. Though Cindy pretended to be knowledgeable about sex and birth control (she had, after all, taken Alyssa to University Health Services for her first exam to make sure she requested the female gynecologist), Alyssa was certain Cindy had been Marc Raymond's freshman year conquest, hers the single name which made it to Marc's short-list. It pained her to re-member how, when Leah had offered her advice on this matter in a mother-daughter talk conducted beside the bed in which her grand-mother, Leah's mother Esther, lay unconscious, doing her best to die, Alyssa hadn't really listened well. She remembered parts of what her mother said, the way love and sex combined made physical union some-thing special, but she'd heard that line as preventative. Her mother's dutiful speech was designed to delay Alyssa's sexual activity because, Leah implied, an eighteen-year-old couldn't possibly feel the deeply mature passion that would transform sex into love-making. What Alyssa remembered best from the whole encounter was the softness of her mother's speaking voice, the way she painted the word "sex" as gently as if she were lightening the background of a canvas with her Chinese bristle brush, how Leah's words had taken on the familiar sing-songy tone halfway into the conversation after she had already said her piece.

The information Alyssa had really wanted concerned the first time, the physical part. Did it hurt, really; did one bleed a lot like a period, or just spot here and there; how long did the guy take to do it. Something about Esther withering on the bed in what was supposed to be her mother's bedroom, something about Gran's old age and her own youth breathing the same air had told her it was the wrong time to ask, selfish somehow, maybe sinful. Beyond that sense of wrongness, it had given her the creeps. What would somebody have thought if they had been overheard? Leah sitting there beside Esther, webbed with support tubes coming and going for practically every bodily function, ex-plaining the mechanics of intercourse to Alyssa, who couldn't meet her mother's dark eyes so instead watched Gran's closed ones, the twitching, crepey lids revealing Esther's mind living on, if only in dream. She was nowhere near sex then, a senior in high school, and she'd told Leah as much, edging herself out of Gran's presence, away from the deathroom smell. The conversation never came up again. Then, with Tony, when Alyssa really wanted to say something, to ask Leah to explain again about that intersection of love and sex, was it real or just fictional, it was just too hard from three thousand miles away.

Because they were already sweeping up, Alyssa followed the rule and bussed her tray. Tony wasn't on the line, but when she stepped through the glass doors into the sunlight on Haste Street he was there, pulling off his food service jacket and folding it so it would drape over his arm, pretending at being her suitor. He slipped on a pair of dark glasses, black wrap-arounds.

"Hey, Alyssa."

"Hi, Tony." She shifted the napkin of cookies into her sweatpants pocket. She didn't care if Tony saw them, it wasn't that; it was just easier to push them into the stretched-out pocket and brush her hands against her hips.

"You through?"

"One more. A take-home."

"Conkey's?"

"Yeah."

"Me, too. You going to write the max?"

"I think. With her, you need to."

"Yeah." They walked the half-block to her dorm in silence. Tony held the Griffiths door open for her. "Cindy gone?"

"She's out for lunch . . . with her mother and Marc."

"Lucky Marc. Dining very elegantly these days."

"Mrs. Cheung's a generous person. He ought to appreciate that."

"I'm sure he does," Tony said, slipping off his dark glasses, leading her to the elevators.

She stopped, backed away. "I've got to pick up a package in the mailroom." The cookies in her pocket were probably crushed by now. Peanut butter crumbs, same difference. She touched the pocket, then lifted her hand to pull her hair back.

"I'll wait for you." He shifted to her other side. "I'll come up with you. How's that?" His hair had grown wild and curly. Once, the last time she'd been with him, she took the scrunchie from her own loose ponytail and wound it around his brown curls, pulling them back to bare the down on his neck.

"I don't think so, Tony."

"Hey. I'm sorry about the last couple of weeks. I *told* you already I was sorry. I *like* you, Alyssa."

"You like certain things about me," she said, thinking of Tricia's flat chest.

"That's not fair. And I could say the same kind of thing to you. You haven't been Miss Congeniality lately."

"I had the flu. Cindy told Marc to tell you."

"He did tell me." He twisted the white cotton of the food service jacket with his strong, pretty, square-edged fingers.

"You're wrinkling that all up, Tony."

"Can I come up?" Little boy, whining.

"No."

"Another time?"

She turned away, heading down the hall to the mailboxes. "Maybe."

"Before I go home?"

"Maybe."

She stood for nearly a minute in front of the boxes, giving him time to leave Griffiths and reach Sherman, trying her combination over and over until she realized she was spinning the lock on 312 instead of 412. 412 was empty, anyway. She fished around the napkinned cookies inside her pocket for the pink slip and realized she'd left it inside her Anthro text. Well, her forgetfulness had saved her from Tony Messina, she thought, although she wasn't entirely sure of exactly what she'd been saved from, except she was positive he'd been dodging her for at least two weeks. One of those rare nights when they were drifting off to sleep together, even Cindy had said something to that effect, that she hadn't seen Tony for a while. It had been a deliberate slight, she knew, his signal for her to back off. She resented this—his need to play the pursued—she'd never been possessive in the slightest, which was why, Cindy said, she'd lasted longer than the others. Maybe that was what had hurt her most, if hurt was the right word: the idea that he thought she cared when she was doing her best to prove to him she didn't. Anyway, she wouldn't have to pull the crushed cookies from her pocket in front of anybody now, and that was something to be thankful for.

She was four pages into her Anthro exam, scrolling through to see how far she'd come on Conkey's convoluted question about competing evolutionary theories, when Linnie knocked on her door. Alyssa gave the file a save, then unlocked the door.

"Tricia's gone?" she asked. Linnie slid through the door and sat down on Cindy's bed, which Mrs. Cheung had made up tightly with hospital corners even though she would soon be unmaking it to pack Cindy's linens, the Laura Ashley florals. "Wait to meet your roommate and then buy your comforter," Leah had suggested in September. "Then you can have matching beds." Laura Ashley was too much for Alyssa, though she and Cindy had gotten along, mismatched comforters and all, for a year.

"Yeah. Lock, stock, and barrel. Her brother came down from Sacramento to take her home, lucky boy."

"Cindy's out with her mother."

"The ubiquitous Mrs. Cheung."

"Hey," Alyssa said. She liked Linnie, admired her boldness, but sometimes, Alyssa thought secretly, she could be too hard. "She's been nice to me . . . all year."

"You strike her as an orphan. You arouse her maternal sympathies."

28

Chapter Two

Alyssa sat down in front of her computer. She scrolled the screen up, down. "I have a mother. And a father."

"Yes, but there have been no sightings."

"So they both live back east. Big deal."

Linnie stood up, peered over her shoulder and pointed to a misspelling.

"I haven't spellchecked yet," Alyssa said. Then, irritated, in a voice she'd never before used with Linnie, "Look, Linnie, do you want to write it for me?"

Linnie sat back onto Cindy's bed, primping the floral shams behind her back. "Why don't you want to go home for the summer? The *real* reason. Is Tony staying?"

"Tony has nothing to do with it. And he's not staying."

"The thing with your mom?"

"What thing?"

"That she didn't drive out with you in the fall, like you planned—"

"My grandmother was dying, Linnie . . . *she died*."

"But are you still mad?"

"Will you stop it! Jesus, I *like* Berkeley. I have a job, I have an apartment. Lots of people are staying over the summer." Lots of people *were*, it was true, but Alyssa didn't know them.

"Okay, okay." Linnie stopped. "Remember to give me your address before you go, okay? If you need help schlepping your stuff over to Dwight and I'm still around, let me help, okay?"

"Sure," Alyssa said, her hands on the keyboard. But when Linnie had latched the door behind her, Alyssa didn't know if she'd find time to do that. She didn't know if she wanted Linnie writing to her all summer long. What could she possible find to write about that would interest Linnie?

It was Friday when Alyssa managed to make it to the mailroom before ten in the morning, the designated deadline for picking up packages.

Baby's Breath

The pink notice was dog-eared, so soiled the old clerk behind the window had to ask for her box number because the pencilled figures were smudged. "Must be Christmas in June," he said, smiling, as he handed her the box, nearly the size of a small carry-on bag.

"Yeah," she said, smiling back, seeing her mother's fine hand on the address label, the Philadelphia postmark.

"You fill out a forwarding request yet?" The clerk asked, extending the card in one hand.

"Oh, no, not yet, thanks."

"Don't fill 'em out, the letters all go back. A crying shame," he said, shaking his head to show just how shameful.

"Oh," Alyssa said, turning, imagining cartons of letters stamped "return to sender," which was really silly when you thought about it because everyone knew freshmen went home in June. She had to be the only student in all of Griffiths who was getting a package from her mother on the last day of the semester.

The elevator and the halls were empty. Most doors up and down the hall opened to bare beds and empty bookshelves. As soon as Alyssa was done packing, she'd meet Howie, the geeky but friendly guy from her comp section who drove over to Cal every morning from his apartment in Oakland in a rusting Chevy Biscayne. He'd had a crush on Alyssa all semester, which made her uncomfortable, though she'd never been anything but kind to him. There was something just a little off about Howie, not the big misses that made people into caricatures, but something just two or three degrees off target. When she was utterly truthful, Alyssa recognized that Howie reminded her of herself. There was some gene they shared that made it easier to be around Howie than people like Cindy, or Tony, or even Linnie. Her kindness was paying off now because he'd been the only person besides Linnie who'd offered to help move her stuff. There wouldn't be more than one load for the Chevy, and Alyssa had promised Howie they'd eat together after.

Chapter Two

Somehow, it didn't bother her that Howie would know her address; it seemed like a safety net, his knowing, just in case.

And now, thanks to Leah, there was one more last-minute box to haul. Alyssa considered leaving it unopened, just stacking it on top of the three boxes of books and treating it as so much more baggage until after the move. But curiosity got the best of her. She scissored off the packing tape and pulled the flaps back. A two-pound Folgers can—Alyssa could smell Leah's brownies—was nestled next to the little body of the bright-eyed, worn-down bear.

Lazzie.

He'd long ago lost the dark red sweater and the knit cap that he'd worn when she was five or six and he was brand new, a Christmas present to her from Cory. His fur was so matted and faded it was hard to tell he'd once been a panda, her favorite stuffed animal, the only one she'd ever been faithful about sleeping with. She pulled him from the box and shook free the packing paper that Leah had cushioned him in, as if she had been setting him up for a fancy burial. A leaf of her mother's stationery fluttered to the ground with the packing paper.

Allie,

I was cleaning out your room and found the boxes of stuffies that we'd packed before Gran died. I couldn't imagine that you'd want them all for the new apartment, but I thought you might like Lazzie's company. Call me as soon as you've moved—I know you're busy.

I love you,

Mom

P.S. I washed him—don't know if it did much good!
P.P.S. If you don't eat the brownies, pay your moving man with them!

She lowered her face into Lazzie's belly and breathed in the familiar scents of the Philadelphia rowhouse: freshly laundered towels, the faintest trace of turpentine, rich chocolate, her mother's dusky fragrance—evoking everything she'd been afraid to leave at the last minute because she couldn't believe it would still be there if California was wrong, if she wanted, or needed, to come home.

She hadn't thought she'd ever *need* home again when she'd chosen Cal, a continent away from the room where Gran lay failing, bit by bit, wizened and weak yet still strong enough to tether Leah to her side with the rope of duty. She'd thought instead about a city by the San Francisco Bay where death and guilt and expectation and duty didn't confuse themselves with simple love. She threatened her mother with this, Alyssa's own need denied, when she told Leah she didn't plan to come home.

"Allie, of course you can come home," her mother had said, changing "won't" to "can" just the way she'd lighten a base coat that displeased her.

"*Alyssa.* I'm not ever going to live here again."

"Of course you're not, honey. But home's always here for you. And so is Carnegie-Mellon. You know what the admissions people said—"

"I know what *they* said."

"Sweetheart, don't be short with me now. If there was any way I could come with you—"

"I know you can't. Just stop it, Mom. I know Gran needs you. I can get to Cal by myself."

"I know you *can*," Leah said. "I just wish you didn't have to."

Even though Alyssa privately believed that a nurse wouldn't have made any difference to Gran in that last month, Leah had chosen to stay in Philadelphia with *her* mother and Alyssa ended up flying to Cal without *hers*, leaving behind the boxed stuffies and half her posters and lots of books because there was no way she could pass those boxes off as luggage to the airline. Throughout the three days of freshman orientation, when she met Mr. and Mrs. Cheung and Linnie's dad and mom and even Tricia's parents, she'd sworn she'd never forgive her mother—

not for staying with Gran, not that—but for refusing to ship the stuffies right away. "It's too much, Alyssa," Leah had said, pulling her hair back from her face with quick hands. "You need to consider your roommate and how tiny dorm rooms are. After you've been there a while, then you'll know if there's room for them." At the time, all Alyssa could think of was how Gran's things had worked themselves into each square inch of the Philadelphia house: pill bottles on every bathroom surface, laxatives on the cereal shelf, diapers in the trash cans, soiled bedclothes in the hamper. Of course, after that, she'd never asked again for the stuffies, and Leah hadn't remembered—until Lazzie. Even when Linnie said otherwise, it was stuck with Krazy Glue in Alyssa's mind that it was the stuffies, not Gran's dying, for which she was never to forgive her mother.

But now she had Lazzie, faded and pulpy as he was, to go with her to the apartment on Dwight. She thought she'd box him back into his cardboard coffin so neither Linnie nor Howie would see him. She would put him into the box and fold the paper wrapping over him like a bunting and neatly tuck the flaps inside each other so he wouldn't budge when they traveled the three uphill blocks to her apartment. But first, with the dorm nearly empty and her door safely locked, she wanted only to eat her mother's brownies and breathe in the smell of home.

CHAPTER

3

These were the excuses she used for buying the two pairs of cotton drawstring baggies. First, every pair of jeans she owned had been bleached white across the belly and thighs after two months of working in the kitchen at Alfredo's, splashed, sometimes soaked by the mixture of Clorox and Pine Sol the kitchen crew used for clean-up. The concoction was so strong it made her woozy with nausea if she didn't manage to divvy up the breaks through her shift to make time to stand in the tiny alley beside the restaurant. There the air reeked of oven exhaust and rotting vegetables, but it cleared her head of the Clorox fumes.

Second, Berkeley had been hot through the summer, hotter than she'd expected, and she didn't own anything cooler than sweats and jeans. Sure, Leah had sent two sundresses from home, but they'd grown too tight across the chest. Alyssa had stopped wearing dresses, anyway. Hardly anybody in Berkeley wore them unless they were patterned with geometric splashes of neon color and short enough to be mistaken for blouses, or shapelessly black and so long that the hems dragged on the dirty streets, fraying and caking fashionably with gutter dirt. Third, fall semester was going to start in less than two weeks, so it was the right time to be shopping, even if it meant brushing shoulders with thin and wiry girls who had no interest in the cotton baggies that Alyssa picked, knowing she didn't have to try them on. The extra large was sure to fit. Drawstring pants were supposed to be formless. That was the point. For the first time in her life, the notion of shopping for school clothes held a certain appeal, the kind of freedom someone tastes, almost like a sugar, when she knows she's playing by the rules, if only the ritual ones. She liked this surprise: the way something she'd always resented, even dreaded, could reverse itself into a reward.

Her mother had given up on the back-to-school excursions some time in high school, probably her sophomore year. Before then, it had been a Labor Day tradition for Leah to outsmart the stores by spending the morning with the colored sales inserts from the *Inquirer* laid out on the kitchen table, studying the prices on Trapper binders and Doc Martens and Gap shirts, finding the best deals in the greater Philadelphia area for Alyssa. Then the afternoon expedition, the marathon rush through the mall, the endless in's-and-out's of dressing rooms, the inevitable disagreement about what looked better, the laced boots or the slip-ons, the green jersey with sleeves or the one without. Leah would stand Alyssa in front of the fitting room mirror, arranging the unbought clothes on her ugly duckling daughter. Her mother's easy beauty charmed every looking glass she faced. Leah's face—soulful ebony eyes, high cheekbones, wide lips—was queenlike, the stuff of fairytale drama. Some mystical power resided in those features, some secret talent Alyssa lacked.

Through it all, what Alyssa remembered: Leah's unspoken *"If you'd only try to look more like me, this would be so much easier."* The excursions stopped, finally, when Alyssa suggested it would be easier for them both if Leah just gave her the money and let Alyssa and Sharon take the bus—Sharon's mother had done it this way forever—and then Leah could paint on the holiday weekend instead of spending it in department stores, which she hated. "I know you'd rather paint, Mom," Alyssa had said, putting the dare into words, hoping that her mother might surprise her, might disagree. But Gran had called out in the burbling voice she kept until the last stroke. Leah turned away from the newspaper, wordlessly pulled her chair back from the table, then went upstairs to what Sharon called the infirmary, the bedroom Leah now shared with Gran and her hospital bed. It *was* her sophomore year, she remembered now, because Sharon had her second holes pierced. Leah had said to Sharon, touching one of the gold studs, "They look pretty, Shar." But later, alone with Alyssa at dinner, louder and not so nice: "No. Absolutely not. Not until you're eighteen, anyway."

The fourth reason she bought the pants, the not-so-good reason she kept tucked away like the snotty Kleenexes Gran used to keep stuffed under the cuffs of her sweaters, was that she knew now why her periods hadn't come for the last two months. The first pregnancy kit said yes, pregnant. She'd seen the commercials—in the Griffiths lounge after General Hospital or sometimes after Letterman—where a series of attractive women express worry and then gratitude over their test results, making it seem like merely purchasing the test kit would get each exactly what she wanted: a baby if she was needing one, no baby if her boyfriend got hard one afternoon when they didn't plan to do it but begged her, *just this once won't hurt, I'll take it out first*—and left her curdled with fear that she might be pregnant because there was no way a baby belonged in her life, not now, maybe not ever.

After the first test said pregnant, she'd bought another one, a different brand, EPT this time, and waited again for the commercial's promise, the right answer. But it read positive, too. Alyssa didn't have the stamina to walk down to the Rite-Aid pharmacy on Telegraph and buy a third. Three's a charm, her Gran used to say when something went wrong, as a yellow scratch cake fell or the watercolors on Allie's paintings ran together in an ugly stain. But three wouldn't be a charm for her, she knew, because it had never been, not even once. Her family was three people big until her dad left, this before she'd reached the age of memory. When Alyssa was older, Leah told her: "He said he wanted room, honey, he needed space." For years, Alyssa thought Dennis had left them for a bigger house, which turned out eventually to be the literal truth, or at least part of it. What started out as her misunderstanding ripened into a teenager's resentment against the narrow rooms of the Philadelphia house which Leah bought herself and loved so much, but which Alyssa saw as a house without room for a father. The resentment turned against Gran when she came, all frail and wobbly, to live upstairs. How could Gran fit into the house, Alyssa wanted to know but never asked, when a father couldn't fit? Why could they manage being three with Gran when there had never been room for a father?

When Sharon started going out with Jason, three didn't work, either. Sharon said they could do things together, she and Alyssa and Jason, but the few times they tried, Alyssa could feel how her presence interrupted the current running between Jason and Sharon, how they were grounded and she was the one taking all the sparks. She and her mother and Gran had managed for awhile, but three didn't save Gran, did it, lying in her coma. Alyssa wanted to laugh the first time she heard her mother, low-voiced and weepy, explain to Cory that Esther was in a permanent vegetative state. "A carrot or a cauliflower?" she wanted to say to make her mother look at her and laugh, to show her relief that it was Gran and not Alyssa who was dying so selfishly, so slowly.

So she didn't buy a third kit. Instead she threw the used ones away, tightening two twist strips around the Hefty garbage bag so nobody— not her neighbor Clara or her landlord Huddie Clark or even the garbageman—would see the colored strips and dots that had betrayed her. She had, unfairly and unwisely, at the age of nineteen, on the cusp of her sophomore year at Cal (straight A's her freshman year), become the victim of some gruesome gag, some cosmic joke designed to ruin her life.

But once the pants were paid for and bagged (the first a blue-striped pair, the second a dark purple paisley that reminded Alyssa of one of her mother's scarves), it was easier not to think about this last reason for clothes shopping, the real one. She had two more weeks of work and early registration and the advance reading for Miller's seminar to get

37

through first. Then she could consider what the pregnancy tests had told her. Then she'd know what to do.

She bought a sugar cone of frozen lemon yogurt to eat on the uphill walk to her apartment. At dusk, the city streets pleased her more. She skirted dog droppings without missing a step or dripping from her yogurt. She wasn't responsible for them, at least. They didn't come from her dog, the long-legged black Lab puppy she'd saved when Huddie found it, skinny and whimpering, beneath the stairs leading to her apartment on the second floor. It was breaking Huddie's heart to take the pup to the pound, so Alyssa told him she'd take it, she'd been wanting a dog, *if* Huddie would let her keep it inside the apartment. The puppy—she'd named him Coffee Bean because that's what his breath smelled like, fresh ground coffee—really belonged to three of them: to Huddie, because he'd found it and then bought the collar and leash and pooper-scooper; to her neighbor Clara, so that sometimes when Alyssa had to work a double shift, Coffee didn't have to go a long lonely day without being walked; and to Alyssa, on whose mattress the puppy slept at night, settled into the crook of her knees when she turned on her side to fall asleep. Sometimes, jerking and moaning with his dog dreams, he'd wake her. But she'd drape her arm over his belly and he'd snuggle up against her and go quiet as she fell back to sleep. He'd grown into something that couldn't qualify as pure Lab because he was too lean through the torso, Huddie said, but Alyssa liked him just as well, maybe even more, when she learned he was a mutt.

When she walked up Dwight Way at night, the street had become so familiar she wasn't offended by the paper trash the wind had sifted against the curbs, or the stray panhandler who'd worked himself off the beaten beggars' path on Telegraph. If there was any daylight left, she liked to stop and face due west, where she could imagine the sailboats on the bay, the rolling whitecaps signaling choppy waters. Good for the sailors, she thought with generosity if it was a windy day, though sailing always made her seasick and was forever linked to her memory of capsizing the catboat her father had rented during a rare summer vacation trip. *Your fault*, he'd shouted, bobbing to the surface of the too-cool and not-so-clean water of Long Island Sound.

She liked watching the Berkeley sailors, whose shouts seemed joyful even when the gusty winds tipped their slender boats nearly sideways. Often the sunsets were so perfectly radiant they pained her, making her ache with the need to describe the vivid range of colors to her mother, to tell Leah how the sun sank against the skyline like a doused flame. The snatches of conversation from the street soothed her, turned inward as her thoughts were, with the shopping bag slapping a gentle beat against her right leg every other step. The last block, from Warring to Prospect, was her favorite. The hill was steep, but the elms overhead were so thick with leaves that at times she imagined herself in a tunnel stretching all the way from the Pacific Ocean to her apartment door.

The tiny gardens between the curb and the buildings were untrained compared to her mother's manicured plot beside the walkway to the Philadelphia house. Next to the symmetry and color of Leah's annuals the Berkeley gardens were chaotic, revolutionary. Here a pumpkin vine coiled lazily around a single orange globe the size of a beach ball. In the next yard yellow and red nasturtiums had twined themselves in and out of the spokes of a child's tricycle. Her own apartment had no flowers, just juniper shrubs which Huddie or sometimes his son Junior kept pruned so they wouldn't block the bayside view of the tenants on the lower floor. Alyssa didn't mind. Because she walked it at least twice a day, often more frequently with Coffee pulling ahead on his leash, she felt the whole block of flowers was hers. She knew each little postage stamp of earth as well as its gardener did and so felt she deserved her share of the bounty.

Coffee barked as soon as her foot hit the first stair. He leapt against her when she pushed the apartment door open, welcoming her with his high-pitched yips.

"Hey, Coff. Hey, Coffee Bean. There's a sweet dog. Good boy. Good boy." He danced around her, slapping the bag with his tail. She sat on the floor and let him lick her face. "That's enough now, Coff. Enough, okay?"

Settled on the board and block shelf against the kitchen wall, the message machine caught her eye: the little red light blinking on and off, impatient as Coffee for her attention. It was probably Howie, calling to see if she wanted to catch a movie, something they'd done throughout the summer, infrequently enough that Howie couldn't have called it dating if he wanted to. Alyssa shook a dog biscuit, the last, from the box on the kitchen counter and made Coffee sit, sit, sit, until he sat, or got close to it, and she gave him the biscuit, stroking his head and sweet-talking praise to him, just the way Huddie had told her to do when Coffee was a good dog. She pressed the message replay button and opened the fridge: a near-empty half-gallon of whole milk, two brown bananas, some tuna from three days ago, three boxes of pizza she'd brought home from Alfredo's last week, or maybe the week before. She'd need to shop.

"Hi, honey. It's Mom. I'm sorry I missed you. I'm calling because I thought I'd go ahead and book your tickets for Thanksgiving and Christmas. I miss you, sweetheart. Call me as soon as you can to give me the dates, okay? I hope you get three weeks at Christmas." A pause. "I love you, Allie."

Alyssa shut the refrigerator door and found, beneath the stack of newspapers on the stove, the tablet she used for shopping lists. Milk, dog biscuits, carrots, some kind of fruit—not bananas this time—macaroni and cheese. She stopped writing, pressed the message button, and listened to her mother's voice once more. Hearing it twice was like scratching a scab or pinching a bruise on her shin. She couldn't keep herself from picking at these places where blood collected, contained beneath the thinnest skin. The tone of her mother's voice was asking, no, commanding her: *love me back, Allie. Love me more.* No matter how many times she told Leah that Allie was a baby's name, her mother wouldn't stop. Even when spoken into a dead phone, recorded on tape, it irked her. *Remember I'm your mom*, her mother's use of the diminutive said. *Remember you're my baby*.

It was close to seven, ten in Philadelphia. She could wait, pretend it had been too late when she got home to return Leah's call, but then Leah would call again when Alyssa might not be prepared, when her voice might inform against her. She picked up the receiver and stroked Coffee, pacified into laziness by his biscuit. The phone rang six times. Maybe Leah wasn't home. Maybe, eventually, when the machine came on, Alyssa would have to leave a recording of her own voice. Or maybe Leah was wiping the paint from her fingers before she picked up, something Alyssa could envision perfectly with her eyes shut, even from three thousand miles away. It never worked, wiping the paint from her hands. The oils always found their way onto the white receiver so Leah's phone had the mottled, marbled look of accidental art.

"Hello!" Her mother's deep voice, live, not recorded.

"Mom?"

"Honey! I'm so glad you called tonight. Hold on just a sec, sweetie, while I get some of this off my. . . . There, how *are* you?"

"Fine, Mom. I'm calling about the tickets." She let the silence lengthen.

"Honey? You there? How are *you*? I've been working like crazy for the Labor Day show, George is hounding me day and night for some new pieces, but I think about you all the time, sweetheart. You have your fall semester calendar, right, so all you have to do is—"

"Mom, I don't know if I can come home." Alyssa reached for the shopping bag holding the drawstring pants and pulled out the paisley pair, flattening the pants against her stomach like an apron.

"Why in the world . . ." Leah's silence, long and hurt, ". . . wouldn't you be able to come home?"

41

Baby's Breath

She coiled the drawstring ends around her index finger, cinching the strings like a noose, pulling tight until her fingertip turned purple. "Well, you know I got this dog and he's—"

"Honey, I *know* they have kennels in California."

"He's just a puppy, Mom. He'd hate it in a kennel. And my landlord said—"

"What about asking your neighbor, the one you like, Clair?"

"Clara. That would be too much. I couldn't ask her." Alyssa unwrapped the noose and started again with her ringfinger, tightening the string and watching her fingertip swell with the angry color of trapped blood. It didn't really hurt at all, strangling your own fingers. It was like pricking yourself with a pin, or pulling out arm hairs, or stretching muscles that didn't want to stretch. At a certain point, past a certain threshold, the sensation stopped, and it was happening to somebody else, not to her at all.

"There's another reason. I know it's not this dog. . . . Is it a boyfriend honey? You could bring *him*."

"No, Mom, I don't have a *boyfriend*." She let the noose go, shook out her fingers. Had Tony Messina ever been her boyfriend? Did thrashing about with a guy on his dorm bed make her into his girlfriend? If anything, the queasiness in her stomach, the tenderness of her breasts, should qualify her as a girlfriend. Could she give this to her mother, such a present of utter confidence: her own swelling body? Or, if she took care of it some other way, the way Linnie's older sister had, would it be safe to let her mother see her, even then? Wouldn't Leah take one look at her and know, as she had always known with an accuracy that seemed unfair, exactly what crime Alyssa had committed?

"But I don't understand how you can not want to come home. Summer, okay, I know you wanted the summer, but Thanksgiving and Christmas both?"

Leah would know. Either way, she'd know. If Alyssa didn't give in,

Chapter Three

Leah was entirely capable of figuring it out from across the continent. The best thing to do was give in, just a little. "Mom. I'll come home for one. Not both. I don't want to leave Coffee that long, and I—I just like it here."

"Gee, sweetie, I was going to keep this a surprise. . . . You know how the light in your room is so good, perfect for a studio? Well, the basement's a bona fide darkroom now. I know you'll love it. It's all set up with lots of room and safelights and—"

"You're using my bedroom for your studio?"

"Oh, honey. I hope you don't—"

"Where am I going to sleep when I come home? Where's my stuff?"

"I boxed everything. I was *careful*, don't worry. It's all labeled. I put it downstairs."

"But where's my *bed*? Where will I sleep?"

"With me, hon. I fixed up my room for both of us. I put your posters up. It'll be fun for us. I know how much you liked having Cindy for a roommate."

"I liked my *room*, Mom."

"You have a room, Alyssa! Your things, the darkroom. . . . They're just different. Honey, you really have to see it. . . . You'll *like* it, Allie, I promise."

Alyssa began twisting the string again, tighter this time, around two fingers, ringfinger and little. "It was *my* room." Tighter, tighter.

Leah's voice rose. Alyssa had succeeded in exasperating her, finally. "But you didn't come home for the summer. You don't even want to come home *now*."

Her mother reached the place she wanted to reach, where she always ended up, winning. Orchestrating every disappointment to be Alyssa's doing, Alyssa's fault, Alyssa's blame. She was never enough for her mother: never slender enough, never neat enough, never nice enough, never bold enough, never loving enough, never grateful enough, never

never never enough. There was no way she could trust her mother with the secret inside her. She couldn't even think of it. She conceded, saying the words which came easiest.

"Thanksgiving. I'll come home Thanksgiving." Then, pushing, pressing, hurting back, "If you'll get Dad to drive down. I want to see him."

Suddenly, walking, standing, even speaking, was too, too tiring. She needed to hang up, to go lie down on her mattress and hold Coffee against her, to retreat to the one sanctuary where she didn't have to think about any of it.

She'd go home for Thanksgiving. That was it. Thanksgiving.

She carried her fall textbooks home from the Golden Bear Bookstore in the late afternoon, shifting them to one hip and then the other until her arms ached. Reaching into her bag for her apartment key, she dropped them all at the top of the stairs, Coffee going berserk behind the locked door. What had started out as a glorious blue day had cheated itself into a mean, wintry gray. A see-through blanket of clouds swept over Berkeley from the west, casting shadows, then tearing itself in half to let the sunlight through, more depressing than a pure unbroken cloud cover would be. At least then, in solid gray, a person wouldn't get her hopes up.

"You need some help there?" Clara stepped onto their shared landing, wiping her hands dry with a green dishtowel. Alyssa smelled garlic and onions browning, heard the faint pop of cooking oil heating over a burner turned high. Clara's door, like Alyssa's, opened at the top of the apartment stairs, so they shared a landing and each other's comings and goings, especially if these were, as Alyssa's was today, fraught with accident.

Clara was the best kind of neighbor, a woman so completely different from Alyssa that throughout the summer they'd slipped into the easy intimacy of opposites, pleasing them both with their unexpected fit. Sixty, maybe sixty-five, a tall woman, strong and thick, muscled but graceful, Clara was the closest thing to a real friend Alyssa had found since coming to Berkeley. She was close to six feet, and Alyssa liked standing close to her, measuring Clara's height with her own. It made her feel less the dependent daughter her mother reminded her to be and more like Clara's chosen ward. This is how it would be if a mother elected a daughter by conscious choice instead of some obligation of birth. Alyssa's height, towering as she did over her petite mother, made her feel gawky. But with Clara she stood up straight and still couldn't meet her eye-to-eye. Age, size, race—everything was so completely different between them that she felt unreserved, as if in Clara's presence she had been reborn, a negative of her old self, a new Alyssa Staton where light turned shadow and shadow became light.

"Oh, Clara, thanks." Behind her door, Coffee howled.

"That dog too big for his britches." Here was something else she loved about Clara, yet another unforeseen gift: the way her speech turned Alyssa from the white girl next door into another woman on the neighborhood stoop. Clara's phrasing treated Alyssa to a world of feeling, a strong and smoky mixment of passion and delight that her own speech could never evoke.

"He misses me."

Clara reached for Alyssa's splayed history text with her amazing hands. *Magical* was the word Alyssa used. Watching them, the beauty of their ropy, outstanding veins, the long tendons under ebony skin, Alyssa wanted her camera in her hands for the first time in months. The black hands, the heavy book, the grey sky. The picture framed itself without her bidding.

"He don't miss you, sugar. He just loud."

"Thanks, Clara." Alyssa pushed her door open with her hip. "Can you come in? I have Diet Pepsi."

"No, I got chicken over there I'm cooking up." She looked down at Alyssa, her face noble, inscrutable. "You look peaked. You wearing yourself down for some reason."

"I'm twenty pounds overweight," Alyssa said, lying even in the confession of something she'd never had the will to say to another person. She was thirty pounds overweight, not twenty. The lie once said made her want, as was her habit lately, to qualify it. "I'm puffing up, not wearing down."

"A person wears away different, every one of us. You, now, you don't eat right, so you's swelling up that way." Clara reached for Alyssa's forearm and gently turned her hand over, palm up. She stroked the paperwhite skin of the underarm and pressed her thumb once, twice, three times, each a different place. "It's salt and fat does that, holds the water in."

Alyssa drew back, rubbing her skin where Clara's gentle thumb prints had left it aching for touch.

"Sugar, you come next door and eat some chicken with me. That pizza ain't nothing like what you need." Clara turned to leave. "Bring that dog, too, if you need to. We take him for a walk after supper, if it don't rain."

Throughout Clara's meal—fried chicken, broccoli, boiled new potatoes with parsley—she watched the magical hands serving and clearing, now and then touching her shoulder. What she liked best about Clara was that Clara didn't ask questions. Not from disinterest—she listened and remembered—but from some kind of adult faith that sooner or later the speaker would get to the important part. Her mother was the opposite. Leah would probe and pull at Alyssa, always had, until Alyssa had to lock herself beneath the stairs in her darkroom, or go to bed (the excuse of headaches helped, she'd always had them), or leave the house to escape the inquisitions. What happened between her and Sharon? Where was the black blouse they'd bought together at Bloom-

46

ingdale's? Did Alyssa think—*no reason, just asking*—she'd be going to the Spring Dance? Even from across the continent, even so busy with her upcoming show, she found time to pose the questions Alyssa didn't want to, couldn't answer. And then, likely as not, once she'd dredged them up, Leah would misplace the answers, or what she thought were the answers.

Clara set a teakettle on the burner. The snap of the gas range igniting signaled the end of the meal, Clara's way of saying she'd appreciated the company, but now she would have her tea, thank you, by herself.

"That was great, Clara. Thanks."

"Plenty left over for you. I'll wrap it. Tomorrow's supper."

"Oh, no, you keep it—"

"Already done."

Clara set a plate of chicken and potatoes down in front of her, crimping the tinfoil wrap around the edges the way Alyssa remembered her Gran sealing the apples inside a pie crust. "You need to drink more water."

"I do drink water."

"Stay away from them soda pops. Coke, Seven-Up, they're all filled with salt. Not the same as drinking water." Clara ran her thumb under Alyssa's eye, tracing the dark circle beneath it. Through the apartment's biggest window, the sister to the one in Alyssa's living room, Clara watched the sleeting Pacific rain. "No walk, I guess. That dog gonna drive you up the walls." She sat down across from Alyssa, straightening the ironed tablecloth with her thumbs just the way she'd pressed the skin on Alyssa's arm.

"I'm kind of tired, anyway. I think I'll just go to bed early tonight."

"You not doing well."

"I'm doing okay."

"The health center, they have walk-in services."

"They do. . . ."

47

Baby's Breath

"You walk in there, sugar." The kettle coughed, then whistled. Clara left it keening while she walked Alyssa to the door. "Couldn't hurt to see somebody," she said, resting her hand on Alyssa's shoulder.

Health Services did have walk-in hours, nurse practitioners who would take care of most anything a student could come up with. But she hadn't been back to Tang Center since Cindy had taken her. That time, she'd left with the wheel of yellow birth control pills she'd never used because listed there, at the top of the list of possible side effects, was weight gain. After Tricia's list, she couldn't knowingly take a drug that might induce weight gain, spinning her out of control of any diet she could imagine putting herself through. Tony turned out to have practiced his own birth control, which was rated pretty high on the effectiveness chart, and she'd never had to go back for the three-month exam. She didn't want to end up looking like the heavy-set nurse who had taken her blood pressure, a blow-up doll, an inflated version of herself.

Instead of trying to give Coffee a real walk in the steady rain, she sat in her yellow poncho at the base of the apartment stairs and unleashed him, letting him snuffle around the parking lot and into the juniper beds. He trotted back and forth across the lot between her and the invisible scents that pulled him away, but he came back as soon as she said his name, deliberately drawing out the two syllables. She was careful to call him back when he strayed too far down the sidewalk, and when he did his dog duty behind Clara's car, she used the pooper-scooper to clean it up. By the time she had locked her apartment door behind her and shook off her dripping parka, it had stopped raining. Coffee had had the next-best thing to a real walk; she figured it wouldn't be neglectful if she called it a day. Lulled by Clara's good food, remembering the brush of the long dark fingers against her own skin, she fell onto her mattress and slept, waking only once to pull the comforter over her head.

*

Chapter Three

If she'd had any idea that Tony Messina would be leaving campus, jogging directly beneath Sather Gate as she was walking in, she would never have brought Coffee to campus for his run. She would have headed in the opposite direction or walked up into the Berkeley hills where the fancy houses hid at the end of gated driveways. Or she'd have stayed home, in bed even, if she'd known there was any chance she'd be talking to Tony Messina on September 5, two days before the semester started.

"Hey, Alyssa!" he called to her without breaking his stride, swerving around the Rastafarian who stood sentry at the Telegraph entrance. Tony was shirtless, wearing only shorts and running shoes. "Your dog?" Then, standing in place, pumping his knees in the showy aerobic insistence of the athletic fanatics Alyssa despised, "Duh. Of course it's your dog. Good summer?"

For a dazed moment until the girl caught up to Tony, she as scantily dressed as he, thin as a bird but as evenly tanned as Mrs. Cheung, Alyssa thought she might be able to talk. Maybe take Tony over to the coffee house in the student union and get iced mochas and talk. Coffee would be snuffling Tony's legs, tickling him and making him laugh, and Tony would say he'd thought about Alyssa over the summer. Then Alyssa could say she'd thought about him too. Pretty soon they'd be talking in such a friendly way that she could tell him about what had happened to her, probably that very last time back in May when they were together. Back when Cindy had leaned out and waved goodbye from the passenger window of Mrs. Cheung's BMW and Tony had said *catch you later* to Marc, Alyssa thinking *what the hell, what's one for the road*? And anyway, she didn't see the point of refusing him what she'd given him plenty of times already. When they'd finished their mochas, then maybe Tony would know what to say and do, and he'd lift her hair and kiss the back of her neck, and everything could go back to normal.

"Hi," the girl said, brushing up against Tony's side like a cat. Her blonde hair was cropped short, bangs long across her gray eyes.

Baby's Breath

"Sandie, this is Alyssa. She was in Griffiths last year. History, right, Alyssa?"

"Right." If only Coffee's leash would break so she'd have to tear after him without making conversation. Tony and Sandie wouldn't think her strange, just concerned about her dog.

"Sandie's a freshman. She's from Fresno, too."

At least Sandie had the manners to stop bouncing in place when she spoke. "I told him he couldn't escape me by coming to Cal. I *told* him I'd follow him to the ends of the earth." She tweaked Tony's skin above the waist, exactly the place where he'd teased Alyssa to measure him with the fat-pinch test, pointing and coaxing: "Not an inch, right? Not even *half* an inch!"

All Alyssa could think of to say was, "The songleader. The picture in his wallet." Lame as it was, Sandie was pleased. So secure, so certain in her boyfriend's eventual fidelity that it could only please her to know another girl, an older woman no less, knew the exact position of her picture in his wallet. Sandie was as sure of Tony as Alyssa was of Coffee. Even unleashed, allowed to roam, he'd come back to his mistress. Like Coffee, Tony would whine and complain, pull against his collar and follow every scent on the wind, but he'd come home in the end. Because Sandie was blonde. Because she was thin. Because she jogged and had followed him to Berkeley, to the ends of the earth. Because she clearly had never allowed herself, her foolish, stupid self, to complicate his pleasure by getting pregnant.

They talked more, words passing back and forth that later Alyssa wouldn't remember at all. Tony was living in the frat house, Sandie in Sherman. Tony was declaring poli sci. Sandie was in psychology. Of course she would be. And of course, to show she wouldn't hold anything against Alyssa, she had called over her shoulder, as she and Tony joined hands and dashed across the street against a red light, "I love your dog."

Leaving them, Alyssa had tripped against Coffee's taut leash. She tugged sharply, though it wasn't the dog's fault that her face was burning with shame. She hung her face, the old high school habit returned, so her hair curtained her features and they couldn't see, when she waved and turned away, how she was crying. In a storefront on Durant, a plate glass window mirrored the street and forced her reflection: the long dark hair hanging to her waist, the shapeless, faceless figure in the T-shirt and striped baggies being pulled off kilter by a loppy, gangly mutt on a blue nylon leash.

She thought later it had to have been an out-of-body experience, the phone call she made that night to Alpha Kappa Lambda. She heard her flat request to speak with Tony Messina. She remembered the delight in his voice when, after his roommate called out "Chick for Messina! Telephone, bro!" he answered with such eagerness that she knew "chick" must stand for "Sandie." Briefly, hanging there outside herself, listening to their preliminary conversation, the meaningless this and that of acquaintances who find each other making nice purely by accident, she wished she knew what it was like to have anybody—a mother, a friend—answer the phone with such delight, such undaunted expectation. And then, angered by the betrayal of her own envy, she blurted out what she had not yet told one living soul.

"I got pregnant, Tony. By you. Absolutely certainly by you."

He had the grace to say oh, no, or oh, god, some suitable expression of manly woe.

She cut him off. "I don't know what to do."

"What do you mean? You haven't done anything? You're *still* pregnant?"

"I'm pregnant."

"Jesus, Alyssa. You've been pregnant for ... four months? You couldn't have let me know before, when it was, when you could—"

She didn't speak. Not when he was making it her fault. Just like her mother would. Just like the fat nurse at Tang would when she'd have to say no, she'd never taken the birth control pills. Why? I didn't want to get fat like you, nurse. Look at me now. Ironic. She couldn't speak to him any longer if he made it her fault.

"Look, I think it's still possible to . . . you know . . . look, I'll go to Tang with you, to find out . . . if you want. . . ."

"You'll go . . . to Tang with me."

"Hey! It's the only thing I know to do! What else could we do? Listen, give me your number. I can't talk now, but I'll call you back. To-morrow. Early. Before—"

Out of body, in body, what did it matter. Tony Messina wasn't going to make it all better, not the way a nice guy would. She hung up the phone and slid to the floor. When it rang again, and again, and again, triggering the machine and cutting her own recorded voice short like the repetitions in very badly done white girl rap, she knew it was Tony, hitting the Star 69 return with his slender, pretty, nervous fingers. Maybe they were sweating. Maybe shaking. Not nice, Tony, not really nice, probably not even to Sandie after he had what he wanted, but smart, responsible enough to keep himself out of trouble. He wouldn't be able to call her forever—he wouldn't get her number from directory assistance. She could wait this out, too, until it just went away. It would—everything else did. She just needed to wait.

She pulled the phone to the floor beside her and leaned her back against the cupboard door that was missing a hinge. Huddie said he'd have to rehang it.

Such a duplicitous word, to hang. To be hung. To hunger.

Hang, hanging, hung.

CHAPTER

4

Dennis still enraged Leah, even after so many years. "Look," she said, switching the phone to her other ear for no reason at all and banging the Dutch oven from the stove to the sink just for the sake of the noise. She liked to think she had too much dignity to shout at her ex-husband, but sometimes it required extraordinary effort. Like now, when she could hardly keep a bandage on the wound of Allie's refusal to come home for Christmas. "She says she'll only come home once, for Thanksgiving. I'd appreciate it if you'd do the traveling this time. You can pick her up and take her out for dinner if you want."

Dennis' round baritone sounded exactly as it had twenty-two years ago when they met, like he was an opera singer rather than a becoming-something-like-famous painter: commanding and wheedling at the same time. "Yes, I'd do it of course, but you see Missy is pregnant—by the way, it's another boy—and I'm loathe to leave her alone."

Not as much as I loathe you, you pretentious asshole. She let the lid of the pot fall from her hand into the sink where it clattered onto its mate. "Well, Dennis, I'm not going to let her use my car to drive to New Jersey when she's only here once for such a short time. Maybe you could get someone to . . . baby-sit . . . Missy. I'll cooperate about which day to make it easier for you." He just wasn't going to jerk her around again about Allie who, thank God, was over eighteen. It had been a courtesy call in the first place, a favor to Allie, one she regretted.

"I don't know if that will be possible, Leah."

"I'm sorry to hear that. I really have to run now. I have a painting to crate for an opening."

"A group show?" His tone was condescending.

"No, one woman. The rest is already at the gallery." Gloating. The sliver of information would fester under his skin, and he'd never ask. As successful as he was, Dennis was that competitive. Especially with Leah. His ascendancy was part and parcel of what had attracted them to one another, mentor and student, man-of-the-world and initiate. Her greater talent, arising, had been unbearable to him, though neither of them explained it that way, not to themselves, not to anyone.

They'd met in October, at one of Dennis' openings at The Ritton Center For The Arts, a modern gallery downtown. He was wearing a tweed jacket and red knit tie, but underneath was a denim shirt, and he'd not cleaned all the paint from beneath his nails. Dennis was a painter truly enough, his splashy abstracts popular purchases as focal points for posh Philadelphia living rooms, his name beginning to spread like syrup beyond the region, but he also consciously dressed the part. He wanted to look like painting was all he cared about, and Leah didn't think he even saw the oxymoron.

He'd been holding a glass of white wine in a blunt hand that looked better suited to hammer and pliers than nylon brushes. He was twelve years older than Leah according to the bio in the show catalog, divorced, the gray lacing his dark hair giving him an aura of expertise.

"The show is wonderful," Leah said, approaching as the cadre of admirers around him thinned when the caterer replenished the shrimp tray. "Your brush technique . . . the movement, it almost looks spiral."

"Thank you," Dennis said, pleased. He must pluck his eyebrows; they were too thick not to straggle toward his nose. Brown eyes and hair like her own, but more fair-skinned, nearly pasty. It wasn't really his looks that attracted her, though he had a good straight nose, and very white teeth he flashed, then covered with his lips, making their afterimage the more noticeable. "Are you a painter? Nobody else has noticed that. I'll be amazed if Zanza does," he said, gesturing with his head toward the *Inquirer* critic who was working his way, notebook in hand, from painting to painting. "He ought to be reviewing worm farms or something he's qualified to look at." He'd been bitter, but then redeemed the tone with a self-deprecating laugh. "Listen to me. I ask you a question and then I don't let you answer. Are you a painter, Miss. . . ."

"Pacey," she supplied, putting her hand into the one he'd jutted into the air. "Leah Rhee Pacey. Leah. Not really, I mean, I paint, but I'm not . . . I was in art school, but I didn't. . . ." What would he care about how and why she hadn't finished? Leah smoothed her black skirt. Damn. One of her stockings had a tiny run creeping from beneath the toe of her shoe.

"Hmm. Modest for one so perceptive. Come on. I'll give you the cook's tour. The first time I experimented with that spiral stroke was really in this piece," he said, guiding her toward a small painting. "I was dealing depth and illusion here—and the notion of the unpredictable and even chaotic whirlpool within, not suggested by the boxy shapes. Do you see?"

"It . . . is it intended to comment on that as part of the human condition, the confinement of our external lives, I mean, well, the stroke also contradicts the cool tones of the boxes, the passion of the inner life as opposed to. . . ." Leah stopped, embarrassed by her desire to impress him. Who was she, for god's sake, to be interpreting a painter's work to the painter? None of her own work was abstract. She'd never particularly thought she understood non-objective art.

But Dennis put his hand on her back this time, to guide her to the next. Leah felt his hand acutely, the firm touch arousing her in a way Elliott—staid, reliable Elliott who she'd been dating five years already, by-the-book Elliott who expected to marry Leah but not until his law practice was established—didn't, never had. "Absolutely," Dennis said.

Baby's Breath

"I think you'd like to visit my studio sometime." There was not a hint of a question mark at the end. It was a statement of fact, and Dennis was quite right.

They'd eloped to New York City three months later, on Valentine's Day 1975, robbing Esther of seeing her only daughter married. "This way, I get you all to myself," Dennis said and moved into Leah's apartment when they got back, keeping his own as a studio. "It's best for me to have a separate work space," he said. "Always has been." He showered and shaved and groomed carefully before he left to go paint, almost as if he were the one who had to show up in a real estate office at nine o'clock every morning. His income was substantial but unpredictable, he pointed out. Her job gave them a steady base and insurance.

For the next two years, Leah learned from Dennis. On weekends, she'd paint alongside him and he'd critique and explain, departing from his acrylic abstracts to quick demonstrations in the oils she favored. "You need more life drawing experience," he said in disgust one Saturday noon. "That's still not right."

Leah swallowed the dregs of her morning coffee. "The design program didn't have...."

"Screw it. You need one, you don't know what's underneath those clothes and it shows. Just sign up for one at Fleisher. You know, that design major was a stupid waste. It's just as well you didn't finish it. A major for frigging wimps without passion or gift or grit." He'd gestured grandly at her chest, then his own. "And you, my sweet, you . . . you have gift, you have passion, and I, I shall give you the heart for it." He'd pointed to her chest, then leaned so his finger touched her left breast. "Hmmm. Yes, I believe your *heart* needs fortifying." He'd cupped the breast with one hand, put his other arm around her back, and pulling her against him, lifted Leah off the floor and spun her around. He was powerful, and even if the spin hurt a little, she felt his erection and her aching, wet answer, a different one than she'd ever had for Elliott. That Saturday, as many, they lost a good part of the best daylight to lovemaking. Dennis said the release made them bolder with the paint when they did get back to work. They'd moved most of Dennis' furniture, better quality than Leah's, into her apartment, but left the big bed in place. Paint was their aphrodisiac, although there were days when Leah was slow to respond, reluctant to leave her canvas, even when Dennis pressed from behind, to arouse her with his hardness against her rear while he reached around to unbutton her shirt, unzip her jeans.

She did take the life drawing class. Maybe it was all that sensuous flesh that made her want to let her whole body draw a life, rather than only having her hand mimic it. Or maybe it was the approach of her thirtieth birthday.

She painted through her pregnancy, relishing the excuse to cut her hours in half at the agency. Cory, third in command back then, had successfully argued that her salary be cut only twenty-five percent. "Consider it a pre-payment to induce you to stay," she'd said, quite seriously, reading Leah's wishes easily as a primer.

And then, in November, a month and a day before her thirty-first birthday, Leah had become Alyssa's mother, and her painting life had been moved aside as decisively as a chess piece in the hand of a relentless master: check and mate.

Not anymore, though. Not anymore.

The summer's work had been the cityscapes she'd imagined. She'd begun with Waverly Street, the iron gate and flowered walled-in walkway to her own door, and then moved over to Panama, the quaint cobbled street designed for carriages, too narrow for cars at all. Then she'd moved in concentric circles into other neighborhoods, into the city, absorbing, photographing, sketching in charcoal. She'd immersed herself in the airy cool of early morning, the silvery cast of that light. Her twilight paintings captured subtle darkness rising off the street while the buildings fought to hold the rose gold of the evening sky, lone figures moving homeward unaware of the play of light on themselves, living cells of the city organism. Flower boxes trailing ivy, massed geraniums in enormous planters, figures tilting their faces sunward as they waited at a bus stop, children under a sprinkler on a tiny patch of lawn: George had seen the potential for a September show as soon as Leah brought in the first three.

At first she'd demurred. "Too much pressure," she told him. "Too many of them aren't *painted* yet. I don't know how long they'll take." She did though, really. The work was flowing, and though she always had a crisis of confidence when one was finished, the life she was absorbing and claiming did seem to be pouring out of her richly, a painting a week.

"The brush work is exceptional. I notice a tad of impressionism, yes? A lighter, quicker feel to the brush, a lighter palette. And the figures, my dear, they *move*. Extraordinary. You can do it. We can pull from other work, you know, if the number is too sparse." His mane stood up as he ran his hands through it, searching for the tack that would convince her to give him the rudder. "You have a couple that would work, I believe, perhaps in another gallery? You can pull those, you know, if they're not spoken and paid for."

She'd hurt him when she'd placed work in other galleries, Leah saw then, and that as much as anything was why she agreed to shoot for a solo show to open the Fall season. It was true; she did have other pieces that would fit well, but the new work would be showcased.

"I won't really need to have announcements ready, or printing done until August. Don't be alarmed; we'll keep it small, but the series is too fine to just scatter. We'll do a catalog," he said. "You need to start being reviewed."

"Thanks," she'd said, knowing the gift she was receiving. Talent, even genius, without the nurture of an experienced promoter usually resulted in poverty, or a day job in something like real estate.

*

Chapter Four

"So how are you going to manage Christmas?" Cory said once her Cobb salad and Leah's tuna melt had been served. The gray-tinted restaurant glass muted the beat of the early September noon sun, and the air-conditioning was cranked up to frigid, which further lifted the hood of humidity. Leah had just told Cory about Allie's insistence she couldn't and wouldn't come home for Christmas, but Leah's plate distracted her. Waving her fork in Leah's direction, she complained, "God . . . once you get through menopause, you won't be able to eat like that, trust me. A couple of French fries anymore, my butt looks like two ferrets fighting it out in a burlap bag. I used to be able to actually eat."

Leah laughed. "Yeah, well. I think I'm about there. Sometimes when I look in the mirror, it's just not me, you know? These lines, they all seemed to just come. Like on my neck, here. And my hands look like my mother's when she was already old. Fifty-one almost. I think of myself as about thirty." She sighed. "It's almost like I keep knowing there's some mistake. This isn't right."

"I know what you mean. But you look terrific. Any hot flashes or signs?"

"Some. Do you take hormones?"

"Oh Jesus, yes. I need all the help I can get. Do you realize how much our turnaround time on properties has increased?"

"Come on. You're being stubborn. Someone else can do what I did."

"Do you know how hard it is to settle, when you've seen what can be done? And for how little money? That's the thing." Every time they were together, Cory told Leah at least once how badly she missed her at the office.

"I wish to hell my daughter missed me half as much as you do."

"Oh geez, I was in the middle of asking you about that, wasn't I? So how are you going to cope? You know, you'd be welcome at our house Christmas Day."

The waitress, a pretty girl about Allie's age, appeared to refill their coffee cups, and Leah waited until she'd finished to answer. Leah wondered if Allie's restaurant in Berkeley was upscale, like this little place, with real plants instead of plastic ones, and not too loud. She couldn't get any real information out of Allie.

"It'll be okay. I hung up and cried a long time, feeling very sorry for myself—you know, especially about the opening. I wanted her to share that with me, but I do understand about classes just starting. But about Christmas, I've realized: she doesn't really know what she's saying. She's not going to really want to spend Christmas away from home. When she comes for Thanksgiving, I'm going to just give her the ticket for Christmas."

"She may get her back up," Cory warned, tucking her bobbed hair behind her ear and taking another roll. "Been there, seen that." She peered over the top of her glasses.

"Yeah, but I don't think so. What kid wants to spend Christmas alone, way away from home? Her friends won't be there, I mean, they'll have all gone home. . . . She's not going to turn it down when the ticket's in her hand."

"Is she with a guy, maybe, that she hasn't told you about?"

Leah paused. "I doubt it. Tell you the truth, I sort of wish she were. I'd send him a ticket too. I hate thinking of her all alone in that apartment. She says it's fine, she likes it, but she's got this pride thing. I don't think she'd come out and say, 'I made a mistake.'"

Cory shook her head. "Do they ever?"

"Make a mistake or admit it?"

"Either."

The mothers laughed.

George had ordered champagne for the opening, and as many hors d'oeuvres as she'd seen at any of Dennis' openings before or after they were married. Elegant. Leah wore her favorite, black. It was practical and didn't require a lot of attention. A wide, hand-hammered brass bracelet and a dramatic matching necklace of hammered brass and onyx made for her by a friend from art school, and medium height heels—which she'd always hated—were what she'd finally settled on.

She was a nervous wreck, childishly grateful when Cory did come early, as she'd promised.

"God, woman, you look stunning! Are you really expecting anyone to care about the paintings? And those nails!" Cory teased.

Leah folded her red thumbnails into her palms, wrapping her fingers around them and then pressing the fists against her outer thighs. The caterer was spreading white linen over a table in the front room of the gallery.

"Don't do that. They look beautiful. I'm only kidding you."

"I know. It's not me, though, is it? My hands are always such a wreck, I just thought I'd try to make them look nice. I got a manicure."

"About time, now that you're reaching the ranks of the rich and famous." Cory hugged her. "I'm serious, Leah. I'm just so proud of you, so happy. You deserve this, and it's just starting."

George popped a cork. "Come, ladies. A private toast before the admiring hordes arrive."

The show did look spectacular. Even Leah hadn't quite envisioned the impact the paintings would make when arranged and hung this way. The frames were simple, as she'd wanted them, harmonious with each other and the paintings. She'd had her work in juried group shows many times and it was always satisfying when the show was a success. But that was a lemon drop on the tongue compared to this, a whole lemon meringue pie. "Enjoy, enjoy," George kept exhorting her, his erratic hair sprayed down for the occasion. Leah tried, but she felt a little like an imposter.

Shrimp. Champagne. Crab-stuffed mushrooms. Yogurt cheese from Amish country. Baked brie. Popping corks. And people did, as George had predicted, bring their checkbooks.

"This is Dennis' speed, not mine," she said to Cory. "He loves being the center of attention."

"Did you send him an invitation?"

"Are you joking?"

"I didn't mean so he'd come. I meant just to show him. . . . Do you ever want to get married again?"

"Some guy's toothpaste spit in my sink? Some guy's dirty underwear wedged behind my bathroom door?"

"Yeah, but how about a wild passionate screw . . . or even a really good backrub?"

Leah shrugged. "Do I believe in love? I don't know, really, except for Allie. That's what broke Dennis and me up, in a way."

"Love broke you up? Or did you mean Allie?" Cory's eyebrows went up. She sipped champagne and waited for an answer. Cory knew how to do that, wait.

"Same difference."

Leah didn't elaborate though Cory waited for more. Seconds later she was pulled away to greet the people arriving to absorb a view of her world, much of which was hidden like Waldo in the paintings.

Leah had wondered sometimes whether she and Dennis would still be married if she'd not had a child. Certainly Dennis had always put himself first, and that had been somehow acceptable to both of them. Leah was potential, future; Dennis was achievement, power.

At first it seemed he'd be a good father. He was doting and even did diapers as long as they were *wet but no poop*, as he said. Of course, what do newborns do, really, but eat and sleep and collect insincere compliments about how beautiful they are, a communal gift to fortify parents for what's to come? And Dennis sponged up those compliments, taking the dusky down on Allie's head as his own achievement, as though Leah's hair were, say, blue. Alyssa, the name to which Leah pushed Dennis, an alternative to his choice, Allison, was one she loved for its softness and how it sounded like alyssum, making her think of *baby* baby's breath.

Chapter Four

Once Allie became mobile, though, toddling and grabbing and whining and spilling, Dennis's patience was a short string with no knot on the end.

Allie was twenty-six months when the marriage finished dying, though it had lurched along and foundered several times since her birth. She was sick again, another ear infection, and her temperature meant they wouldn't accept her at the day care. Leah had already taken too many days off and was reluctant to take advantage of Cory's understanding for another because Allie's fever was low and her spirits were good.

"I really need to go in today," Leah said to Dennis as she pulled cereal from the cabinet and milk from the refrigerator, wiped Allie's nose, and started to make herself a bologna sandwich to take to work. "I've already missed Monday and Tuesday, and there's the Raymer house to do; it's supposed to be ready to be shown next week, and I haven't been able to do up the plans, let alone get the work orders done."

Dennis' mouth tightened. Leah braced.

"Not today. Really, it's just too disruptive to the flow. I'm sketching the new piece."

Leah set the milk down hard. In her highchair, Allie whined and squirmed. Dennis hadn't fastened the safety belt again, Leah noticed, and hurried over to do it before Allie stood up. "I've told you, you've got to do the belt. Honey, I'm sorry, but I really need you to keep Allie today."

They'd bickered about it a bit more over Cheerios and toast—their meals already centering around what Allie could or would eat—while Leah monitored Allie's progress with her tippee cup and the toddler-sized bites Leah set a few at a time on the tray in front of Allie, who had smeared butter and jelly off her toast wedges into her thickening sable curls. Dennis, rumpled as sleep in his old white terry robe, looked Leah up and down, and Leah knew it was registering in him that she didn't intend to be overruled this time: she was ready to go, in a long tweedy skirt, black sweater and and her good black boots, dressed for an "out day," when she'd visit new listings, sketch pad in hand, to plan a makeover. If she had the slightest intention of staying home with Allie, she'd have been in sweats so she could be down on the floor building Lego cities. Since it was Leah's job that kept them in health insurance and often paid for Dennis' studio, this was one of the rare arguments she would win.

"It's good for you and Allie to spend some time alone together, you know?" Leah tried to placate a petulant Dennis as she kissed Allie good-bye. Even though the pharmacy labels on them were clear, she wrote out instructions for the baby's decongestant and antibiotic and placed the note like a bomb on the kitchen table. Neither she nor Dennis was used to her drawing a line. She got outside their apartment door by steeling herself against Allie's crying and putting one foot in front of the other like soldiers.

The first time Leah called home to check on Allie during the day, she wasn't alarmed that Dennis didn't answer the phone. He could have been changing Allie. Leah herself often didn't sprint for the phone if she was engrossed with Allie. But the second time, she wondered about it and was distracted as she compared paint chips for the Raymer house and sketched a rearrangement of the living room furniture. The third time, the black worry thread began to fray.

Leah took an early lunch between visiting houses and went home. There was no sign of Dennis and Allie, though a quick look reassured her Allie's diaper bag was gone, which she took to mean whatever had taken them out hadn't been an emergency. She told herself she was being neurotic and decided to go back to work. Her heels made a hollow click on the hardwood floor of the hallway.

The office was empty except for Alice, the receptionist, and one agent who was eating a tuna fish sandwich at his desk, the smell widening until Leah's stomach rumbled. Her bologna sandwich had no appeal, though. She sat at her desk, fidgeting and unproductive. When the phone rang a little after twelve thirty, she answered it half through the first ring.

"Alyssa just managed to get the top off a gallon of Turpinoid. It's all over the place—and her."

"Oh my god, that's poisonous. Did you get it off her? Where is she now?" Leah could hear Alyssa scream in the background, her worked-up yowl only Leah could settle by rocking her, stroking her hair and cheek.

"She's all right. I washed her hands. You'll have to come get her. I can't work this way."

"Did you check her breath—make sure she didn't drink any? Call 911 if there's any chance that she took *any* in. I'm on my way."

"Good."

Leah sped, ran a red light, prayed, even though she didn't really believe God answers such prayers.

In the studio, Allie's busy box and a couple of stuffed animals lay on the floor. Dennis was in the work area, soaking up Turpinoid with paper towels. Allie was across the room, still crying, hiccups added in like a slow metronome. One side of her face was too red.

Leah snatched Allie into her arms, caressing her. "What happened to her face?" she demanded, but keeping her voice calm as a lullaby, and sitting to use her body as a rocking chair for Allie.

"I was checking her breath, *like you said*," Dennis snapped.

Leah studied Allie's cheek, but Allie twisted away and buried her head back into her mother's shoulder.

"You were supposed to take care of her at home," Leah said.

"You don't seem to understand. I have work to do. I brought stuff for her to do. There's no reason a child shouldn't be able to behave. If she wasn't so spoiled. . . ."

Leah had stared at him then. When Allie was all the way calm, Leah dressed her in her snowsuit and took her home. Within two months, she'd signed and filed the divorce papers Esther's attorney had drawn, the ones that specified—against adamant legal advice—no alimony, no child support, just a trust fund for education. The only dividend from her marriage she took for herself—and it grew just like blue chip stock—was the right to despise Dennis, to turn him into a running joke for Cory. So what if she exaggerated, stereotyped, demonized—it made Cory laugh. It made Leah laugh. And she never let loose around Alyssa. Never. She'd sworn she wouldn't rob Alyssa of a father twice.

George's hand on her arm startled Leah as if from a dream of falling. He had to incline his head up slightly to look her full in the face. His eyes, slightly buggy behind his glasses, were light-full, happy.

"You see? Shouldn't you be admitting now how right I was about a show? There'll be a write-up in *Philly Arts*, you know. I expect an *Inquirer* review, too. And they'll be good, trust me."

Leah felt out of place, an imposter, but a gratified one. She flicked her hair back with the startling manicured hand. "Thank you, George. Really, just thank you."

George grinned. "You mustn't stand over here pretending to disappear. People want to meet you. My dear, we're *selling*. Have you seen the red dots going up? Four already. *Vespers, Child's Play, Panama Street*, and *Canopy*—I told you that dappled light was extraordinary—are spoken for."

Glasses tinkled as the caterer set more out. How many openings of Dennis' had Leah been to, and how long ago? It had taken her more than twenty years to navigate the detours, but this one was hers. She was here now, and she was staying.

CHAPTER

5

Leah had called the airline twice. In spite of the weather in the middle of the country, where O'Hare was slow as planes were de-iced in a November freezing rain, Allie's direct cross-country flight was expected to be only forty minutes late. And just in case they made up time, Leah was at the airport nearly an hour before it was even scheduled.

She bought coffee and let it get cold while she fidgeted in a seat by the gate Allie's flight would come into, after she'd tried to pass time in the bookstore, brushed lint from her coat, and gone twice to the ladies room, where she'd also brushed her hair and checked her teeth. She needn't have bothered to bring the latest issue of *Philly Arts*; she was too excited to read, though Leah blamed the din of the holiday-crammed airport. Seven months, three weeks and four days. *I'm never going this long again without seeing her.*

When the plane was finally announced and passengers began to deplane, Leah positioned herself to get a glimpse as they straggled out. Allie's seat was in the back half of the plane, Leah knew, since she'd bought and mailed the ticket in September to seal the details of the visit as unchangeably in Allie's mind as in Leah's heart.

Finally, Allie in the jetway. Leah couldn't see her face but recognized the curtain of hair, duller than its usual high-gloss onyx, hanging over her features. Allie looked at her feet as she walked, a loaded backpack in place. She wore baggy sweatpants, her old navy peacoat—though

Baby's Breath

Leah had given her an L. L. Bean field coat last Christmas—and hightop sneakers from her high school wardrobe.

When Allie finally looked up to swing her hair out of the way with her old gesture, a clump of passengers still protecting her from her mother's frantic bear hug, Leah thought how pale she was, how raccoon-ringed with fatigue her eyes.

"Sweetheart, oh, honey, let me look at you . . . I've missed you so much." The carry-on bag in Allie's hand blocked Leah's embrace, but Allie extended her other arm and the pressure of it around her mother's shoulders felt intentional, not overly quick. Leah said nothing about how exhausted Allie looked, or the extra weight—always a sore point—but simply linked her arm into Allie's and held out the other to take the carry-on.

"That's okay, Mom, I've got it," Allie said.

"You sure? That backpack looks heavy. Can't I carry something?"

"I've got it."

"Okay, then, honey. Let's pick up your bags. Are you hungry? We can stop on the way home for something to eat."

"I didn't check any bags."

"That's all you brought?" Leah eyed the small carry-on. "Oh, I guess you've got the rest in your backpack."

"That's books. I've got finals coming up, you know. I don't need much."

Leah had never fussed much over clothes herself, though Esther had, so she kept it neutral when she said, "Maybe we can get in a shopping trip, pick you up just a few new things."

Allie shrugged. "I'm okay, Mom."

"Oh, sweetheart, I know you are. Just put up with me fussing a bit, okay?" The sallowness of Allie's complexion, the smudges beneath her eyes made Leah long to rock her daughter to sleep and then cook an irresistibly fragrant pot of chicken and dumplings, to find her little Allie again, the one she could take care of.

Chapter Five

From the time Allie was a toddler until long after she really outgrew her mother's lap, she'd want Leah to sit in the rocker and let her climb on so she could snuggle chest to chest with her mother. She'd bury her face in Leah's neck, legs bent into kneeling position and feet sticking out past the end of the chair, one to each side. The closeness had been almost too much for Leah to endure, so unthinkable the chance of losing it. Leah had stroked Allie's downy hair, making note as it coarsened with time, until braids snaked their way down her daughter's back.

"I can't wait to hear about school," Leah said as they matched strides down the concourse past The Steak Hut where customers stood in line. "Oh, doesn't that smell good? You didn't tell me if you're hungry."

"Mom, too many questions at once," Allie said, but not unkindly.

"Sorry, honey. Are you hungry?"

"I could eat something."

"Let's stop on the way, then. Or would you rather have home-cooked food?"

"Whatever's easiest. I really don't care."

"Can you hold out until we get home? I made you a lasagna—but it'll keep if you're starved."

"No, that's okay. I can wait."

In the car, Allie was too quiet for Leah, but she tried to keep the tone light and remember not to ask too many questions. Allie sat facing forward, twisting the button on her peacoat.

"School's fine."

"The honors seminar."

"No, I'm still majoring in history."

"No, I'm not dating anyone, special or otherwise."

"Not really." The last was in response to whether she'd made friends with any of the neighbors in her building.

"So did you put your dog in a kennel?" Leah asked. "What's her name again?"

"He. *His* name is Coffee Bean. No. There's a woman in the apartment across from me who likes dogs. She's taking care of Coffee."

"I thought you said that would be an imposition?" Leah said, and immediately regretted it. She shifted her hands on the steering wheel and peered at the car ahead of her, trying to think of something to say that would distract Allie, preclude her snapping back. "Um, so lasagna and a salad, I think, and I've got garlic bread sticks, too."

"No, it's not an imposition. She *wanted* to do it." Allie's voice held something like an accusation. Leah resisted a response.

"Well, it certainly is nice of her. Maybe we could get her a present."

"I'll take care of it, Mom."

Leah reached over and patted her daughter's thigh. "I know you will, honey. I'm sorry."

"Speaking of presents, though, I brought you one." Allie reached into her pocket and pulled out a little box wrapped in blue with a silver tie around it.

"For me? Sweetheart, thank you. What is it?"

"I guess you'll just have to suffer the agony of unknowing—that's what Professor Miller calls it," Allie teased, sounding like her nine-year-old self, the happy year Leah returned to in her mind as a touchstone.

"Will you steer? Or better and safer—open it for me?"

"Not now, Mom."

"Come on, honey, I can't wait!"

"Mom." The teasing tone to Allie's voice was gone, sucked out through the window her daughter had cracked as if she weren't getting enough air. "It's no big deal. It can wait till later."

Silence claimed the rest of the ride through Philadelphia evening traffic. Leah had hoped to hear details about school and friends, but Allie switched on the radio. Leah sighed. She'd let it go for now, with the little blue box resting weightless as an egg in the nest of her lap. They'd connect better over dinner. Allie was probably tired, but Leah hoped

Chapter Five

she'd be pleased with how she'd fixed up the bedroom, with the carefully shared bureau top and drawers, the divided closet. Even Allie's daisy head poster up now, by the scowling dreadlocked rock singers. And she'd had her contractor put up two shelves to the right of Allie's side of the bureau. Leah had left them empty, for Allie to use however she wished. She'd offer to get new comforters for the twin beds, let Allie pick the pattern.

And she hoped, she dearly hoped Allie would be excited about the permanent darkroom in the basement. Excited enough to want to come home more often. Excited enough to compensate for the bedroom she'd lost. Leah felt a stir of guilt about the room, but reminded herself Allie was, after all, an adult.

*   *   *

On the bottom stair, Leah stopped. "I'm just going to put that lasagna in. I'll be up in a sec. You want me to bring you something? Cranberry juice? Orange?"

Alyssa started to say she wasn't thirsty, but her mother's glowing face, upturned in expectation, caught the refusal in her throat. "Orange is fine, Mom." She saw her mother as a photograph, black and white, a perfect portrait: pure light framed by hair still as dark as Alyssa's own, one slender, pale hand on the newel post. Her mother who looked more like her sister, Sharon used to say.

"Okay, sweetheart. You've got all the drawers Gran used to have . . . in the bottom of the bureau? And as many hangers as you need in the closet. We'll fill them up, right? We'll max out my credit cards—"

"*Mom.*"

"Well, we'll max out one credit card . . . how's that? Sweaters, a skirt? Something new to wear when you see your dad? They've got some cute wool jumpers at Macy's—"

"You don't have to remake me just to see Dad, Mom."

"Oh, honey, I know." Leah turned to the kitchen. "I do know that.

I'm just . . . feeling like I want to give you anything you want. *Just because.*"

Just because. This was their game from as far back as Alyssa could remember, up until high school when it didn't work anymore to have your mother swoop down on you in public and cover your face with kisses. "*Just because,*" Alyssa used to say when tired or sleepy or yearning for touch and she'd slide under Leah's arm, nudging the book from her mother's lap and locking her arms around Leah's neck. "Well then, just because," Leah would say back, pulling her into the nest of her lap, pressing Alyssa against her breast, ignoring the book when it dropped to the floor. They never needed to talk then, and Alyssa couldn't remember her mother ever spoiling "just because" with questions. Now she heard the echo of tenderness in Leah's voice, but one question circled, bleaching the fondness even from memory: *What's wrong with you?*

"I think I can find my way around," Alyssa said, reaching the top of the stairs.

"Oh, sweetheart, I know you can."

She passed the door to her mother's bedroom—their bedroom, Leah corrected her when they had turned onto Waverly Street and Alyssa unsnapped her seat belt in anticipation. She dropped her backpack and slid the duffle bag off her shoulder, letting them sit in the hall where they fell. As soon as Leah topped the stairs, she'd pick them up and carry them to wherever it was she had decided they belonged. She'd probably never stop. It was some biologically determined instinct for a mother to pick up after her child. Two or twenty, it didn't matter how old. In the bedroom that had been Leah's alone and then Gran's and Leah's and then Leah's again before it was theirs together, her mother would settle Alyssa's bags into whatever corner she'd decreed should be Alyssa's, squaring them neatly with the bedroom walls. *Let her.* Let her pick up after me if it makes her happy.

Since college, especially after her summer in the Dwight Way apartment, she'd found she could relinquish more and more of the customs of home. With daredevil ease, she found herself breaking the old household conventions, Leah's habits of doing that had always seemed as coded as laws. In Berkeley, she kept butter on the counter instead of inside the fridge. Who wanted to spread refrigerated butter's half-frozen chunks on toast that turned stone cold before the butter softened? She left the toilet brush in full view instead of hiding it demurely inside the bathroom cabinet. Everybody had a toilet brush, what's the big secret? And why not use every plate and fork in the kitchen before you washed the dishes? Economy of labor and conservation of resources both excused that choice, one hundred percent politically correct in California.

But her breaking of customs didn't entitle Leah to the same. Even as she realized the unfairness of the thought, she couldn't cease believing that her room, exorcised of her once-upon-a-time presence and transformed into a studio, constituted an act of personal violation. For God's sake, Mrs. Cheung still bought an occasional porcelain doll to add to the collection on the glass shelves in Cindy's untouched lemon-yellow bedroom in Pacific Heights. Cindy still kept clothes in her closets at home; *her* mother did Cindy's laundry, motored across the bay from Berkeley every weekend. Alyssa should have known. Leah had expected her to wash her own clothes since she was ten. Ten!

So she had to see the studio first, without Leah standing beside her, measuring, tempering Alyssa's response with her expectation. She wanted to feel whatever she would feel by herself, without her mother's prompting. No kisses, no bandages.

Standing on the bare hardwood floor of the room that had just six months earlier been carpeted exactly the way she chose, she was overwhelmed by homesickness. Canvasses, some clean, some finished, leaned against the wall in place of the bedstead where she and Sharon had tacked pictures and posters and once, when Sharon was furious with her own mother, a whole pack of Zig-Zags, one thumbtack for every paper. She had wanted to leave, yes, insisted on choosing a school three thousand miles from Philadelphia, but she hadn't intended her mother to believe she was leaving forever. Leah should have left it just because it was *hers*. Now, except for the oily reek of turpentine, it wasn't even recognizable as a part of the house she remembered. A hot balloon inflated in her chest, a helium bubble of fragile rage threatened to bursting by a pinprick of sorrow.

Only the view from her windows was the same: behind the bare oak limbs, the lights in the Goldman's bedroom across the cobbled street winked at her. She used to watch their shadows, Elise and Peter, the muted figures of shadow puppets behind the curtains. Now they're putting on pajamas, she used to say to herself. Now Peter is brushing his teeth. Now Elise is getting into bed. Now Peter has turned out the lights. Then, her own bedroom lights long since extinguished, she would cuddle Lazzie and fall into utter sleep, as if Elise and Peter were her own parents, all three of them sleeping safe and sound under the same roof. Had Leah ever noticed them, Alyssa's dream parents? Had she suspected Alyssa's desire held tight against her daughter's fickle heart? Suspecting disloyalty, had it been easier for Leah to wipe out her daughter's place, erase it with brush and paint and her selfishness?

Leah had coated the bedroom walls a creamy white. Of course she would have obliterated the fingerprints and smudges that might remind her this was really Alyssa's room. Except for her little mahogany bookshelf, which no longer held her *Stuart Little* and *Charlotte's Web* but was stacked with supply catalogues and her mother's paint-stained Gray's *Anatomy*, all her furniture was gone. The makeshift bookend, a Mason jar vase of dried flowers, held charcoal pencils, too, in the infuriating partnership of neatness and mess marking her mother's studio. If everything has a place, she would say to Alyssa, taking a brush or a tube of paint from her daughter's hands, that makes it easier to be tidy. Put it back where you found it, Allie. If you borrow something, make sure you return it in better shape than you found it, honey. Now Leah had

Chapter Five

broken all her own rules. Turned them upside down and inside out to have a studio. Alyssa touched the canvas leaning against her mother's painting table. It looked to be a man walking in *her* park, where she'd learned to ride a bike and later, sitting with Sharon on the swings during her riot girl phase, where she'd learned to smoke grass. Leah had taken her space there, too, putting that shadowy man into the empty park. As always, her mother's painting left her out. Nothing of hers was left. Nothing. She could tear the canvas to pieces with her bare hands.

Her mother's easel and palette looked larger than they had in the dark, low-ceilinged basement where Leah used to paint. Like the two trailing vines which Leah had hung to either side of the windows, they were greedy for sun and space, eager to spread their roots, intent on taking up even more room than they were given.

"What do you think?" Leah said, touching her arm. "Hey! I didn't mean to startle you!" Orange juice spilled. Her mother set the dripping glass on her painting table. "I should've warned you." She dabbed at herself, the floor, Alyssa's shirt. "Sorry, honey . . . involuntary christening—"

"I'm going to change, anyway."

"It's nice, huh?"

"It's great." She stepped away from Leah. Another touch and she would break, she felt that brittle. "Where am I going to sleep?"

"With me! Remember I got another twin bed, come see! New sheets, too, navy blue, your favorite—"

"It's not my favorite."

"It used to be."

"A lot of things used to be." She turned, too fast. The hem of her unzipped sweatshirt caught against the dried flower heads in the Mason jar, which fell, shattering against the hardwood floor. "Sorry."

Leah knelt and picked the straw flowers from the thick shards. "It's okay. It's just a jar. Doesn't hurt a pencil to drop it."

"It wouldn't have broken if you'd left my carpet." Pushing, pushing.

75

Baby's Breath

"I can't paint on carpet. You know that." Leah's voice came quick and hard. She'd almost lost it over that lousy jar of flowers.

Better to back right out of the room, shut the door, just stay away, go to bed. "I'm going to take a shower."

"A quick one, all right?" Soft again, wheedling. Leah wouldn't let Alyssa spoil her studio. "Dinner will be ready in about fifteen minutes."

In the bathroom, she let her clothes drop to the floor and left them. Her mother had taken all the time in the world to get rid of *her* bedroom, but the chrome piping that Leah had installed for Gran still circled the tile shower, robbing Alyssa of space so every time she turned to rinse, she hit her elbow or her hip on the cold silver rail. Getting out, she was careful to turn so her swollen stomach didn't touch the cold metal. She was careful not to look at herself in the mirror when she dried and wrapped her hair in one of the clean towels her mother had left folded on the toilet seat after slipping into the bathroom when Alyssa was showering. New, navy blue to match the sheets on the twin beds.

She must be, would be careful. There was no privacy for her in this house.

They found a space on the fourth floor of the elevated garage downtown, finally, after winding up and around the tunneled lanes so many times that Alyssa felt carsick.

"Did you bring film? We can stop at Gower's and get you some black and white if you didn't." Leah turned back to the car. "Did we lock?"

"We locked." At the elevator, Alyssa waited for her mother to catch up. "I didn't bring my camera."

Leah pushed the button for the ground floor and took Alyssa's hand. "Do you want to use mine, then? For your visit with Dad? I was so sure you'd want to use the darkroom." She squeezed Alyssa's fingers. "No towels, no duct tape, no ruined exposures! A real sink!"

It was a real darkroom. A photographer's dream. But, like the shared dresser and the twin beds and the stupid posters hanging on the wall in Leah's bedroom, it struck Alyssa as a payoff for something her mother had taken without asking. Another rule of her own Leah had broken: *always ask first*. She hadn't asked, had she? She'd just taken. Alyssa would never use the darkroom, its space created by the theft of her bedroom. "I don't think I want to take any pictures of Missy, thanks."

Her mother laughed. "I take it we're not stopping at Gower's." Leah's failure to play the unrequited gratitude card surprised her.

"No, no stop at Gower's."

The elevator stopped on the third floor. Two joking, spotty teenaged boys stepped inside, altering the elevator space. Alyssa edged closer to her mother, pressed to Leah's side by the instinctive inclination to move nearer to blood kin when strangers enter the scene. She begrudged Leah this dependence that surfaced at the oddest times, the umbilical cord saved from rupture by flesh and history. The boys looked once, quite boldly, at Leah's face, but it was Alyssa who stared them down until they dropped their gaze and turned away.

"It's been a while since you've seen Caleb and Missy, hasn't it? Caleb will be changed—"

"And Missy will be very pregnant," Alyssa said, and quickly wished she hadn't.

Leah must find Missy an irritant too. Though they'd never spoken badly of her, Alyssa suspected her mother's assessment of Missy was identical to hers. Too young, too naive, too fawning. The perfect clone of Tony Messina's Sandie. *Usurper* was the word she thought of for Missy. Then, resenting the way Leah's slender figure had earned the attention of the boys in the elevator, she attached it to Gran and Leah, each usurpers in their own way.

"Should we get the comforter first? I didn't think you'd decide to sleep downstairs. Do you want new sheets, too?"

"Mom, I don't care about the sheets." Alyssa pulled her hand from her mother's as though the real reason was to fix the shoulder strap of her backpack. The elevator doors slid open to the ground floor. "I'm used to sleeping alone now."

Often, with the tension between them as frail as a membrane, she wanted to tear it with her voice: *just leave me alone.* But waking up groggy and headachy after the first night at home, she'd sworn she wouldn't. When Alyssa awoke, Leah had been mixing buckwheat pancakes in their favorite blue bowl—the cookie bowl, Alyssa used to call it. *She's making an effort. Don't spoil it.* When the tension eased and they laughed or fell into the nonsensical games of childhood, only at those moments did she admit to herself that it felt good to be babied. When she wasn't flushed with resentment, it felt good to be home.

Inside the bed and bath shop, Leah pulled her to the comforter display. "What's your favorite color now, honey? I'll bet we find it here."

"What?"

"Your new favorite color. Since it's not navy. . . ."

"Oh, anything."

"Look at this." Leah touched a thick blanket in green and yellow. "Do you want stripes? Flowers?"

"Can I take it back to Berkeley?"

"Oh—of course you can."

"Never mind. We can just get something that matches the couch."

"It doesn't have to—"

"This one." Alyssa picked up a thick, plastic-bagged comforter in splotchy patches of brown and cream. "It looks like a painting, doesn't it?"

"An abstract, I guess." Leah wrinkled her nose. "You're sure you want this one?"

"Mom. Let's just get it."

"Okay, honey. Okay."

The clothes were harder. Leah thought Alyssa should wear a jumper, a dress, a long skirt even, to dinner with Dennis. Alyssa thought pants were just fine. They compromised on a pair of billowy long black harem pants that Leah saw in the window of Kountry Kasuals, even though they agreed the store's intentional misspelling to stress the alliteration was contemptible. They laughed about that and slid clothes back and forth across the racks while they whispered to each other. Phoney Phinesse, Alyssa said. Hair and There, Leah coughed, muffling her chuckles, lifting her own hair onto her head in the mimicry of a bouffant. Easy Sleazy, Alyssa shot back, crossing her eyes. Racey Lacies, Leah said, pulling her sweater tightly across her breasts, posing like a pin-up.

Leah didn't ask her about size, just handed her two pairs of the black pants from the end of the display rack, where the L marker separated the XL's. "Let's find some blouses, huh?" she said, handing the pants to Alyssa. "As long as you're dressing up. Oh, look!" She pulled a short silk jacket from a rack and held it up to Alyssa. "It's darling, honey!"

"It's too short."

"No, it's supposed to be cropped like that."

"It's still too short."

Leah rehung the jacket. "You want something longer, sort of flowing like the pants?"

"Whatever. I'm just not the cropped type, Mom."

"How 'bout this?" Leah held up a sheer, sparkly, long-sleeved silver sweater. "Kind of elegant and simple, don't you think?"

It was too much like the silver jacket Cindy Cheung had made her buy in San Francisco, too much a reminder of Tony Messina and all she didn't want to think about, especially not now with her mother two feet away.

"No, not silver."

"Gold? They've got one in gold."

"Okay." Shopping was losing its luster.

"Let's go try them on."

"*I'll* go try them on."

79

Baby's Breath

"But I want to see! I'll be your fashion advisor."

Alyssa took the sweater. "Just let me do it."

"Can I at least find another top? Something you could wear here or at school? For Thanksgiving dinner?"

"Okay, okay, okay. Find another top—"

Chirpy but too old for her purple suede miniskirt, the petite sales clerk called from the cash register, "You ladies ready to try something? Oh, those are beautiful pants, aren't they? We've got some red blouses—"

Alyssa felt short of breath. Hyperventilation, she'd learned in the first-aid class she'd taken her senior year. You need to slow down, sit before you fall down. "Where's the fitting room, please?"

"Just follow me, babe. Right here."

She latched the door behind her, tugging at it twice to be sure it wouldn't swing open to a waiting shopper as it had when she was twelve years old and trying on her first bra in the lingerie department of Macy's. That had been her mother's fault, not locking the door, but Leah just laughed and said, "Oh, Allie, she didn't see anything she hasn't seen before." Yet the shopper's amused face and her barked "Sorry!" had stayed with Alyssa for years, polished pearl-hard by the same shame she felt now as she tested the door a third time, just to be sure.

As if in reparation for past injustice against her, the pants in the extra-large size did fit. The elastic waistband stretched uncomfortably taut against her belly button, but if she rolled it down below her waist, the way she'd been doing with her cotton baggies, the pants were comfortable enough. She was becoming a master of disguise, she told herself, turning from side to side in front of the dressing room mirror. A master of deceit. She looked fat, but she didn't look pregnant. With the long gold sweater draping down to her thighs, she could pass. She could show her mother this, she guessed, and unlocked the door. "Mom?"

Chapter Five

Holding two more blouses, Leah came from the cash register. "Oh, honey, that's it! You look beautiful. Très élégant!"

"*Mom.*"

"I mean it. It's a stunning outfit."

The sales clerk came up behind Leah, who turned to her, welcoming a second opinion. "She looks like a very different young lady than the one who came in with you, that's for sure. That outfit hides about twenty pounds, I'd say."

Leah's eyes locked on Alyssa's face. Sharp-edged, steel setting the lines of her mouth, she pushed the sales clerk on the shoulder, an aggressive push that might have been considered a punch in another setting. "Thanks, we won't need you anymore." Then, turning back to Alyssa, who'd retreated behind the locked door, "She's a moron, honey. She ought to be working in Phoney Phinesse."

Alyssa couldn't shed the pants fast enough. She pulled her own sweatshirt over her unbuttoned flannel shirt and hung the sweater and pants crookedly on their plastic hangers. "Mom?"

"Honey, I'm right here. Just hand them to me. I'll pay and you wait over at Java Jitters. We'll eat, okay? You want burgers, a salad? I know you don't want pizza."

"Thanks, Mom."

"She's a moron, sweetheart. A frigging moron."

After all that, the day wasn't as miserable as it might have been. In the Poster Outpost, Leah bought a Van Gogh reprint when Alyssa said she appreciated the thought behind Leah's preservation of the Radiohead posters, but she didn't listen to them any longer. They decided "Irises" was too obvious a choice, so bought instead "Portrait of a Young Man," joking that at least they'd have one handsome man in the house. Leah tried to ask her, then, about dating, and Alyssa thought Howie might count as dating and talking about him might please her mother. She told Leah about Howie's alcoholic parents, how he had a full scholarship to Cal but couldn't move out of their Oakland house because they'd kill each other for sure if he were to leave them unguarded. Leah said yes, but he's just a kid, he doesn't deserve that, and Alyssa said true, but try to tell it to Howie. It was what she liked about him, she told her mother, the way he had these caretaking qualities that most boys didn't. It's nice, Leah agreed, you have a friend like that. Daddy was never that way, was he, Alyssa asked. And Leah said no, he wasn't, but how smart Alyssa was to recognize the difference between men who had that capacity and men who didn't.

Alyssa thought her mother sounded a little sad when, sitting on the living room couch with the new comforter draped across her knees, Leah said to her, "I wish I could have given you a better father, honey. I wish I'd done better by you there."

So sad that Alyssa stopped clipping the price tags from her new clothes and reached for the hug first, the only time since deplaning at the airport when she really wanted her mother's arms around her. She murmured, deep into the familiar, poignant smell of her mother's hair, "You couldn't have known, Mom. How could you have known? How can anybody?"

CHAPTER

6

Leah hadn't seen Dennis since shortly after Allie got her driver's license. She'd let Allie do the driving to practice the run to Dennis and Missy's old house in New Jersey a couple of times while she had her temps, but never to the newest house, the grand one bought and paid for by Missy's parents. A dowry, Leah thought. Dennis had managed to marry a woman with a dowry. Even though she didn't like her daughter driving a freeway, once Allie had her license, Leah's relief at not having to see her ex-husband was greater than her caution. She'd already taken to leaving the house if Dennis came to get Allie. The way he blew in as if on a white steed, asking rhetorical questions and wearing his attentive father persona, made Leah crazy. Several times she'd been unable to shut herself up in time to spare Allie what Leah was determined to spare her.

When Leah opened the front door the afternoon after Thanksgiving, shock made her stare. Dennis' hair, salt and pepper when she'd last seen him, was fully white. Still luxuriously thick, with the same wave of forelock arranged to look casually fallen. Leah knew how he toyed at it with thumb and forefinger. She imagined he sprayed it into place, maybe shaped it with Missy's styling gel. Surely Missy used styling gel.

He was early or Leah wouldn't have been there. "Allie's . . . Allie's just gotten into the shower," was all she managed.

Baby's Breath

Dennis arched his eyebrows and checked his watch, conspicuously inconspicuous.

"I'll, uh, tell her to hurry." Leah fingered the silver necklace Allie had given her on the way home from the airport. She hoped she could avoid asking him in.

"I hope she won't be long. The opening of Alfie's exhibition is at three, and we do have dinner reservations after that. I tried to allow plenty of time. After Alyssa's interest in portraits last year, I spoke to him about her."

This was nice. Classic Dennis: keep 'em off balance. Alfie's photographs, particularly the portraits for which he was famous, were in high demand. "She'll really enjoy that," Leah said, meaning it.

"This is all portraits of artists at work. In fact, he did one of me last year for my spring catalog. It's in this show . . . I'd, uh," Dennis laughed, looked down. "I sort of wanted Alyssa to see it." *Let me have this*, he was telling her. Let me be something for my daughter *now*. He nodded back toward the street. "Missy and Caleb are with me."

Leah tried to smile, knew she failed.

"Missy, ah, I don't think she can wait. The baby, you know. Might she use your bathroom?" Dennis' eyebrows were still salt and pepper. His eyes, though. Leah tried not to let Dennis see her puzzling. His eyes were blue instead of brown. He must have gotten blue contacts to replace the wire-rimmed glasses he'd taken to wearing, first reluctantly, then quite fashionably, in his early fifties. That was it. The contacts were almost turquoise, the unlikely color of the most tropical sea. *The vain old fart*, Leah thought, uneasy at how handsome he still was and aware that neither of them had proffered the obligatory comment about how good the other looked.

Too long a hesitation. Leah rushed to fill it in. "Yes, sure, okay," she said, thick and clumsy.

"I'll get her then." Dennis walked back down her walled entryway, which she'd painted white to set off the greenery of her plantings and the black wrought iron of the gate. He eyed the hand painted ceramic tiles she'd put up at intervals along the way. Critiquing them.

A moment later Missy, to whom Leah spoke rarely on the phone and even more rarely in person, was following Dennis toward Leah's door, a two-year-old boy in hand. She looked to be in her fifth or sixth month, big, but not yet lumbering, still able to look lithe, like a pretty adolescent. If she'd been holding Dennis' hand instead of the child's, they could be taken for daddy and daughter. *How very sweet.* She wished she had someone to dish Dennis with. She'd call Cory later.

"Hello, Missy. It's good to see you after so long. Come on in. The bathroom's over there, under the stairs. It's tiny. . . ." Leah pointed diagonally from where she stood just inside her front door, across the narrow blue and cream living room warmed with touches of burgundy, to the closed door which anyone would mistake for a closet. Allie's old put-up, knock-down darkroom, which she'd never wanted Leah to share. Leah wondered if Allie's gal-pal stepmother would be welcome there.

"Hi, Leah. What a lovely little home you have. Thanks for the use of the potty. This is Caleb . . . Caleb, this is Alyssa's mommy. You don't remember her, you were so small last time." The little boy pulled fingers from his mouth and lifted his arms to be picked up. "Dennis . . . get him please," Missy said. "Honey, you know it hurts Mommy's back to pick you up now, such a big, grown-up boy."

Missy turned her elfin face, bracketed with long blonde hair, to Leah and beamed. "Goodness, how it must feel to have your child in *college.* I can just hardly believe it." Leah couldn't read her intent but didn't really care, awash with irritation. Apparently Dennis had tried to match his eye color to Missy's. She guessed his face-lift would be next, though she couldn't see where he needed it. She knew exactly where her own could do with a boost.

"Allie! Hurry up, honey. Your Dad and Missy are waiting for you." She threw her voice to the second floor, edgy.

"And Caleb!" Dennis called while the boy squirmed in his arms and Missy shut the bathroom door. Caleb whined, and Dennis set him down. Immediately, he scampered to the glass elephants from India on the coffee table and began moving them to a heap on the floor. Dennis smiled at Leah, shrugged witlessly as if to say, *what's a dad to do?* Allie had never been allowed to touch them. Maybe Dennis was capable of change, after all.

Leah would go upstairs and drag Allie down naked if that's what it took to end this.

"So, you, um, were in a little show a while back?" Dennis said.

"Oh, did you see the review in the *Inquirer*?" Leah said, hoping to score.

"No, can't say as I did. We take the *Times*. I didn't see a mention." Of course there'd not be, not of a Philly opening in a New York newspaper.

"Allie! Did you want to sit down, Dennis?" She hardly wanted Dennis a step inside her gate, let alone seated in her living room, but Caleb was fingering an arrangement of silk flowers Leah had fussed to get exactly balanced. The toilet flushed, water ran, and Missy emerged from the bathroom.

Allie came down the stairs. She wore the harem pants and loose sweater they'd bought, and more: a green and gold scarf, black dress boots from Leah's closet. She'd piled her hair up on her head, securing it with a fancy gold clip, also Leah's. The dangle earrings were new to Leah, who hadn't seen Allie wear earrings for a good three years. Dennis gave a wolf whistle, and Leah thanked him silently for paying attention.

"Hi, Dad. Hi, Missy. Hey, Caleb." Leah was gratified Allie didn't cross in front of her to hug Dennis.

"You look gorgeous, sweetie," Leah said. "You all have a lovely time." She made a point of hugging Allie good-bye.

But then she made the mistake of hurrying upstairs to look out her studio window—she had no idea why, really—to follow them all to their silver Volvo. Dennis let Missy attend to putting Caleb in his carseat. He turned and put his arms around Allie, who not only put both of hers all the way around him, but put her cheek on the lapel of his tweed sport coat, closed her eyes and rested a long moment, neither stranger nor guest, a child at home.

*   *   *

Even inside the new Volvo where Missy's perfume—maybe it was hairspray—hung heavy as fallout, the foul smell of the chemical plants straddling the Jersey turnpike like radioactive metal boils curdled her stomach. It didn't help that Caleb was staring at her, blowing crab bubbles from his pressed lips, dripping spittle from his chin. He didn't resemble her dad at all. He looked like a cross between Missy and Mr. Mincher, her seventh grade science teacher whose hair, or what remained of it, was fine and yellow, stretched over a scalp as fresh and falsely pink as Caleb's stuffed rabbit, which had fallen into the footwell. Now it was pushed halfway under the driver's seat where her father nudged the car up to eighty-five whenever Missy's attention was distracted, stroking his own wavy white hair as if he were petting an animal whenever she asked him to slow down. Caleb's hair, his bangs streaked liberally with spit, was straight as a cornstalk.

"Caleb, Mommy said stop it now." Missy chided him half-heartedly from the front seat. "Your sister doesn't want you spitting all the way to New York."

"He's okay," Alyssa said, forcing a smile, but Missy had already turned back to Dennis. "What's this?" Alyssa asked Caleb, picking up the rabbit.

"That's the infamous Mr. McGregor," Dennis said, turning down the tape of the New York violinist whom, he said, he'd met at one of his shows several years back. "Don't speak for her, Dennis!" Leah used to say when Dennis would return Alyssa after one of her rare visits to his

Philadelphia apartment and, authoritative, tell Leah his daughter was hungry. But Dennis was the kind of father who would not relinquish speaking for his children.

"But Dad, Mr. McGregor was a man." This wasn't what Alyssa really wanted to argue. What she really wanted was to ask her father if he had ever in the course of Caleb's short life read *Peter Rabbit* in its entirety, something she couldn't recall his doing for her. Leah had been the reader, and Alyssa suspected Missy did all the reading duty in Dennis' household. If she *could* read, Alyssa thought, only a moment before she chided herself for unkindness. Missy had been perfectly decent to her, had never tried any stepmother tricks. Of course that would be pretty hard to manage with somebody only ten years younger.

"Ah, the artistic perspective isn't fixated on petty distinctions. Just like you, Alyssa, Caleb's inherited some pretty creative genes."

"Denny . . ." Missy turned to her husband, her profile to Alyssa. "He's just a baby," she said, protesting but pleased.

"Maybe I got Mom's genes," Alyssa said, looking slant-eyed at Caleb, who'd decided to spit onto Mr. McGregor instead of his chin.

"Maybe. She's got a good sense of shadow, the ambiguity of darkness. Hey! Lyssa, you're going to love Alfie's showing!" This was Dennis, always compensating every piece of praise he expended on someone else with a delicately orchestrated but eventual return to lavish self-interest. When she was smaller, Alyssa thought it was because she wasn't smart enough or pretty enough or good enough to hold his attention. For years she thought it was her fault that his visits were infrequent, often slapdash trips to the local McDonald's or Toys R Us. She used to believe if she'd only been a better daughter, he would never have left her and Leah at all. Then, self-conscious with plumpness in high school and uneasy at hulking over Missy, whose fine bones even pregnancy didn't pad, she decided she didn't want to see him and let the visits grow more and more rare.

"Have you brought any of your work with you? I mentioned to Alfie what you'd done in Philly, the Youth Arts Award. We could see if he'd take a look, not today of course, but—"

"I didn't bring any prints." Alyssa picked up the rabbit, the third retrieval, and set it beside Caleb's car seat this time. "I haven't been shooting too much."

Another lie. The truth was she hadn't touched her camera, not since she had hidden the positive pregnancy tests in the garbage. Somehow, right then, she'd lost the desire to frame the world in black and white. Color didn't interest her; it never had. Now, without the set of distorting lenses that would cost an easy thousand dollars, she found black and white disturbed her. It made the world too clean. She never showed up at the advanced photography class for which, prompted by Howie, she'd registered, promising to let him borrow her Canon if he'd register, too. She justified her no-show by telling herself it was only an elective, she'd make it up later, she'd rather use the afternoon lab time to walk Coffee. Howie was smart that way and didn't believe her, but Dennis did, far too easily, when she explained to him how she'd let her photo section go because she'd run out of time. They were crossing the George Washington Bridge by then, anyway, and Missy was complaining she had to pee, and Caleb looked as if he were ready to puke, and all Dennis could seem to think of was whether or not Alfie had hung his portrait on the front-facing wall of the SoHo gallery.

"Why don't you come home with us?" Missy said, raising her voice above the din in the coffeehouse where they'd taken Caleb after he'd thrown up, twice, on the gallery floor. Dennis came close to tantrum, which he controlled by ignoring the entire vomit scene and leaving Alyssa and Missy to deal with a whiny Caleb and a dearth of paper towels. Bored by Alfie's portraits, too cold and silent for her taste, embarrassed by her father's publicly displayed lack of sympathy, Alyssa wanted out by then, too. She'd picked up the little boy and told Dennis she and Missy would wait across the street for him.

Baby's Breath

Missy was distracted—Caleb still did look a little green around the gills—but her offer sounded sincere. "We could skip dinner out and just take you home with us for the night. Sound good?"

Alyssa stirred the whipped cream into her mocha. She let her hair fall over half of her face until she decided. She could try it, going back to Princeton Junction with them. She'd never seen the big house Dennis and Missy had bought together, or Missy had bought for Dennis, or however it had happened. Caleb, sickened by the ride on the Turnpike, had turned much more likeable than she could have predicted. He lay beside her on the cushioned seat of the coffeehouse booth, his head in her lap, almost asleep. She traced his earlobe with the tip of her finger. Peach fuzz, she thought, and told Missy okay, she'd just call Leah first to let her know. Maybe at home when he wasn't compelled to play the big shot, Dennis might listen to her. After Caleb was in bed, maybe Missy would make some tea and Dennis would light a fire and Alyssa would try to say something to them both. After all, they were having a baby too, and might know what to tell her.

"Come here, my little man, my fallen soldier," Dennis said, hefting Caleb's sleeping body from the carseat. It surprised Alyssa that she didn't feel envy when she watched her father kiss Caleb's sweaty forehead, then settle the child against his shoulder while Missy scurried ahead to unlock the front door, screeching she was about to pee her pants. It surprised her again when her father took her hand and tucked it under his arm as they crossed the wide lawn on a brick walkway. "We'll get this little guy to bed and then, what, have a glass of brandy?"

"Dad. I don't drink."

"Oh, Missy's not supposed to either, but she's not adverse to a sip of spirits now and then. How about you?"

"No. I just don't like it, that's all."

"We'll find something else. Then we'll finally have time to hear

Chapter Six

about California and you burning rubber through those honors classes—"

"Who told you that?"

"Your mom. Who else?"

"Just wondered."

Palatial was the only word that suited Dennis and Missy's house. The entire first floor of the rowhouse would fit inside the foyer, which was completely bare except for four of Dennis' big paintings, hung on walls so stark and tall they could have been those of the gallery they'd left behind in Manhattan.

"Faux riche," her father said sheepishly when Alyssa stood staring at the top of the winding staircase where Missy had just disappeared. "A little on the ostentatious side," he said, shifting Caleb to his other shoulder. "But Missy likes it." He leaned closer to Alyssa. Woven with the faintest trace of vomit from Caleb's shirt, she smelled her father's cologne. "Her people, you know," whispering, apologetic, "they come from a long line of big houses in Princeton."

Always, just when she was ready to give him up for his dandying, preening, self-aggrandizing ways, her father pulled something like this. He would say something so perceptive, so self-deprecatory, that she couldn't help but be tempted to love him, Leah's opinions to the contrary. He'd been truly happy when Missy proposed her overnight to Princeton; he'd sung Caleb to sleep on the drive down from New York. Badly, yes. Botched lyrics and flat melodies, but he'd been happy to have her spend the night.

"Daddy! Don't! She'll hear you!" She couldn't believe her own voice. Laughing, she sounded like a five-year-old. A happy five-year-old.

She followed him upstairs to Caleb's room, what seemed to be an enormous playroom with a trundle bed tucked into a corner beneath— Alyssa had to touch it to believe it wasn't real—an eight-foot tall stuffed giraffe.

Baby's Breath

Missy came down the hall, whispering her apologies for bolting inside when Alyssa was there as a guest. "Bladder control. I thought it was bad when I was carrying Caleb, but it's completely gone now," she said, pulling Caleb's shirt and sweater off while Dennis untied the midget Reeboks and pulled them from his son's feet. He dropped them onto the floor. Alyssa knelt to pick up one of the tiny shoes. Squatting, she lost her balance and reached for her father's leg to stop her from tumbling onto her seat. Dennis steadied her by capping her head with his hand. The sole of Caleb's shoe fit into her palm as perfectly as the beaded white baby moccasins that the vendors on Telegraph Avenue sold to tourists and doting hippie grandmothers, as perfectly as her father's hand crowning her own head.

"You have the most beautiful hair, daughter," Dennis said, stroking. *This is the moment. It's going to be all right.*

"I need to pee every fifteen minutes, don't I, Daddy?" Missy said.

Dennis took the shoe from Alyssa and set it down beside Caleb's bed, squaring it with its mate. "Don't believe Missy." He pulled Alyssa up from her crouch. "We're the single biggest investors in Depends in the nation."

Missy put her hands on her hips, leaving Dennis to tuck Caleb into his sleeper pajamas. "Your dad thinks he's so funny."

Dennis stood back from Caleb's bed, surveying his work. He put one arm around Missy and one around Alyssa, turning them toward Caleb's bedroom door and walking them down the hall to the stairs. "Alone with my girls," he said, squeezing. At that moment, with Missy beaming foolishly up at him and his long arm circling her shoulders, Alyssa found it possible to believe that in this sweet and fecund world he'd made with Missy, there might be room for her.

Downstairs, Missy went off into the kitchen, calling behind her, "Roast beef sandwiches okay? I've got good French rolls."

Dennis walked Alyssa into a room where a fieldstone fireplace stretched across a far wall. On either side were oversized oak shelves where Dennis' heavy art books rested in stacks between ceramic vases and pictures of Dennis and Missy and Caleb framed in heavy silver. The drapes were closed against the night, but their dimensions belied an enormous picture window which must open to the sprawling lawns wrapping completely around the house. Dennis set Alyssa down on a long leather couch. He sat on its partner, placed at right angles to make a conversation island in the middle of the room.

"What do you think of Caleb?" he said, nudging a bowl of unshelled peanuts across the coffee table to Alyssa's couch.

"He's great, Dad."

"Looks like me, doesn't he?"

"I—he does. Around the eyes, especially."

"And Missy's pretty darn great, herself."

"She is, Dad. She's . . . nice." White lies, harmless ones, what Professor Miller called social cement. But they came so easily.

"So, Lyssa, tell me what's what in California. The trust fund is covering tuition okay? I leave that up to your mother—"

"It's fine. I'm fine for money. I like Berkeley, Dad. I like California, too."

"Traitor." He laughed, yawned, put his feet up on the coffee table.

"But there is something—"

"You know, hon, when you were small, Caleb's age, I couldn't, well, relate to you. Kids just—let's say they're tough for me to comprehend. But now that you're a veritable adult, I feel like we can talk, well, just as easily as Missy and I talk." He leaned his head against the couch back and shut his eyes. "I get a little testy with small kids. You won't remember, but it was a heck of a job trying to paint and watch you at the same time."

"I . . . don't remember that. I remember Mom, and then Gran."

"You send some prints to me, I'll be sure they get into Alfie's hands. He's an influential photographer, could do you a lot of good."

"I'm majoring in history, though."

"That's right! History."

"Dad?"

Missy came through the double swinging doors that led to the kitchen, holding a tray piled high with thick sandwiches and whole dill pickles and a basket of pretzels. "Denny? Will you go get the drinks? Beer for you and sodas for us, right, Alyssa?"

"Sure."

Dennis pulled himself up from the couch, stiffly, and Alyssa saw what she hadn't noticed through the afternoon: her father was becoming an old man, far too old to be having children with a child-bride. What was it Leah had said, almost incidentally, in one of the chit-chatty phone conversations Alyssa allowed her on Sunday evenings? *Your dad gets away with a lot, but he's not getting any younger.* When Caleb was her age, Dennis would be eighty. Too old.

Missy plopped herself down on the couch where Dennis had been sitting. "They're already out, glasses and ice, just bring them in." She looked down at her belly and flattened her blouse against it, just staring. The cat who ate the canary, Alyssa thought, and then felt badly because really, in the right situation, there would be nothing wrong with gloating over what Missy had to gloat over.

"Missy?" Maybe it would be Missy, not Dennis, who'd know what to do.

"Yes?"

"Before Dad, did you?"

"Did I date? You bet. I know what a lot of people said about him robbing the cradle to get me, but the truth is, I just didn't get on with men my age."

"No, I meant before you got pregnant—"

"He couldn't wait to get pregnant. For me to, I mean. From the very beginning—oh, Alyssa, is it all right if I talk like this with you?"

"Sure."

Chapter Six

"He was hoping for me to get pregnant from the first time we, you know, as soon as. . . . He wanted a son, he said."

"Of course." Because he couldn't comprehend children, Alyssa thought. Because having a couple more with Missy might make them comprehensible, somehow.

"Oh, honey, it's nothing against you! He's so proud of what you're doing, majoring in art out there in California—"

"I'm majoring in history."

"—but he thought, I guess all older men think this, he thought he'd be a better father this time."

All she could see was the set of Dennis' face when Caleb buckled over his arm and spewed his lunch across the gallery's polished floor. "And has he? Been a good father?"

"The best!" Dennis boomed from the kitchen doorway, a bottled Heineken under his arm, a tall glass of iced Coke in each hand. After uncapping the beer, he lowered himself onto the couch next to Missy and helped himself to a sandwich. "Missy? You know what I've been thinking?" A lettuce leaf fell from the sandwich and landed in his lap. Missy picked it up and tucked it into her small mouth. "We could send Alyssa to the Sorbonne if she wanted. That's where Alfie went." He paused to chew.

Alyssa watched the muscles in his jaw, mesmerized, and thought of Cindy's boyfriend, Marc Raymond. Her stomach churned. "Where's the bathroom? I think I should wash my hands," she said, standing, setting her Coke dead center on the cork coaster that Missy had pulled from a red enamelled Chinese box on the coffee table.

"Go through the kitchen doors, then to your left," Missy said, holding a pickle up to Dennis' mouth.

Alyssa paused before the swinging doors and looked back. Missy and Dennis were clinched in a kiss. Missy's wrist leaned against Dennis' shoulder, the pickle dangling from her hand. She said, so softly they probably didn't hear, "I'm a history major. A history major." Then she pushed through the kitchen doors and headed straight for the antique phone which rested on the counter right next to Missy's cookbooks.

Leah wasn't mad about the drive. It was very late, sure, and she said she'd rather not do it, but she wasn't mad. Dennis was, when Alyssa came back into the family room or whatever it was and ate her roast beef sandwich and some pretzels and then said, cool as she could, that she'd called Leah to come pick her up because she wasn't feeling well. Missy was disappointed, it seemed, but Alyssa couldn't tell if it was because she was losing Alyssa's visit or any visitor, period. They wanted to wake Caleb so she could say good-bye to her brother, but she wouldn't let them. And that, in the end, was the saddest part. Back on the turnpike, turned sleepily to the window, she thought that maybe the best thing about her aborted visit was Caleb, how she ended up liking him best.

*　*　*

"Mom, I told you. I'm not coming home for Christmas. I can't."

Leah had broached the fragile subject as if it were one of the plates she was washing on the evening before Allie had to go back to school. She wiped her hands on a towel. "Alyssa, honey. I think when the time comes you'll be sad and want to come home. Lord knows, I want you home. I can't imagine Christmas without you. Or, wait—is that it? Do you want me to come out there to you?"

"No, it's not that. I just have so much work, and my job . . . it's just not a good time." It was sharp, quick-edged when she spoke.

Leah felt the pressure of tears behind her eyes. She turned back to the sink, ostensibly to finish the dishes. Allie sat at the kitchen table, not even clearing up the condiments that needed to be refrigerated. "Could you take care of the salad dressing and margarine?" Leah said, using the weight of insubstantial matters to anchor herself. "Can you see why

96

this is so hard to understand? I'm your mother, it's Christmas. You don't want to be with me either here or out in Berkeley?"

Right then, Leah felt it. Maybe it was a change in the charge of the air, maybe a slight shift in Allie's body position. Allie was weakening. Leah knew to let it all sit, let the guilt-stone sit on Allie's shoulders for a bit. If that was the only tool she had, so be it. As long as it was really in Allie's best interest, Leah would do whatever she had to. And there was no way it was best for Allie to be all alone. She'd wait and bring it up again tomorrow.

Leah was troubled through the evening. Unresolved matters always bothered her, though she'd learned Allie's timetable for working anything out was always longer than hers. Allie could put things off forever, a difficult habit to accept for Leah's take-charge-fix-it-now nature. Still, if she could hold out until Allie brought it up—or was at least ready—the results were usually better.

But sometimes Allie just didn't, wouldn't, couldn't act. The older Allie got, the more Leah had to practice the foreign art of waiting. She'd wrap her tongue in cotton batting if that's what it took to keep silent now, patient as snow, and wait until tomorrow.

Although she'd fallen asleep quickly, Leah awoke a little after midnight, then couldn't get back to sleep. A painting she'd scarcely begun was propped on the easel in the studio, and now she sensed she knew what it needed. She could translate this plaintive yearning into a sweeping brush stroke that stopped short of completion, carrying both hope and hopelessness. To do an entire painting with the motion and to lighten the value of the hue at the top of each stroke: might it convey the feeling she was after? The subject was a figure in the urban clearing of a nearby park, a stranger she'd photographed as she walked toward the last of a lemon twilight. It was this same feeling of longing and despair she felt about being with Allie that Leah had felt possible as the complex emotion of the scene. Maybe she could use it now.

Baby's Breath

She'd not painted while Allie was home. Foolish, probably. Allie likely wouldn't have noticed or cared. But Leah had tried to avoid anything that might stir the old embers of Allie's resentment into a flare. She wanted to get the feeling right with her daughter and save it there, as if something could be resolved, some old anger of Allie's, mysterious to Leah who saw her failures outweighed by the gold of her intent on the other side of the scale. Maybe her mistake all along had been the business of trying to capture and hold what felt too precious to lose.

Perhaps she could try to paint the idea of loving what she saw even while she released it into another mutation. Quicker brush strokes, yes, the movement of light within the scene.

Leah got out of bed and slipped past the bathroom into her studio. Allie was asleep on the couch in the living room, another wound, although she had put some of her things in the drawers Leah had cleared for her. She'd made no comment on where her posters hung, and Leah hadn't asked for one, another stalemate.

She lit only the focused high-intensity lamp on her painting table, moving it up onto a shelf, arching its neck like a swan's over her canvas. She'd use Allie's figure and this sense of something fleeting, incipient loss. Leah picked up her sketchbook and began to work on the shape of her daughter for the painting. Within forty-five minutes, she couldn't stand it any longer, she thought she understood what she was after. She squeezed paint onto the palette.

She didn't know how late it was, but she heard the toilet flush before Allie appeared silently in the doorway, almost ghostly in a voluminous floor-length white gown, her hair wild and loose as dreams around her shoulders, down her arms.

"Sweetheart! Hi, I hope I didn't disturb you. I . . . had this idea and thought I'd get some work in while you were sleeping."

"Oh, no. I got up to go to the bathroom."

"I hate to see you go back tomorrow. I miss you, Allie."

"Alyssa."

98

Chapter Six

"Alyssa. I'm sorry, hon. I don't do that on purpose. It's just such long habit, you know? Remember when you were little, you wouldn't even answer to Alyssa? You thought it was somebody else."

Allie smiled and shook her head. "Things change. . . ."

"Ah, yes, but not everything. How about a midnight snack? Remember those? Good thing Mom slept like cement."

Allie giggled. "It's more like three than midnight."

"So what? New rules. Mother and daughter required attendance pre-dawn pig-out. I've got those frosted brownies in the freezer, and cocoa mix. I've even got marshmallows," Leah tempted, wiping her hands on a Turpinoid cloth. Allie didn't seem to be on a diet, and Leah had tried to be sensitive about not suggesting she needed to be. This was the first flat-out wicked indulgence she'd proposed, and she did it out of the memory of old moments when Allie couldn't sleep and Leah would stop painting to make her hot chocolate.

Allie averted her face. "That smell."

"Turpinoid? I'd think you'd be used to it by now. Want to come downstairs with me or shall I bring stuff up to us? Maybe you can get in bed, and we'll really break the rules. Remember what a fit Gran used to have if there was any food upstairs?"

"Oh god, yes, Okay, let's. Eat in bed. Gran would shit a brick."

"No problem. The cemetery people will call if she rises from the grave to come after us. See, it's part of a pay now, die later plan that Mom bought. The cemetery ensures notification of relatives should the deceased experience resurrection of the body due to the reappearance of Jesus." Allie giggled, all the encouragement Leah needed. "Now, I believe we can also assume that if a body rises in response to an unthinkable breach of proper decorum by surviving relatives, we'll be notified. It only makes sense, wouldn't you say?" *I must be punch-drunk,* she thought. She'd never made fun of Esther's fundamentalism like that.

"I'm cold. I'll wait in bed, unless you want me to help."

"No, honey, you get warm. This'll just take a sec—I'll nuke some milk while I get the brownies out. Anything else you want?" She was already halfway down the stairs. "I'll be right back." When she looked over her shoulder, Allie was just going into the bedroom—their bedroom. She gave a little wave.

Leah dug out two marshmallows for Allie's hot chocolate, and carried their mugs and brownies upstairs on a bed tray she'd had for Esther before it was apparent Esther wouldn't ever be off a feeding tube again. Allie was already in bed, the twin of Leah's, but she'd pulled the navy top sheets out to make them appear one. Leah handed her the tray and peeled off her socks and the gray sweatshirt she'd put on over her nightgown when she first got up.

She climbed into bed next to Allie, who propped pillows into readiness. "Well, thank you. Where'd you get the extra pillow?"

"No, thank *you*, in your closet."

"No, thank *you*." Another old joke, like *just because*.

"No, thank *you*."

"All right. You win." Leah said.

"Mom!" Allie touched the silver chain around Leah's neck, Allie's "nothing special" present which Leah hadn't removed since she pulled the silver paper off the little gift box and found the delicate loop of jade attached to a braided chain. She didn't think it was a stretch to see the jade as heartshaped, a warm and polished whole. "Mom, you can't wear jewelry to bed!"

"Ya wanna bet I can't?" Leah put her fists up. Allie smiled at her—another game remembered—and Leah brought her mock gloves to Allie's cheeks and cradled her daughter's chin.

"Do you like it?"

"I love it." A fragile moment, too tender to risk. For a moment they each sipped their cocoa, Allie chasing marshmallows with her tongue.

"Nothin' better than hot chocolate, is there?" Leah said. "I was chilly, but I didn't want to wake you by going downstairs to turn up the thermostat."

"Nothing wakes me. And sure there's something better. What's the matter with you?" Allie said. "Hot chocolate *and brownies*, that's better. Now this is a meal. I'm sort of a lousy cook; I eat at the restaurant when I can."

Leah thought to renew her shipments of care packages. Maybe she'd include a cookbook of easy recipes and canned or boxed ingredients for them. That would be different.

"Okay, so you're a lousy cook. Me too. Big deal. The only decent cook in our family was Mom. So what's new and exciting in your life? You haven't really told me anything."

Allie licked the remains of a brownie off her fingers. She hesitated. Then she scooched over closer to Leah and put her head on Leah's shoulder. Leah shifted to extricate her arm, but only so she could put it around Allie's shoulders and draw her closer.

"Things going okay, sweetie? Do you have a best friend? I was surprised you and Cindy didn't room together again. Did something happen?" Leah sensed Allie was about to answer. *Don't ask a bunch of questions*, she remembered Cory cautioning. *They hate questions. You never hear anything about anything that way.*

"No, not with Cindy."

"Then what happened?" She was doing it again, the questions. It was an exercise in tooth-pulling, laborious and bloody, to get anything out of Allie. "I'm sorry, honey. I don't mean to pry. I just want to hear about, well, anything."

Allie was silent. She tucked her face against her mother's breast, hair spilling over her cheek and eye.

"I put another copy of the Mary Cassatt print right there so I'd see it when I wake up," Leah almost whispered, not mentioning she couldn't bear the thought of one of those rock stars glaring at her with their perverse hostility. "It always makes me think of you. Oh! Honey. Can I show you something? I'm putting you in a new painting—not like a portrait, but just this feeling I get about you, just missing you, I don't know, wanting to be close to you. I'll just show you the sketch, okay?" Leah swung her feet out over the floor and pulled her arm from around Allie. "Don't move, I'll be right back."

It wasn't ten seconds. All she brought in were three sketches, one of a hand detail and one that studied the angle of a torso. The third was recognizably Allie by her hair and something very subtle in the facial profile, even though it appeared middle-distance and headed away. Leah knew she'd caught it and hoped she could do it as well with the brush. It had to be Allie: some essence of Allie was what this painting was *about*, this current of touching and missing halted for a heartbeat. She'd done Allie's body without all the extra weight, so Allie would know she was the same to her mother.

Leah handed Allie the sketches as she got back into bed and tried to get her arm back around Allie. But her daughter had straightened, the pliancy gone. She was studying the sketches.

"Really, it's the one on top that's the study for the painting. The middle distance one." Leah said. Allie was studying the close-up of the torso.

"That doesn't look anything like me."

"Honey, look at this one, see? It's elusive, and that's the thing, but that profile, the way the hair is moving, that's. . . ."

"I've gotta get to bed," Allie interrupted. "I'm exhausted."

"Okay, well, let me brush my teeth again—I've got brownies stuck in there—and we'll turn the light out."

But Allie got out of bed. "That's okay. I sleep better downstairs, anyway." And that quickly, she was out of the room, her nightgown flapping around her feet.

"Allie! Honey, please, can't we?" Leah trailed off, frustrated. What had she done wrong? Or was she doing it again now, trying to hold on to what she had to release?

Chapter Six

When Leah returned from taking a too-quiet Allie to the airport, she headed upstairs to her studio, wanting to lose herself like a stone in the creek of new work. She'd tried again in the car but didn't know how to do it without asking questions. Whatever she'd missed with Allie, well, she'd missed it. But Allie had softened some about Christmas, at least the one time they'd talked about it, and Leah would work on her a little at a time.

Cold sunshine streamed through the skylight onto something stuck to old paint still tacky on the palette. The plane ticket for Christmas was on top of the ragged-edge sheet of notebook paper. Allie's writing was cramped, tiny as if she'd needed space. Which she hadn't for what it said:

> I really can't come for Christmas,
> and it won't work for you to come to Cal.
> I'm sorry.   Allie

An oily blotch stained the page.

CHAPTER

7

It was Howie, finally, who said it to her after Christmas break. Not Tricia, who had nearly flattened Coffee on the corner of Dwight and Etna one day in a roller-blader's oblivion. Not Linnie, surprisingly, even though with their spring semester schedules they crossed paths frequently enough in Wheeler Hall. Not Cindy, who had tried repeatedly to get Alyssa's Dwight Way address in order to mail her a birthday card. (Finally, two weeks late, Marc Raymond delivered it by sending it down the aisle in the auditorium in Tolman Hall as their Intro to Psych professor waxed forth about the self-help culture's popularization of denial mechanisms.)

It was Howie, part-geek, part-brother, who said to her just as they had finished eating dinner in the Burger King on Shattuck, "Hey, Alyssa. Are you just putting on weight? Or are you, like, pregnant?"

Because his words hadn't the irony that anybody else's would have and because she could tell he was making a joke with it, she just took the last two fries off his napkin, swabbed them through the puddle of catsup on her burger wrapper, and said in the lame jokester's voice that Howie had used, "Pregnant. Sextuplets. Bobbi McCaughey style."

Being able to say it like that, out loud to Howie, even though he couldn't know she'd told the truth, made it easier to ignore. It was almost like reverse psychology, only she was spinning the story for her own sake. Tell everybody, she thought, draining the last of her choco-late shake, aiming the gurgles straight at Howie. Tell the whole frig-ging world—Leah even—and they'd probably do exactly what Howie did. They'd roll up their burger wrappers into a paper and cardboard burrito, swipe the table top with the spare napkin, and dump the whole thing—Alyssa's confession included—into the grease-smeared swing-ing flap on the Burger King trash can. It was that easy.

She'd worn a flannel shirt topped by her oversized zippered black sweatshirt constantly since she'd returned from Thanksgiving in Phila-delphia. Without the frilly maternity blouses Missy wore, Alyssa thought she looked innocently fat, not fashionably pregnant, and she counted on the tender mercy of everyone she knew—even Clara—not to mention what must surely be construed as an embarrassment, a roll-ing, out-of-control weight gain, the pounds gathering momentum like a rock slide. Howie, though, he'd been the one to say it because of those missing synapses. And just as easily he could let it go, trashing her an-swer with the crusts of his cheeseburger.

Even Tony let it go when she'd run into him weeks ago at Togo's, when he'd taken her arm and pulled her into a booth and grilled her like she'd committed a crime. She just told him, flippant, the same way she'd spoken to Howie, that she'd taken care of everything.

"But—" Tony said, his eyes falling from her face.

"Jesus, Tony. I'm just fat. Okay?"

"You're—"

She'd stood up. Looking down at him, she lowered her voice, but spoke clear and close so he could hear her through the jukebox din. "Just leave me alone from now on."

"I—"

"I wish you'd left me alone to begin with."

So fat she was, and this was why, four weeks away from a due date that nobody but Alyssa had ever calculated, she just stopped remem-bering she was pregnant. She was fat. Tricia could put her on any list in the world—she could hang a banner from the Campanile for all Alyssa cared—but she was *fat* now.

That didn't seem fair. She'd done everything right, she thought, for most of her life. She'd been a good student. She hadn't, until the past summer, lied too much to her mother. She'd been sincerely sad when Gran died, careful not to blame Gran for the betrayal of her own body, the smells and sounds that worked their way into every room of the Philadelphia house that last year. She didn't envy Missy, but that might be damning with faint praise considering the kind of husband and father Dennis made. She did her own schoolwork, even when the competitive academics at Cal drove ditzes like Tricia to the Internet paper bank. She'd been a good employee at Alfredo's, so good that now when she stopped in to say hi to Sal and the kitchen crew, she never left without a vegetarian supreme—"On the house for you, gorgeous"—in her hands. She'd always given blood like clockwork, once a month. She never failed to pick up Coffee's poops, no matter how far from the apartment they were. She'd trudge the long way home, Coffee towing her on the taut blue leash, and drop them safely into the garden refuse bin that Huddie would haul to his own house up in the hills for his compost pile.

When everything else that mattered was tallied up and accounted for, it didn't seem fair she'd grown so heavy. She'd learned the trick of averting her eyes from mirrors and store windows, of glancing up at Howie or across the street at the Rastafarian when she walked by the storefronts on Bancroft on her way to class. She brushed her teeth at the kitchen sink to avoid seeing her graceless, flushed face in the bathroom mirror. She dressed and undressed in the dark. If the moon was full or Clara's porch light lit, she would shut her eyes for those moments between dropping the dirty clothes and putting on the clean ones in that cool caesura of air against her skin. Then she felt her own unwanted ripeness, the tender swell of her breasts above the unfamiliar hardness of her stomach. Not womb. She didn't like to call it that. More and more often she didn't bother to change her clothes. What did it matter if she slept in her sweats or her drawstrings? Who made the law that said free American adults had to wear designated pajamas? When she fell onto the mattress beside Coffee still wearing clothes tainted with Berkeley's stink, it was that much easier to find sleep, the route to sweet darkness that much quicker. There was a lot to be said for not scrutinizing your own reflection. Once a person learned to avoid looking at her face, it was next to nothing to believe that what was going on with her body was the effect of too much food, too much sleep. She was what Professor Miller quoted from Plath, "a melon strolling on two tendrils."

Howie'd taken her joke about the McCaughey sextuplets and launched into a long dissertation on the faults of the adoption laws in California ("Look at me! I'd a been better off adopted. Hey! You think somebody will adopt my mom and dad?"), a diatribe that lasted nearly six blocks when she didn't have to do more than nod and walk fast to keep up with his longer strides. Just days after, she woke from sleep with her stomach twisted up into crazy knots like she was going to die from one of those intestinal blockages that had floored her sixth grade teacher in the middle of a blackboard lesson on direct objects. The illuminated numbers on her alarm clock said 2:30 AM, reminding her where she was—safe on her mattress in her apartment and not in hell, in which she didn't believe but which had some power over her more convincing than disbelief. Coffee lay beside her, his breathing gone deep dog quiet. Envying his stillness, she blamed him for not feeling her distress, for not circling and whining as Lassie would have done. When the second cramp or twist or whatever it was caught her sharply across her pelvis, she turned and pushed him off the mattress, roughly, with a hard backhand for which she could later excuse herself because of the fire burning inside her belly.

Then, as if her wishes really worked, the burning lessened, backing off in the ebbing, recursive lapping of a saltwater tide. Afraid to move, she pressed her hands against her abdomen, keeping herself whole by soldering her splayed fingers hard upon her own skin. Coffee, sleepy and forgiving, crawled up beside her and curled against her side. Exhausted by her sickness—that was the best word for it—falling into sleep, she felt a slow Morse Code against her fingers, the thud, thud, thud of an S.O.S. tapped out in flesh and bone.

"Alyssa, you home?" Clara's voice pulled her to the surface of sleep. "Alyssa, that dog of yours going wild. Alyssa?"

Alyssa pulled herself up from the broken-backed couch, caught her tangled hair in one hand. Her sweats were soaked through. Had she peed herself? Pinned against the couch, her spine splayed by cramps, had she never made it to the bathroom? Water, she thought to herself. Water, not pee.

Dizzy, careful! The dizzy spells overcame her when she stood up too fast; she knew better by now. She stepped around Coffee, who *was* going wild, and across the living room floor, littered with the ice cream carton Coffee had torn to shreds, and made her way to the door. She stepped in something. Wet, soft, but not the ice cream which had melted into the carpet faster than Coffee could lick it up, though he'd tried. She remembered watching him. How long ago? Yesterday? The day before?

Dog shit. Her apartment reeked of it. Not his fault, poor dog. Hers. Too sick to move, she hadn't been able to take him outside. She tried to call out to Clara, to tell her for God's sake stop calling her name. *Alyssa, Alyssa.* She knew who she was, damn it. But her mouth was dry, junk caked on the corners of her lips. She raised the tail of the flannel shirt she was wearing and wiped her mouth.

"What, Clara?" she managed, twisted in half by the wide wingspan of pain which beat inside her skin. She didn't open the door. She leaned against it, though, and propped her hot forehead on the beach towel she'd thumbtacked up to curtain the glass panes. Good, good. The curtains drawn, the towel up, Clara couldn't see her.

Chapter Seven

"Honey, let me inside there."

"No, I can't . . ."

"Alyssa, honey, you let me in and I'll take the dog out. Dog needs his run, sweetheart. You sick, I'll take him for a run."

"I'll—I'm just taking him now. You don't need to." Alyssa thought she could feel Clara's hand pressed against the glass, against the opposite side of the pane where her forehead touched. Clara's beautiful, muscled, strong hand. Just on the other side of the pane, an eighth of an inch away from her skin.

"Honey, open up. You need somebody in there with you."

Alyssa raised the foot with the shit between its toes. Where could she? Yes, against the leg of her sweatpants. She wiped, streaking the black pant leg. Not *her* foot, somehow. Her feet had been detached by the clapping wings inside her body. Not even *her* body.

"Honey, I'm going to go next door and get my key."

Alyssa waited for Clara to move. She felt her there, tall and determined, waiting.

"Clara?"

"Honey?"

"I'm . . . I've just been sick."

"Open up, sweetheart."

"I can't."

"It's just Clara. Open up for Clara."

"I'm just . . . getting into the shower."

"Open up. I'll take the dog. Then you have your shower."

Coffee stood on his hind legs, whining. His claws scrabbled against the door. Big scratches. Huddie wouldn't like that. One more person she'd be letting down.

"Here. I'm letting him out for you." Alyssa unlocked the door, pulled the deadbolt. "Clara?"

"I'm here, honey."

"Don't look inside . . . at me. Just take the dog."

Baby's Breath

"Honey—" Coffee nosed his way through the cracked door. Alyssa slammed it behind him. "Honey, you—"

"Clara, go away now. I mean it. Go away."

She felt Clara move away from the door, heard the sharp whistle calling Coffee back from the parking lot. "Go away," Alyssa whispered, shooting the deadbolt home. "Just everybody go away."

Through cleft curtains, Alyssa watched Clara leave. Coffee darted off and then returned to jump against her. When Clara and the dog were beyond sight, she felt badly about her rudeness, about her dereliction of duties toward her forgiving dog, about the shameful smell of the apartment. Between spasms she made herself move, do penance. She used a whole roll of paper towels to swab up the spilled food and the dog shit, sealing the soiled towels and her soaked sweatpants into a kitchen garbage bag. On the floor of the bedroom closet, next to a pair of broken sandals, she found the flowered gift box holding Dennis and Missy's untouched birthday present: a bottle of Giorgio. She emptied it, perfuming the air and the floor and the carpet and the walls until the air choked her.

She picked up the phone just once. To put the receiver back on the hook, she told herself, but then it felt like she should be calling her mother for something, maybe to ask Leah to start sending the baking again, to tell her mother she'd missed the cookies and brownies, had only asked her to stop because she didn't want to share. Could she say something like that to her mother, who expected such perfection? Didn't perfection mean you were beyond need of salvation?

Then, because it seemed the only thing left she could do that would make any difference at all, she stumbled into the bathroom and stripped. Under the shower, she soaped and soaped and soaped herself again, shampooing her hair and scrubbing her feet until the water ran cold from the spigot and she stood, wet and shivering and heavy and clean. Clothes on. Socks and shoes. Ready.

Leaving, she could hear Coffee and Clara inside Clara's apartment.

Chapter Seven

Music was playing on the radio, acoustic guitar and mouth harp, she thought. Coffee was safe, then. If she didn't get back soon—well, Clara would keep him safe. Alyssa couldn't say for certain what day it was. But she could decide it was easier to walk downhill than up, her steps measuring the throbbing come-and-go of the wingbeats tearing at her back. She kept her head down, her damp hair over her face. Its tips touched her downhung hands. If she wanted to—needed to—she could pull it hard from her scalp, tearing it away like a thatch of dark ropy weeds. She'd failed even the dead now, violating Gran's orders against going out with wet hair. But never mind—because it was drizzling. And though she'd remembered to shoulder her filled backpack, she hadn't thought to pick up her umbrella or rain slicker. More violations.

The traffic was so light on Telegraph that it had to be Sunday. Yes, that was right; Clara's day off was Sunday. By the time she reached Shattuck and turned left, the rain had shifted gears from drizzle to downpour. She wasn't sure if she would take the rapid transit subway east or west. What seemed most important was to keep moving. Only movement kept her from cracking right in half. She stumbled once, on the top of the BART stairs, and clutched at the railing to stop herself from falling headlong into the tunnel.

"You drunk?" The woman was small, not small enough to be a midget, but too small for sixty or seventy, which was what she looked. Someone intended to be a dwarf who hadn't quite made it.

"What?" Alyssa said, steadying herself, looking down at the pruney face, the wisps of flyaway white hair that poked from the pink stocking cap.

"Drunk as a skunk. Never get away with it. Drink up all the kitchen money and he'll hit you, hard. Whiskey, gin, port if I had to."

"Excuse me," Alyssa said, stepping down too hard on the step. Her thighs were burning. She couldn't stand much longer. "Let me by."

The dwarf cackled. "Let her by! By the by! On the run, made for fun." She stopped her screeching and came up the steps so she stood head-high with Alyssa. She reached out to Alyssa's hair and combed it with her curled hand. "Don't mess my kitchen, darlin'. Leave it clean as you found it."

The restroom wasn't clean, but it was empty. It wouldn't have mattered had it not been. *She had to lie down*. When she closed the stall door behind her and slid to the tiled floor, she thought it was funny, really, how much of her recent life had been spent hiding in bathrooms. Just a little longer, and she wouldn't need to hide anything. Just as soon as she pulled the dark brown towel from her backpack and worked it beneath her so her bare skin, her clean skin, wouldn't touch the grimy floor. Just as soon as she braced her knees against the metal walls and gave her battered muscles permission to push into the pain, to float downstream with the flood current, out to sea with the tide. Just as soon as she took her Swiss Army knife—Daddy's present to her: *good camper, Alyssa!*—a red knife, a red rope, cut, that's easy. Just as soon as she could find a way to stand and to wipe the rubbery, gluey stuff from between her legs, first with the toilet paper and then, when the paper was gone, with the crisp toilet-seat covers.

Just one more thing. She took the clean towel, the green bath towel tucked into the bottom of her backpack because by now the brown towel was dripping, and she triangled its corners like an envelope. That's what she was doing: making an envelope, putting the little package inside. It moved, so she was careful not to bind the envelope too tightly. Don't want it too tight. And she didn't cover where the sounds were coming from—that didn't seem right, either. She lifted it—a loaf of bread? a china doll?—and leaned it against her breast, just a moment there, when she needed one hand to unlock the stall door. Yes, a big bin, nearly filled with used towels, stood next to the sinks. She settled the neatly wrapped bundle onto a layer of the used towels. But the towel dispenser was empty—the dwarf, probably, cleaning her kitchen—so she had to pull used towels from under the envelope to make a basket-shaped hollow in the trash, like a bowl or a nest. No sounds now. That was better.

She had to sit again, this time on the toilet, where she lowered her head to her knees and tried not to smell. She held her breath, remembering what she'd do when she had to use the restroom in somebody else's home. She would synchronize her tinkling with the flushing so nobody could hear the intimate betrayals of her body. If her needs were different, she just wouldn't go. No way would she scent the air in the house of some stranger, somebody whose forgiveness wasn't bound to her by blood. She listened to the toilet flushing once, twice, three times and four until the water swirling in the vortex of the ceramic bowl was distilled clear as rain.

She let herself look in the mirror, finally, when she was rinsing and rinsing her hands, after she'd pulled her hair back and splashed water against her face. She propped her hands against the wet sink and leaned into the mirror. Pale skin. Round face. Dark eyes. Cupid lips, her mother used to say, but blanched now, almost gray. She looked a little sick, but she looked like herself.

Alyssa Pacey Staton. Admitted with honors at entrance. History major. First row, second seat from the left in Professor Miller's seminar. Blood donor. Library Literacy volunteer. Tenant at 2787 Dwight Way, apartment 2B.

She started to leave, then walked back to the trash bin. Inside the other bathroom stalls, the ones she hadn't used, mounted above the toilets were filled containers of paper seat-savers. One at a time, like petals, she pulled them out and mattressed them beneath the tiny package in the trash. Then, crimping the last of them into a doll-sized quilt, she tucked it around the towel-wrapped package like a blanket.

Alyssa Pacey Staton. Her mother's daughter.

CHAPTER

8

Leah hooked the dangle earrings Allie had left on their bureau into her ears. She didn't dress up often now that she worked at home every day, and her flared long wool skirt, high-heeled black boots, and low-cut cream top weren't office wear anyway. She had a date. She'd painted all day, then scrubbed her hands with Turpinoid, taken a scented bubble bath, and even polished her nails, "Brownberry." A stemmed glass of blush wine was on the bathroom counter. She put the evening news on the radio after the Vivaldi violin concerto she'd listened to in the tub had reached a crescendo and ended. Stocks were down but so was unemployment, Ken Starr had unearthed another bimbo, there'd been an arrest in the most recent neonaticide, Saddam Hussein was ruining another day for the United Nations' inspectors. Leah listened, none of the news heavy on her shoulders, while she applied light brown shadow, a touch of eyeliner, mascara, blush, and a muted red lipstick, more color than she usually wore. But she felt, well, *colorful,* light and sexy. "Leah in Ecstasy," Cory called her, teasing when Leah couldn't mask her happiness with how her life was finally turning out.

It was, of course, Cory who'd set her up with a single man, a widower whose children were in college, recently transferred to Philadelphia by his company and looking for a house—and a friend. Leah couldn't begin to remember how many times she'd said no in the past. *No, thanks, I have another engagement. No, thanks, I need to be with my daughter. No, thanks, my mother is quite ill and there's no one but me on duty in the evenings.* Sometimes what she'd said had been true, and sometimes she was using an excuse because it seemed so pointless to start a relationship she couldn't sustain in the unlikely event a first date—a blind date, for heaven's sake—turned out well.

"Exactly why not?" Cory had said, in the entry of Albert's Italian, their favorite downtown restaurant, hand on her hip in exasperation when Leah trotted out, *Oh, thanks anyway, but I really can't,* her amorphous, all-purpose answer since her mother's death.

Exactly why not? Leah had to stop and think.

"There's no good reason, is there?" Cory pushed. "You're just so used to refusing, you don't even stop and think before you answer. He's a nice man and he has paintings—I know that because he mentioned them when I was showing him a house on the north side, and he said he liked the wall space in the living room for his paintings. So anyway, he must like art."

"Oh god, he's probably got framed paintings of neon unicorns airbrushed on black velvet."

"Hey, wait up here. Maybe they're from a really good place. Kmart had some darling prints on sale last week. . . . If you think I'm going to let you be a complete hermit. . . ."

Leah interrupted. "Honestly, you're worse than my mother ever was," she said, but she was turning it in her mind like a stone. Little sparkles of mica caught the light. Why not? "Will you leave me alone if I just do it?"

And she actually looked forward to it while she was engrossed in the painting she'd conceived when Allie was home for Thanksgiving, which she set aside after Allie was offended by the sketches. Leah had thought Allie would like the earlier, lighter version of herself, but saw, finally, that a much deeper interpretation of Allie was called for—demanded, really, by Allie herself. She'd need to do it with the added pounds but the figure still beautiful, to convey the elusive presence of

Chapter Eight

Allie, her Allie, and Leah's own preoccupation with holding and losing her, wanting and yielding her.

Leah had let the incomplete painting sit face to the wall on the floor of her studio from after Thanksgiving through Christmas, while she did other work and let her mind puzzle out how to do it. Then she decided to start over, stretching a new, larger canvas, and priming it with gesso. Only the sketches she'd done of the three-quarter face and the posture of Allie's neck were exactly the daughter who'd come home too briefly. Leah tacked those up on the bulletin board.

An idle memory of Missy coming up Leah's front walk gave Leah the notion of realigning the balance of the figure. *That* was it: people who put on a lot of weight quickly had a different center of gravity; the angle of their backs changed, so they looked less at home in their bodies. That was why she'd not gotten it right. But she didn't want the painting to convey discomfort. She wanted the poignant, elusive quality she felt with Allie and the pain of being with her, even as Allie was always and ever leaving. Her new idea was to paint Allie in the urban thicket, in that extraordinary early gold twilight, as Leah conceived Allie could *become*: still self-contained, but more peaceful with herself and her separate world as she moved toward and into it. Show her with the extra weight, but moving, agile and supple, into her life. Do a minimum of preliminary drawings. Let the struggle of the process of becoming—for daughter, for mother, for the painting itself—be revealed in the finished painting, part and parcel of its integrity. Leah could imagine herself giving the painting to Allie, maybe for her graduation, or on her wedding day, or when she had a daughter of her own. She'd never sell it, that much was for sure. This was the painting by which she'd make peace with this Allie, the distant, inscrutable one who carried the New Adult membership card and had to wave it in her mother's face by not coming home for Christmas. *All right, Alyssa,* Leah thought, *I'll show you that I get it.*

Finally, Leah thought she had it right, both the complicated feeling and the simple sketches done directly onto the readied canvas. She created a palette with the Winsor and Newton oils she'd graduated to as soon as she could afford them. She was elated at what was emerging. Her usual self-doubt didn't claim any attention, though she'd gone back to the park in several more waning afternoons to absorb the dialogue of the light and color, the silence of the shadows. The work itself had taken over, the vision larger than anything else in her mind, except Allie's reticence about returning her mother's calls.

Especially since Thanksgiving, it had been virtually impossible for Leah to talk with Allie. She left messages on Allie's machine—*call back, reverse the charges, honey*—but Allie didn't. Something was going on between Allie and Dennis while Allie was home, Leah thought. It was no more like Allie to submit to dressing up to please Dennis than was the last minute phone call saying she was going to spend the night at his house, or her late call to Leah to come pick her up. None of that computed, although, as Cory said, *What can you do? She's an adult, he's an adult. When you have no hold at all, hell, Leah, you might as well let it go, you know?*

And Leah had. Had tried to, at least. The worry wasn't constant any more, though it probably crossed her mind daily and bothered her deeply a couple of times a week. She was learning to accept what was, even while she left her plaintive messages on Allie's answering machine. *Call me, please. You can just put a message on the machine if I'm not here, Allie. I need to know you're okay.*

She was quite ready when the doorbell rang. Cory had told her Bob was tall, well-built, mustached, and, she pointed out, the fact that he still had hair, let alone that it was blonde, gave him several bonus points. "He's charming and funny, though I sense a potential for moodiness, so watch out for that. And call me tomorrow," were her last words on the subject.

Chapter Eight

Leah drank the last of her wine, straightened her skirt, checked her teeth in the mirror, and went downstairs to open the door.

Cory had been right about the description, Leah saw immediately, although Bob's hair was an ashy light brown. But he had a warm smile and engaging manner when he introduced himself and told Leah how much he'd been looking forward to the evening.

"Would you like to have a drink here before we go out?" Leah offered.

"I made reservations at Nichting's," he said. "I thought we'd go to the lounge there before dinner. But I'd really like to stay here. I'd like to see some of your work. Cory told me you're a painter."

"Let me take your coat," Leah said, stepping back and gesturing to the living room where three of her paintings hung. "It's nice that you're interested."

Forty-five minutes later, they were in an animated discussion of David Hockney, whose acrylics Bob admired greatly but Leah found plastic-looking. "Yes, he's British, but his work just shouts California to me. That's where he lives now, you know," Leah said, while congratulating herself on a good decision to go out with Bob. Cory was right, damn it. Leah was going to have to confess to her.

Bob glanced at his watch. "Whoa! We'll miss our reservations if we don't get going," he said.

He was holding Leah's coat for her when the phone rang. "I'd better grab that," Leah said. "I've been leaving messages for my daughter. I'll be quick, but it could be Allie. . . ." She hurried into the kitchen and grabbed the wall phone.

"Hello?"

"Mrs. Staton?" A woman's voice. Black.

"Uh, no, this is Leah Pacey, but . . . who is this?"

"I thought this was the number, maybe I read it wrong."

"My daughter's name is Staton. Is that who you're looking for?"

Baby's Breath

"Is this Alyssa Staton's family?"

"Yes, yes, this is Alyssa's mother. Who is this? What's wrong?" Leah could hear her heart pound in her ear, pressed hard against the phone.

"My name is Clara Edwards. I live in the apartment across from your daughter. Alyssa?"

CHAPTER

9

Alyssa thought of Caleb at first, that somehow her little brother Caleb was outside the door, crying for her to let him in. She imagined his hands scrubbing his teary eyes, the flush to his sweet round cheek, his fine blonde hair matted from bad sleep, from nightmare or tummy ache.

But that wasn't right. Missy and Dennis wouldn't let Caleb wail for so long, thumping and kicking on the other side of the wall as if he were throwing a temper tantrum. Missy and Dennis had Caleb in Princeton, safe in the bedroom in the big house where he was waiting—he'd told her this, sitting on her lap when Missy asked for a second bowl of ice cream in the cafe in New York—for a little brother. It couldn't be Caleb raising the ruckus, waking her to the shadowy box of the rented room and the ache in her own stomach—her heart?—and the blood soaking the gritted gray sheets beneath her.

She sat up and tightened her sweatshirt around her breasts. Binding? Was that the word, from Anthro, the binding of the breasts? Sore and stiffly ponderous beneath her dampened flannel shirt, they seemed too big, not hers, their weight a punishment for something she had forgotten doing but which, failed memory aside, she must deserve: her guilts made literal flesh and blood beneath her own skin, stinking the rented room, driving her from sleep to the dull morning that sifted light through a single window.

Baby's Breath

She was in San Francisco, the Tenderloin. That much she could remember, though she'd forgotten the name of the street and the hotel—without private bathrooms, could it be called a *hotel*? All she could think of after stumbling out of the BART Station at Civic Center was finding a place to lie down, to sleep; she hadn't thought of how badly she needed a bathroom, a private place with water and towels where she could get herself clean and stop the blood she could feel leaking from between her legs with every step. After four blocks, the T-shirt she'd folded into her underpants in the Berkeley BART was soaked through, and the purple neon sign reading "ROOMS DAILY/ WEEK" had seemed a gift, even though in the lobby she'd jostled her way past people whom, in another time and place, she knew she ought to fear.

Last night, she'd found a toilet at the end of the hall and used it because she had no choice, but it must have been the men's, it smelled so bad. Glued to the inside of the toilet bowl was a flattened condom, coiled against the blemished porcelain like the outgrown mantle of some deep-sea mollusk. She'd mopped up her own mess with the coarse paper towels stacked atop the toilet tank. They were framed with the stain of dirty water or rust. She hadn't wanted to tuck them inside the last pair of clean underpants she'd pulled from the zipper pocket of her backpack, but with the blood dripping stubbornly between her legs, she had done it. *A bandage*, she thought, layering the open towels and then folding them in thirds into a stiff stack. *Bandages* are for *wounds*. She put her ruined sweatpants into the rusted trash can and splashed water on her face and legs, what Gran used to call, after tickling her with suds from the kitchen sink, a spit bath. With every last towel gone, she stood and shivered herself dry before she tugged on the faded Levis that she found rolled up tight and packed on the bottom of her backpack. She gave up trying to button them, just folded the waist down like lapels and pulled the tail of her flannel shirt down low. Even after that, with

Chapter Nine

her tiny room's flimsy door locked behind her and her skin itching with imagined contamination, she remained thankful.

She lay back, dizzy with the effort of remembering the exact facts of the previous day, trying to determine her responsibilities to only the moment at hand. The crying and thumping from the room behind her head stopped, but it seemed as if the wall was wheezing, bellowing foul air. The jeans she'd struggled into in the nasty bathroom were sticking to her skin and to the sheets of the single bed; unbuttoned, they'd worked their way farther down her waist while she slept, anyway, squeezing her hips, tattooing stitch lines into a blue seam on the slack white skin of her abdomen. Still too fat. She had to be clean, presentable, if she were going to leave this room and find what she needed, pads and clean clothes and something to drink. So that was the first thing to accomplish, getting cleaned up. And that meant back to the mucky bathroom.

When she rose from the bed and flipped the light switch, she pierced her finger on the broken plastic toggle. More blood. She found a grim humor in deciding that, most probably, her blood wasn't the worst substance this room had seen. Shouldering her backpack, she opened the door into the dank hallway, badly lit by a single bare yellow bulb.

"Hello, Miss America." The words were slurred. It took Alyssa seconds to see the person, woman it seemed, leaning against the wall two doors down. She was thin as a rake and her face spooky pale, haloed by jet-black curls. Her faux leopard coat hung loosely, caped across her bony shoulders. As Alyssa watched, she sunk to the bald carpet in one elegant movement, like mercury falling. "Give me a hand, hon?"

"Excuse me?"

"The bathroom, doll. Help me to the bathroom." Her stick legs poked straight out from the leopard coat. She was barefoot, stockingless. Bruises latticed her shins to her thighs and disappeared beneath the coat hem.

125

Baby's Breath

What can you do when someone asks you for help, surprising you with her neediness at the very moment you are most desperate yourself? Help her, Alyssa knew, sliding her key into the lock of her own door, as though there were anything in the bloody room that somebody might want to steal. Lock your door and help her.

"Pleased to make your acquaintance," the leopard lady said, reaching for Alyssa's arm and pulling. She wasn't slurring her speech; it was a southern voice that drawled the words whispered into her ear. "Take me to the bathroom? Before he wakes up?"

Alyssa staggered backward against the wall, bracing her back while the leopard lady seemed to crawl up her arm, threatening to offbalance them both. "Lean on me," she said, taking handfuls of the leopard coat, cinching it closed around the lady like a hoist.

"You got your own problems, sweetie?"

"Are you drunk?" It slipped out. In any other world it would have been rude, but not here.

"I am not drunk." She didn't smell drunk. Alyssa believed her. "I have been . . . incapacitated briefly." She leaned heavily on Alyssa, as if her weight were all in her bones and not her flesh.

The bathroom door was locked. Helpless herself, Alyssa said, "It's locked. It's locked!"

"We'll wait," the leopard lady said, and sealed her promise with a wink. The toilet flushed, the occupant groaned, and the door crept open. A small man, brown and ratlike, rushed from the bathroom, eyes downcast.

Alyssa held the door open. "Do you want me . . . to . . . inside . . . with you?"

"If you would, darlin', I'm a little feeble here." Briefly, grotesquely, they hugged each other, sliding through the doorway together. Alyssa locked the door behind her and let her backpack slide to the cleanest patch of tarnished linoleum she could find. She felt too sick to wait for whatever ablutions the leopard woman had to perform. The close air,

the ratman's smell, was too, too much. The pattern on the green linoleum kaleidoscoped. She reached for the lip of the porcelain sink, felt
something caked and lumpy beneath her hand.

"Is there a woman's bathroom here?" Her words, phlegmy in her
throat, threatened to gag.

"Ought to be, but ain't. *Isn't*, I should say . . . Oh, easy there, doll, sit
down yourself, easy." As if Alyssa's weakness had furnished her with
new strength, the leopard lady dampened some paper towels—replenished by God, Alyssa thought—and soothed Alyssa's face. "You're going to need more washing up than this, Lord knows, hon."

"Uh-huh." For just that moment, suspended in grace beneath the
leopard lady's hands, she wished for her mother, the cold washcloth
cure for fevers and headaches, the cool, fine, painter's hands—*Mommy's*—that had dipped and wrung for baby and then mother, satisfying
grace with a baptism of love and duty.

"We're a fine pair," the leopard lady said, brushing Alyssa's hair back
from her face.

"Are you better now?"

"Will be, in a minute." She rustled in the pocket of her coat. A tiny
vial, like one of the amber antique prescription bottles that Clara collected, appeared in her hand. "You go ahead and do your business"—
she pushed Alyssa to the toilet—"there."

Because the yellow walls of the sorry bathroom were patterned with
stains that matched the leopard lady's bruises, and because the decay
spiralling from the slow-draining sink said nothing could embarrass
her, not here where there was no shame to be had, she pulled down her
stiff jeans and sat. The clotted paper towels fell from her underpants,
but the leopard lady didn't see. She was brushing her teeth—no, not
that—rubbing baking powder on her gums, shaking it from the vial
onto her palmed hand as though she were measuring gold flakes.
Watching her—oh, cocaine! Alyssa wondered if she too rubbed the
white powder into her gums, tongued it into paste and swallowed,

would it ease the piston of cramps that was expelling the fist-sized clots of her own blood into the toilet with the condoms and the ratman's excretion.

"Do you have some Tylenol?"

The leopard lady sucked on her finger, then used it to spatula clean the insides of the vial. She leaned against the sink, looking as if she were trying to focus, missing the big picture. "Not at present. . . . Maybe Lenny—maybe I could find a Percocet?"

Alyssa took a stack of the paper towels and wedged them into her jeans. "Okay." Enough was enough. She had to take care of herself. Survival of the fittest. She flushed the toilet, twice in a row so it didn't stop running.

"Give me a moment and I'll help you out, hon." Slurred now, Southern. Alyssa doubted the words. "There's a Rite Aid on Market. About three blocks down."

Alyssa closed the toilet seat. The leopard lady sat on it, her head between her knees. The coat slipped from her shoulders and arranged itself on the floor like road kill from another continent. Her bare arms were mazed with bruises, yellowing older ones imprinted with bright blossoms of new color like petals blooming against a pale background.

"Take it."

"What?"

"My fur. Take it and wear it to the Rite Aid, then . . . if you can't find me, you leave it with Lenny at the desk downstairs."

"I—"

"You ain't gonna make it a block looking like you do, hon. Just bring it back." She leaned down and stroked it, petting the thick lapels. Alyssa ached for Coffee—no, she'd left plenty of food and water, and Clara wouldn't let—"I know you're a girl won't steal from me, will you?"

"I won't—no."

Chapter Nine

"Get going then. Shut the door behind you. Tell Lenny I'm here, would you, hon?"

"I'll tell him."

"Hon?"

"Whatever you done—to be here—you shouldn't be. You don't belong here, hon. You get out . . . before you can't."

A wolf in sheep's clothing, Alyssa thought of herself as she waited outside the grilled door of the Rite Aid Pharmacy on Market. OPEN AT 9:00, the placard hanging at eye-level inside the glass door said. The coat covered her stained jeans so if people stared, they stared at the leopard skin, not at her, not at who she was. And if they didn't stare, well, it was because she *did* seem to have the potential to fit in with the street people; she could become one of them pretty damn easily. At least nobody tried to panhandle, but you wouldn't, would you, ask for something from someone who looked as though she might have even less than you. And that was what she looked liked: a girl with nothing, no past, no future, nowhere to go. She studied her image in the glass behind the Rite Aid grill, which quartered her reflection like a Picasso portrait, a misogynist's dismemberment. She recognized the hair, hanging lank and unclean down to her elbows. The dark eyes were sunken, set into a face that looked whittled from bleached bone. The white neck disappeared into a leopard collar, buttoned to the top. In reflection she had become a target for the ire of the animal rights activists who wouldn't detect the faux fur's polyvinyl sheen: an overexposed print's delayed failure of reality. They'd stone her for what they thought she wore, what they suspected she was. They'd be wrong.

Behind the grill, her reflection—no, not her reflection, a real person's, a live woman whose pared-down scalp sprouted hair extensions like Medusa's snakes—shook a prison-sized ring of keys at Alyssa in mock aggression. The glass door pulled open. The clerk unlocked the storefront grill and pushed it back against the wall of the entryway alcove, first the left, then the right gate. Wordlessly, she ushered Alyssa into the fluorescent light of the pharmacy. It was so warm inside Alyssa felt dreamy, like she could crawl behind the counter and hide herself to sleep.

But she marched one sore leg after the other and found the aisle with sanitary pads, where she scooped up two boxes under her free arm, blue-packaged Always Super. Two words she swore she'd never use again. She passed another clerk on her knees restocking cough medicines, and found the painkillers. The last bottle of Extra Strength Tylenol on the shelf was waiting for her. She fisted it in her right hand, shifting her backpack to her left shoulder. Back to Medusa, holding the pads and the Tylenol out like an offering—look! I'm not a shoplifter!—she spoke. "Do you sell, um, women's underpants?"

The clerk looked at Alyssa's legs and shook her head. For a moment Alyssa thought she was signing no, no underpants. But she was just cranky, or critical, or suspicious of a white girl who'd shown up at opening on a Monday morning shopping for underpants. A *fat* white girl. "Aisle four, past the baby bottles."

Coming through the cramped, soiled lobby in the Bay Breeze Hotel— she saw the sign this time, working her way up from Market—she had to lean against the plywood wall forming the clerk's cage to catch herself before she dropped, or slumped, or fell to the floor in whatever verb would best describe the slow motion tiredness grounding her like double gravity. She couldn't find the leopardess—she would barely make it up the stairs to her room—so she set down her Rite Aid sack and shrugged out of the fur and rolled it up, lining outward as Gran had taught her to handle a good coat. "This is—"

"Dara's coat." Lenny, tall and paunchy like Steinbeck's Lenny (but he was *fiction*; this was *real*), reached through the window and pulled the coat in, snaking it over the counter to his side of the cage. "Her Dalmatian costume—Hey, you okay?" She crumpled to the floor; she wasn't okay, and for what Lenny would later tell her was maybe ten minutes, she lost connection with the story in which she was a character, what somebody like Lenny would surely call a player, this spacy plot infiltrating her life.

Water helped, after Lenny had half-lifted and half-pulled her to the row of stiff wooden chairs against the back wall of the lobby. She thought it was possible to get faint-headed from dehydration, and she couldn't remember the last time she'd had anything to drink. At the apartment, before running water into the big bowls she'd put down for Coffee? Had she taken a twice-used tea bag from a yellow cup and rinsed, then swallowed down some water? She knew she hadn't taken water from the bathroom in the Bay Breeze; the stained, pocked porcelain of the sink and the fumes rising from the clogged trap had stopped her dead from cupping her hands and drinking, the way Daddy had taught her to when she didn't have a cup, but only when the snowmelt could be trusted. Lenny brought her the unopened bottle of Calistoga water, uncapped it, and put it to her lips. Then the leopardess was there, telling Lenny to get this girl up to her room, and suddenly she was in her room, only the sheets had been changed and two cellophaned turkey sandwiches were leaning upright against the uncovered pillow like little stuffed animals. Positioned on top of the pillow, like the fancy mints at some posh hotel where Dennis and Missy might stay, were seven red and white capsules. Barber poles, Alyssa thought, just before Lenny scooped them up in his big hand and shrugged her onto the bed.

Then the leopard lady—Dara now, wearing a pink jogging outfit— shooed Lenny from her room, and helped her to the bathroom, and settled her into the bed with its cleaner sheets, and fed her the Percocet, and made her drink more water. Again Alyssa felt the ministrations of a cool, damp cloth to her forehead. It seemed right, this part of the story, that a lumbering idiot had carried her upstairs and a coke freak was nursing her.

Baby's Breath

But even in this safety of sorts, taken under wing and tended to, she could see that something was terribly, terribly wrong. Just before she slipped off, she thought she heard Dara say again, ". . . leave here. Before you can't. . . ." And then something came to her about baby bottles—why had the clerk at the Rite Aid told her about baby bottles? She hadn't asked about baby bottles. And then, for the longest time, she was out.

The call from Clara Edwards had aborted Leah's date with Bob, icy fear instantly dousing the new pleasure. "My daughter seems to be . . . missing," Leah told him, trying to level her voice, when she hung up. "That was a neighbor of hers. She said Allie's been gone since yesterday. Left her dog, it's not like her."

"My god," he'd murmured, and put a hand on her shoulder. "What can I do?"

"I think . . . I'm sorry, I just can't go out tonight. Maybe another—"

"Well of course you've got to be here."

"I'm sorry. I would have liked to."

"No, wait," he said, as Leah started toward his overcoat. "I'm not going to leave you alone now." Concern raked across his forehead. "Look, I've got kids, I know. Let's sit down, figure out what to do. I'll help. Should you call her father?"

He took off his sports coat and loosened his tie, signaling he wasn't about to leave. Leah would have been uncomfortable with an offer of kindness, but given no choice, could welcome it. As if she'd been taken ill, Bob led her back to the couch in the living room. He sat next to her, his calm like the good blue she'd mixed that afternoon, an anchor.

Leah took a breath, tried to slow the horrors hitched to stampeding horses. "It's probably nothing. I don't know this woman, she's an adult, not a student or anything, but maybe she's an alarmist. I know she's taken care of the dog before. Probably Allie just . . . spent the night at a friend's. It's inconsiderate, but she's been inconsiderate lately."

Chapter Nine

"Aren't they all," Bob said. He smoothed his mustache. "They have no idea, do they? How they scare us. Are you and your daughter close?"

Leah hesitated, pulled at a strand of hair fallen forward, then flipped it back and fingered her earring. "Not so much. I don't know. She's pulled away. I had my mother here before she died, I don't think Allie wanted that."

"They all pull away," Bob had said then. "It's normal."

He'd gone out and gotten them Chinese in white cardboard cartons, rooting through Leah's cabinets for plates while Leah willed the phone to ring. Clara had promised to call if Allie showed up, and Leah had called Allie's again, demanding an immediate return call this time, not her usual deliberately casual, warm-voiced request. But the whole evening, the phone taunted her with silence while Bob told funny stories, both of them knowing exactly how much of her was paying attention. Still, his presence comforted her and she tried to define it. Something that doesn't change what you're feeling but is better to have than not. Chicken soup when your body aches with flu. A perfect eulogy when you're grieving, she thought, and then panicked, afraid the thought was an omen.

"What exactly did this Clara say?" Bob asked while he picked up their plates. Leah had rearranged the Moo Goo Gai Pan and rice he'd dished out for her, eaten four or five forkfuls.

"She just said that Allie had been gone overnight without telling her. She was keeping the dog anyway, but she wanted to know if Allie had told me where she was going, or when she was coming back. She said Allie hadn't done this before, and, well, then she said she was sorry to worry me. She said she'd taken the dog out for a walk for Allie, Allie wasn't feeling well, and when she came back, Allie was gone. Maybe she just went to a friend's, you know? Clara said she'd put out lots of extra food and big bowls of water for the dog. I mean, obviously, Allie meant to be gone."

Baby's Breath

"How'd she get your number?" Bob asked. His white shirt was rumpled now, as if her worry were his own.

"I don't know. I guess, she's got a key to Allie's . . . maybe Allie's phone has speed dial. I really don't know." One more thing.

He asked to see a picture of Allie, and Leah took him upstairs to her studio and showed him the sketch studies for the Allie painting, still evolving. When had she shown a man, well, shown anyone, really, her heart's hideout?

She slept in the lapses of her pacing mind after Bob left at midnight, and in the morning she tried to paint. She didn't call Cory for fear of Clara or Allie getting a busy signal. Didn't call George about the Bradshaw commission. When the phone did ring the one time, at noon, it was Bob's warm baritone.

"Heard anything?"

"No, I need to. . . ."

"Yes, well, I'll get off to keep the line open. Will you please call me?"

A good man. *See, Leah?* Cory's voice in her head. *There are good men.*

And then part of Leah was angry, a compartment next to but separate from the terror place. How many times had this happened? Sometimes it seemed Allie had internal radar warning her if her mother was about to be happy, and she'd produce a crisis that whined to Leah, *No way. Don't even think about it. Don't you dare have a life.* Here Leah was supposed to be working on a painting for the Bradshaw Foundation, an important commission, a fat one, though George had reminded her that where it was to be hung, *that* was the coup. And she met a man, had the temerity to accept a date, had the nerve to like this man and even after the first hour, to know she wanted to see him again. Somehow, from three thousand miles away, Allie had smelled it: *Oh god, no, my mother is happy. Can't let that happen. Got to fix that. Guess I'll take off, let her sweat, teach her a lesson.*

Another wave of panic: she'd be punished for her resentment in the

Chapter Nine

great Catch 22 of mothering, the one that said, oh yes, this business will take every drop of emotion you've ever felt and then an extra ocean or two of new ones, but make sure they're unselfish. Just love, give, *love, give.*

Love, give. Give. Love.

When the phone rang at four o'clock, she startled and flew at it, guilty. She'd dozed, the white screen behind her lids empty, exhausted.

A telemarketer. Not Allie. Not Clara to say Allie was back, no problem, no harm done.

At six, Leah had a glass of wine on an empty stomach and called Berkeley information for a Clara Edwards, giving Allie's address on Dwight Way. Clara answered on the second ring, almost as if she, too, were waiting for a call. Leah knew it was her, recognized the buttery, round tone, a rich alto.

"This is Leah Pacey, Clara. I'm sorry to bother you. I'm wondering if Allie's been. . . ."

"No. Not hide nor hair. Miss Pacey, I know you must be worrying."

"Yes." Twisting the phone cord, feeling it, that Clara knew something more. "You said she wasn't feeling well, but could she have gone to a friend's? I mean she's mentioned a boy named Howie . . . maybe he's become a boyfriend?"

"Lanky boy? Big white whale of a car? Once, out in the parking lot, I saw a boy drop her off."

Leah's little jealousy dissipated. At least Leah recognized Howie's name. So maybe this Clara wouldn't really know if Allie had done this before. Maybe Allie had just asked someone else to watch the dog other times. Or taken the dog with her.

But then Clara went on. "But she's been feeling poorly. And looking. . . ."

She rubbed her forehead, oily. She'd not even washed her face that morning, just started in on coffee and a worry sandwich at daybreak

135

and kept right on going. There were hard little grains in the corners of her eyes. She swiped them out as she spoke, her voice notching into anxiety.

"Do you think I should come out there? I could, I mean, if she's sick?"

Leah didn't realize how fully she'd expected Clara to say no, she was sure that wasn't necessary, Alyssa would show up any moment, until Clara answered on the tail of too much silence.

"That might be the right thing to do. Yes."

Then, the list of tasks became the mercy of diversion. Call George because she'd have to delay the Bradshaw work. Call Bob because he'd shown care to her, a stranger after all. Don't call Dennis, because he'd been a stranger for years. Call Cory, because she needed someone, not a stranger, and the face that looked back at Leah from the bathroom mirror when she finally washed her face in cold water wasn't one she even recognized. Call the airline. Pack what? Jeans, black slacks, black pullover, red pullover, white Oxford, and a painting shirt, for no rational reason. A sketch pad, automatic. A sweater. What was the temperature in California in February? A nightgown, shampoo, toothpaste, toothbrush. Leave a note for Dave Allen to get her mail, watch the house.

Cory insisted on driving her to the airport and Leah boarded the six-thirty flight to Oakland International, scarcely twelve hours after Clara said, *yes, maybe that would be a good idea, come*. Another day was cracking the rim of the horizon, about to lift the lid on another world.

Frantic barking was the first answer to Leah's knock. A tall black woman came to the door, shushing the barker before she gave an inch to ascertain Leah's identity, and then opening it widely to her, a stranger. Either she was an unthreatening presence or Clara thought the big black dog up on its back legs, scarcely restrained by her hold on its collar was protection enough.

"Clara Edwards?" Leah said, though she was sure already.

Chapter Nine

"Come in. You're Alyssa's mama." Her forehead was broad and shiny. Wide-shouldered, big-breasted, ageless, though Leah checked Clara's hands by habit and saw she was already past middle age. "Coffee, you quiet now. Down."

"This is?"

"This here sure is," Clara smiled, patting the dog's head as he sniffed Leah's legs. "Alyssa's dog."

"I'm sorry she left you to take care of . . . without asking, I mean." Leah stumbled through the beginning of an obligatory apology. She *was* embarrassed. "I can't imagine what . . . but have you heard from her?" She'd convinced herself that the trip would turn out to have been unnecessary, but she'd turn it to good use, a mother-daughter interlude of getting to know Allie's life.

"Nothing."

With the one word, Leah's confidence went cold.

"You come sit a minute," Clara said. "Will you have something to drink?" She gestured toward the kitchen and Leah followed the sweep of Clara's hand and arm, looking into the next room even as she shook her head. The apartment looked like a house, settled, long lived-in, old-fashioned. A little worn, maybe, but really, it was just *dated*. A doily on the back of the overstuffed chair. An old *Hammond Atlas* on the table in front of the couch. Coasters. Braided scatter rugs. Leah saw framed pictures of black boys and girls at various ages, and a hand-colored portrait of an ancient black woman. There was an aura of permanence. Leah sensed what attracted Allie to this unpretentious place and felt herself a failure; she'd not given Allie enough of a stabilizing history, always looking ahead as she'd been.

"No, nothing thank you," Leah said, though her stomach had started complaining during the taxi ride. But she didn't ask for the key to Alyssa's, or move to leave.

Clara noticed. "Just sit a minute, won't you? I'll tell you what I know."

Leah nodded. Without asking again, Clara moved the few steps to the kitchen entrance. "I'll just make us a cup of tea, if you don't mind. I need a little something. You come with me, all right?"

Leah followed, numb and grateful. She took off her jacket and folded it onto the back of the tweedy green couch, a sort of modified Early American. There was a stale taste in her mouth, and her silk blouse needed a wash. Leah herself needed a wash, oily-faced and fuzzy-teethed as she was, with her deodorant on overtime and threatening to quit. She gathered her heavy black waves into one hand, resting the ponytail on the back of her neck a minute, as if she thought anything might stay in place, which she didn't.

Ten feet away, Clara switched on the stove and pulled out a kitchen chair for her. "I felt bad calling you. I wouldn't if I didn't think it needed to be." She opened the refrigerator door and began taking out small packages. The kettle made little creaking noises of beginning. Coffee, who'd finished his restless sniffing and clicked across the kitchen floor after Clara, plopped down to watch.

"I'm thinking I should call the police," Leah said, trying the idea, wanting Clara to argue her out of it.

Clara shook her head in the negative, gratifying Leah, but only momentarily. "I don't know about that. You don't know how they do people, the police. My son . . . he . . . well. And even my late husband, one time."

Leah took this in, confused, and suddenly so exhausted she couldn't make her mouth connect to a single coherent thought. The women were silent a minute, Clara's hands . . . beautiful, Leah noticed, long-fingered and swiftly competent, busy. A knife hit a wooden board with a muffled thud four or five times, and then, while Leah closed her eyes a moment after she wiped the grit out of the corners, there was the sound of wax paper rustling. Clara set a plate between Leah's place at the table and what would be her own. How could Leah argue with the woman feeding herself? She eyed the little squares of ham and cheese, the saltines and sweet pickles.

"I'm hungry myself just now," Clara said. "Maybe you won't mind sharing a snack with me."

Leah knew that Clara had seen right through her. She went on around the embarrassment over her own transparency, over the loud growl her stomach made, back to Allie, who was the point after all. "It sounds like you don't trust the police. But would Allie? I mean, well, wouldn't they help *Allie?*" She meant *a white girl.*

Clara's silence and the way she kept her back to Leah while fussing with the tea bags and cups, were unsettling. Finally she turned and came toward Leah with teacup in one hand and kettle in the other. "Didn't quite boil, but it should be hot enough," she said. "You do what you think best about the po-lice," she said, inflecting the word so it sounded like *poe-leece*. Myself, I won't call them, or I'd a done it."

Leah was torn between taking some small offense and being grateful for the advice. Just too tired to figure it out, she took another cracker and layered ham and cheese on it. "Thank you," she whispered, "You were right, I was hungry. Am."

"You get you a good night's sleep. Tomorrow's soon enough to take it on." Clara sipped her own tea, and didn't elucidate. She edged the plate an inch closer to Leah. Coffee padded over and stood with his chin on Leah's knee, begging.

Leah woke at daylight in Allie's bed, the mattress on the floor. Not in it, actually, but on top of the cotton India print spread; the bottom sheet was stiff, as if Allie had spilled Coke and just left it to dry. After Clara had let her in, well after dark, even Leah's curiosity about this place that was Allie's had been overtaken by fatigue. Just a warm water face wash, a scouring of teeth, and the time to peel off her stale clothing and pull an oversize T-shirt over bare breasts and underpants had separated her entry into the apartment from the dead sleep into which she'd sunk.

Now Leah lay still a few minutes, her surroundings so unfamiliar she was initially unable to remember where she was. Then she heard a yip out in the hallway and the sound of a door closing. Coffee. Clara had insisted on keeping him another night. "You don't know the neighborhood, where to run him, I mean, and this here dog wants out at the crack of dawn," she'd said. "I'll keep him tonight. You get yourself settled."

"I'm hoping Allie will be back anyway," Leah had said then. "I just can't imagine . . . but I keep reminding myself there's no reason to think something's wrong. It's not like she has to check in with her mother. She's been on her own out here for a year and a half." Clara hadn't said a word, just unlocked Allie's door and handed Allie's mother the key.

She sat up and looked for the details of the small bedroom as they took shape in the gray light. When she saw how little Allie'd done, she felt guilty, like she'd taught Allie nothing about making a home. Bare bones, really. No personal touches, no little pretties in here, no pictures for color or the evocation of a memory. Mini-blinds unrelieved by curtains at the window. A lot of plants, though; maybe they counted as an effort. Some drawstring-type pants, half-in, half-out of an open drawer in the one small bureau. The closet door ajar to a jumble of stuff on the floor: athletic shoes, dirty socks, a yellow bra, a notebook, an inside out T-shirt. A jacket, hung next to the sundresses Leah sent last spring. That was all.

She was lightheaded with hunger. The refrigerator was a bust; mustard, ketchup, pickles, wrapped-up pizza, stale bagels. A quarter carton of milk, just souring, and no cereal to put it on anyway. That last was strange, because Allie loved granola with raisins and bananas even for lunch or dinner. Coffee, however, could have lived forever on the amount of dog food Allie had set out alongside a mixing bowl and a Dutch oven both full of water. Obviously, Allie knew she was going somewhere. Maybe Allie had left a note on Clara's door that had come down without Clara seeing it, a note that asked her to let the dog out, the whole thing that easily explained.

Clara was out in the hallway once, but a strange embarrassment kept Leah from opening the door just then, before she straightened the disorder of the living room that had been obscured by darkness and her noodle-boned tiredness last night. As if Clara hadn't already seen how Allie'd left it. But it would be too much like she was wanting something, maybe for Clara to feed her again. She needed to get the dog from Clara, though. She needed to get hold of herself and make some decisions.

Dizziness waved over her. All right then. She'd get the dog, and get something to eat. There must be a little convenience store within walking distance. Maybe even a grocery store. She'd figure it out. And she could start looking for Allie. There. That was how she'd start. She'd talk to people in the neighborhood, show Allie's picture around. She must have friends other than Clara . . . girls Allie's age. Of course she wouldn't have confided in someone that much older.

She showered quickly. Allie had left towels on the tile floor in there, moldy-smelling. There was a linen closet, but no clean towels or sheets in it, just some cleaning supplies, though from the look of the apartment they'd been one giant waste of money. Allie had shampoo and conditioner in the shower and Leah used both. Strands of Allie's dark hair slowed the tub drain, just as they had when Allie lived at home. Leah remembered the time Allie'd taken scissors and cut off the braids that hung down her back right at the base of her neck. *Why, Allie?* Leah'd said, over and over, as if something were going to make sense. *Why would you cut off your beautiful hair?* When she stood naked, making do with hand towels to dry her body and sop moisture from her hair, Leah suddenly bent double drenched in memory, fear and tears. *Just tell me why.*

A knock sounded at the apartment door. Leah struggled into underpants and jeans calling out that she was coming. The white Oxford shirt fought her, damp and braless as she was, hurrying to cover herself as she headed across the living room to answer the door.

It was Clara, holding a thick mug of black coffee and a plate fragrant with hot corn bread, a pat of butter melting on top, a knife balanced diagonally alongside.

"Oh Clara, how good of you. How nice. Thank you so much," she said as Clara extended both hands. Clara smiled.

"No trouble. I figured you must be hungry. Alyssa always likes this cornbread, so I thought her mama might too."

Leah tried to remember if she'd ever once made Allie cornbread. Maybe not. She'd made some good things that Allie loved, though, hadn't she? It was Allie who said to stop with the care packages; her mother could have kept sending them and then Allie wouldn't have been sniffing around strangers' kitchens for homemade anything. Now she was being petty.

"Please, come in. I mean, this'll sound silly, but you could bring your coffee over here. I haven't found that Allie has any, but, honestly, I haven't really looked. I just got up and showered." An embarrassed shrug.

Clara was wearing a simple dress, long, a print that looked African. Her hair was long, not an Afro, but not exactly straightened either. The top was pulled back from her face. Long silver earrings dangled. Leah, who was almost never self-conscious about how she looked, suddenly felt her own disarray. She tried to wrap the small towel she'd carried with her around her head, which of course didn't work and made it all worse.

"I could do that if you'd like a few minutes company."

"And why don't you go ahead and bring Coffee—the dog, I mean— along with your coffee. I thought I'd go out looking for Allie, and I'll take him with me." It seemed only polite to ask her in, though Leah wanted to get ready and move on with the business of finding Allie.

142

Chapter Nine

Clara hesitated a minute, then said, "Sure. I'll get him."

When she reappeared, the dog was scampering around Clara in eager circles. Clara had another mug of coffee in one hand and a newspaper tucked under her arm, which she set on what passed for a coffee table in Allie's living room. The front page blared about Monica Lewinsky and the hunt for the mother of the newborn baby girl found dead in the BART station.

"Thought you might like to see the paper, too," Clara said. "You can keep it, I'm through."

"Thanks. How could that girl not see how far in over her head she was?" Leah sat down across from Clara and gestured at the paper with her hairbrush. She could at least get her hair brushed out and her shoes on while she had the coffee.

"None of us know what goes on in people's lives, I figure. She's probably just a girl, don't know where to go, what to do."

"She was working at the White House, I mean, she'd graduated from college. It's not that I blame her, so much as, well, I just think she should've been more careful about what she was getting into."

"Oh, you mean ... I was talking about the baby's mother," Clara said. "That subway station, it's near here, it's been on my mind. Such a thing to face."

"Oh, I was talking about the Clinton thing."

Clara looked at Leah a minute, then looked away. "How can I help you?" she said.

"Can you give me directions to campus? I thought I'd ask around. I have a picture of her."

"It's awful big," Clara demurred. "I worked over there seventeen years. Never did even try to learn which every building was."

"I have to start somewhere."

Clara gave Leah her searching look again. Leah didn't know how to interpret it, but logged the expression in her memory. Inscrutable. She could paint it.

Baby's Breath

Clara led Leah to the picture window, which was on the side of the house positioned toward the bay, and pointed out the beginning of the route to campus, down Dwight Way to Telegraph to Sather gate. They looked to the west. "Can't see it now," she said, "but sun's gonna run off that fog; from the hills you'd be able to see the bay. You get a sense of it wherever you are. Whole town wants to slide right in." Leah stood with Clara, cornbread in one hand, coffee in the other. "You keep yourself straight looking for where the bay is. That's always west. To get back home, go uphill, make sure it stays behind you. Gonna be a good day, but you'll be wanting a jacket. You got one? That heavy coat you had yesterday just wear you down."

"I brought a sweatshirt and a jacket. Clara, look, thank you. Really, thanks. This is delicious, and I just appreciate all you've done. For Allie, I mean. And now me." She was ashamed of the jealousies that ran through the dark cavern inside her like underground springs.

"It's nothin', honey. We got to help each other." Clara glanced at the newspaper and shook her head. "I'll get out of here now. You'd best keep Coffee on a leash. You had dogs?"

"No, never really could." A stupid thing to say. Here, Allie kept one in an apartment. "But, it's okay, we'll get along. I like dogs." As if to show her sincerity, she bent and patted the Lab, who'd followed Clara's heels to the window.

Once she was there in the lingering remnant of morning fog, Leah saw what Clara meant. It had been a fine lunacy, the notion she could find Allie on this sprawling campus. After the first hour, Leah gave up approaching the younger-looking girls with Allie's high-school graduation picture, and began scanning for Allie's height and hair color, working from Greek Revival buildings to California Mission style at a far end. Later, off campus, she studied the hippie-looking sorts who had sidewalk tables set up on Telegraph Avenue to sell jewelry, leather crafts, tie-dyed T-shirts, incense. This must be where Allie'd bought

144

Chapter Nine

her necklace. Leah saw the same jade and silver combination, though none seemed exactly like hers and she was glad for that. She reached up to roll the jade between her fingers. Allie. *Allie, honey, come home now.* When she was little, Allie had come promptly at her mother's summons. Sun rolled up the carpet of mist. Behind her now, it skulked into the hills. There seemed no point to show Allie's picture anymore, even to obvious students, uniformed in jeans and heavy black backpacks. *Needle in haystack department here, Leah.* Clara had just been too gentle to tell her what a stupid notion it was. Coffee jerked the leash; a butterscotch cat crossed in front of him, insolent and at her leisure.

Leah found a grocery store and bought as much as she thought she could carry back to Allie's apartment and still manage the dog. When she came back outside, the leash she'd tied to a parking meter was wrapped around one of Coffee's back legs and he was barking frantically. "Not a good plan, huh boy," she said, untangling him. She wasn't doing this right. Maybe she *should* call Dennis.

Back at the apartment, she put away the wheat bread, bananas, granola, sliced turkey, tea bags, ground coffee, and two frozen chicken entrees she'd bought. She opened the new box of Milk Bones, and Coffee sat, whining his anticipation. She had to think. She had to be much more organized. Why hadn't she put up photocopied *Missing* posters while she was wandering around like an idiot?

She could call the Registrar's office and ask them to find out if she'd been in class. She could go through the apartment and look for the names of friends. Just be methodical, Leah, she told herself. Methodical and calm.

She started straightening and cleaning the apartment, looking for where something might obviously belong, and then taking that excuse to examine whatever cupboard or drawer she'd created the occasion to open. She watered all the plants on the shelves under the big window so she'd not feel she was only snooping. Allie had a way with them, she could see; ivy and ferns were flourishing and they were hard to grow.

Baby's Breath

There were jade and aloe, and some viney sort Leah couldn't identify. A tiny ficus was putting out new shoots and turning them palms up to the sun. Leah didn't even know how many of those she'd killed herself.

There were bill stubs on Allie's desk under the streetside window. Leah didn't see anything overdue. She gathered them together in a paper clip and opened the top desk drawer. Inside was an organized disarray of papers that seemed to be in discrete piles. Children's writing: staggering, crayoned, illustrated with stick people and lollipop trees. Letters to Allie along with a Certificate of Appreciation from the Library Literacy program, honoring Alyssa Staton's work as a reading tutor. *I love you*, two of the letters said, from little girls named Lashonda and Tiara. Another, thinner stack of papers, had to do with giving blood, acknowledgments, and times and locations of blood drives. There was a card identifying Alyssa as a donor, type B positive. Not the rarest of rare like some exotic orchid, but not garden variety as was Leah's own A positive.

She trashed the fast food bags and picked up the clothing on the couch and floor. A pair of shoes came together after she found one under the upholstered chair and one in the kitchen under the dinette table. Leah went through the garbage before she carried it out, then, fighting guilt, compulsively dusted the living room. An old vacuum cleaner was upright in the back of the one big closet. She went over all the carpet, matted and thready as it was, like it hadn't been cleaned in weeks, maybe months.

She washed a backlog of dishes, crusty-ringed glasses that argued against relinquishing their remnants. Putting those away gave her entry into each cabinet, but the contents were impersonal. No yield there.

Leah carried the clothes she'd picked up and folded into the bedroom. Of course she should just stack them on the dresser top, clear as a handwritten note saying, "I wouldn't invade your privacy." Instead, she began opening the drawers one at a time, assessing what belonged in each, and sorting the clothes, except the obviously dirty ones, into drawers. As she did, she first pulled out whatever was rumpled and re-folded it into neat, smooth handkerchief squares. That way, she got herself to the bottom of each to see if Allie, woman-like, had tucked away talismans of joy or shame.

Neither, it seemed. Until she got to the bottom drawer. There, neatly stacked, was a little pile of pictures and papers. A snapshot of Dennis on a sailboat, when his hair was still dark. Another picture of Allie and Leah. Leah remembered this one, taken by Esther before she died, out-doors on Easter Sunday the year Allie was nine, the good year. Allie's arms were wrapped around Leah's waist, and Leah was hugging her, both of their faces turned sideways to grin at the camera. The shine off their hair was lustrous, the picture alive with delight. A happy birthday florist card signed *Howie* in draftsman's print was with the pictures. A few of the letters Leah had written Allie in the last year were there, but Leah saw no particular significance to them, no clue as to why these were the ones saved. They were just newsy, ending with how much she missed Allie. Nothing unusual in that.

Behind all of this, in the back of the drawer, something was wrapped in sheets of plain tissue that Leah was careful not to tear or leave with telltale wrinkles. A tiny pair of white moccasins, beaded in white, min-iatures really, emerged from under six or seven layers.

Later Leah looked back on the moment thinking if she'd just slapped her forehead or could sketch in a lightbulb over her own head, the dawning would have been almost funny. And she'd not once thought of it. Had Clara?

The baby moccasins in one hand, she knocked at Clara's door with the other. Sharp, almost accusatory knocks. When Clara opened it, Leah held out the little shoes on her outstretched palm. Yes. She knew. Leah saw the slightest flinch on Clara's face before Leah's words even formed.

Baby's Breath

"Clara, is Allie pregnant?"

"Could be," Clara replied softly. "Yes. But I have no reason to . . . why don't you come in? Maybe we can figure something."

"I'm calling the police," Leah said. How dare Clara not tell her right off? "I'm reporting her missing. I should have done it right away."

"Miss Pacey, you might be bringing a whole pile of trouble on your daughter's head," Clara said. Coffee yipped from behind Allie's door.

"If she's pregnant, I'll help her. Being pregnant's not against the law, for god's sake."

CHAPTER

10

The morning when Alyssa felt she could stand up straight long enough to put on the new black sweatpants Dara had left on top of her deflated backpack with the change from Alyssa's twenty-dollar bill, Dara told her it was Thursday.

"You've been asleep *forever*," Dara said, passing Alyssa in the hall. She wore a sweater and a pair of jean shorts, her skinny legs shining with cheap hose, a sad imitation of somebody's suburban mother gone mad. "I brought you water, hon, like you asked."

"I asked?" Her mouth held a metallic tang, almost painful, as if she'd been chewing on tinfoil. She wanted to rinse it out, brush her hair.

"Percs, percs, percs. They'll do you every time. Feels a lot better, though, don't it?"

"What?"

"The pain, baby. Your brain's all fuzzy. You got four or five more, in the cup on the dresser. Courtesy of Lenny. What you get for paying rent a week in advance."

"I need to get going," Alyssa said, catching back a rope of her hair, so dirty her fingers felt slick when she pulled them away from the oily tangles.

"Of course you do. You got things to do. Places to go. . . ."

Alyssa held her hairbrush against her heavy breasts. Her shirt was soaked. She could smell herself. Probably Dara could smell her too. Probably didn't even care.

"... People to see." Dara sang out, operatic, her arms raised in one of the odd moments of elegance she summoned up from some long gone, happier past, hijacking Alyssa's attention from what needed to be done.

" 'Things to do,' " Alyssa echoed, flat-voiced.

"Then you need to go. Get packed, then scoot."

"Thank you, Dara." She remembered her manners, even here. *Doesn't matter who you're talking to, Alyssa*, Gran would say. *Remember your manners.*

"Bless you, my child," Dara said, kissing her forehead. She smelled dusty, her arms a bony hug inside the sweatshirt sleeves. Alyssa thought of *ghoul*, then took it back, ashamed. Dara and Lenny weren't so bad; she'd remember them, might come back. Dara said the rooms on five had their own bathrooms. That would be something. That was worth considering.

She sat in the Greyhound lobby of the Transbay Terminal on Mission for most of the day. If you didn't want to stand out, she understood, you put yourself in the middle of people nobody else much cared about. And you watched their comings and goings, their vague gruntings and scratchings. You listened for an occasional squeal or angry word in the hope you'd find out something about yourself. As she watched, she combed her unclean hair with her fingers and braided it into a loose plait. She had no scrunchie, no rubber band, but her hair was so heavy with dirt the braid was held in place by its own inertia. When night fell somewhere beyond the city's skyline, she felt she could recess from watching the crowds, from searching for the sign that would tell her exactly what she was expected to do.

It came, finally, in the guise of a legless man's dog, a longhaired little curl of an animal dancing on two legs outside the McDonald's across the street from the terminal. When the clock above the ticket counter

Chapter Ten

read six-o'clock, she'd thought of ice cream for dinner, a chocolate shake, to wash down two of the handful of Percocets Dara had pushed into her sweatshirt pocket as a farewell gesture. Her legs ached, up and down, so badly that she imagined if she were to pull off her pants in the gaudy fluorescent restroom of the Greyhound, she would find them as bruised and battered as Dara's. Though she wore four layers, every dirty shirt she had, topped by her sweatshirt, her leaking breasts had soaked through T-shirts and flannel so she bore a stiff vest of cold fabric across her chest. The milky smell, the obvious damp, didn't worry her—at home as she'd become in the no-man's land of the displaced and the freaked-out—but her bulky breasts hurt, a steady, committed, pulling pain that seemed knotted to the innermost organs of her chest, her heart and lungs. The falling-off feeling of a Percocet would fix this; Dara had promised from the beginning the Percocet would be balm, and it had been. She left her station on the plastic bench to trudge across Mission and order a shake, a medium. Resting her backpack on the littered surface of an empty table, she fingered two Percocets away from the lint in her sweatshirt pocket and mouthed them, swallowing the syrupy, thick chocolate mix. Coming out through the heavy glass doors, she'd let the cup slip—she'd had enough, anyway, it was too sweet—and down it went, splashing the legless man on his little rolling table. But the dog was happy, doing its eccentric dance, and that was when, already numbing from the pills, lighter on her feet, she was given the sign: go home and check on Coffee.

From then, it was easy enough to buy the round-trip ticket to Berkeley and shuffle onto the bus in a line of passengers as raggedy as she. She wanted to sit by herself—her soppy, sour smell—but the bus driver seemed to wait forever, ushering in more and more older people looking like refugees from an urban war with their taped-over cardboard boxes and their paper bags smudged with grease. Only when the seats were full was the driver content to start the engine and queue up behind the other outgoing buses. For the stop-and-go drive across the bay and

151

into Berkeley, she shared her seat with a heavy woman, fatter than she, maybe a little older, whose wheezing, asthmatic intakes of air were followed by softly expelled "uh's" as measured as the tick-tock of the metronome Gran had kept on the living room bookshelf in their rowhouse, a placeholder in memory for the upright piano that just wouldn't fit.

She was glad it was night. In her room at the Bay Breeze, under the thready covers of her single bed, night and day hadn't made much difference. What did it matter if you slept under sun or moon? In Berkeley the lower scape of the old buildings on Shattuck enabled it to be real night, so that when she turned up Dwight there were patches of sidewalk enveloped in true dark. She'd take Coffee over to the Clark Kerr campus and let him run on the lawns. At night, she could usually get away with this. It was safe, set off the street by the old dorms left over from the school for the blind, and she could let him have a good romp without worrying that she felt so sluggish, sort of seasick and headachey. It would be best if Clara wasn't home. She didn't know about talking to Clara, not just yet.

She didn't realize the kitchen light was on until she'd unlocked the door. Coffee scrabbled against it so eager and impatient that she worried he'd break it down before she had turned the deadbolt. Then she'd be in trouble with Huddie, too. Coffee barked and kissed her and barked some more, so all she could do was drop her backpack and sit down on the floor with him, which is why it took her so long to realize the kitchen light was on ... and her apartment was *different*.

Coffee was all right. He smelled good and clean, and he didn't seem to be begging, not for food, anyway. That was the first thing she saw—the Dutch oven and the extra bowls of food and water weren't on the floor in the kitchen where she'd left them. A bowl of water and a licked-empty pan that must have held Gravy Train were matched up neatly on the floor to the side of the sink, like a tidy pair of shoes in somebody's closet. And the counters were clean—except for a two-cup drip filter perched on one of her thrift-store yellow mugs. *Goldilocks,*

Chapter Ten

she said to herself when Coffee pressed against her legs for more love, and she had to shut her eyes tight to keep from screaming. *Who's been sleeping in my bed?*

Two bananas resting in a mixing bowl. Inside the fridge, fresh milk, sliced turkey, three oranges, a tinfoil cover pinched onto one of Clara's mixing bowls. Coffee edged closer, sniffing at the turkey.

"No, Coff. No, boy." She shut the fridge door. That's when she remembered the kitchen lights—that the kitchen lights had been on before she'd come inside. As soon she stepped across the vaccumed carpet and into her bedroom, she knew it was Leah. It was true: her mattress bed had been stripped of its coverings. Sealy Posturepedic: Extra Firm read a blue label where her pillows should be and Lazzie now sat, his chin nodding disconsolately onto his chest. Her mother's soft black carry-on bag—the one Allie used to take on overnights to Daddy's— rested half-empty on the bentwood chair in the corner.

She'd be back.

Alyssa thought, no shower now, and turned to the bathroom. The towels she'd counted on—the towels that she'd left piled on the bathroom floor—were missing. Pads, then. She thought she'd left some under the sink from before—well, just from before. But there were none, just a new four-pack of toilet paper. She'd need soap back in the Bay Breeze if she rented one of the rooms with a private bath, upstairs on five, so she took the fresh bar from the sink: Dove, her mother's brand. And she'd need shampoo, too, so she lifted the half-empty bottle from the shower. Hanging from the inset soap dish beneath the spigot, framing it like a little altar, was the silver and jade necklace she'd given her mother at Thanksgiving. *I love it,* Leah had said, kissing the heart with her fingers. Alyssa reached for the polished corner of jade—*I see a heart, don't you?*—and lifted the chain from the hook of the soap dish. Suspended from her fingers, it swung back and forth to the beat of her pulse like a hypnotist's charm. She coiled it in her palm and slipped it into the smallest zipper pocket of her backpack.

Baby's Breath

Very little time.

She couldn't find her grey sweatpants, not in her closet or in her dresser. But her dark blue ones, torn in the crotch, were folded neatly in her bottom drawer. She set her backpack on the mattress and took the pants and two flannel shirts from the drawer and stuffed them into the bottom compartment. Then the shampoo and the bar of soap. Clean underpants, a handful. A jar of peanut butter from the kitchen cupboard. On second thought, the unopened box of granola she found there, too. Which left just enough room for Lazzie at the top of the pack where, if he wanted, he could poke his head through the open zipper to breathe.

Coffee, mistaking her urgency for the signal to walk, yipped, high-pitched. I can't wait, he was telling her. Take me with you.

She would take him. She'd find his leash and put some Gravy Train into a freezer bag and take Coffee, too. But she had to find his leash. *Think like Leah.* Everything in its place, put back where it belongs, better than you found it. Where would Leah put his leash? Not in the drawer with the silverware, not on the table in the living room. Nowhere on the counter. *Think. Think.* She went back to the bedroom where she found a neat gap in the row of hanging clothes in the closet. Hers on the left side, her mother's few things on the right. A pullover jacket, a black sweater, Leah's painting shirt with the cuffs rolled up. The jacket—she might need a jacket on the windy streets of the city. Alyssa pulled it from the hanger—*hurry*—and started to tug it over her head. A clinking in the jacket raised Coffee from a sit. He bounded against her.

"Down! Down!"

Inside the front pouch of the jacket—*like kangaroos, Allie!*—there was the leash, the leather handle wrapped around the chain.

Leah had walked her dog. Not only walked him, but let him loose at some safe point as well, maybe close to home or in the dead of night when the traffic died, then slipped the leash into her pocket, where it hung, not properly put away, forgotten until the next walk.

Leah had fed her dog. She would have brushed Coffee, too, if she'd found the dog brush on top of the refrigerator. Would Alyssa be able to do these things for him, cooped into her tiny room in the Bay Breeze? Would the streets of the Tenderloin be as good for him as the funky up-and-down sidewalks of Berkeley? Was there anyplace in the city where she could let him run unleashed the way he could at Clark Kerr and People's Park?

Coffee was safer here with Leah. And Clara. They were women who knew what to do, how to take care. She herself wasn't fit—not now—for custody. Her dog would be better off with Leah. He'd miss her, but she'd come back soon, and then it would be all right. Just now, there was something she needed to check, and she couldn't afford to see her mother. Too many questions she wasn't able to answer, not right now. She'd just take her things, and say goodbye to Coff, and slip out of the apartment before anyone knew she'd been there.

A biscuit would keep his heart from breaking, she thought, and sure enough, there was a new box of biscuits in the cupboard, right where the empty one had stood for weeks. She pulled out two. Coffee sat, un-bidden, and waited.

"Good boy." She touched the biscuit to his mouth. "You're growing up, Coff." He was already ready for the second, and she crouched down and hugged him, hearing the quick swallow in his throat, feeling his slathering kisses across her face. "Be a good boy for me, Coff."

But she made the mistake of looking back to the kitchen where he sat, politely, hoping for a third biscuit. On the counter by the telephone Leah had repositioned, like ornaments or mementos on view, were the white baby moccasins she'd bought from the HIV table on Telegraph, where with every sale they gave out a brochure on community involve-ment in the fight against AIDS. She thought—she couldn't be sure of anything, could she—that she'd left them hidden somewhere, under clothes or behind books.

She crossed the living room to the counter, picked them up, stared hard at them, how they balanced in the bowl of her cupped hand. Such little, little feet they would fit. Baby's feet.

Newborn baby's feet.

Leah had taken the sheets and towels to the laundromat on Haste Street, that was all. How long had she been gone? An hour? An hour and a half? She'd sat there waiting for the washer first, then the dryer, all the while sketching Clara's face with its inscrutable look, full of unspoken knowing. It put Leah off that Clara didn't entirely trust her, though she didn't entirely trust Clara, so fair was fair. Still, she'd let Clara talk her out of calling the police again. "Give her time, Miss Pacey," Clara said. "She's got nobody far's I can tell, except you, and maybe that lanky boy . . ." and me, Clara, the woman who looked after her, unsaid in the charged air of the hallway between the apartments, as if Clara knew Leah's heart. "I'm thinking she'll be back, when . . . I'm just thinking she'll come back on her own. After the dog, make sure he's okay."

"But . . ." Leah interrupted, "she's been gone way over twenty-four hours. It's pushing four days, now. That's what missing persons departments are for, you can call in a missing person after only twenty-four hours." I don't need Clara's permission to call them, Leah reminded herself, yet had stood there while Clara pressed on through her reluctance.

"Miss Pacey, my son got arrested for drugs." Clara's features were composed, but there was suffering and the remnant of shame there. "The po-leece charged him up, seven felonies, so the defense would have to bargain and they'd be sure to get their jail time. Miss Pacey, I know on my soul that my son was doing drugs. I know just as sure that five of those seven charges were fake, so's he wouldn't be eligible for the treatment program, only for the jail. They say treatment's easy time. I wouldn't believe it myself, except Eddie, my husband, he talked to a black officer—Eddie'd worked with his Dad for years—that boy looked into it for Eddie, told him, yeah, our boy made the cops mad, they went for him and the D.A. climbed right on. . . ."

Leah began to sputter another protest. This wasn't the situation with Allie at all.

Clara shook her head, and urgency laced her voice. "They get some-thing in their minds, Miss Pacey, and they don't care who needs what or even what's true and what's not. I wouldn't tell you this if I just thought it. I've lived here all my life, heard it from too many people. Most of 'em black, that's true, but you don't know what fix Alyssa's got herself into. I wouldn't be helping them go after her, just in case."

"Please, call me Leah," Leah had murmured, all she could say. "I don't know, Clara, I just feel irresponsible not having professionals looking for her." Clara had backed off then. "I know you have to do as you see fit. I'm only talking to you mother to mother."

But it bothered Leah enough that the two times she'd picked up the phone to report Allie as a missing person she'd ended up putting it back down. Clara's distrust of the police seemed out of character with her restraint on everything else. The Registrar's office at Cal had said they didn't know if they could provide information on whether Allie was at-tending classes, because she was, after all, an adult. They'd check and get back to her. Another day. I'll wait another day.

And she had waited, most of the day on Thursday, nervous energy leaking from her pores like so much sweat. She'd scrubbed the kitchen floor on her hands and knees, the grout of the bathroom tiles with a toothbrush and bleach; she'd washed the windows and the inside of the refrigerator. Finally, when evening came and it was too late for the Reg-istrar's office to call, she'd stripped the bed and gathered up the hand towels she'd used herself into a heap with the ones Allie'd left on the bathroom floor. Leaving Coffee at home because it took both hands to carry the laundry basket, Leah walked two blocks to the WashN'Dry and waited out the machine cycles rather than hike back and forth. In the first place she needed the towels, and secondly, she was tired of sleeping on top of the cotton spread because the stiffened sheets were discomforting and, truth be told, a little repulsive. Who knew what Allie'd spilled?

Coffee barked as Leah made her way back up the stairs to the landing Clara and Allie shared. She'd used fabric softener in the dryer so the towels and sheets, crisply folded and laid in the laundry basket, were pleasantly scented. A small warmth still emanated from them, seeping from the middle of the pile. Leah carried the basket to shield her abdomen and chest from a dank winter offshore wind, wishing she'd worn her jacket. She was slightly out of breath from the awkward position, and relieved enough to be back in the apartment that she didn't immediately notice the open kitchen cupboard. She'd not have left it that way herself, compulsive as she was about order. First she thought Clara had been in, perhaps to borrow something. She crossed into the kitchen to close the cupboard; the box of granola was gone. It was strange but not alarming. Clara had a key. Allie had told her she and Clara borrowed from each other, though she guessed it was most often Allie who did the borrowing.

As Leah moved through the apartment to the bedroom, though, little things seemed wrong. In her own home she would have known instantly what had been moved or was missing. In Allie's apartment, she had to think, study, remember. When she went into the bathroom to put the towels away, it took a good three minutes to identify that the shampoo was missing. So was the bar of soap from the holder by the sink.

In the bedroom, a drawer was open. Leah knew right away what was missing: a pair of sweatpants had been there. She was sure, because it was one of the items she'd considered washing, and decided no, they were clean.

Chapter Ten

Leah debated, circling the obvious conclusion. Surely Allie wouldn't come home and leave again. It would've been perfectly obvious her mother was there. Absently, Leah's hand went to her neck to finger the silver necklace while she thought. It wasn't there. For a frantic couple of seconds, her hand flailed around her neck, disbelieving the bad luck of losing it, until she remembered that it had tangled with her hair when she was in the shower that morning; she'd finally had to take it off in the process of freeing it. It was still draped over the soap dish.

But it wasn't in the bathroom either. Was she remembering wrong? She tried to picture when she'd last seen the necklace, needing to find it now, Allie's gift, from which she'd last taken hope.

Coffee's nails tatted like knitting needles against the floor as he followed her back to the kitchen. Maybe she'd carried it out there when she was pulling out the hair knotted with the links. She searched the kitchen counter. Something else was missing. It took her another long minute to catalog. The moccasins. The little white baby moccasins. She'd left them on the counter. Allie had been here. She'd taken the moccasins, and she'd taken the necklace. She'd taken soap and granola and sweatpants. She wasn't somehow lost or injured or off having an abortion. She knew her mother was there, and she had to know her mother was frantic. She'd come in and taken this odd assortment and slipped out without so much as a note.

Later, Leah would think back and acknowledge that it was the liquid of anger—how could Allie behave this way!—that finally combined with the dry lumps of bewilderment and fear in the bowl of her chest for the chemical reaction that transformed her indecision.

"I'm calling to report my daughter missing. She's been gone since Sunday. I think she's pregnant."

Alyssa went south on Piedmont at first. All she could think of was putting distance between herself and the apartment where Coffee's stop-and-go barking agitated the night air, a living burglar alarm in search

159

of a lawbreaker. She'd been lucky; the windows to Clara's apartment were dark. The new weight of her replenished backpack pulled at her shoulders, but she pocketed her hands in the pouch of her mother's jacket and leaned against the wind tunneling up from the bay through the manmade valley of Parker Street. At the corner of Derby and Piedmont, she leaned forward and lifted the straps of the pack from her shoulders, easing the cutting burden. Her shirt, warmed during her brief sojourn to the apartment, was cold again. Her new sweatpants, too, felt damp between her legs. The pads—she hadn't found pads, hadn't thought to stuff a T-shirt or dish towel there, driven as she'd been by Leah's coded messages throughout what had been her private place: *I'm here. I'm looking for you.*

The wind washed her mother from her head, unworking the lank hair from the makeshift braid. Head bent, one foot after the other, she worked her way down Derby toward Shattuck. She'd find water for Percocets and what—whatever it was she'd set out to do when she'd left the city—and she would sit down as soon as she had a moment, slip off her backpack, give her shoulders a rest. She passed a gaggle of black boys, jiving each other, bumping shoulder and hip across the sidewalk. They cut their formation, let her through, but called after her: "You, bitch! You uglier than sin, girl! Sheee-it! Whooey!" But it couldn't be her they saw. She was, at this moment, invisible behind the hulking, smelling, dripping thing that put one foot after another and parted ill-meaning gangs with silence. Cars passed her, headlights brightened, then lowered as if the one look had been enough for each driver. Like the black boys, they were signaling her to go on, move through, pass by. They wanted her out, gone, blackened into the red glow of their tail-lights and vacuumed into memory by streams of exhaust.

On Shattuck, breathing hard and feeling what she thought was hunger behind the rack of her ribs, she turned down Adeline. A kitchen, she remembered, a kitchen that she was supposed to keep clean. And something else, something to do—to check. Coffee's water? Water

Chapter Ten

Clara's wintered geraniums? No, done. Not that. Not necessary. Not that. It nibbled at the edges of her mind, what she was supposed to do. Once she'd figured it, then easy enough. She'd be able to rest, and eat, and sleep somewhere quiet, for a long time.

A clot of couples at the top of the BART stairs blocked her way. The men wore suits, dark and important. The women's faces—glass cheeks under sleek, short hair, gold at their ears—hardened when she inched around them, her backpack held against her stomach now, its shape a remembrance of something, something. The women backed away from her, slender legs on spike heels, and pulled their coats tight around their necks, as if protecting themselves against a windborne virus. Alyssa took each downward step slowly, one foot finding the other, standing on a single stair, steadying herself against the railing before she shuffled one foot to the next. Beneath the ground, removed from the wind, all the blowzy parts of herself collected and recomposed themselves: her heavy hair against her shoulders, the runny nose she swiped with a cold paw of a hand, the backpack rounded against her front like a restored ballast. The passengers from a westbound train disembarked. She flattened herself against the corridor wall to let the riders pass upstairs to their lives above ground. Pulled by memory, by the gravity of the backpack's forward weight, she edged toward the bathroom entrance. Finally, she remembered where she was headed— she had something to check. In the kitchen.

The dwarf woman at the sink was familiar. She wore a yellow coat, a pink stocking cap, navy blue knee socks and brand new Keds, kelly green. Like a child had dressed her, or dressed herself, Alyssa thought. The dwarf turned from her wizened reflection in the mirror and let her loose eyes roam over Alyssa in a spastic, nervous examination of parts, drifting from her face to her backpack, back to her face, then to the dirty ropes of dark hair falling to her waist, never once fixing them- selves in focus.

"Messed my kitchen. Messed my kitchen. Messed my kitchen." The dwarf keened, her voice rising. "Messed my kitchen. Hell's bells, hell's bells, hell's bells."

Alyssa let the backpack rest on the floor beside her feet. Lazzie, sad-eyed, white-faced, poked out from the zipper opening. She fingered two Percocets from the damp pocket of her sweatpant. Blood on her hand. A bath would be good. Drinking water first, bath water, somewhere. After she found—

"Ain't no children allowed. No children allowed, the little bastards, the little beggars." The dwarf knelt, childsized, beside Alyssa's backpack. She poked at Lazzie with an outstretched finger. "The little bastards." She stood up and pushed Alyssa against the half-closed door of a stall. "Get out!"

Alyssa sank backwards, onto the toilet, and kicked the stall door shut with her foot. She slid the chrome bolt home and listened to the flush of the toilet beside her stall. Then the rustling of paper, the user's low "Fucking paper! Christ Jesus." Beneath the stall door her backpack appeared, slid across the dirty cement by the dwarf's mottled, horny hands.

The dwarf's voice overlapping, faster now, from outside the restroom entrance: "Ain't no children allowed! Messed my kitchen! Cut that filthy hair, anyway. Cut that hair!" Shrieking now, pumped with excitement. Other voices layered over the dwarf's.

"Lee, watch her, she's nuts!"

"Why didn't we take the car!"

"—the awful mess parking last week—"

"Lee! Don't!"

"—to call Henry Porter, you know, the shelter's director. . . ."

"We saw a cop—"

"Burton will go. . . ."

One of the Percocets stuck sideways in her throat. She had tried to save up her spit, the way Sharon had taught her in eighth grade, but she managed to swallow only the first one all the way. The second lodged in her throat, like words that wanted out before they were gulped down by accident. She could unlock the door and get water from the sink, but the dwarf might come back and start yelling again. She'd left something here, she knew, but now it was clear to her that the dwarf would not have taken good care—*what a mistake!*— not the way Alyssa took care of Coffee, so Alyssa would get it back, start all over again the right way. And she had the moccasins this time, and she had a secret place to live, and she even had Dara and Lenny.

She was cold, though, wet shirt and wet pants. Beneath Lazzie in the backpack were the flannel shirts. One she put on herself, over the wet layers that scaled against her skin like penance. One she shook out and flattened across her knees. If she were cold, *it* was probably cold as well, and the flannel would be soft, a Good Housekeeping seal of clean warmth.

The next-door stall was empty now. Sink water ran, somebody coughed. Somewhere, away, Alyssa heard the dwarf's voice, but so faintly it barely reached her, so didn't matter. ". . . bastards . . . cut the hair . . . clean . . . clean. . . ." The Percocet inched down her throat. She thought of grammar school science, the mouse inside the corn snake, the way the snake's jaws unhinged to encase the struggling mouse, the rippling, one-way musculature beneath the snake's skin. She pulled the flannel shirt across her wet breasts. *Where was it?* Lazzie's size, almost. Not furry like Lazzie. *Not a bear, silly!* The dwarf's words returned, coming closer and closer, a circling buzzard. "Wha'cha gonna do, wha-'cha gonna do, wha'cha gonna do—"

"Enough already, Molly. Just show me." A sane woman's voice, confident. Professor Miller?

"Bastards!"

"In the stall, huh."

"Stall, stall, stall!"

"Got 'em cornered, Moll." Someone rapped against the stall door. The metal walls vibrated. "Hello? Police Officer here. Can I help you?"

Baby's Breath

Alyssa took Lazzie from the backpack, laid him against the flannel shirt opened on her knees.

"Miss? I'd like to help—these people outside are concerned about you."

She folded the shirt over Lazzie's chest, snugly, and tucked the v-shaped tail at his feet beneath his torso.

"Miss? If you'll just speak to me, I'd like to know you're all right."

In the side pocket of her backpack, she found the moccasins. She held one in each hand, studying the fine beadwork. Of course they wouldn't fit on Lazzie's feet. He was a stuffed *bear*. They were *baby* moccasins. Where was Lazzie's baby?

"Miss?" The voice came from the stall beside her. She felt the metal partitions shudder. Then the voice was above her head. "Miss? You need some help? Open the door, please, so I can help you."

The officer was pretty, blond like Sharon, scarcely older than Alyssa. It wasn't true what the boys in Tony's frat house had said, that only lesbians went into criminal justice. This officer had a sweet face, a girlfriend's face. Yes, here at long last was somebody who would help, who would listen.

She tipped her head, shook a lock of hair from her face, rested the moccasins in her backpack, smiled back. She heard the officer clamber down from the toilet. Then Alyssa stood, Lazzie tight against her sopping breasts, and slid the bolt back. The door swung open slowly, pulled by its own weight. The pretty officer stood facing her, still smiling.

"Miss? Some people up on the street were concerned about you—"

"Bat outa hell!" The dwarf sputtered. She was moving down the line of sinks, turning each faucet on full blast, leaving them running as she moved on to the next. A train hummed through the tunnel, eastward toward the Valley. If it kept going, if there were a BART tunnel beneath the continent, it would reach Philadelphia, Princeton Junction.

Chapter Ten

"Molly! Turn them off, please." The officer spoke without moving her eyes from Alyssa's. "Now's not the time, Molly."

Alyssa extended her arms, so tired now, and offered Lazzie to the officer.

"You got a stuffed bear, here, honey?" The officer took Lazzie, eyes on Alyssa's face.

"I couldn't—you know—take care, so I left. But I came back. . . ." The words came hard, squeezing up and around the molten Percocet in her esophagus.

"Somebody hurt you, miss?"

"I came back to take—"

"Who hurt you? You can tell me. I've got the bear. What happened to you?" The officer's eyes moved down, measuring the stain on her sweatpants, up to her breasts, the dampness darkening the clean flannel.

"I came back."

"Miss, is that blood on your pants?" The officer touched Alyssa, lightly, high on the thigh, looked at her thumb. "Miss, you're bleeding pretty badly here. Can you tell me what happened?"

"But somebody's taken it. Not *her*." She cut her eyes sideways at the dwarf, "She's not—" Alyssa tilted, wobbled against the officer's shoulder. A sturdy hand took her arm, kept her from falling.

"You better sit down, Miss. Careful, there." The officer kept her hand on Alyssa's shoulder, squatted with Alyssa as she lowered herself to the floor. She faced Alyssa; she smelled good and clean. Pretty golden hair, cut square beneath her chin. "I need your name and address, hon. You have some ID?"

The *hon* did it. This was going to be easy street. Sit down, square her tired back against the wall, her hands free because the officer had Lazzie, was holding him the right way, not letting his head flop how it would if you didn't support it with your arm. The officer handed her

165

backpack to her, set it down beside her. She found her wallet and pulled her Cal card from it. The officer smiled at her, and again Alyssa thought, this is finally so easy, finally when somebody calls you *hon* and asks you straight out and all you have to do is answer, go along.

"That's good, now Miss—Alyssa, it is, right? I'm going to get somebody here to help you—you just sit there, okay?"

She didn't even have to answer, this officer understood her so well. The two women who stood at the restroom entrance and stared, gawky faced and rude, they didn't know a thing about communication, and Alyssa was glad when the dwarf flew at them, waving her arms and shooing them outside. She and the officer were having a conversation. It wasn't their business, not any of them.

"This is Sanders, in the BART on Shattuck. I've got a girl here, disoriented, bleeding badly." The officer's voice lowered, her lips pressed against a black box. ". . . Looks like violent rape, I'm guessing. She's not coherent . . . I don't know. I don't see any visible signs, no paraphernalia. . . . She's got ID, though. Yeah, a mobile to the hospital." The officer listened, then turned to Alyssa as she holstered the box with one hand, Lazzie nestled into the crook of her shoulder with the other.

"I—" Alyssa started.

"You want him back?" The officer settled Lazzie into Alyssa's lap. "Sure. Somebody's coming to help you, Miss." The officer rested her hand on Alyssa's shoulder. "You and your baby, both."

Alyssa looked into the sweet Sharon face, heard the kindness in the voice swelling over the word "baby," like it was the most natural thing in the world to speak of.

"My baby," she said, shifting Lazzie. "My baby."

Coffee's head jerked up, and his ears rose on each side of his broad forehead. Seconds later he began his warning barks, even as Leah felt the dull resonance of several people out on the stairs. Still the crisp knock on the apartment door was quite unexpected; the late news was over, Letterman into his monologue. Leah, legs folded beside her on a bristly-with-dried-something couch cushion, was ready for bed in a T-shirt and a huge pair of drawstring baggie pants out of Allie's dresser.

She approached the door. "Who's there?" she called, trying not to sound frightened. The wind had been blowing, trying to slop the bay up where it didn't belong and rip branches loose. Leah had never liked wind much.

"Police, ma'am."

When Leah cracked the door, a wallet opened to a badge was waiting, eye-level. She unhooked the chain. "I thought someone was going to call me tomorrow morning," she said to the man and woman standing on the landing. Neither was uniformed.

"Sorry for the hour, ma'am. Are you Leah Pacey?" The male spoke and Leah nodded as she focused on him. "I'm Detective Pat McNeill. This," he inclined his head toward the woman, only a little shorter than he, "is Detective Barbara Halsumae. You reported your daughter missing?"

His sportscoat, a colorless tweed, managed to look baggy in the shoulders and too tight to button. His shape said he liked his dinner, and then maybe another one the same night. A tired cop's face—under thinning brown hair—complete with bulby nose. No brogue, but a whiff of its history in his family. His voice wasn't aggressive, but neither was it too friendly.

"But they said. . . ." Leah held Coffee by his collar as he lunged to examine the visitors up close.

"May we come in, Mrs. Pacey?" The woman interrupted, her voice kind, cultured-sounding. She was a bandbox sort, impeccable in her mid-fifties, chiseled cheekbones, blue eyes, and tall, reedy flexibility of a former model. Wavy salt and pepper hair shorn-up, like a man's. A sliver of Leah's mind registered her own Medusa hair, ridiculous outfit, bare-feet, scarcely-restrained dog. She felt old and frowzy next to this

167

woman in a neat blue pantsuit. Once, Leah had had control of her life, too. Some, at least.

"You found her? I was sure she was here tonight."

"Let's talk, Mrs. Pacey. Do you have a picture of your daughter we can see?" the woman said again, and Leah, anxious, backed herself into the apartment, scanning their faces for a clue. Once inside, the man gestured at the couch and raised his eyebrows asking permission to sit down. Leah nodded. She dug in her purse and pulled Allie's high school graduation picture from her wallet. The woman took it and handed it wordlessly to the man.

"That's almost two years old, but it's still a good likeness," Leah said. "Except her hair would probably be down. I told them on the phone, it's very long. You can't miss that hair." Leah switched off the television and turned on the small lamp on the desk, which wasn't bright enough, but the reading light behind Allie's stuffed chair would have illuminated only Leah. This way, all of them sat outside an amber circle, the detectives next to each other on the couch and Leah perched on the upholstered chair with the tearing-loose cord.

"Have you found her?" she said.

"You mentioned your daughter came home, though?" It was the woman, gentle, enthusiastic at this news.

"But I didn't see her. I'm worried because I'm pretty sure she's pregnant. This isn't like her, not at all."

"What made you report her missing if she came home today? How far along is she?" The question seemed concerned, as if it rose over a cement foundation statement: we're only here to help.

"I don't know. . . . I didn't know she was pregnant." A confession.

"What makes you think she is? Have you talked with her?" said Detective McNeill. An Irish tenor, Leah thought. The question sounded like an accusation to Leah, though that was irrational, she knew.

The first question was too complicated. She just skipped it. "I told you, I didn't see her. I was at the laundromat. I could tell she'd been here."

"How?" he pressed.

"She took some things, her things, I mean, not like stealing." She tried to soften her own defensive tone. "I've just been so worried. . . ."

"What did she take?"

"Not very much. Soap, a box of granola . . . um, some pants . . . underwear. Oh, a little pair of baby moccasins. That's what made me think she was pregnant. I asked her neighbor, and the neighbor said yes, she could be."

"When did you last see your daughter?" he said.

"Thanksgiving. She came home to Philadelphia for almost a week."

"And was she pregnant then?" asked Detective Halsumae, leaning out over her knees.

What kind of mother wouldn't know the answer? "She didn't say anything about it. She had gained weight. . . ."

"Why did you report her missing after she'd been here?" It was McNeill again. Leah felt him after something, like Coffee nosing under the couch.

She thought a moment. She considered the truth, that she'd been angry, and was ashamed of it. "I . . . I don't know . . . I mean, she's, well, she's not behaving rationally. If she's pregnant, she's going to need help. She hasn't even told me. I've been so worried. I thought that's what the Missing Persons Bureau was for."

The detectives looked at each other. Coffee sniffed the crease in the man's pants. The air felt charged to Leah, like an invisible force field had been activated, but doubtless it was her nerves. McNeill spoke. "We're not from that department, ma'am. We're following a different case."

"What case?"

"Can we get to that later?" The woman again. They must do that, alternate talking, to keep your head bouncing like a tennis ball from one of them to the other. Leah wished the woman detective had come alone. There was a better chance that a woman, especially a mother, would understand. She should have specified she wanted to talk to a woman who was a mother.

"I don't understand. What's this other case? What does it have to do with Allie?"

"We'll get to that."

Smooth as a razor, the woman spoke out of her turn, cutting off Leah's questions. Her voice was gentle, shaving gel for her words. She was the kind of woman whose legs and underarms were shaved even in the dead of winter. (Not like Leah, with her stained fingernails and toilet paper stuffed in her underpants because she'd started menstruating this evening, seven weeks after her last period. She'd not been able to find a single pad or tampon in Allie's apartment. Her own yeasty woman-smell came to her when she shifted to cross her legs.)

"Can you tell us more about Alyssa ... Allie you call her? Who might be the father of the child?"

Again, what kind of mother wouldn't know the answer? "I don't know. She's mentioned a boy named Howie, that's all."

"Do you have an address or phone for him?"

"No. I've been looking myself, around here." Leah gestured vaguely at the desk and then toward the bedroom.

"Who's this neighbor, the one who said she was pregnant?" Detective McNeill cut in, the pad he'd taken out of his jacket pocket open and at the ready.

"No, she just said she might be," Leah corrected, a little sharply. "Across the landing, Clara Edwards."

"Do you mind if we look around?" Maybe if the woman had been the one to ask, Leah wouldn't have heard Clara's voice. *You don't know how they do people.* Wary, she hesitated.

"This isn't my apartment," she said. "It's my daughter's. I really don't feel I have the right. I'd rather you didn't. I'd like to know what this is about."

"Has Allie been having any personal problems that you know of? Does she use drugs, or alcohol?" McNeill's questions were offensive to Leah, but they were probably standard. They're helping me, Leah reminded herself.

"No, no, and no. She's an excellent student, honors, has a job, or had one before school started back up. No, she's been fine."

"Any trouble with the law?"

"No!" Leah landed on the word, and edged forward on her seat for emphasis.

"So, she hasn't confided in you."

"Well, of course, she confides in. . . ."

"About her pregnancy," he said. Was there a hint of contempt in that? Picking at her wound?

"I don't even know for sure that she's pregnant. I do know she's missing and I'm scared and I'd like to know what you're going to do." Leah gestured and shifted her weight again, raw.

It was the woman who told her, after all, using her first name, as a woman would. "Leah, we have your daughter in custody. A girl fitting the description you gave Missing Persons was picked up at the Shattuck BART stop earlier today. Her ID named her as Alyssa Staton. I questioned her myself. She's at the police station."

Leah stood so quickly her feet tangled. She caught herself as she pitched forward. "Oh my god. Why didn't you tell me?" She picked up her white sneakers, put them in front of her and sat back down, cramming her feet into them. "She's all right? I'll go get her. Oh, I don't have a car . . . no, that's okay, I'll get a taxi."

Pat McNeill started to speak, but the woman interrupted him with a hand on his upper arm. "Wait. Please sit back down a moment." Barbara Halsumae's face softened toward pity.

"What is it?" Leah said, still standing, ignoring the man now, speak-

171

ing directly down to the center of the other woman's eyes, black, impossible to read in this dimness. Then Barbara stood up herself and took a step toward Leah, as if she were going to touch her.

"We think she's had the baby, Leah. We think she had it in the BART station."

"When you found her?" Leah felt as if the lights were either too low or too high, as if the shadows were moving in her peripheral vision.

"No, we think she had the baby on Sunday."

"But this is. . . ."

"Thursday night," Barbara supplied, almost a whisper.

"Where is the baby?"

"She left it, Leah."

"You mean . . . but where is it? Who has it?" The force field between Leah and the detectives was expanding, and Leah saw the woman's mouth move, but couldn't hear over the white noise in her ears.

Seconds passed and the woman's mouth moved again. The part Leah made out was, "I'm so sorry." The wind outside picked up again; that's what must be obscuring the detective's words. The heavy breath of God.

CHAPTER

11

Betrayal.

The police officer from the BART station had betrayed her. This wasn't *help*, this big bright place looking like the oversized waiting room in a dentist's office. She stood sandwiched between the two officers who'd driven her from the police station, heavy glass doors locked behind her, identical glass doors locked in front of her. Waiting for entrance, the officers spoke as if she were deaf and dumb, as if she weren't even alive. Outside it was still dark, the sidewalk they'd covered on the way from the parked car spotting with raindrops.

"He don't pick lookers, that's for sure," the black one said, thumbs hooked into his waistband, a sheaf of papers pressed under one arm.

"I think Monica's cute!" This from the white one, the driver who'd capped her head when she stumbled getting into the car because her hands were chained in front of her. They'd walked her from the police station and driven her here, *to the jail*, transported her in the back seat caged as if she were a rabid dog. That wasn't right. Coffee had his rabies shots, the whole series, good for two years. She'd taken care of *that*.

"I'd take her for a spin, myself," the white one continued. He held her backpack, Lazzie pushed into it upside down, stuffed tight so the zipper would close all the way, not handled with care the way the blonde lady officer had done. But the blonde lady had turned into a liar, they all were. Alyssa had shut down back in the police station when the woman with the cropped gray hair kept on asking her questions about Lazzie and a baby, pretending like she cared. She wasn't going to talk to any of them. They were making about as much sense as the dwarf, who at least had *acknowledged* her with those flittering, loose eyes, had shown she knew Alyssa was there, alive and listening. *Feeling*.

"That Tripp, whew."

"He didn't do her, too?"

"Nah, held the line there." The white one laughed and shifted Alyssa's backpack from one meaty hand to the other. "You still seeing Lupe?"

"There's a nice girl."

"Can't be too nice, you dating her."

"Damn right."

The glass doors in front of her opened, magically, it seemed, of their own accord. The officers took her by each arm and walked her to an island in the waiting room. Beyond the island, like an altar positioned before church pews, a big screen television broadcast flashing color portraits of a man and woman arguing, the shots moving from face to face in a seductive rhythm of light and shadow. Scattered through rows of sistered metal chairs sat men and women who recalled the human cargo on the Greyhound Bus she had ridden across the bay. Fretting people, their agitation subdued by the big screen, their angry energy defused by the tension of the onscreen characters. The air smelled of sack lunches, orange peels and turning milk, like the community classroom in the Berkeley library where she'd tutored in the literacy program, reminding her of second grade, Miss Wilson, and the postered alphabet beginning with a capital "A," just like her name. A woman watcher broke connection with the television and craned her neck around, staring hard at Alyssa before breaking into a jack-o-lantern's grin checkered by missing teeth both top and bottom.

"She's all yours," the black one told an inside officer who wore a name badge above his pocket, "Hopkins" printed in bold letters. *"H" is for hat, that you wear on your head.* The black one handed Hopkins the papers he'd carried folded underneath his arm.

"Thank you, gentlemen," Hopkins said. "You on 'til 6:00?"

"Oh yes," the white one answered, dropping Alyssa's backpack at Hopkins' feet. Lazzie couldn't breathe, she thought, as he lifted her hands and unlocked the bracelets of chain from her wrists. " 'Til the butt crack of dawn."

"What's your name, address?" Hopkins said to a clipboard he took from the island. He wasn't speaking to *her*, was he?

"This one ain't talking, Hop," the black one turned back from the glass doors, which were opening to release him to the sidewalk and the parking lot and the car that would take him and the white one back to Berkeley. *Take me with you*, Alyssa wanted to say, but she wasn't talking, like he said. She licked her dry lips instead.

"What's her story?" Hopkins asked.

The black one breathed in, blew out, rolled his eyes upward. "The BART baby."

Hopkins bent his lean, gray face to look at her as if she had suddenly materialized, flickered into living color like the tempting images on the television screen. *"B" is for baby, that sleeps in the cradle.*

"One of those," he said softly, speaking not to the departing officers, now sealed safely beyond the pair of glass doors, but to her. "Talk or not, we're going to book you now, little lady." He unfolded the papers and began to copy, not in Miss Wilson's even, loopy hand, but in chicken scratches. *"C" is for cow. "C" is for cow, and coward, and car.*

"I don't belong here. Please," she said to Hopkins, touching his sleeve with her hand. She watched it tremble, her nicked nails, the scar on her ring finger from before she could remember, when Leah said the car door slammed too fast and Gran wrapped her bleeding hand in paper towels and took her for stitches. *"C" is for car.* "I want to go back with them."

Baby's Breath

Hopkins squinted at what he'd written. "Nobody *belongs* here. Or so they say." He tucked the pen into his pocket. "Get over it."

He motioned Alyssa against a white sheet hanging from the wall like an unfurled school map, waiting for a picture of the world, or, she recognized with a fluttering pain in her chest, like an expectant canvas in her mother's studio. "Toes there," he said, looking away from her face, pointing at the strip of white adhesive tape on the tiled floor. "Picture time." She hesitated, turned sideways to catch the Jack-o-Lantern's simper. "For your ID card. Face me, please." He patted the pocket of his own khaki shirt. "Put it here when you dress out . . . and wear it at all times."

Alyssa matched her toes to the line of tape. "You must show your card for count, to go to visiting, or to go to court. . . ." A camera flashed; Hopkins motioned her to follow. ". . . Or at any time at the request of any jail staff member." He returned to his island desk and wrote again on his clipboard. *About her, probably. About what they said she'd done.* Then he was back behind the camera—an expensive Polaroid mounted permanently on a grey plastic trunk, corners rounded to match the design of the desk and the walls and the chairs and the counter across the room. A model like the one in Passport Photos in Philadelphia where she and Leah had gone before their vacation to Cancun. Mugging, they'd tried for straight faces. "Book em, Dano," Leah had said, cracking a smile at the exact moment the flash went off. For her picture, Alyssa kept a straighter face, but couldn't keep from giggling herself dizzy as they teased each other all the way home: What's *your* crime? No! What's *your* crime! Never again, Leah had said after the two weeks in Mexico, when she and Alyssa were itching with sunburn in their wing seats in the sky above the Gulf. Too many tourists, she complained, pulling a face that matched her passport photo, too much sunshine. A merciless sentence, two weeks in Cancun. No shade, no shadows.

Hopkins pulled the film from the Polaroid and waved it dry, then clipped her portrait and sealed it into credit-card size with a laminator. She wouldn't take it from his open hand. She didn't want that, a picture of herself. An *ID*.

"You'll do a whole lot better in here if you just follow the rules," he said softly, looking full face at her for the first time since the transport officers had left. "You're going to have it hard, never been in here before. You don't have to talk to me, but sooner or later," he thumbed toward the worshippers seated before the television, "you're going to have to talk to somebody." Jack-o-Lantern had turned back to the screen. "And you do have to listen. Just listen and do what you're told."

Because he looked at her now, treated her like she was somebody real, she took the ID card from him and followed Hopkins across the room to the long counter where he took each of her fingers—*this little piggy had none!*—and rolled them one at a time across a stamp pad and onto an index card. She watched him write her name and a series of numbers—7236—to match the number, her number, on the ID card she had better wear if she were going to do what she was told. When he gave her a folded packet of bright orange polyester and a pair of blue slippers—like what Gran had worn because of her corns— and told her to dress out, she did exactly what Hopkins said. "In there," he told her, opening an aqua door marked by a blunt, black number 1. She listened hard, didn't question, just did it.

Inside, the four tight walls suggested a fitting room in a very bad department store. Thinking this, imagining she was inside a store, it was easier to take off her own soiled, matted clothes and stand naked in a strange place. Like stripping the blackened, banged-up peel of a banana, she was getting rid of skin she didn't really want or need. She kept only her underpants on, the clean pair they'd let her take from her backpack in the hospital after the examination, when she'd wanted so badly to get rid of them and their endless, tiring, confusing questions that she'd said yes, she would sign whatever they wanted and let them take her blood, as if they didn't have enough of it already, soaked through the black sweatpants she left in the biohazard can in the examination room. After the examination, they had given her pads and the under-pants and blue sweatpants from her backpack. That was the last she'd seen of the blonde officer, and that was when she'd decided on silence, until the gray-haired lady brought her an egg sandwich and Diet Pepsi at the police station and said, like a teacher or a mother, stern and un-smiling, "Alyssa, we have to talk."

But the gray-haired lady with the fine skin and the ropy veins in her hands—like Clara's, like the picture she'd wanted to take of Clara's—had talked instead, so many questions turning to assertions, mixing it all up so she couldn't say for sure where she'd been on Sunday night, what street the Bay Breeze Hotel was located on, when did she ride the Greyhound back to Berkeley, why were the moccasins in the backpack with Lazzie, *what had she done to the baby*. She tried, first, to tell the gray lady what she could. Telling the right answers got you "A's," and "A's" turned Leah's attention from the canvases back to you. It was always the best way to get her to put down her brush and pull you into a painty embrace because you were such a smart, good girl. She learned to save this—telling her mother—and to time the telling so she could pull Leah from the basement studio with her good news. So she'd tried with the gray lady, too, to save what she hoped were the right answers. But the gray lady, who must be somebody's mother with her hair gone shades of iron and her clasped, veiny hands like a gardener's in prayer, had grown impatient, so Alyssa stopped trying. *Leave the answers you're unsure about blank; if you have time, go back and make your best guess.*

There hadn't been time, though, and the gray lady's perfect face wrinkled in exasperation after Alyssa had eaten half the sandwich and spilled the Pepsi because her hands didn't seem to be working. She said, "We're going to hold you, then, Alyssa. Until you can tell us what we need to know."

Holding, she thought, when she slipped on the orange pants and pulled the shirt over her head. This wasn't *holding.* The fabric of the

Chapter Eleven

suit—styled like surgical scrubs, but the wrong color—was cool against her skin, her white arms plump, obscene extensions. She hadn't worn short sleeves in public since forever, since the Freshman Fatties list. Good thing there weren't any mirrors in the fitting room, though. She gathered up her discarded clothes as if she were going to do laundry and opened the door.

Hopkins was waiting. "You can make two phone calls," he said, looking at the clothes she held in a jumble against her breast. He pointed to a line of telephones mounted against the wall behind the camera's podium. A man was being photographed: caramel skin, thick neck tattooed the color of the blood veins in the gray lady's hands. "Collect. Dial the area code first." Hopkins motioned to her clothes, to the backpack he'd held while she changed. "Then we inventory your possessions and you're ready for intake." He moved forward to take the clothes from her arms. Confused, she held on, linked to Hopkins by a tug-of-war over the soiled span of fabric. Elbow jutting, he motioned to the counter, *put it down.* When she let go and her clothes crumpled onto the counter, he jerked his thumb back, hitchhiker style, and sent her across the room to the telephones.

Do what they say. Follow the rules. A photocopied white page postered behind the phone shouted BAIL BONDS: PHONE US COLLECT in thick black letters. In smaller print, a blue sheet listed Alameda County Court numbers. Stuck catty-cornered at the bottom of the blue page with a piece of dirty Scotch tape was a card reading Public Defender's Office, phone, fax, and e-mail. The police had offered her one of those, the same card, only cleaner, but she'd said no just to get them to stop, stop, stop talking about what they'd found in the BART station, under the paper towels.

Phone somebody. She knew Daddy's number, by heart, in New Jersey. She knew Howie's number in Oakland. She knew her own Philadelphia number, of course. She knew her apartment number where Leah was looking for her. And she knew the number of Clara's apartment,

179

where the old desk-style cream-colored phone sat on top of the thick Oakland directory in the kitchen, where more often than not something smelling good—cornbread or pork roast—was baking in the oven, and Alyssa was always welcome to share because a child with a good appetite was a cook's delight. She took the receiver off the hook. Her hands, faced with a familiar task, shook less now, and she dialed. Two rings.

"Hello?" It was Clara, two rings away, so close to the phone. "Hello?"

Alyssa swallowed, bitterness coating her throat.

"Hello?"

She opened her mouth. A croak whispered from her dry lips.

"Alyssa honey, that you? Your mother—"

She hooked the receiver with a hand stiff as steel and turned to Hopkins. "Nobody home," she said, shrugging.

"You have another call coming."

"Nobody home there, either," she repeated. They couldn't force her to phone, could they, any more than they could force her to talk.

Hopkins sighed. "Whatever you say," he muttered, as if she were an ingrate, a fool, a hopeless liar. "It doesn't get much better," he told her, discharging some duty with his warning. "Come with me now."

Back at the counter where she'd left her fingerprints, the spiraled, inky Rorschachs that belonged to her and her alone, Hopkins asked her to lay out the soiled clothes. She should have been embarrassed by the stained shirt and the sweatpants with the ripped crotch she'd never bothered to mend, even though Leah had sent her a miniature sewing kit in a care package and Cindy had exclaimed how cute the baby-sized spools of brightly colored threads were. But Hopkins just told her, back in his flat proctor's voice, to empty her backpack while he inventoried her belongings on another of the endless NCR pages held thickly on his clipboard. He acted like there was nothing he hadn't seen before, no dirty secrets that would faze him in the slightest. Until she lay Lazzie on the counter, face up next to the dented, unopened box of granola.

"They took his moccasins," she said, moved to language by the softening features of Hopkins' face. "They ... took them away." Took them, and the stained pants from the biohazard bin in the hospital, and the Percocets from her sweatshirt pocket. *Evidence.*

"You'll get the bear back," Hopkins said. He seemed to catch himself then, pull himself back from the comfort he'd just spoken. "You can release to a third party. Forty-eight hours notice."

"I'll keep him. Nobody else will."

"You're not listening. You can't keep him, any of this. It all gets sealed and stored. Unless you fill out a release form. You want to do that?"

"What?" She kept her hand on Lazzie, stroked his natty fur.

"No personal possessions in Intake or General Population. Just you and the clothes we give you. Understand?"

"I wouldn't do any—"

"Honey." Hopkins looked as if he might cry. "I got daughters, four of 'em. Being here ain't no picnic. You keep straight, do what they say, cooperate with the PD, you won't be here long." He paused, rubbing his temples with his hand. A gold band had sunken into his ring finger. Like forgotten wire trussed around a growing tree trunk, it was inset into the skin. If he ever wanted it off, somebody would have to cut it with a jeweler's saw, she knew that. She didn't want him to cry.

"Do I have to sign it—the release—now?" She waved her hands, which were trembly again. She didn't think she could hold a pen.

"No, whenever you decide. Plan forty-eight hours notice, is all, if you got someone coming special." He pushed her clothes, along with the granola and the bar of Dove, into a large ziplock bag. "We'll put the rest with him, in here," he said, shaking out a second bag. "Nice and easy, just like this." He laid Lazzie atop the flattened backpack and slid them both inside. He hadn't checked the side pocket with the silver necklace, but Alyssa thought it wouldn't matter. He'd been kind with her; she wouldn't tell, if it ever came to that, that his inventory was off an item or two. She could do that for him, break just one rule to keep him from crying.

Later, though she never saw him again after being booked, she'd think more clearly of Hopkins. She'd believe that his kindness had been intended to save her from what was to come. In giving her his guarded sympathy, he had been letting her know the worst part was still waiting for her, so she'd better be prepared, just the way you'd brace yourself when you realized, too late, you were about to fall.

Alyssa knew—Hopkins had told her—that she'd have to wait for a while, maybe a couple of hours, before they came to take her to Intake Housing.

"Intake?" she asked, her mind birdwalking to breath, to breath-lessness, to the Saturday CPR class she'd taken with Howie when they'd messed up their practice saves because the mouth-to-mouth felt too much like kissing, embarrassing them both.

"Where you'll be classified," Hopkins said. "Let you know which pod you're going into."

Pods. Pea pods, pod people. "Pods?" she asked, stupid.

Hopkins was gentle. He would be, wouldn't he, four daughters, none of *them* in jail. "Housing unit. They'll decide should you be in general population or not." He paused. "That's all it is. My guess is you'll make GP after intake." He looked at her, tired, about to sign off from his graveyard shift. "Sixty-some women, a couple of men—in there with the women because, you know. You don't need to tell any of them," he waved at the television watchers, "what they say you done, you might . . . might be better not to."

Which was just fine, because she couldn't place it herself right then, *what she'd done.* The orange suit was too light. She was beginning to

Chapter Eleven

shiver, to wish for flannel and Leah's jacket, now sealed and marked as her property, but the truth was it might as well have been stolen from her. She longed for Dara's Percocets and her mattress bed and Coffee huddled up close against her back, calming when she lifted a sleepy arm and stroked him back to peace from a dog dream.

When Hopkins left her to process the drunk woman who kept pulling her muddied dress up over her face, time slowed to an ache she measured with her thumb pressed hard against the pale skin of her inner wrist, as if she were taking her own thudding pulse. She wanted to sit, to wrap her own arms around her shoulders and be still. She found a chair in the back row of the television theatre, as far away from Jack-o-Lantern as she could place herself. She had nothing of her own, not unless she counted the underpants she wore or the soggy pad between her legs, pressed against her by the hard seat of the gray chair. Having nothing, no smell or texture to recall her to herself, she grew colder, and the shivering shook her down to her feet clad in the rubber-soled canvas slippers. The television images faded to commercial; the drunk woman, fighting against the restraint chair, barked a string of profanities. Alyssa watched Hopkins set her in a chair and strap her down. No, Alyssa's mind jumped, it couldn't be an electric chair. You have to have a trial first. Then, exhaustion falling like the Percocet numbness she had wished for, like radioactive fallout so silent and invisible, she couldn't pay attention any longer. Sitting, chin against chest, the mantle of dirty hair closeting her face, her arms linked loosely across her stomach, she slept. By the time a hand neither rough nor gentle roused her by grasping and shaking her shoulder, morning had broken. Through the glass doors of the jail entrance, the heavy-lidded, unforgiving sky looked almost purple, the color of Gran's breakfast prunes. Scratchy-eyed, cotton-mouthed, Alyssa couldn't remember how in the world she'd come to this place where not a single soul looked familiar, where not one foreign face was smiling.

*

183

Baby's Breath

"Women's Intake," Solis answered when Alyssa asked where the two officers were taking her. Solis was small and dark, like a pretty cat. Her twice-pierced earlobes were bare, but Alyssa imagined them studded with diamonds when Solis was off-duty, dancing with her boyfriend the way she described to the bigger woman officer when they stood waiting for the electronic eye to see them. Solis pressed the tarnished button beside the discolored metal speaker plate on the door to Intake. "Inmate coming," she sang into the speaker. The door swung slowly open. Solis took Alyssa's arm and steered her over the threshhold. "Watch your fingers around these, " she said, nodding, and Alyssa thought she could see the imaginary diamond baubles sparkle. "They close no matter what."

Another counter for the shuffling of papers, close to the wall of an open, two-storied indoor arena the size of the gymnasium of her high school in Philadephia. *Coliseum*, Alyssa thought, catching the impression of a balcony surrounding the second level, aqua doors with bold black numbers against white walls like some tricolored surrealistic art show. A carpeted coliseum. Another pair of officers, another cramped fitting room, but this time they told her, both of them standing inside the closed door, staring: "Everything off."

When she hesitated, unclear—did everything mean her underpants, too, like you were seeing the doctor?—the male officer said it again. "Everything means everything, Staton," and turned away to look out the little vertical slice of window centered in the locked door. Alyssa wouldn't look at his name tag, didn't want a name attached to the man who would watch her undress.

"But I—" she waved one hand. Could she say period, or menstruating, or bleeding to a man who'd called her by her last name as if she were a dog?

"Everything," said the woman. Middle-aged, dull, the features of a tired short-order cook or a clerk at KMart. Alyssa took in her name,

Chapter Eleven

Ostrom, and raised her eyes from the tag to Ostrom's face. She fixed the large mole that was placed off-center on Ostrom's cheek, too high for a beauty mark.

"But I'm . . . you know." Alyssa pointed. Couldn't they understand? If she could make them understood, they wouldn't make her undress like this.

Ostrom shook her head, her taut, high ponytail bouncing, contradicting the age of her sallow face. "Strip search every time you enter or return to a unit," she catechized. "You don't want to be treated like a criminal, you shouldn't get into trouble. Clothes off." She locked eyes with the male officer. "Isn't so bad. They all get accustomed."

If they had touched her, she would have fractured, too broken for the King's horses or Mommy's kisses to ever make her right again. They didn't touch, but their instructions—how to bend, what to spread, when to turn this way and that—were like probing fingers anyway, poking at the private parts she'd done such a good job of hiding for so, so long. She thought of a frying chicken, laid out on a cutting board in Clara's kitchen, Clara's strong hands pulling at wing and leg, splitting the breast with her wooden-handled boning knife. She saw her own armpits, the hair grown out nearly two weeks long. *Gross.* And between her legs, bared of the soiled pad tossed onto her stained underpants, when she turned around, and around once more, well, it was just better not to be in this cramped room so close to the officers she could smell their breath, old meatloaf and rotting leaves. So she floated higher and higher until it wasn't Alyssa being seen and seen again in poses that Alyssa would never strike for herself, even fully clothed. They pretended they weren't really watching her, their cold eyes tracking the bloody trickle down the inside of her thigh that prompted Ostrom to explain how the commissary worked, but she knew what they must be thinking: *dirty girl*, can't keep herself clothed, doesn't deserve any better than this. Ostrom kept talking, saying that she'd be provided certain

185

items, anything else she'd need to order and pay for with the money on the books, she did have money on the books, didn't she, college girl like she was. *Smarty pants. Dirty girl.*

When they told her to put on her suit again, she was shivering, her teeth knocking. Her brittle fingers tugged against the orange fabric, pulling the thick elasticized waist around her shrinking stomach. She was withering, wasn't she, shriveling herself to Gran's dying size, her body good only for discharging snot and pee and shit and blood just like Gran, just like what happened to everybody when they died and their families had to watch it all, and clean it up, and pretend like it was just love they were feeling, like they weren't appalled into nausea by the goopy miasma of human cells that insisted on having their own uncivilized way with every rude gasp and groan and grunt. They were watching her die, just the way she'd watched Gran, calling it anything but what it was. *Gross.*

The man motioned to her to come out. She made herself sink back to earth and follow him. She'd left, just floated away, during the violations committed in another world, one where she didn't want to see or hear or be who she was, splayed like bloody giblets on a cutting board. She was sorry she came back, then, as she watched Ostrom scribble down words about her, about her most private parts and their shame, her shame. The words glued her down, kept her from floating.

Beside the computer counter, Ostrom gave her a stick of soap, a toothbrush, and a jar of baby shampoo—*baby!*—and pointed above Alyssa's head. "You use Shower 2 upstairs. Good personal hygiene is mandatory. Clean up and I'll show you your cell, go over the rules." Ostrom elbowed toward a clot of women playing cards at a table, sistered by their orange suits. "See them at the tables there? This is a Direct Supervision facility, Staton. Means you try to get along." She turned to the computer screen and tapped the keys. Alyssa didn't move.

Ostrom stopped typing. "Upstairs? The door says Shower 2?"

"Why did you give me baby shampoo?"

Chapter Eleven

Ostrom stared, reassessing. Not so smart, this college girl, not the smarty pants she'd thought. "Your hair, Staton. Your hair stinks and you need a shower. We run a clean house here. Follow that?"

Navigating by Ostrom's pointed hand, she passed the table of card-players. They looked up, eyes moving from her ID to her face and back again. The only blonde face among black and brown ones, waiflike, short-haired, winked at her and slapped a handful of cards down on the table.

"Read 'em and weep," the blonde said, fanning her face with her hand.

"Ah, go on, Joey."

"You lie, boy!"

"Sheee-it! Yo, fancy pants, you playing Guttierrez tomorrow, sure."

Alyssa climbed the metal stairs to the balcony. *Catwalk*, she thought, stopping at the aqua door marked Shower 2, looking down at the card-players. Joey—*Josephine? Jolene?*—was shuffling the deck of cards, her thin shoulders hunched. She threw back her head and laughed, a sharp, unexpected Adam's apple rising and falling in her pale, slender neck. Beneath her orange top, Joey was wearing a long-sleeved thermal shirt. Maybe Alyssa could ask Ostrom for one, too, if she was still shivering after the shower. Maybe Ostrom wouldn't be so hard when Alyssa was cleaned up, oriented.

She turned on the faucet in the tiled white shower stall to let the water run, then stepped back to strip off her orange suit. No shower curtains, no shower door, just the brightly lit stall and the water coming down, steam rising like bay fog. The same as the dorms in Griffiths, sort of, but here it was as if with every windowless wall and open cell door they were insisting on watching everything, the architecture saying to the inmates: *nowhere to run, nowhere to hide*. She hung the pieces of the orange suit on a silver hook, where they dangled like a deflated wind sock. Funny, really, when she'd never cared about clothes, to find that she would hate the polyester skin so much it was a relief to stand naked.

Baby's Breath

Her breasts were cool. Still heavy, still too solid inside her taut skin, but they'd stopped leaking. Some time last night, she remembered, right about when the gray lady had insisted on talking about a baby, a baby, a baby. Alyssa said back—had she shouted, had she really raised her voice—*okay then, a baby!* Some time about then, it was as if a little hand had reached up inside her and turned down her heart and along with it the aching, hollow pull that made her breasts weep. She touched her stiff, dry breasts and rested her hand in their cleft, then traced down the center of her stomach. How long since she'd allowed herself this: the touch of her naked body, her own hand tracing the contours of her bare skin. How long since anyone—except the sullen, pony-tailed doctor in the emergency room with the police, and he didn't count—how long since anyone had stroked her, rested a hand against the back of her neck and just let her be still, surviving the touch of a foreign hand?

"Staton. Here's your bedding and towel." Ostrom stood in the shower room, blue sheets and white towel extended like a tray.

She calmed her urge to cower, to drop her head and let her hair cover the parts of her it could. What did it matter if Ostrom saw anything now, she argued against the vestiges of modesty, of privacy. Ostrom had already seen everything there was to see of Inmate 7236 and Joey downstairs and everybody at the card table, too. Seen it, probably bored stiff by it. Alyssa took the stack of linens, didn't even try to shield her breasts.

"Check the sheets for damage," Ostrom said, turning. "You don't report it, you'll be responsible for any."

"Thank you," Alyssa said.

"When you're clean, I'll show you your cell. Forty-two, follow the numbers."

"Okay."

"Staton? You don't need to let the water run to heat it. Not like home. We have industrial heaters here. One of the perks of jail residence. Hot water twenty-four hours a day."

Ostrom was right. The hot water was a gift, steady and unending.

Chapter Eleven

Inside the stall, she bent her head and turned completely around and once more again, letting the water soak her hair and blind her to the door from which Ostrom had exited and to everything else outside that belonged to the world she could choose to float above when the people in it cut too close to her bones. She opened the bottle of baby shampoo—hotel-sized, baby-sized—and emptied it onto her head, working the suds up first on her scalp, then down the long ropes of hair, her hands massaging the locks, then lifting them into the stream of water, rinsing. She worked up a lather with the tiny bar of Ivory soap and coated herself, scrubbing and scrubbing again. She repeated this until the bar was so thinned that it cracked. She folded the two halves against each other and kept scrubbing.

The meager towel Ostrom brought was damp all the way through even before she lifted it to her hair to matt the dripping ends. Without creme rinse, her hair knotted against itself. Her brush was in her backpack, sealed by Hopkins, so she combed her hair with her fingers. She put on the orange suit and folded her towel in thirds and collected the empty bottle and the remainder of soap. Just once, before she left Shower 2, she touched her breasts, her stomach, and felt them transformed beneath her open palm.

It wasn't more than a cubicle, her *cell*. An emaciated mattress on a shelf, really, and another shelf, paint-scratched metal, like a table. No sink, no toilet, not like what they showed in the movies because, Ostrom told her, these were *dry* cells. Dry like her breasts now, dry like the new pad she wore between her legs, dry like her throat was, almost as if she'd been given the chance to drink water and had forgotten to sip, been so distracted she'd failed to recognize her own body's need. Ostrom explained: the inmates shared the common bathrooms, like summer camp. She'd been to summer camp, surely, a girl like her? But no roommate, not for her, she'd lucked out and been placed in a single.

Ostrom stood inside the cell and gave her instructions, directions, restrictions, a drill sergeant speaking to a dull-normal recruit: "You are responsible for the cleanliness of your room."

"Walls and vents are to be kept clean and free of all materials."

"All damage and defects we find during inspection will be noted here." Ostrom held the rule book up to Alyssa's face, bound bright orange to match her suit. "If your room is found unclean or damaged, you may be held criminally liable."

Criminally liable. For keeping a dirty room. Alyssa remembered Sharon's mother, redfaced, close to breaking, yelling at Sharon in front of Alyssa: "Your room's a crime! You're grounded!" The gray-haired lady, emotionless: "We believe you to have committed a crime, Alyssa." Leah, her face flushed, in love with her child, delighting in her daughter's laughter: *What's your crime? No, what's your crime?*

Ostrom stopped her singsong recital; her voice dipped. "Consider this your home, Staton. Keep this like you would keep your own home." She turned from the cell and moved onto the balcony, grasping the rounded metal rails constructed like the separating fences that kept children's hands from the chain links of the lion cages at the Philly zoo. Flexing her arms, Ostrom scanned the living area below, where the cardplayers were breaking up and moving to the television, catcalling, jostling each other. Joey's blonde head bobbed among the dark ones. The steamy smell of boiled meat seemed to enter the cell from the vents, a heating system gone awry, and Alyssa sat down hard on the bare mattress which was to be her bed.

Ostrom nodded, satisfied with her survey. "We're all one big happy family here, Staton." She rubbed the bridge of her nose, human for the first time, somebody's disappointed mother. "One big happy family."

After Ostrom left, alone for the first time in years, it seemed, Alyssa wanted to lie back on the mattress, sink her head into the flat pillow covered by the pin stripes she had always thought prisoners wore until now, until the orange suit hanging clammy against her skin. But the mattress had a smell, the dusky, unpleasant odor of stale smoke in a ho-

Chapter Eleven

tel room where somebody had cheated, snuck a cigarette and then discovered too late that the windows didn't open. She shook out the blue sheets and made the bed. She stuffed the pillow inside the pillowcase, then sat down again. On the floor, beneath the desk-shelf thing, was a rubber band. She reached to pick it up and caught a bundle of dust, someone else's long brown hair. She wasn't to blame for this bad housekeeping. She'd just moved in. She shook the fluff from the rubber band and pulled her damp hair behind her shoulders. The band would only wrap around once because of the thickness the snarls made, but she managed a sloppy ponytail. If she couldn't brush her hair out, she'd keep it bound, at least.

"Welcome to Camp Alameda, home of the brave by the beautiful South Bay." Joey slipped around the door, her fisted hand held to her mouth, mimicking a microphone. "Where all are one, and one is less than nothing." Joey extended the microphone, tipped her head, whispered. "She give you the one big family line, hon?"

It didn't seem senseless to her at all when she answered, speaking into the mike of Joey's hand, "The family line? Oh, that, the . . . yeah, she did."

Joey, taking her answer for the offer of friendship, sat down beside Alyssa, her light frame electric. "Your first time in, huh?"

"I haven't really. . . ."

"Tut, tut, tut." Joey laid a finger across her own lips, rimmed on top and bottom by long, downy hairs. "We don't do denials here, only affirmations." Joey looked at the bare cell, the made-up bed, Alyssa's ragged ponytail. "You could really use a comb, you know. You get them at the Commissary. For a whopping thirty-five cents, if you've got it."

"Or I could cut it all off, like yours," Alyssa said, like a ventroliquist had taken possession of her vocal chords. Joey's face crumpled.

"I'm sorry, I didn't mean . . . I'm just sorry." She *was* sorry, too. She wasn't just pasting in cement to make the conversation last. It wasn't Joey's fault, every bad thought she was barely keeping from stinging at her brain like wasps. It wasn't Joey's fault Alyssa, floating away from her own feelings the way she was, had overlooked that anybody in here could be capable of being hurt.

"Sure, okay, I know how it is . . . the first time," Joey said, extending her hand. "Joseph Michael Diehl. What's yours?"

The meat smell sifting through the air vents had meant lunch at a long table set and cleared by the inmates. Joey, Joseph—so stupid that she hadn't seen it earlier—sat beside her, introducing her around as if she were a prize. Alyssa Staton from forty-two, most recently of Berkeley, formerly of Philadelphia. They liked that, her being from Philadephia, and the others launched into long travelogues of where they would be from, soon as they got out of here. Acapulco, said one of the cardplayers. No, no, no, New York City for me, said another. Joey didn't say for himself, just touched her hand when a woman down at the end of the table had yelled, "What they got you for then, Staton?" So she'd filled her mouth with a spoonful of powdered potatoes and pretended she hadn't heard. The meal over, she bussed just like the others, sliding the trays onto the rolling cart pushed and pulled by two inmates who disappeared with the cart through the metal security doors.

"That's what you wanna be," Joey said, watching the rattling tray.

"What?" She couldn't follow anything, she who'd been so smart, so clever in past life.

"Trustee. They make you trustee if they trust you." Joey laughed.

"What makes them trust you?" She'd try to follow. *The only stupid question is the one you don't ask, Alyssa.*

"Do everything right. Follow what they say. Do good time."

"Do you?" she asked. Joey's face seemed a cipher. "Do good time?"

"Sure I do. Every time." Joey scratched his head, turned toward the television. "But they like you to be able to spell." Joey twirled his pointing finger, the children's signal for crazy, then pointed to his head. "I switch things around . . . inside here." He moved toward the televi-

192

sion and waved to her. Maybe he thought he'd told too much. He didn't know her, after all. She didn't know him.

So many strange people in so little time, so much talk about nothing and too much had exhausted her. She climbed the stairs to the balcony and returned to her cell, shutting the door behind her. Alyssa lay on the blue sheets and curled around the flat, sad, smoke-smelling pillow, the meal she'd eaten without tasting rising in her throat, threatening. Pressed against the flat mattress, her cheek felt wet. Her first thought was her hair, how long her hair would take to dry when bound in its secondhand rubberband. The next thought, widening like a door ghosting open, was tears.

Her cheek was wet with tears.

CHAPTER

12

Leah heard the police knock on Clara's door, felt sorry to have brought it on her, but not sorry enough to wait so she could apologize. She'd dressed hurriedly in her black slacks, a blazer and flats, thinking she should look respectable. She'd never been inside a police station in her life. Probably Allie would be sitting right by the door, just waiting for her or for the ride she'd provide. But she must have been—be!—so scared, Leah thought. She paced, looking out the window on the street side for the yellow cab she'd thought would come immediately since it was after midnight. It was nearly a half-hour, though, before it slid in next to the curb and gave a short horn tap. The wind still roiled.

The streets were muted compared to the color and motion that churned them during the day. Even the people who were out were hustling for cover as large rain began to splat down here and there, their scurrying motion animal-like in the dark.

At the police station, Leah handed a ten-dollar bill over the seat and asked the driver to wait. It would be much better than calling for another cab. She'd go in, maybe have to sign something, collect Allie and get her home safe. During the ride she'd cautioned herself, no firing questions, no recriminations, not now. This was all, obviously, wrong. An extra hug, a cup of tea, maybe some toast, a quiet on Leah's part that signaled understanding and acceptance—the right atmosphere for Allie to open up. And if she was too done in to explain tonight, all right,

Chapter Twelve

first thing in the morning would be soon enough. She'd find out what had really happened, and then she and Allie would unkink the chain. She had to let Allie figure it out, that she could have, *should have* confided in her mother right away. Kids were like that, always learning the hard way. It didn't seem to Leah, though, as if she herself had ever had the luxury of behaving stupidly.

She ran up the brilliantly lit steps into the police station entrance. A uniformed officer, tired-looking, largely bald, was behind a counter, a glass wall rising from its raised edge to the ceiling. Leah spoke through the glass, exaggerating the motion of her lips.

"I'm here to pick up my daughter."

The policeman gestured to a small microphone set in the glass, a speaker on either side. He pushed a button and his voice came at her. "Into the mike, please, Ma'am."

Leah looked around, spotted it, took a step and positioned herself. "I'm here to pick up my daughter, Alyssa Staton."

He consulted his clipboard. "Did we call you to come get her?"

"No, but two detectives were at her apartment. They told me she was here."

The officer consulted a piece of paper.

"I don't show her here now. Let me check for you." He picked up a phone, but Leah couldn't hear what he said. He turned back to Leah when he was finished and switched on the speaker again. "Ma'am, she's been transported to county. You can see her after two o'clock tomorrow. . . ." Then he consulted his watch. "I mean today, this afternoon."

"County?" Leah said, her pitch rising. "What's county? Why isn't she here?"

"I'll ask one of the detectives to come up to talk to you, ma'am. I don't know the situation. Please step through the door and come around."

He buzzed open a glass door to one side of the small lobby area.

She approached the counter, which enclosed the officer. He stood higher than she, on a platform behind the counter. She felt like a child, looking up to entreat this man looming over her. "What is county?" she repeated, agitated. "Why isn't my daughter here? Those detectives said she was here."

"That'd be the county jail, ma'am."

"What?" Leah struggled to make her mind work through the haze of a blank dream.

"The jail, ma'am, over in Hayward . . . the detective'll answer your questions." He gestured behind Leah, and before she turned, she saw relief on his face. "This here is Detective Brynner, ma'am," he said. Leah turned around as the policeman spoke over her shoulder to the big man, rumpled and mushroom-faced, who was approaching. His eyebrows were a straight slash angling from his forehead down to his cheekbones, which seemed to slant up in answer, making the upper half of his face diamond shaped. "Hardy, this is Mrs. Staton," the officer at the desk said.

"Pacey. Leah Pacey. I'm Alyssa Staton's mother. Where is she?"

"Mrs. Pacey, if you'll come with me please, I'll give you the rundown." Detective Brynner gestured back the way he'd come.

"I . . . the cab is waiting. I can't take Allie home now?"

"I'm afraid not. Did you pay the cabbie yet?"

Leah nodded.

Detective Brynner signaled the officer behind the counter with a wave. "Joe, send Mrs. Pacey's cabbie on, will ya?" He looked back at Leah and gestured down the hall. "This way, ma'am."

It was an interview room, not the office she'd imagined, to which he took her. A table, four or five straight-backed chairs, a one-way window, unadorned walls. "Can I get you a cup of coffee?" he said.

"No, thanks." She brushed the offer away with one hand. "Please, what's going on? Where's Allie?"

"I think you spoke with Detective McNeill and Detective Halsumae, didn't you?"

Chapter Twelve

"Yes, at my . . . at Allie's apartment. They said she was here."

"They would have explained that we believe she gave birth on Sunday and abandoned the infant." The detective spoke with no discernible emotion.

"That's a mistake," Leah said, and then repeated, "That's just a mistake. She might well be pregnant, but the idea . . . no, there's no way."

The detective seemed to take her measure. Leah wondered if she looked like some sort of nut case. Stay calm, she told herself. He had to believe her.

He ran his hand over the top of his head, a gesture of fatigue. "I know this must be hard, ma'am. She's had a baby. That's been confirmed by medical examination. She was picked up and taken to the hospital because a beat officer thought she'd been mugged or raped. She was disoriented and bloody."

"But the other detectives said she was all right. Is she all right?"

"Yes, ma'am. They got her cleaned up and dismissed her. She's not wounded . . . the bleeding was just from . . . after having a baby."

"Where is Allie's baby?"

"We believe her baby is the one found at the BART station last Sunday. She signed a consent to take blood and tissue samples when she agreed to be treated. What we've been able to check so far does suggest she's the mother. She's a match for blood found at the scene."

"If you'll just let me talk to her, I'm sure we can clear this up. This is a mistake." Rain slanted suddenly against the blackened window, wind-driven, loud.

"She's in custody, ma'am. She's not been arraigned yet, but. . . ."

"Then you have to let her go." Frustration and exhaustion were holding hands, beginning a dance in her head.

"I'm sorry, Ms. Pacey, but bail isn't even set until arraignment. She's been arrested for child endangerment and possession of a controlled substance, but I expect she'll be charged with manslaughter at least.

197

Maybe murder. That's someone else's call. Anyway," he sighed, "we've got probable cause. You might want to know that she'd also ingested street drugs."

"Allie doesn't take drugs." Leah's hair had fallen forward over one eye and now she shook it back and raised her chin. This proved it to her absolutely; this was all wrong. Allie was famous for her disdain for druggies.

"Perhaps you've . . . lost touch with her a little. It happens, ma'am."

"I need to see her. I'm going to go see her now."

"That won't be possible until two o'clock tomorrow afternoon."

"I can't see her?" Incredulous.

"Not until then. I'll give you a booklet about the policies and procedures at County. In Intake, there are no visitors until two in the afternoon."

Leah stood, wanting to fly at his face with fists, wanting to scream her outrage. Her metal chair clattered backward, teetered. She caught it. Picking up her purse, she said, "This can't be legal. This can't be right. Where's your booklet?"

"Before you go, maybe you can clear something up for us. Would you wait a minute?" As he spoke, Detective Brynner stood, carefully pushing his chair back first, and left the room. She heard him speak to someone in the hall, but the words were indistinct.

He came back in with an opaque blue plastic bag. He set it on the table and removed a bloodstained towel with frayed edges. "Is this familiar to you?" he asked. "It has a monogram . . ." he said, and pawed through the folds until he found that edge. EPR, the diamond shaped stitching proclaimed. Diamond shaped, like the detective's face. Esther Rhee Pacey.

"No," Leah said.

He squinted at her. "You've never seen this?"

"I don't recognize it," Leah said.

Chapter Twelve

"Well, then. I'll walk you out and pick up that jail information for you at the front desk on the way." He opened the door again and motioned her through first. "Uh ... Ms. Pacey, I hope you'll talk to your daughter about cooperating with us. It's in her best interest. We can't help her otherwise."

"If you wanted to help her, she'd be home now."

Leah hadn't wanted the detective to walk her out, hadn't wanted to accept the booklet he'd handed her, hadn't wanted to accept a ride in their squad car, but she'd done all three. Swallowing bile, she'd gotten in the car because calling a taxi would have meant using their phone and waiting in their station until it came. Thirty more seconds would have been too long.

There was nothing else she could do tonight. First thing in the morning, she'd think it through. Now, though, back in the apartment, she headed for the bathroom and sank her face into the pool of water she made in her cupped palms. It was after three in the morning. Eleven hours to wait. She stripped down to underpants and stuffed them with fresh toilet paper. In the morning, she'd have to go buy tampons. Her eyes were scratchy; her head and neck ached. She pulled on the T-shirt she slept in, doused the light, and fell back on the pillow.

Something was nagging at her about the bedroom. In the twilight realm between consciousness and sleep it came to her, so disturbingly that she sat up and turned the light back on to check. Yes. She was right. Lazzie—Allie's comforter, the keeper of her tears—was gone.

The rain had cleared out by dawn. Leah woke fuzzy-headed, gritty-eyed, unrested, hung-over with the aftertaste of bad, unremembered dreams. She got up and showered, a pointless sense of hurry driving her. She took the newly-washed bath towel off the shelf, then hurriedly replaced it and dried herself with two hand towels that didn't burn her mind with what they matched. As she pulled on jeans and a shirt, she tried to focus on a short shopping list—tampons! coffee, granola again—but couldn't remember what it was she needed, or be logical about what she and Allie would need once Allie was home.

Coffee whined and nosed around the door. She'd forgotten to walk him. "Okay, boy," she said. "We'll go to the Quick Stop. Maybe I'll know what we need when I see it." She had to stay calm and stay busy until she could take a taxi to the jail, straighten all this out, and bring Allie back with her. What she wanted was someone to talk to, at the same time she dreaded it, and she especially dreaded seeing Clara, who'd warned her the police were quite ready to use a table saw on the truth to make pieces fit their notions. If Leah hadn't reported Allie missing, she'd not be in jail right now. And it was her fault the police had gone to Clara's last night, late as it was. Even as she was dialing for a cab, Leah had heard the knock and Detective McNeill's brusque "Police!" then the opening and closing of Clara's door.

It seemed whatever Leah most wanted to avoid—a divorce, say, or nursing an invalid mother, having her daughter arrested, running into Clara—that's what was guaranteed to occur. She was out on the landing closing the apartment door softly behind her when Coffee spotted a squirrel in the parking lot. A feral mock-growl splintered into shards of barking. If his tail hadn't been waving like a parade flag he'd have been one fierce dog.

Clara's door opened. She wore black pants and a red tunic top, her hair pressed into neat waves. She's been sitting there waiting for me to come out, Leah thought, panicky.

"Good morning, Clara. Coffee's desperate . . ." she said, and tried to head immediately for the stairs. She could at least put it off.

"Miss Pacey, Leah, wait a minute. I'll walk him with you," Clara said. Leah started to protest, then let it go, a hope whose time had come and gone in the same instant.

"All right," she said, "but I'm headed to the store, too. I need to get in some things for Allie."

Chapter Twelve

Clara left the door open as she went into her apartment in long strides. A gray car coat was folded over the back of one of the chairs. So she had been waiting.

Neither woman said anything as they went down the stairs in single file, Coffee first, Leah propelled by his forward pull, and Clara only a little slower behind her, using the metal banister.

In the parking lot, Leah tried to get it over with. "I'm sorry the police came to you last night. I never thought they'd involve you. I only mentioned . . . anyway, I'm sorry."

"That's the smallest part of this trouble," Clara said, and Leah wondered what she meant.

The morning was crisp and chill, a weak sun trying to dry last night's wet residue and enough breeze that there was no fog. Leah could take a deep breath without feeling she was suffocating. She'd been ready to feel a little better until Clara said that.

"I really am sorry," Leah said again.

"It's nothing. Don't you think about that." And then Clara was silent, as if she were back to waiting for Leah.

"They said they have her at the jail," Leah said. "This is all such a mistake. They said I could go at two o'clock, but as soon as I get some food in the house for her, I'm going to go on ahead. I've got to straighten this out." Coffee lifted his leg by a little gated yard where the brown remnants of a zinnia bed cluttered the ground. Someone had just given up, that was all. Anything could be cleaned up with dedication.

"It's gonna take more than you," Clara said. "Here, give him to me a minute," she added and reached for Coffee's leash, giving it a quick jerk and release. "Get back," she said sharply and Coffee stopped straining ahead, making his breathing loud and raspy, choked by his collar. "He's just learning, but you best not let him get away with that or he'll drag you right into the bay." She handed the leash back to Leah.

"What do you mean?" Leah said, consciously giving a couple of little tugs so Coffee would know she expected him to stay by her side.

"About the dog?"

"No—Allie. What's going to take more than me?"

"This business with Alyssa. Time and lawyers and more patience than anyone's naturally got," she said. "First thing is to see about bail. Can't do that 'till she's arraigned, though."

"Bail? No, Clara, this is a mistake. What did they tell you?"

"Little as they could, that's all they ever tell you. I could just see where it's headed."

"Well, for one thing, I've got to find out if Allie's even pregnant. I mean, they're saying she had a baby, and . . . well, she just wouldn't, not ever."

"They're way ahead of that. They wouldn't ask if they didn't already know." A pigeon landed on the sidewalk in front of Coffee and he lunged forward. Leah reined him back hard and quick, like Clara had.

"But Clara, what if they've set her up? I mean, you told me yourself they do that sort of thing. They don't know my daughter. I do. You don't understand, they're not only saying she had a baby, they say she abandoned it, that she left it to . . . you know, that one that's been in the papers. There's no way."

"I know," Clara said gently, looking straight ahead. "I don't like saying this to you, but better I do. I think it's the truth."

It was strange, Leah thought, how things you know can stand alongside what you've never seen or dreamed: they were passing maples and oaks and elms here, the familiar trees of home, alongside ones she couldn't begin to identify. A towel from back home, something on it she'd never imagine. "How can you think that? She'd never hurt a living thing. Why, when she was little. . . ."

Clara didn't exactly interrupt, but when Leah paused to order examples to describe how sensitive Allie'd been, she filled the space in, speaking deliberately, letting the ideas sink like separate stones in water. "She was looking poorly. The pounds, her wearing all the baggy clothes. Lately, started t'stay away from me. And last Sunday? When I took the

Chapter Twelve

dog? She was real sick. Maybe she didn't know labor, maybe she did. Scared, prob'bly. Either way, real scared. Poor child."

"Clara, she'd have come to me." Defensive, scared again herself, but differently. Clara didn't even know about the towel, and she thought Allie had really done this. They were coming into a more commercial area, the sidewalk more peopled, and Leah was conscious she didn't want anyone to overhear.

"I don't know about that. People get scared enough, shamed enough. . . ."

Leah didn't say anything more. Her mind raced. Was it possible? No! Slow down. Was it possible? She tried to call up the image of Allie in the harem pants, long sweater. And then suddenly she remembered how she'd struggled at Thanksgiving to get Allie's center of gravity identified for the painting, the different carriage, the different walk. Possible? Leah's cheeks burned. Dizzy, then, and nauseous. "I . . . need to sit down," she said to Clara.

"It's all right," Clara said. "We'll find somewhere right now." Clara took the dog's leash from Leah without asking, shifted the dog to her far side, and put her free arm around Leah's shoulders to bolster her. The older woman felt sturdy, big, to Leah, like her father's physical presence years and years ago. "I know a place just ahead," she said, "where you can sit and catch your breath."

Clara had taken Coffee back to the apartment while Leah walked up and down each aisle in the Quick Stop, putting a few essentials in the metal basket and a few things only Allie liked, in case there was a chance, still a chance, it was all wrong. A half-hour earlier, Leah had been dumbstruck, dry-eyed, seated in a booth in the little coffee shop where Clara had gotten her first a glass of water, then a cup of tea. The fact that the idea made sense, that it fit Clara's instinct about the course of events, didn't mean it was true, but Leah had to allow the possibility.

She kept trying, but there was no image that matched the words.

Baby's Breath

When she got back with the bag of provisions, it wasn't even ten yet. She knocked at Clara's door to get Coffee, and, though she didn't particularly want to talk, she couldn't be alone any more so she asked Clara to come over while she put things away and made a pot of coffee.

Maybe she did want to talk. She kept starting sentences in little jerks and stops that made her feel like Coffee switching directions to chase something new.

"What should I do?" she said finally, the gears stuck a moment. "I should get out there right now, shouldn't I?" She'd just poured Clara a mug of coffee at the rickety dinette table in Allie's little kitchen, the first time Leah had sat there. It would be easy, Leah saw, to bring the kitchen up: a blooming violet in the center of the table to brighten its pale gray surface, an arrangement of baskets hung artfully on the wall, a print with blue, lavender and green over there, next to the refrigerator, a rug on the floor in front of the sink. Yes, and a spider plant hanging in the window over the sink. She'd do that, and more, before Allie came home. For Allie. Oh god. Not a spider plant, the way they were always having babies. Oh god, oh god.

"No point, honey. When they say two o'clock, they don't mean one minute to," Clara was saying. Had she missed something?

"But I can bail her out, can't I? I mean, that just takes money. I have money, or I can get it."

"Depends." Clara said. "If they do her like my son and most others, they'll charge her up high as they can. Then there's a hearin' to set bail. All's you can do 'til then is see her at visiting. They give you forty-five minutes, that's all, no matter how early you go. First couple days visiting's forty-five minutes, just between two and five. After she been classified, you can go after nine in the morning . . . but still just the forty-five minutes."

"Forty-five minutes," Leah echoed. "Isn't there some way I can. . . ."

Clara shook her head no.

Chapter Twelve

"And you be prepared; there's only what they call no contact visits there, a glass between you and her."

Leah's eyes teared. Clara reached across the dinette table and covered Leah's hand with hers.

Leah tried to pull herself up. "I know I've got to get hold of myself," Leah said.

"Best you do," Clara answered, "in my experience." She looked older as she sat quiet, Leah knowing her just well enough that it wasn't rude to stare. Her lips were thinner than most black people's, thinner than Leah's, too. If she ever painted her, she'd use umber to make the lines from nose to mouth form parentheses around their stillness, like they did now.

"Are you tired this morning?" It wasn't right that everything should be about her and Allie.

"I got a call about four," Clara said, a slant answer. "I think it might have been Alyssa."

"Allie? What did she say? Why didn't you tell me?"

"Didn't say a word, just a sorta rasp, and then hung up. Just a feeling it was her. And about when they'd be givin' her the two phone calls."

Leah was stung. Then, Oh! but Allie doesn't know I'm here. And no one home in Philadelphia. Would she call Dennis? "I need to call my house, check the machine. God, I should have been doing that right along. What's wrong with me?"

But Cory was on the machine, and then Bob, and then George (Call me. I've got another commission in the works), Cory again, and then the beeps to say there were no more messages. Leah considered, then rejected, calling Dennis. Why bring him down on them? She'd wait until she'd seen Allie, probably brought her home, even, and Allie could call him herself.

She was headed back to the kitchen table to rejoin Clara when the knock came. She looked at Clara who said I don't know by way of an oddly graceful motion, light palms up and extended out from the dark of her arms.

"Who's there?" Leah called, approaching the door.

"Police."

Leah swung the door toward herself. Two uniformed policemen stood, one holding folded papers. "We have a search warrant, ma'am."

"Clara?" Leah turned with the question. Clara had already gotten up.

"Let 'em in, honey."

After the police left with their paltry triumph, the bath towel Leah hadn't used, the phone rang. Maybe this was Allie, using her phone call. Leah picked it up.

"Is this the Staton residence?" Male, young-sounding. Howie?

"Yes, it is."

"To whom am I speaking?" the voice said, a slight edge of excitement in it.

"This is Alyssa's mother."

"Ms. Staton, would you comment on your daughter's arrest? We have a tip she's the mother of the BART Baby. Can you give us any information on that?"

"It's absolutely untrue," Leah said, and hung up. She paced uneasily for a few minutes, thought of renting a car, just as she'd thought of calling Dennis, but rejected both as unwarranted. She called for a cab, flushing when she gave the driver the address of the jail, three towns south of Berkeley. She had to get to Allie; this had to stop.

"The county building's over there, right?" the driver said, looking at her in the rear view window.

"Yes," she said, and was glad for light traffic on the freeway.

The jail was large and stark, adjacent to buildings labeled Administration, Sheriff, and Coroner's Office. Was that where the little body was now? Razor wire topped the compound, and a guard tower imposed itself on Leah's awareness. She went through the double glass doors and looked around. There were small clusters of people sitting in the lobby area, while four or five small children were chasing each other like puppies, laughing. One of the women got up abruptly to grab a boy about five years old by the arm, swat his rear and deposit him roughly into one of the chairs while she scolded him in a burst of Spanish.

Leah approached a glassed-in area labeled Visitors' Registration. A uniformed officer said, "Pass your identification through" and, guessing, Leah took her Pennsylvania license out of her wallet and put it into a little metal drawer that opened in front of her. "I'll need your purse, too," the officer said. Was she imagining a sneer on his pulpy lips? He looked to be in his twenties, swollen-faced from sex or alcohol or both.

"Have you been here before?" he asked.

"No," she said, and her voice stuck so she had to clear her throat and say it again. "No."

"Okay, then. We keep your purse here while you visit, ma'am. If you'll give me the name of the inmate you're here to see, I'll have them notified while you go through security." He didn't say it in a condescending tone. Maybe she'd been unfair.

"Alyssa Staton."

"Would you please sign, ma'am? Here's the receipt for your purse. At two o'clock, you can proceed through security, over there. You get forty-five minutes."

Leah signed the visitors list, flame-faced when she wrote *mother* in the space that asked her Relationship to Inmate. "I know," she muttered.

"Did you want to put money on the book today?"

"I . . . she'll be coming home, I'm sure. I've got to talk to her first."

"All righty then. Have a seat." He smiled then, Pendleton, his name tag said; his teeth were crooked and very bad.

Leah had twenty minutes to wait. She sat, knees primly together, straight-backed, examining the lint on her black pants. She'd worn her blazer again, the same clothes she'd worn to the police station to make a respectable impression. Fat lot of good her respectable jail-visiting outfit had done. How had she and Allie come to this?

At two o'clock, she got into the line forming for admission to the visiting area. Another officer checked her through a metal detector. "When you get into the tube area, have a seat and wait for your inmate to appear," he said, and Leah answered okay in what came out a whisper.

The tube? She was afraid her voice would fail again. Instead of asking, she hung back a little, mutated into a woman wispy and insubstantial as gauze, so she could follow a man of perhaps sixty who looked as if he knew where he was going.

Her unwitting guide led Leah to a set of elevators which they and a couple of the others from the waiting room took to the second floor. Leah followed him to an area of partitioned booths, each with a chair, a phone, and a window to the other side.

Leah took a seat in one of the cubicles, trying to keep a distance from the visitors who were likewise choosing booths. This was like nothing she'd imagined; she thought she'd see Allie, touch her, not *through a glass darkly*, but face-to-face. The old words from one of Esther's passages came into her mind. She was powerless, in a twilight of unreality where nothing she'd learned in fifty years gave off light. The tube. Even the name was claustrophobic.

A uniformed woman, matronly-shaped though her hair style— long, high-ponytailed—argued she was much younger, appeared at the entrance to the inmate's side of the room. A young woman with dark hair—Allie?—yes, it was Allie—hung behind her, a bright orange

Chapter Twelve

uniform drawing Leah's attention. Allie shook her head no as the officer pointed, but the officer took her by the arm and seemed to lead her toward Leah. How much weight she's lost. Her whole body is different, thought Leah, longing to hold Allie against her own body to reclaim their connection—her child, a life she'd made out of herself. It was unthinkable, this strangeness, this unfamiliarity. She picked up the telephone on her side of the booth as the guard pointed to the receiver on Allie's side.

Allie sat, head down, hands in her lap out of Leah's sight. Her hair, shining, lush, an onyx river, was bound back in a long ponytail with a naked rubber band, though so softly and loosely clasped that the sides draped forward like a memory of Allie's customary curtain. Leah thought she had never seen hair so rich, so . . . fertile was the word that came to her. Tears leaked into Leah's eyes. She tapped lightly on the window and pointed at Allie's receiver. Pick it up, she mouthed. Pick it up. She repeated it when Allie didn't move and tapped with the nail of her forefinger again, like the peck of a little bird.

Finally, in a slow roll, Allie lifted her neck slightly, her eyes more. She still didn't move at first, but when Leah pointed again, imploring her with her eyes, Allie reached for the receiver and—another agonizing slow motion—put it to her ear.

"Allie, sweetheart, are you all right?"

No response. Allie's face vacant.

"Are you all right? Are you hurt?"

A barely perceptible headshake, no.

"Allie! You've got to talk to me! You've got to! I've got to know what's happened so we can work it out." Leah felt dizzy. She switched the receiver to her other ear and tried to breathe.

"Mom." Allie's voice came from the bottom of a well.

"Honey, I'm here, tell me . . . what's going on?"

"I already told . . . them." Allie sounded as if each word were a boulder to move. '

Baby's Breath

"You told them?"

"What happened."

"But they said you haven't. . . ."

"I did! I already did!" Frustration gave her energy. "They look at you naked . . . they don't give you a comb."

"Listen to me. Did you have a baby?"

Allie looked her full in the face then, with what seemed to be wild loathing. "All right!" she shouted, the receiver crackling with the force. "I had a baby! Didn't they tell you that?"

"Where is the baby, Allie?"

"Alyssa. I'm not a baby."

Leah exhaled, consciously loosening the grip she had on the phone. Her arm and shoulder and neck were stiff with its tension, and her ear hurt from how hard she was pressing it there. She picked up words she could string across the white noise on the line. "All right. Alyssa. Where is your baby?"

"I don't know." She mumbled it, flat and lightless, into the receiver.

"What do you mean you don't know? Allie, for god's sake!"

Allie shrugged. Deliberate, stony, disinterested, now, a lift and release of the shoulders. "I . . . don't . . . dead."

"I don't know? It's dead? I'm dead?" Leah repeated what she thought she'd heard in the garbled s and d sounds. It was the mumble again, Allie's mouth right up against the receiver where the words got tripped and distorted. "Allie, speak up. These phones. . . ."

Allie stared at her. Leah couldn't interpret the expression, both stony and constantly changing by infinitesimal, indiscernible degrees.

"Do . . . you . . . hear . . . me . . . now?" She pronounced each word, each syllable exaggerated.

Leah nodded.

"I said dead."

Chapter Twelve

The word, dead, came as an aimed blow. Dead. Leah recoiled before she struck back. "Don't you care? Allie?"

It happened again. Allie just looked at her, shrugged, a gesture that said no, not particularly. Then she set the phone on the cradle, stood up and left. Nothing else. She turned her back and walked out the door she'd come in. It closed behind her, a silent repudiation.

CHAPTER

13

What could she do after all? Leah sat, unbelieving, in the little cubicle, but Allie didn't come back. She actually knocked at the window as if some kind Being would appear and explain this cataclysm in which she found herself alone. When there was no response, she let her head sink down onto her arms, splayed on the tabletop at which she sat. She hunched her shoulders and sobbed, stifling the noise, clinging to the small privacy the partitions provided. Someone else was crying, too, and somewhere else a man shouted, *I don't give a shit*.

She had no tissue, of course; her purse had been taken away from her. All she could do was use her hand and the sleeve of the white shirt under her blazer. She poked at her hair, gathering it at her neck (*like Allie's!*) with one hand while she tried to compose herself.

No one else was leaving. It wasn't even two fifteen yet, and she had until two forty-five. Leah made her way back down the elevator, stopped in the women's room to splash cold water on her face, collected her purse from the guard who must have seen blotches and swollen eyes before, and traced her way back to the waiting area. She'd told the cab to come back at three. Now she had time, but no heart to press for information, to ask about arraignment, lawyers, procedures. The look of Allie's eyes, stark, and the uncaring shrug: Allie had a baby and had killed it.

Back at the apartment, her normal repertoire of thinking and feeling

212

scraped out, Leah lowered herself onto the couch. She let time go, tried to let her racing mind run out of gas.

She was dozing lightly when the phone rang, interrupting a half-sleep dream of a small, floating dark-haired child. Leah argued with herself but decided she had to answer.

"Alyssa Staton's residence?"

"Who's calling?" Leah said, wary.

"This is Heather Guard, from the Associated Press. Is this the Staton residence?" The voice sounded youthful, perky, sweet. A young woman who wouldn't kill her newborn.

Leah hung up.

I need to eat something, she thought. Maybe a warm bath. Maybe if I take a sleeping pill and go to bed, I'll wake up tomorrow with an idea. As she was turning that notion to let it glisten like a piece of fool's gold in her mind, the tiny light of a comfort, the phone rang.

"Hello?"

"'Lyssa! How's my girl?" A sonic boom.

Leah hesitated, but saw no way out. "Hello, Dennis, it's not Alyssa, it's Leah," she said, twisting the cord, then picking up the whole phone from the desk and heading from the living room toward the kitchen for no reason other than to move.

"Leah. I didn't know you were visiting." Petulant. "Why didn't you let me know?"

She just reacted, not meaning *not* to tell him, just answering the question and it didn't come up. "It wasn't planned in advance."

"Oh . . . Well, put Alyssa on, will you?"

"She's not here." Absolutely true, she'd think in retrospect. She hadn't said a word that wasn't absolutely true.

"Then have her give me a . . . that won't work, I'm about to leave and I left the cell phone at . . . can you take a message?"

Leah headed over to the desk for paper and pencil, still carrying the phone in her left arm. "Um, sure. Go ahead."

213

Baby's Breath

"Missy's had the baby!" Dennis paused for her reaction. Leah imagined the lift of his chest, how he was squaring off his shoulders even talking on the phone. He'd produced another masterpiece.

"Congratulations." She tried to infuse her voice with something resembling enthusiasm.

"They're both fine. His name is Justin Dennis. Eight pounds seven ounces ... are you getting this down?"

"Yes, I am," Leah said, though in fact she'd put the pencil down and had taken the phone over to the couch where she was laying her head back against the rough fabric, eyes closed.

"Length is nineteen inches. Born this morning at six thirty-seven. His Apgar scores were nine and ten ... pretty amazing, huh? Missy was just a trooper."

"... a trooper," Leah repeated, hoping to get by as a parrot.

"Now you tell Alyssa I'll send pictures as soon as I get them. I did photographs in the delivery room myself...." Dennis, proud of himself for not fainting, probably. "You got all that?"

"Yep, got it." If Allie had even gone to a hospital at the very last minute, Leah would be calling Dennis—and Cory, and George, and possibly even Bob—reciting birth weight and length, and the sweet detail of the name, which makes a newborn a *person*. A baby girl, the police had said. She could have been the one calling to tell Dennis he was a grandfather. Too bad to miss the opportunity because *that* would have finished him off. He wouldn't make it to pick up Missy and the baby at the hospital because he'd be at a beauty shop getting his hair dyed. *Oh god, oh god.* Now she was crying again.

"... can't wait to get them home, of course," Dennis was saying. "Leah?"

"Yeah, right here. That's ... wonderful news, Dennis. Congratulations."

"Have you got a cold?" Dennis didn't wait for an answer. "Okay, well, I've got to run. Tell Alyssa I'll talk to her soon."

Chapter Thirteen

She'd think about telling Dennis tomorrow. Right now there was nothing else she could endure. The eastern sky was fading toward night. She'd take a bath, heat up the plate of good food Clara had put in the refrigerator, and go to bed. Maybe she'd see something in the light of morning.

But when she woke from the sleep into which she'd finally drugged herself, nothing was clearer or even different. Clara had pushed a note under Leah's door saying she was going over to Oakland to spend the day babysitting for her daughter's children and might be late getting back since her son-in-law could drive her home. *Be careful if you go out,* she'd finished the note. *There's people in the parking lot looking for you. If you need help, call the building manager, Huddie. He'll come or send his boy to walk Coffee.* And she'd written out Huddie's phone number.

There were indeed people looking for her. Even from the second story window, Leah could tell they were reporters. A white car, Channel 8 News Teamwork stenciled on the driver's door, was parked by the bushes flanking the drive. A youngish man seemed to be circling the building. He gestured several times to another man who had a video camera on a tripod. Inside another car, this one unmarked, someone had her head back, sleeping.

Within the next hour, there were two more video cameras and several more men and two women standing around in the parking lot in weedy clumps. Leah lowered the blinds and closed them, though every now and then she sneaked a look through the gap at the side. Once, when she looked, they'd all moved back beyond the low hedge onto the sidewalk. *Maybe I could set up a show and sell some paintings. A private outdoor art fair, since they want something to look at so badly.* Then she wondered when she'd ever paint again. If.

The phone rang. Leah stared at it, a thin layer of anger over her fear like a skim of ice over black lake water, nearly thick enough to support her weight. *Once. I'll answer it once.*

"Hello?"

"Mrs. Staton?"

"There's no Mrs. Staton here."

"Is this Alyssa Staton's residence?"

"Who's calling?"

"This is Kim McBride from the Telegraph, ma'am. Would you be willing to comment on Alyssa Staton's arrest."

"No. Please don't call here again," Leah said and hung up.

She stopped answering the phone. She'd let it ring a couple of times, pick it up and abruptly bang the receiver back in the cradle. By midday she started answering every fourth or fifth call; it was always another reporter. Coffee paced and whined. She inhaled deeply and called Huddie using the number Clara had given her.

"Yeah. Clara stopped by t'tell me to help out. I tried to run 'em off, but all I can do is make 'em get out the parking lot," he said. "Me or my boy'll come up and get the dog out for you. Do you want I should use the master key if you're not there?"

"I'll be here," Leah said grimly.

"Wha'cha gonna do?" he said. His voice was deep. "Can't hole up forever."

"I don't know. I haven't figured that out yet."

"Tell Alyssa . . . just tell her from me t'keep her chin up. She's a good girl."

She sketched when her pacing made her more nervous. She thought in circles, like Coffee after his own tail before he finally plopped down and sighed. She made herself a list: call Cory, call George, call Dennis, finally, but did none of it. She looked in the yellow pages under Attorneys. There were pages of them. She was as much a prisoner as Allie. *Just as much*, she thought, and the thought made her angry. She slapped the book shut. *Stay there, Alyssa. You're where you belong.* What would she do if a lawyer did get Allie out anyway? Bring her back to the apartment? A mute belligerent girl who'd left her baby to die? Whose own

Chapter Thirteen

mother didn't know her? Who'd hidden from police? Whose responsibility would Allie be? Without even Clara to talk to, ashamed to call anyone else, Leah sketched and paced and waited for it all to end.

All weekend there was a gaggle of reporters outside. Leah realized they were taking shifts. The phone rang frequently. After a full day sandwiched between two nights of waiting for the cup to pass from her, she started to dig in. When a brazen reporter knocked at the door, she opened it and spoke calmly. "I have no comment nor do I intend to have one. I would appreciate your respecting my privacy."

The reporter argued, and a photographer stepped into sight as Leah started to close the door. A flash popped, and Leah realized he'd probably caught her image.

She'd go see Allie again. Whatever she felt, it was her job. The monstrous thing her daughter had done was something she'd have to set on a high shelf like a forbidden object, to be taken down and examined only when she could bear it.

And she'd have to call Dennis.

Another knock at the door, but the voice letting her know: "It's Clara. I brought some breakfast." When she opened the door, Clara stepped in with a plate of bacon, scrambled eggs, and toast. She wrapped an arm around Leah's shoulder. "Got to be more than a body can take," she said. "I'm sorry I was gone yesterday. I know you've got no one here."

"Thank you," Leah said. "I hope you had a good time with your grandchildren." The word struck her as she said it, sank like a stone into her consciousness, but she turned her mind off. "This is nice of you. . . ." She nodded toward the meal.

"Hush," Clara said. "People help each other." She carried the plate into the kitchen and set it on the table. "Did you make you some coffee this morning?"

"Not everyone does," Leah said. "Yes, there's coffee in the pot. Have some with me?"

"What goes around comes around." Clara patted Leah's back. She took two mugs from the cabinet and filled them both. "Black, right?"

"That's . . . not comforting right now. Yes, black. You have a good memory. I don't know how she could do such a thing, Clara. My mind can't get around that. She did it. You were right. She's thrown away her life and her baby's . . . a newborn, Clara, a little girl . . . and mine."

"Can't let that happen," Clara said, putting a mug down by Leah's plate and getting a knife and fork out of the drawer.

"It already has. I raised her and I don't know her."

"You're in shock, I know." Clara said. "I was like that when my boy got locked up. Like it separated me from the rest of the world. Never been that alone, even though Eddie was still alive then. I couldn't even talk to him. Sit now, get some food in you." She pulled lightly on Leah's upper arm.

Leah sat, but didn't pick up the fork. "But your son didn't kill his baby."

"No," Clara said. "He didn't. And prison for drugs doesn't mean the same as prison for killing, I know. And we don't know, maybe that won't happen. You get a certain kind of shock, though, and more almost makes no difference. You can't take it in, right?"

"No. I just can't." A sob took Leah off guard, and she couldn't breathe for crying then. Clara got up and came around the table to hold her like a mother, one strong hand bracing Leah's head against her cushy chest, the other stroking Leah's hair. Coffee whined softly, nosing around Clara's legs, jealous.

The talk with Clara had bolstered her. When she started to feel, to believe, just how long this was going to take—not just another week or two as she'd said to Cory and George—Leah read over the list she'd made on a pad from Allie's desk. The colorless imprint of something

Chapter Thirteen

Allie had written with heavy pressure was illegible but present on the top sheet, ghostly.

She penciled on several more items, found a phone book in a kitchen drawer, and began.

It took only two calls to lease a car, she found, if one paid no attention to the cost, only the proximity of the dealership. Her third call was to the telephone company to arrange a new unlisted number. Cory, who said, "Yes, it's all over the paper. I'm sorry, Leese," was next. Cory was the only person who'd ever nicknamed her, and Leah thought she'd used it now on purpose, to say something more than, "What can I do to help?"

She asked Cory to get her house key from Dave Allen, pack some more clothes—the clothes she used to wear to the office—and ship them. The call to George was harder, delaying the commissioned painting, and not being able to tell him when it would be done. Just as she hung up, the phone rang and she picked it up by reflex.

"Leah, Jesus Christ. I've called probably thirty times. What the hell is going on? You've got some nerve lying to me. That's why you're there, isn't it, goddammit. What's this crap all over the newspaper, this ridiculous story about Alyssa?"

Leah sighed, set her pad and pencil down on the kitchen table, and sat down. "Dennis, I'm sorry," she began. Her coffee was half-gone but she wrapped her free hand around what was left of the cup's paltry warmth.

✳   ✳   ✳

Saturday. After dinner, hot dogs and potato chips eaten to the background noise of the nightly news, the crowd of television watchers tuned to an hour-long segment of *Entertainment Tonight*. The hosts (the girls in Alyssa's freshman dorm had nicknamed them Plastic Face and Wax Mouth, courtesy of Linnie's bitter wit) were reciting celebrity birthdays. But the afterimage of Alyssa's face—round-cheeked, sol-

Baby's Breath

emn, and pale in her Franklin High graduation photo—lingered on the screen, the wrap-up story in the Channel Eight local broadcast. Beneath Wax Mouth's lavish make-up, her lips as red as movie blood, Alyssa detected her own portrait burned into the monitor. Behind the vividly colored frames of the tabloid coverage, the title of *her* story loitered. In case anybody *Cindy or Linnie or Tony or Howie or Dennis or Clara or Leah* had missed it this time around, the updates on the BART Baby tragedy would return, when her round white face would be suspended to the meter of the newscaster's words. Hands to her cheeks, turning away from the television, Alyssa sought the circles of bone beneath her eyes, the cartilage forming the bridge of her nose. If she pressed hard enough, she could break the bones, scar the skin, repattern the configuration of eyes, nose and mouth into features nobody would recognize and no mother would ever claim.

She couldn't sit down in front of the television, though Joey patted a chair beside him. She shook her head and went upstairs to her cell. Brushing her teeth in Shower 2, she let the bristles scrape back and forth against her gums until they bled and her spit ran pink in the bottom of the aluminum bowl. Before dinner, Ostrom had told her she had money on the books now because they'd credited the forty dollars they'd inventoried from her wallet. Alyssa asked for a comb and toothbrush, that was all, but Ostrom had given her a kit of bath items, the kind you'd find nestled into a wicker basket in a hotel bathroom. "Good hygiene is mandatory, Staton," Ostrom said, repeating herself. Alyssa wondered if she still looked dirty. Reconsidering, she decided no, Ostrom was just remembering her from the strip search; she couldn't erase that Alyssa and fill in the blank with the new one, the clean one.

In her cell, she laid down her toothbrush on the shelf next to the toilet items from the commissary and picked up the comb. After shaking her hair loose from the rubberband, she started on the sides and worked back, untangling, then combing out a strand of hair at a time. Maybe

Chapter Thirteen

Ostrom thought it was dirty, having so much uncombed hair. Maybe that was it. Maybe Ostrom didn't know that hair was just dead cell matter, excreted from your pores, like sweat, just dead stuff all prettied up.

I didn't know it was dead.

She'd said those words out loud into the telephone mouthpiece smelling of soiled palms and old money. She'd said them to her mother's face on the other side of the glass in the visiting room. Leah hadn't heard, but she'd said them just the same.

Friday afternoon, after Ostrom woke her from the sleep she'd fallen into like a craving and walked her from the cell to the tube, she'd had to keep from running. Alyssa slowed herself, dragging behind Ostrom to the little room where Leah was waiting on the other side of the glass panel. At first all she'd wanted was to tell Leah how awful it was to be in jail, how the toothless woman from booking, the Jack-O-Lantern, had found her and stared into her cell for the longest time after lunch, how the housing officers seemed to expect her to do bad things, how every rule in the whole place assumed the inmates were just dying to do bad things every chance they got. The glass between them, the smelly telephone in her hands, it was all so wrong compared to what she'd needed from her mother, the scene she'd imagined would follow when Ostrom told her, "Staton, your mother's in the tube, waiting."

Not sweetness and light. She hadn't been so stupid as to think Leah would be happy, but she wasn't prepared for her mother looking as if she were going to erupt in molten rage. Her dark eyes flamed, her full lips thinned in exaggeration as if she were speaking to a deaf-mute. Questioning, the worst kind, when Leah already knew the answers but was going to drill Alyssa anyway because *it's the principle of the thing.* In her disappointment Alyssa *did* become deaf, and nearly dumb, and glad of the glass panel separating her like a SWAT shield from her mother's sealed wrath. All she had to do was shift the receiver, speak with her lips tight against the phone, nudge the mouthpiece beneath her chin. Speak up, speak up.

Baby's Breath

I didn't know it was dead.

She'd spoken up. Had Leah heard her? Of course Alyssa *cared*—but that was it, the blow that severed flesh, her mother's accusation that she didn't care. Leah always presuming to know what she, Alyssa—*Allie*—should feel.

Don't you want the blue pants, Allie?

Wouldn't you rather have a salad?

Shouldn't you give Sharon a call back, hon?

If you spend it now, you won't have it later and you'll regret it.

She didn't have to speak to visitors any more than she had to speak to police detectives. She could—would—the next time Ostrom or a trustee called her to the tube, say that she wasn't going. She didn't have to go. She hadn't read in the orientation handbook that they could make you visit if you chose against it.

Her scalp was sore. She couldn't tell if the soreness came from her brain, a worm weakening the insides of an apple, or from her snarled hair, pulled out by the roots like Leah insisted crabgrass had to be. That was it, she recognized, leaning back against the mattress of her bed: she was caught between rotting and uprooting. She could be shrinking down to nothing like the Wicked Witch of the West, melted by water. Or she could be ready to fly to pieces in the centrifugal force of her spinning brain, stripping the gears that gave traction to forward movement, to a place she couldn't yet make herself go.

She lay back on her bed and planted her slippered feet high against the wall. If she let the blood run back from her feet and legs toward her heart, they stopped aching. If they stopped aching, her mind would cease playing its game of musical chairs. Then maybe she could sleep. She could feel the music wearing down, the number of chairs declining: Coffee's okay, he's with Clara. Missed something due in Miller's, can't remember now. Mom's here, Mom's here. They took the moccasins. They took Lazzie. The BART station, the screeching dwarf. Dara and Percocets, gone, gone. The BART station. The moccasins. The hinge on the kitchen cabinet, Huddie said he'd fix it. The BART station. Mom's here. The BART station.

"Hey, Numero Forty-Two." Joey stood framed in her open cell door. The lights in the living area blinked once, twice. Bedtime warning blinks. "Hear they're moving you to GP tomorrow."

Alyssa swung her legs down and pulled herself upright. "GP?"

"General Population. Women's Unit. Until trial or whatever."

Hopkins had told her; he'd explained it. Unless you were incorrigible or really nuts, like the drunk lady in the restraining chair, you went into GP. And if you were gay, like Joey, you went into the GP Women's Unit because, well, she could figure it out, couldn't she?

"I'm going, too. Most of the players are."

"Why do they even bother?"

"Bother what?" Joey hefted himself onto the shelf, and neatly pushed Alyssa's bathroom things aside with his slender thigh. He sat, toes pointed, legs swinging in a one-two rhythm.

"Why do they need to classify *you* every time, Joey? It's not like it's your first time."

"Rules. By the book. Laws, maybe." Joey rolled his shoulders. "And people can change, I mean, can't they? Somebody come in all drugged up, breaking down walls, but be sweet as peach pie the next time around." He stopped the shoulder rolls. "People change."

"Do you, Joey?" This was the safe path, the traveled road, away from her game of musical chairs and the chance she might be left standing, nowhere to sit, caught out by the deadened music. "You don't, do you?" She set the comb beside her on the mattress as if it were a jewel.

"Man, you're cold." Joey stilled his swinging legs.

"But you keep coming back."

"They keep *making* me come back."

"This isn't chicken or the egg. You keep ... doing what you do ... and that brings you back. That's not change. That's cause."

"You gonna be a professor?" Joey sidestepped, as clever as she.

Alyssa shook her head.

"What, then?"

"What do you mean, what? I'm here now, I'm not going to be anything in here."

"What'd you do, anyway, Alyssa?" Sharpshooter. Right between the eyes. Not malicious, though. Not like the Jack-o-Lantern, brushing so close that static had sparked between their uniform sleeves, who had whispered *famous now, ain't you, Staton?*

"I . . . I'm . . . I can't talk about it."

"Holy Apostolics say it's the only way."

"I'm not an Apostolic."

"Neither am I. But it gets you out of here for a couple of hours on weeknights and Sundays, if you're interested."

"I'm not." Alyssa picked up her comb, spiderwalked it between her thumbs and pointer fingers. Church on Sundays made her think of confession, the atonement of sin, the achievement of grace—the language of her freshman year Philosophy of Religions course. But the words which had before been only decipherable textbook abstractions turned themselves into shovels, digging at earth that didn't want to submit itself to plowing, wouldn't even loosen under the lip of a rusty spade.

Joey's Apostolic escapes from jail wouldn't save her; she was feeling enough to know that much.

GP was different, but identical, too: the open area surrounded by cells, indoor-outdoor carpet counterfeiting the decor of a rundown rec room in a suburban basement, another big-screen television. The same speech about cleanliness, order, the same rules against contraband. *Contraband*, sounding like the spoils of war, as though there were anything Alyssa could hold hidden in her hand that would dull the knifesharp blades of the bared facts being whispered around by women whose hard faces averted from hers without greeting: she was in jail be-

224

cause they found a dead baby in a place where she'd been. A baby the police said she killed. *Baby Killer.*

Ostrom had been reassigned to General Population, too. Out of choice, Alyssa thought at first. Out of spite for her, Alyssa, personally. When they were lined up in their matching orange suits and marched like third-graders across the jail grounds to the new unit, Joey corrected Alyssa's thinking about Ostrom. Shifts and staffing assignments were rotated, that was all. Just coincidence they moved when Ostrom did. Stuff goes down when people get too familiar, Joey said, wincing at what he'd left unvoiced. But good for you and me, now. We get Ostrom again. The Iron Woman. Nothing's going to happen to nobody. Not on her clock, at least.

Alyssa thought of Hopkins, almost made herself homesick hoping to see Hopkins again until Joey told her no, booking was different—the officers in booking didn't see any inmates long enough to get to know them. Except somebody like me, Joey said, laughing. The revolving door syndrome. For a moment, as they were setting up for a lunch that smelled like pressed turkey roll and green beans, Alyssa wanted to quiz Joey, get him to admit he was capable of changing his ways, could give up turning tricks for something else, anything else. She wanted to ask him why the Apostolics hadn't saved his soul yet, but the trustees rolled the trays in, and the inmates were sitting down to eat, and the black woman with the corn-rowed hair, a crack addict who went wild-eyed to medical twice a day for her methadone treatments, was demanding grace in her fierce and unforgiving voice.

Because they'd moved units on Sunday morning, Joey had to miss his Apostolic Tabernacle and his escape to Educational Unit 5. Lucky Joey, though; he found a friend with a shaved head from the Oakland streets whom he welcomed with a rocking, two-armed hug and a sit-down talk that excluded her, politely but clearly, from their reunion. Once more Alyssa was given a cell assignment to herself, almost as if the officers were protecting the other inmates from the dirty college girl who'd ended up inside where nobody wanted her, who couldn't get outside because nobody believed her when she said she hadn't done it, hadn't killed that baby whose moccasins she was carrying around in her backpack like a keychain. Maybe they were thinking, give her a cell to herself and nobody will have to look at her, hear her breathing, smell her body sweating, inexplicably, whenever somebody nudged against her with hip or elbow, sweat collecting beneath the thin orange fabric as if she'd just run Coffee all the way home from Sather Gate to the apartment on Dwight.

"Arraignment Tuesday for you, Staton. You going to give someone a call, get her to bring you something other than that to wear?" Ostrom said when she checked out Alyssa's linens and took her completed commissary request form at the computer station in GP. *Poker cards*, Alyssa had marked. *$3.15.* She wanted them for Joey, so Joey could start his own games instead of waiting on the Jack-o-Lantern's crowd.

Ostrom had a disconcerting but deliberate habit of looking everywhere but straight in Alyssa's face. Now she let her eyes fall to Alyssa's chest, waiting.

"Arraignment?" Alyssa repeated, fixed on Ostrom's mole, the rolling muscle of her jaw moving as Ostrom chewed a piece of gum, Juicy Fruit, it smelled like. Maybe the officers had a rule, a secret one not printed up in the orientation handbook, about handling college kids, *dirty girls*, seeing through them, making them invisible.

"Court. Prosecutor. Your attorney," Ostrom's eyes rose from her clipboard to Alyssa's breasts again, "pleads you ... You got an attorney yet, Staton?"

"No, I—they said—I didn't. . . ."

"Refused your right to preliminary counsel, huh," Ostrom said, motioning Alyssa to the side so the inmate behind her could reach for the next stack of blue sheets. "How you planning to plead, then?"

"She have to plead guilty, leaving her own baby like garbage," the

Chapter Thirteen

inmate behind her said, the short one, the shadow to Jack-o-Lantern, a woman whose arms were pocked up and down with red sores.

Alyssa felt the punch against her lower back, a curled fist or a sharp elbow drawn back and slammed against the softness to the left of her lower spine, a blow executed so deftly and so quickly nobody who hadn't felt it would know it had happened. She shielded her breast with the linens and stepped sideways out of line, away from the counter. Ostrom hadn't seen—*Joey said they were safe with Ostrom*—yet Alyssa didn't understand what good it would do to confront the pocky shadow woman.

What could she say if she turned and faced her accuser?

I went back.

It wasn't garbage.

"Staton. Visitor in the tube." Ostrom appeared in her cell door. She sniffed, maybe at Joey, who was sitting beside Alyssa on the bed, painstakingly using a dark blue pencil to trace the words Alyssa had recorded from his dictation in faint, oversized print onto a yellow legal pad. More likely she sniffed at Alyssa, who felt the rush in her veins that meant she was going to begin sweating even though the unit felt so cold that Joey had to wear a T-shirt and a thermal shirt beneath his prisoner's top. ·

"Visitor, Staton," Ostrom repeated, clicking her silver pen in and out with her thumb. The inmates weren't allowed pens, only pencils, because they'd use anything to tattoo themselves, *anything*, Joey said. Ostrom's pen clicked one-two-three-four.

"I don't want to see anybody."

"It's your *mother*, Staton."

Joey cut his eyes at Alyssa, then moved the blue pencil over the letters she'd printed for him, so he could trace the belly of the lowercase "d" and remember it went to the left, to the hand with which Joey ate and wrote.

Baby's Breath

"I don't want to see . . . my mother." Alyssa held her breath. Joey finished the word, *dedicate*, and ran his fingertips over it as if he were reading Braille.

Joey looked at Alyssa, raised his eyebrows and stared hard. *Tell her why.*

"I don't feel well. I was . . . was just going to lie down. My back—" It was true: her back ached. The punch had grown a softball-sized bruise, turned a perfect circle of skin a grim gray-green color. After she'd made up her bed with the blue sheets, she'd pulled her orange top up and twisted herself around to look into the mirror inset over the sink in the shower room. It had marked her as clearly as the badge on Ostrom's uniform marked Ostrom a guard. *Rotten.*

"Your decision, Staton," Ostrom said. She'd had enough. She wasn't going to beg Alyssa to see Leah, she'd make that clear. "Goes into the computer, you refusing a visit. You don't want to make a habit of it. You get flagged *pattern of resistant behavior*, you won't be playing school with Diehl anymore."

"How threatening," chirped Joey when Ostrom's footsteps resounded on the balcony stairs. "No more playschool."

"Joey. Can we do this later?"

"No problemo. You don't want to see your mom?"

"No."

"I'd see mine if she came down to visit. She don't, though."

"Look—"

"Hey, it's all right. It's all right." Joey stood. He touched her, then stroked the thick ponytail that had splayed itself over her shoulder. "It's all right, Alyssa. Thanks for the . . . you know . . . *secretarial assistance*." He twirled his hand, a deliberately fey gesture that made Alyssa forget herself and smile. "I think I can finish it myself now, anyway. A half-wit can trace, right?"

"You're not a half-wit. You're dyslexic."

Chapter Thirteen

"In Special Ed . . . the other kids used to say stupid." Hands on hips now, playing a part, *wanting her to raise her laughter.*

"You're not stupid."

"Dyslexic?"

"It means—they think it means—your wires are crossed." She rewarded him then, lightening the explanation with a half-grin. "You have to work harder, is all. Rewire the connections, sort of."

"Thanks."

"I'll help you more, just not now."

"Hey, I get it. I get it." He walked to the cell door, his slippered feet scuffing the carpet. "Alyssa?"

"Uhh?"

"You going to see her eventually, aren't you? Your mom?"

"Go on, Joey."

"Okay, okay, it's just that . . . she'll keep coming back, you know?"

But Alyssa didn't know.

*   *   *

Her Sunday afternoon route to the jail was direct enough, but Leah lost herself twice. A brilliant sun made the world look almost normal. *I've got to do this,* she thought. *Like before, right after the divorce and I had to do it all and do it alone. You might as well take hold because you have to cope.* She remembered visiting her mother in the hospital after the first stroke, when exhausted and lonely, it was hers to calculate odds, make decisions, monitor the monitors.

The protocol at the jail was easier for being slightly familiar. Leah surrendered her purse in the area that looked like a ticket counter, collected her receipt, and signed the registration. "She's in General Population now," a different guard, a woman, said. "Just moved out of Intake. Follow the sign when you go up to the tube. Did you want to put money on the book today?"

"Uh, does she need it?"

"You can check the computer yourself—over there—or I'll look for you. . . ." Without waiting for an answer, she used a keyboard and checked the screen. "Oh, sorry, no. She can't have any more anyway. But whenever you want, you can use those computers over there anytime you want to check something." The way she said *whenever* sounded like a lifetime.

Leah found her way up to the tube and picked the most private booth she could find. A good five minutes passed, then a uniformed woman came in without Allie and, from the door, scanned the inmate side booth until her gaze stopped on Leah. Leah recognized her as the one who'd escorted Allie to the visiting area on Friday. The same high ponytail and mushroom puff of teased bangs, incongruous over a thickening body. The green trousers and khaki shirt of the uniform strained at both pants zipper and middle blouse button. Leah, too, was in her uniform: the blazer, white blouse and slacks she'd adopted as respectable, setting her apart from people who committed unthinkable crimes.

The guard crossed to the booth and picked up the receiver on the inmate's side before Leah could guess why. She motioned to Leah to pick up on her side.

"You're the lady here to see Alyssa Staton?"

"Yes." Only a small flush, maybe unnoticeable.

"She's not indisposed to see you, ma'am."

"What?" *Indisposed?* "Is she sick?"

The officer's name tag said Ostrom. Insignia decorated her sleeve, but what caught Leah's eye was the dark mole that protruded from her cheek where a high school cheerleader's dimple might be. The guard didn't look like she'd ever been a cheerleader. Of course, neither had Allie, neither had Leah.

Ostrom looked defensive, though surely that made no sense. "No, she's not sick," she said. "She has no desire to see you ... she's *in*disposed." She said it as if she were explaining the word.

"I have to see her. How am I supposed to know what's going on?"

"You can check the computer." Ostrom started to turn.

"Wait! Please, can I ask you some questions?"

The officer looked back at Leah. "What?"

"I don't know what to do. Does she need a lawyer?" Dennis had been enraged that Leah hadn't engaged an attorney at all, let alone a top defense man. "How do I get information if she won't talk to me?"

Ostrom said, "She's down to be arraigned on Tuesday. There'll be a PD there ... Public Defender. That's a lawyer."

"Should I get her another lawyer, one of her own I mean?'

"Lotta people do. All the ones with money." *Was there a sneer on her face, or something else?*

Leah squeezed the bridge of her nose with her thumb and forefinger trying to think. "Can I um, send one to talk to her here? Can a lawyer get her out—with bail I mean?" Dennis had been insistent. *Of course they set bail*, he'd shouted.

"Sure a lawyer can talk to her. They come into the tube just like anybody else. About bail, the judge at arraignment decides that. Depends on what they say she did, if she's a flight risk."

"Can you advise me? I've never been in this situation. I don't know whom to ask. Why won't she see me?"

Ostrom scrutinized Leah a moment, lowering her eyes to Leah's expensive tailored jacket, white silk button-down shirt. Leah wanted to squirm, to say *stop looking at me*. She sat as still as she could and waited.

"What do you expect?" Ostrom said.

What do you expect? Dennis' words exactly. *It's not like I can come there, not now, anyway*, he'd said. *I've got Missy and Caleb and the new baby ... for god's sake, Leah. Do you need money?*

"What do you mean? I expect her to ... I don't know. Explain."

Baby's Breath

"You think people got an explanation for what they do? I never heard one in here that made any sense. Just a pile of excuses. They all got 'em. You'd better leave her alone. She don't want t'see you? Don't come here." There was an edge to Ostrom's voice. Did she resent the silk blouse? Did she have contempt for a mother whose daughter wouldn't see her, even in jail? Did she scorn Leah's naiveté, the questions she'd asked? Did she find Allie loathsome? Of course she would. Anyone would.

CHAPTER

14

Clara offered—asked, *wanted*—to come to the arraignment with Leah, but she'd declined. "I'd rather . . . have somebody to come back to," she said. "I do better by myself."

It had been shame, really, dictating that response. The image of Clara next to her when the charges against her daughter were read: drugs, abandoning a baby, *killing,* made her feverish with humiliation. Guilt by association and guilt by blood linked her with this. She'd hoped to sift anonymously into the arraignment, quiet as air, to meld with the faded plaster and the bland institutional tile.

Wrong. Wrong. Wrong. The press recognized her thanks to that one shot a quick photographer had flashed off as Leah was closing the door of the apartment on the brass balls of a reporter. Clara could have helped her push her way through the forest of laced dress shoes and dark mid-height heels, which is what she saw with her head in its "push-on-and-don't-look-at-them" position. Of course that would have put Clara on the local news or the network feed too, hardly fair.

The hearing room had been almost empty twenty minutes ago but now people were trickling into little pools. Ostrom had told her they usually took the high profile cases in first and quickly, but maybe only Ostrom still thought that was a secret.

Allie was brought in through a door to the side of the bench, which was on a raised dais, a throne-like desk flanked by an American flag and another one, whose red edges draped over a white field like a barber pole. Even though she was seeing Allie for the second time in the neon orange jail clothes, the shock wasn't easier because now something else twisted her stomach and dizzied her with unexpected pain: Allie was in chains. The links around her waist were narrow enough to pass as a faddish belt, except that extensions from it bound her wrists to her waist rather than to each other. Her gait was too short, and Leah realized, an instant after she identified the waist rig, Allie's legs were shackled. Didn't defendants usually get to wear regular clothes? Her head was down; she was trying to use the loose drape of her hair to hide her face, but the sloppy ponytail was in place.

A tall, suited man followed Allie into the courtroom. They took places behind a table, and the guard—a blonde boy wearing a gun!—unlocked Allie's hands. In another world, he could have been a boyfriend holding her hand, and Leah would invite him to dinner. Leah was distracted by a woman who laid a briefcase on the table across from Allie's, on the other side of the aisle. She sat alone at a table with room for three on a side, while the man with Allie—he must be the public defender—turned his seat to face Allie instead of the judge's bench and talked animatedly. He opened his briefcase and reached in, but he didn't spread out manila folders like an oversize hand of cards the way the woman was doing. Once his head, with its inverted U of a graying hairline, bounced. He must have laughed, because Leah saw a small smile flicker on Allie's profile. It disappeared immediately, and the man patted Allie's shoulder.

"All rise! The Superior Court of Alameda County is now in session." A robed man, Asian, with a shock of black bristle—as if he'd been a military Colonel yesterday—entered from the left, where the bailiff was posted, and sat behind the wooden bench.

The woman with the briefcase stood. "Marcelle Ward Fayler for the people, Your Honor." Ashy hair, highlighted, in a simple backsweep

Chapter Fourteen

sprayed into place. Aquiline nose, wide lids on her eyes, and a jut of chin. Navy suit, all business. A low-pitched voice that carried well, even with her back to the spectators—mainly press, if Leah could judge by the poised notebooks. The one who'd knocked on the apartment door was there. When their eyes met, Leah flicked hers away.

The balding man with Allie stood up. "Jeffrey Earle for the defense, Your Honor." A good voice, rich, like a singer's.

Leah watched Allie, who examined her hands while the attorneys and the judge went on in their formal language. She flexed her wrists a couple of times, shifted in her seat as if she were uncomfortable, then settled into stillness so Leah couldn't tell if she were paying attention or not. Once Allie seemed to sneak a look behind her and Leah flushed, as if she'd been hiding, but Allie turned forward again without registering her mother's presence.

Allie slumped when the last complaint, as they called it, was read. (*Complaint. Such an innocuous word. "What are you complaining about Allie?" "I'm not a baby, there's no reason I should have to be home at eleven." "What are you complaining about, Mom?" "There's no reason in the world that you can't hang your towels up after your shower."*) Murder in the first degree. That the defendant did, knowingly and with malice aforethought . . . Leah had heard the first autopsy report—the baby had bled to death from an untied umbilical cord—and a murder charge might grow from it, like a choking vine extending wider and higher than its *possession of a narcotic* and *child endangerment* roots. Allie must have known it as well, yet Leah recognized Allie's slump. Leah felt it too, that word, *murder*, like a whip crack, a shot. *Not soft like paper towels all over a baby girl while her life leaked into them.*

"Are you ready to plea?" The judge looked at Jeffrey Earle.

"Not guilty, Your Honor. Request that bail be set at this time."

"The prosecution objects to bail. Defendant is a flight risk. Your honor, after the. . . ."

"... want bail." It was Allie, interrupting. Only the end of her sentence about wanting bail reached the back of the courtroom. The judge and Allie's lawyer both looked startled. Jeffrey Earle stood.

"Your honor, if I might have a moment to confer with my client?"

The judge nodded, and Jeffrey Earle sat back down next to Allie, moving his chair to mostly face her again—if she'd look at him—leaning forward, elbows on knees. Leah saw Allie's head, resolutely front, shake a *no*, then Jeffrey Earle's same movement. He gestured, persistent, and Allie swung her head side to side again. Was he explaining—maybe insisting—to Allie that she wasn't supposed to talk?

Earle stood again. "Your Honor, the defense withdraws the request for bail at this time."

"The record will so note," the judge responded, the surprised look erased now.

What? She doesn't want bail?

Leah felt cotton-eared, stunned by Allie's not wanting bail. How *could* she choose that? Psychiatric examinations were requested and ordered; there was dickering about court calendars and trial date. Allie was impassive now. Sometimes Leah could hear what they were saying, sometimes she couldn't, and sometimes she just wasn't focused on anything except the young woman in orange who had been *her* baby girl once, a black-capped squall of noise and motion whose birth-mottled skin quickly evened into a pale blush rose.

The judge banged his gavel and marked some papers. After a sort of lull, people seemed to know it was all right to stand and move. The blonde boy-guard led Allie out. Jeffrey Earle, who never had unloaded his briefcase all over the table the way the Fayler woman did, slid a single manila folder under his arm and headed for the side door Allie had been taken through.

Leah hurried to catch up with him. "Excuse me," she said. "Excuse me!" He turned and waited.

Chapter Fourteen

"I'm Leah Pacey, Mr. Earle. Alyssa Staton's mother. Please, I need information."

Blue eyes under odd brows that stopped unfinished on their first upward slant took her in. "I'm sorry," he said. "First off, I really don't know anything. I've just been assigned the case. But you should talk to your daughter ... there's nothing outside of the public record I'd be able to tell you without her permission anyway."

"I want to ... and her father wants ... to get her a lawyer. And the bail. . . ." Leah flushed. "Oh. I know you're a ... I'm sure you're very good. I'm sorry, that didn't come out right. I meant, we can get her a. . . ." She was messing this up, bumbling.

Jeffrey Earle laughed, head back, as she'd seen him do with Allie. Then, straight-faced, so Leah could read the laugh-lines, "Can I quote you to my boss? And my wife? Just that one part, about how good I am?"

"I really am sorry," Leah said, trying to recover. "How do I find out about how to do things? Can I talk to her?" Then, a confession that strangely embarrassed her. "She wouldn't see me when I went on Sunday."

"Alyssa calls the shots. She's made that clear. I need to talk with her myself," he said. "Here," he said, raising his knee to use as a table, the file still pinioned by his arm. He opened his briefcase and rooted around until he pulled out a business card. "Take this. Give me a call. I'll try to give you some direction."

"Thank you very much. Is later today all right?"

"Any time you can catch me in." He shut the briefcase, still balancing it from his stork position. The locks spoke in turn as he juggled to click each one down. "And it's fine for you to get her another lawyer, Mrs. Staton. I knew what you meant. I just take care of her until you have someone in place. Look," he said, eyeing over Leah's head, "why don't you follow me? I'll show you another way out. They'll think we're meeting and maybe you can get away."

237

Baby's Breath

"Thank you," she said. "Thank you so much." He motioned her through the door ahead of him. "There'll be no comment," he called and closed the reporters away on the other side.

* * *

Alyssa found herself drawn to Jeffrey Earle. From the moment he'd opened his briefcase and pulled out a green rubber alligator the size of his graceful hand, she felt her lost curiosity rising like mercury in the old glass thermometers Gran had insisted on using throughout her childhood, even after one had broken in her mouth, shattered by *Alliegator's* baby teeth. Absentmindedly he'd set the alligator aside, as if it were the most natural thing in the world for a lawyer to be carrying around, and continued shuffling through his papers. Waiting for the next surprise to unfold, she felt something chug and start, like the reluctant engine on Howie's Chevy Biscayne, as if her insides were a sticky carburetor and Jeffrey Earle the mechanic who'd coaxed the mixture of fuel and air into sparking. She wouldn't dare pick the word *excite*, it didn't seem right. But when she labeled her own curiosity, *thrilling* was the word she chose, hope and pain woven together like the bittersweet pins and needles tingle of a numb leg. It hurt, but the anguish meant her blood was circulating. She was still alive.

When the judge entered the courtroom cloaked in robes the color of death, Jeffrey Earle scooped the alligator from the tabletop and slid it back inside the briefcase. "Judge has a thing about reptiles," he whispered to her, his voice muffled, so close his breath lifted the pleat of hair from her ear. "This is a lizardless courtroom." She had to smile, then. She couldn't help but like him.

When he led her into a courthouse conference room so they could talk—that was all he wanted, to talk before the arraignment, he said—she felt him waiting for her with the same patient anticipation. He didn't pose his questions to get to a destination he'd already picked, the way you set up a calculus proof to reach the only acceptable answer. He watched her, sizing her, as if she might have some toy or trinket hidden in the pocket of her jail suit that would reveal her to him. He positioned his briefcase on the dark, shining expanse of the wooden tabletop, unlatched his briefcase, and stared into it. The contours of his face were in transition, as if after forty some-odd years of being round they had decided to turn themselves lean. What would it be like to photograph his face, its boyish cast exaggerated in white light, its lean maturity emphasized by shadow? She wondered if Jeffrey Earle had ever wanted to mold his own features with his bare hands to disguise himself, to twist his own flesh and tear it into a model of somebody else's face.

He held a folder up, what the suited lady in the courtroom had called the police jacket. "Alyssa Pacey Staton. Nineteen years old. Birthdate?"

"November 12."

"1979?"

"I'm nineteen."

"Do you understand my role here, Miss Staton?"

"Alyssa. Please. Nobody calls—"

"Alyssa then. And I'm Jeff. You know what I'm doing?"

"You're . . . defending me." She thought of the fist-sized bruise gone shades of yellow and plum, how she'd taken to skirting the Jack-o-Lantern's crowd, keeping her face forward, her back to the wall. *Defending.*

"Today I'm defending you. The court-appointed defender." He leaned against the back of the heavy mahogany chair. Alyssa felt his feet knock the table legs and settle into a resting place. "Your mother would like you to have a private attorney—"

"I don't want one."

"It appears your father, also, would prefer—"

"I don't want somebody else. I don't deserve to have the money, it would be expensive ... and my mother doesn't ... my mother's a *painter.*" She wouldn't take any of it, Dennis's money, the private lawyer, Leah's intervention.

But she liked Jeffrey Earle. For a single abridged moment in the courtroom when he'd made her smile, she'd recognized herself. With somebody else, she might lose the way back, miss the trailhead. "I'm nineteen. I can decide."

"That you are. And that you can." He sighed, pulled himself forward and planted his elbows on the conference table. "What's your major, Alyssa?"

"I haven't—I hadn't—declared."

"But you had an idea?"

"History."

"I went to Cal, too. Studied herpetology."

"I don't—"

"Biology major. Herpetology is, you know, chameleons and turtles ... dinosaurs are the really spectacular reptile family ... that involves some history."

"And then you became a lawyer."

"Yep." He wasn't going to talk any more about himself. It wouldn't be natural, she realized, startled from the safe place the conversation had put her. None of this was natural. She couldn't expect this conversation to follow the ordinary back and forth it might in the outside: a little about me, a little about you. She was *inside.* This was all about her, about what they said she'd done to the baby.

"So you don't want bail."

She shook her head, felt the angry points of pain on her scalp where the rubber band caught single hairs and tugged. A headache coming on, her stomach resentful, burning.

"Because?"

"I don't want bail because. . . ." She could do this, fill in the blank, it was all in the context. *Read the context to guess the identity of the missing*

Chapter Fourteen

element. "Because everybody knows . . . the television? And it's just better for me to stay . . . where I am."

Jeff didn't coax her to go on. He didn't raise his funny half-eyebrows in question. He waited. *Often during verbally administered examinations, the instructor's posture will indicate the correct answer.*

"They think I'm a . . . monster already, the women in the jail? Even the ones that did terrible things themselves . . . they hate me. Outside . . . with my mother . . . the people who knew me. . . ." She put her hands to her face in the peekaboo gesture, palms over eyes. "I just don't want to see them."

"The other inmates have threatened you?" His pen, a cheap, ink-stained Bic missing its cap, was poised.

She couldn't see the alligator; it must have been hidden by the open flap of a file folder. Alyssa pressed her back against the wooden spine of her chair, deliberately targeting the bruise she couldn't see. She kept pressing until the hurt there fused with all her other pains—the headache and sore legs and leaden breasts and the hollowness, the hollowness of her insides like the vortex of a black hole.

"Because we can get you into sheltered housing if you're being threatened." The Bic in his hand slackened.

"I don't need to be . . . in sheltered."

"Like you don't need bail?" This came quick.

"Nobody's threatened me. They say things, about what the . . . television . . . what the police said I did."

He opened one of the folders. Of course he needed a distraction. Because how could Jeffrey Earle bear her after she'd brought it up. He could see she didn't deserve bail, didn't deserve sheltered housing. *Dirty girl.*

"I need to talk with you about that, Alyssa. About what the police say you did."

She slumped. She didn't have to find the wounds; he was going to do it for her.

241

"We need to go over this information. . . ." He gave a backhand wave to the folders skewed across the tabletop. "After we've talked, I'll arrange for you to talk to some other people—"

"Shrinks." He thought she was crazy. He thought she was insane. Only a crazy person could—

"Shrinks. A psychiatrist and psychologist, actually. The psychologist first, with some written tests." He paused, found the alligator beneath a file folder, swung it by the tail between two fingers. "Actually, a couple of shrinks, the prosecution's pick as well." His voice and the tick-tock of the green alligator lulled her. Was he tricking her?

"Because the point is," Jeff went on, "that the evidence shows . . . there's no argument you had this baby?"

The alligator stopped swinging. She couldn't swallow. He talked through her silence, repeating the same words, their inflection shifted from question to statement: "There's no argument that you had this baby."

She nodded. If only she could loosen the rubber band tangled in her hair, she'd drape it across her face and make herself unreadable.

"So the issue at hand is what exactly happened from the . . . birth . . . onward."

She struggled with the catch in her throat, the words turned sideways, bridging themselves like a logjam.

"The police detectives—you spoke with Halsumae, I think?—and the D.A. have their surmise. But we—you and I—need to talk about that, what exactly happened."

She nodded. Her hands were twisted together in her lap, so damp their sweat had stained the orange slacks of the jail suit. *Baby killer*.

"Can you do that with me, Alyssa? Walk me through . . . what happened a week ago Sunday night?"

She nodded; she wanted to find the right answers, ace the true/false section. But she couldn't get it straight in her head—the cold night and

Chapter Fourteen

her sick stomach and the tile floor of the restroom in the BART station, Coffee's barking, the knife in her backpack.

The dam in her throat broke, but instead of words what rasped from her mouth was a moan, a harsh and ragged moan that stopped her from breathing until Jeff came around the table and put his hands on her shoulders.

"Stay with me here, Alyssa. We'll talk again tomorrow about this . . . the sequence of events. You stay with me, now."

CHAPTER

15

The blackboard in the Education Unit where she was taken to meet the psychologist was only half-erased, as if the board monitor's arms weren't long enough to reach the highest writing or he'd gotten tired and had just given up. Scattered above the swipe marks of the rubber eraser were echoes of grammar school lessons: direct object, subject complement, linking verb.

Jeffrey Earle had warned her the pencil test would be long, she shouldn't feel rushed, just follow directions and work through all the questions. When she sat waiting for the psychologist to be ushered into the room, she took comfort from the blackboard's vestigial messages, from the familiar rows of student desks bolted to the floor like props in a stage play whose script she knew inside and out. "You can do this, Alyssa," Jeffrey liked to say when he ended their conferences, the late afternoons in the tube that had become a sundial for measuring the dark days following her arraignment.

When the psychologist, looking like a lost twin to Gran, entered the classroom, Alyssa started to believe Jeffrey's prediction. "Dr. Cantrell," the psychologist said, sliding between the rows of lecture chairs to offer Alyssa her knobby hand. She wore a navy blue skirt and a lumpy, hand-knit cardigan sweater embroidered with absurdly colored farm animals, dancing blue pigs and flying red cows, the at-ease uniform of a kindergarten teacher. Her legs were slender, smooth and shapely as a teenager's, a white pump on her left foot, its match in navy blue on her right.

Alyssa rose to take her hand. Gently tugging at their handshake, Dr. Cantrell asked, "Why don't we move to the table, there, Miss Staton. You can spread out. Then we'll both be more comfortable." Facing her, Alyssa saw that Dr. Cantrell was taller than Gran; she and the psychologist met eye-to-eye. Had she ever stood head-high with Gran before the strokes had lamed her, then left her bedridden so Alyssa had to sit on a stool by her bed, leaning her face into Gran's ear for their nightly reading sessions? She couldn't remember what favorites she'd chosen to read. Pearl Buck? *A Tree Grows in Brooklyn*? The failure of recall made her anxious, evoking the blankness striking her just before an essay exam, the split-second of self-doubt gripping her before reclaimed knowledge flooded the lined pages of her bluebook. She thought of Jeffrey, his promise to stay with her if she would stay with him. She thought of Leah, the flush of pride when Alyssa had handed her the SAT scores. Ninety-fifth percentile. Verbal and mathematic. Good enough for any Ivy League.

When the handshake loosened and she glanced down, distracted from doubt by the mismatched pumps, Dr. Cantrell gave a fluttery laugh. Alyssa started, "Did you know—"

"Oh, yes, I've been doing it for years and years." Dr. Cantrell smiled and settled her black nylon bag on the table, where she motioned to Alyssa to sit. "Just something I do to . . . to keep myself . . . oh, human."

Alyssa sat, slid her chair against the table, locked her slippered feet against each other. She listened hard to the simple instructions Dr. Cantrell gave in her animated voice: 500 items, true false, go with your first answer, no time limit.

"Any questions for me?" Dr. Cantrell said when she'd finished the instructions and pulled a book from her bag, a hardcover jacketed in blue and aqua, the same designer colors the architects had chosen for the jail. Maybe Dr. Cantrell was as premeditated about color-coding her reading material as she was about the mismatched pumps, invoking a crazy sanity with the deliberate choices.

"How long does—will this take? My mother comes in the afternoon."

"You're seeing your mother today?"

"Yes, I . . . yes." Go, go, Joey had told her on last week's Monday, just returned from his bimonthly HIV screening, when Ostrom announced that her mother was back. She'll keep coming, Joey predicted, accurately. See her, Jeffrey Earle had said. It's going to help you do what we need to do, Alyssa. Grateful for her mother's intentionally displaced afternoon small talk—Coffee's walks and Clara's dinners and the potted pink cyclamen Leah'd bought to bloom on the apartment window sill—Alyssa's afternoons had grown thick with expectation, her anticipation of Leah's voice on the grimy tube telephone fueled by a stuttering, unexpressed gratitude.

"Can I let her know? So she doesn't drive from Berkeley for nothing, if I haven't finished?"

"We'll watch the clock. She usually comes when?"

"About four." In the dead time between lunch and dinner, when the cell grew too small for Alyssa's thoughts. She'd set the regular time for the visits. Leah had agreed with a single wry reference to their untested survival strategies: *it isn't exactly as if we have anywhere else to be.*

"The guard outside will go with you to a phone. I'll let you know, say, at two? Does that give you time to reach her?"

"Yes. Thanks."

"Any other questions?"

"No, I—can I ask you if I think of one?"

"Yes, of course. I'll be here . . . reading my book-of-the-month. She displayed the cover to Alyssa: a swimming pool, two floating figures. "You can start now." She opened her book, then looked up at Alyssa. "If we get thirsty . . . or something . . . we can ask the officer."

Chapter Fifteen

"Okay." Alyssa picked up her pencil, straightened the scantron beside the thick test booklet. "Thank you . . . Dr. Cantrell."

Dr. Cantrell gave her Gran's nod. *Go on, honey. Do your best.*

At first the questions were easy. She kept her head down, her pencil poised, alert to the correspondence of the digits beside the scantron bubble to the digits of the question she was reading. On some assertions she slowed, the sharp true/false distinctions growing bleary, the arbitrary cutoff between truth and falsity frustrating.

It takes a lot of argument to convince some people of the truth. Argument about what? Capital punishment? Yes, she could argue that, but where were the proofs to be found? In the antiseptic linguistic acrobatics of philosophy class? In the boxy, closed quarters of a dry cell, confinement to General Population except for chain-up and visits to the tube, or walk-arounds in outdoor yards walled by basalt blocks reaching so high they shadowed what little winter sun found its way through the persistent fog? Argument about what? Arguments about her college major, Leah's insistence on Alyssa's declaration of Art, when all she could hear was the subtext of her mother's refrain: *be like me, be an artist.* Convincing whom? She bubbled, blackening the circle for true.

Sometimes some unimportant thought will run through my mind and bother me for days. The moccasins. She'd bought them in January at the table on Telegraph, the leather goods table manned by the aged hippie couple who told her, take your time, yes, each pair handmade, graying old longhairs sitting on white plastic lawn chairs behind the card table, eye level with her swollen belly distending the baggy cotton pants. You like the white ones? Darling, aren't they. Twenty-two dollars. She'd paid with cash, her own money saved from the job at Alfredo's. Were the moccasins unimportant? She bubbled: false.

My parents and family find more fault with me than they should. Family. Leah had delivered Dennis's message: call me, Lyssa. Call me and

247

Baby's Breath

Missy, any time of the day or night. He had only ever praised her in his muddled, proud, out-of-touch way, so she couldn't make the phrase, *finding fault*, apply to him. Until now she had always been his talented, quiet, long-distance daughter. Easy enough for him, even now, to overlook faults in a person he rarely saw. She didn't deserve his blind approval; she couldn't bring herself to dial his number, inviting his undeserved support with her collect call. It seemed Leah, Leah who'd flown three thousand miles but couldn't touch her, even Leah was backing off from the fault-finding mission of her first few visits. Maybe it was the distortion of the tube and the glass wall, the telephone and the waiting guard, her own stifled yearning which made Alyssa feel that her mother had stopped wanting to push her into some place, some thing, some body that she wasn't. She rewrote the question in her mind. *My parents and family should fault me more than they do.* She found the same satisfaction there she took from pressing her thumb against her bruises until tears leaked from her squeezed-shut eyes. And then turned the question inside and out and back to the letters on the test booklet, answering the question as it was written, False.

I often feel as if things were not real. Easy answer there. Sometimes, lying on the thin mattress in her cell, listening to the murmured conversation of the guards making night count, she could barely make herself believe she was in jail with Jack-o-Lantern and the pocky woman and the crack addicts. Joey was somebody she'd made up, like a sprite or a good goblin. Her mother's face, broken in two by the distortion of the glass wall between them. Was Leah real if Alyssa's hands couldn't reach her, couldn't hook themselves around Leah's neck in a fit of wretched urgency uttering the solace of a single word, *Mama*? Wasn't it unreal that the dozen moments she'd wanted to crawl into her mother's lap, she'd been stopped by glass and her own inability to say what she felt, wasn't that unreal? And *often*, did that mean this month, or always before, or forever from now on?

I sweat very easily even on cool days. True, true, true. Even now, across

248

the table from Dr. Cantrell, lost in her book, her white shoe bobbing at the end of her crossed leg, Alyssa's hand left a damp imprint on the test booklet. And every time Jack-o-Lantern sidled past her, before meals or on the way to the shower, Alyssa went cold then hot waiting for the whispers that came more and more often, rising like the dark chorus in the musical of Dr. Faustus she'd seen with Howie at the Berkeley Rep. Once, raising herself from the lunch meal, tray in hand, she'd felt the bite of a bony knee driven into her thigh. Her tray had tipped, the plastic plate holding her untouched hamburger slid to the floor. *Eating off the floor, now, college girl,* the whisper behind her head when she bent to pick up the spewed pickle and lettuce, to blot the stain left on the carpet by the dressing from the meat patty, mayonnaise or mucous, she hadn't eaten it anyway. Could eat hardly anything, the sweat coming on like fevered nausea. True.

At times I have very much wanted to leave home. She let her pencil rest on the true bubble. She had left home twice now, first Philadelphia, then Dwight Way. But she hadn't wanted to leave the second time; the second time the leaving had happened by default. It was hard to tell if choosing Cal had been about leaving something old or going to something new. She couldn't really separate them. Didn't growing up and going to college mean that you wanted to leave home? Then true would be the right answer. But if the question were asking about the second time, her exodus the night when, well then, she hadn't desired that or chosen it, which made the answer false.

"Miss Staton?" Dr. Cantrell's aqua book was closed, index finger marking her place. "Bubble the answer that appears true upon first reading."

Alyssa looked at the clock. It had been nearly an hour, yet she was only working question seventy-eight. "Am I going too slowly?"

"You need not belabor the questions. The first response is generally the, uh, *true* one." Dr. Cantrell gave her fluttery laugh, pleased by her pun.

"But sometimes these questions seem . . . I mean sometimes they're true *and* false at the same time, I can't—"

"As I explained earlier, you want to select the response that is most typically descriptive of your behavior or attitude. Most typically doesn't have to mean always."

She'd speed up, then, and stop quarreling with the semantics. *There seems to be a lump in my throat most of the time.* True. *I like to go to parties and other affairs where there is lots of loud fun.* False. *Much of the time my head seems to hurt all over.* True. *I have never been in trouble with the law.* False.

I have had periods in which I carried on activities without knowing later what I had been doing. Tell me what happened, Alyssa, Jeffrey Earle would say, settling into his listening position, long legs outstretched, when he began their conferences. And she had told him the best she could, though every detail was like pulling her foot from quicksand, the slow strain of muscle threatening to tear and leave her sinking. So it was true, wasn't it, that she'd had periods—San Francisco, Dara fading and reappearing like an apparition—when she had not known what she was doing, when she'd lost herself in conflations of time and place whose red fragments of memory taunted her like flags.

Much of the time I feel as if I have done something wrong or evil. The statement caught her by surprise, like a voice projected from behind the curtains in Oz. The dulled pencil was slick between her fingers; she had to put it down, wipe her hands along her thighs. Dr. Cantrell glanced up, then looked back at her book and turned the page. Failing people, that was wrong. Lying, too. Yes, she felt as if she had done something wrong. Unbidden, Coffee came to mind, his slathering, constant affection. What he must be thinking in his dog thoughts, abandoned and forgotten. Could he feel the same kind of lonely hunger that took hold of Alyssa when Leah left the tube after their visits? Yesterday when Leah had turned, saved one tearful backward glance for the moment of their forced parting, Alyssa had done the same. As the impatient guard spooned the keys and chains in his pocket, she turned back to her mother, torn by uneasy longing, by the tension formalizing their parting: *what she'd done wrong* the starchy stiffness they had yet to iron out.

It was wrong of her to abandon Coffee, but evil, evil came from somewhere else. What they'd said she'd done, that could only be evil, leaving a baby to die, bleed to death, *exsanguinate*. No wonder Leah's eyes, searing her like brands in the uneasy silences subverting their visits, held something back. *You haven't told me everything.* Even though they'd all told her again and again, even Jeffrey had told her, she couldn't picture it yet: the baby wrapped in Gran's initials, the lightly layered paper towels, the bloody smears in the restroom at the BART station. That was evil, that had to be, yet somehow, still, it wasn't Alyssa Staton who had done that.

I don't seem to care what happens to me. The shower room, after dinner, two days ago. She had brushed her teeth and pulled the rubber band—Joey's treat: a coated green one made for hair—from the thick loose pile at the back of her neck. The first hit, a fist meeting her breastbone, set her down square on the damp tile floor of the open shower. The second blow, this time a foot, slippered but rigid, caught her in the stomach. After that, she didn't count, just fixed her open eyes on the strange can-can performed by the pairs of orange clad legs, the up-and-down lift of the knees, the awful grace of the slippered feet moving in and out, in and out. She didn't care then, didn't even cradle her head because it would have required a volition she couldn't master. They were careful not to bruise her face or her arms, and that too became part of her not caring because she couldn't see how it would change anything if she were to show the bruises on her belly or the latticed swelling on her back to Ostrom. Joey found them, patting her too hard during one of their reading sessions with Louis L'Amour. He'd tried to make her care enough to tell, but that didn't work, either. She imagined the next time: receptive, unfolding herself, blooming for the kicking ballet. *Baby Killer.*

251

Baby's Breath

"Miss Staton?"

"Um?" She'd laid down the pencil, lost her count on the questionnaire.

"It's nearly two." Dr. Cantrell rose and knocked against the classroom door. She mumbled to the guard, then stretched both arms above her head. When the guard took Alyssa from the room, the psychologist's modest calisthenics, the lifting of arms and twisting of torso, made Alyssa think of kindergarten, recesses, rainy day physical education, Leah's open arms at the end of the morning.

At the pay phone mounted on the wall outside the education classroom, she dialed her own number collect, didn't hear the phone ring even once, just Leah's voice, subdued, "Hello?"

"Mom?"

Warmer, softer, as if hers was the call Leah'd been waiting on. "Honey, what is it—have they . . ."

"It's nothing, Mom, except I'm taking this test, this psychological profile, and I won't be done by four. I didn't want you to drive in."

"Oh, Allie, should I come later? After dinner?"

"If you want, Mom." A heartbeat of hope.

"Do you want me to come then, sweetheart? *Do you* ?"

I don't seem to care what happens to me. As soon as she hung up the phone, she would ask Cantrell if she could sharpen her pencil. Then she would bubble in *false*, a dark bullet, an unblinking eye.

"I do, Mom." What she couldn't say: *Mama.*

She understood the psychiatrists were reporting to the different attorneys like opposing spies. Jeffrey had explained that she was to answer the questions as honestly as she could, no matter who was doing the asking. The prosecution's gangly silk-suited woman doctor made her think of an oddly elegant female Ichabod Crane, and though Alyssa made a point of facing her directly, at least when she was certain she knew the answers, the woman had seemed more deeply intrigued by the erasings on the blackboard than by Alyssa's story. Except when Alyssa faltered. Fingering the lapel of one of the many dark jackets whose only deviation from its predecessor was a change in color, dark blue to black, the psychiatrist would lean across the table as though she were the magnet and Alyssa the iron filings of memory she was intent on attracting.

Today it was Dr. Stojanovic—a really nice guy, Jeffrey'd said—who sat across from her at the table in the familiar classroom of the Education Unit. After the sessions with the social worker and the prosecution doctors and the evening meetings with Jeffrey and the tutoring time she spent with Joey before his basic skills class, she'd begun to think of it as *her* classroom, a world apart from the General Population where the Jack-o-Lantern flickered in and out of sight like a shadow-puppet silhouetted by flames. In GP, at meals or in her cell, in the television opiate after dinner, she lost the cord she was using, rope-burned hand over hand, to pull herself up from the well of silence. In the classroom, she felt she had the answers, or, bracing herself against the pain of the ropes stripping her palms, at least that she could find them.

Dr. Stojanovic looked at her straight on with twinkling dark eyes beneath wild, wiry silver eyebrows. He'd stood a full head shorter than Alyssa when he'd risen to greet her after she entered the classroom, paperclips and a pencil dropping from his straightened lap and rebounding against the linoleum floor. His voice boomed like a big man's, though, and it and the sparkle of his eyes made her think of an unkempt, offseason, seventy-year-old Saint Nicholas.

"Good morning, good morning. Miss Staton?"

"Yes, but nobody—"

"—calls you miss, of course they wouldn't, not in this day and age. It's Alyssa, then?" He pulled a chair back for her, sweeping the air with a gesture more graceful than comical despite his stature, indicating she should sit.

Baby's Breath

She sat.

"I'm Dr. Stojanovic, as you know. Your attorney, Jeffrey Earle, would have told you this, yes?"

"Yes." Just answer the obvious questions, she thought. Can't go wrong there.

"I know it feels strange ... these interviews. And sometimes the questions are very hard. You're a college student?"

Alyssa nodded. They always began with the obvious, as though they could trip her up on some blatant point of fact and then be able to say, as Jeffrey warned her the district attorney would: *See? She's lying.*

"I imagine it's very hard, all these questions, what is happening." He paused, letting the words sift through the air and settle like dust motes.

"Yes," she said finally, uneased by the long silence.

"Do you know who I am?"

"You're Dr. Stojanovic. You're the psychiatrist for the ... for my defense."

"Yes. Do you know why I'm here?"

"You need to make a report on me, on my ... state of mind."

"Yes. Do you understand that what we speak of will be nonconfidential, that I'll be making this report for the court which will be available to both your defense attorney and the prosecution?"

"Yes."

Do you know what day it is, she predicted. *Who is president?* Dr. Stojanovic wore rubber bands around his wrists, like punk bracelets or memory triggers for chores too often forgotten. Or maybe, she thought more gently, he'd slipped them there after removing them from the file folders that sat catty-cornered on the table in front of him.

"Do you know what holiday we're approaching?" he asked.

"St. Patrick's Day."

"And it is?"

"March 17." She watched him watching her, the wiry, out-of-control eyebrows raised. "Next Wednesday."

254

Chapter Fifteen

"Thanks, Alyssa. I appreciate your putting up with these silly formalities." Again his smile made her think of Santa Claus, Christmas morning, unopened presents. "Count backwards from one hundred by sevens, please."

"One hundred, ninety-three, eighty-six, seventy-nine—"

"Good enough, good enough, thanks." He opened a folder and scanned its pages. "I notice Dr. Cantrell didn't do an I.Q. test." He waited for her, as if she might be able to explain Dr. Cantrell's omission, then went on. "She rarely leaves that out! You must be very smart indeed!"

He was babying her. "She knew I had honors at entrance at Cal. You know, too, don't you?"

"You've caught me out." He marked the notes inside the folder with his finger. "Honors student. History major. 4.0."

She shrugged. What she wanted to do was jump and run, but then Dr. Stojanovic would record that, too, and tuck his observations into the file with the Rorschach results and the Thematic Aperception Test answers. "I'm flunking now. You'd know that, too."

"Withdrawn, I believe. Not flunking. You have to fail to flunk."

"Same difference."

"A blessing or a curse?" he asked, stepping over her petulance.

"What?"

"Being gifted . . . being smart. I would think it might be a little of both, at different times and in different circumstances."

"Are you smart when school is easy, when you don't have to try very hard?" She could ask questions, too, since she was such a smart girl, a college girl.

"What do you think? How would you answer that?"

She paused. He wouldn't let her off the hook like the spindly prosecution shrink who'd been so intent on her own kind of detection that she hadn't listened to silence, had overlooked how the half-shaped answer built with the wrong words can speak its own kind of truth. Dr.

Baby's Breath

Stojanovic was mining Alyssa, the real Alyssa, not the penciled notes stacked in file folders, snapped tight with rubber bands.

At first she talked hesitantly, withholding. If you cut the insides out of a story, you could check if someone was really listening. She'd known this from way back, from the beginning of memory. When she'd been small, nestled against Leah's breast at bedtime, her mother's hand outstretched across her lips to stifle a series of yawns, Alyssa had learned to listen for the skipped passages in *Pooh* or *Stuart Little*, her mother's sly omissions used like litmus paper to measure the degree of Alyssa's sleepiness and mark when she could lower the book and turn out the light. Alyssa would hear the break in narrative, always, and she'd take the book in her own hands and read, not yet fully decoding the words on the paper pages but from memory. Leah would fall back against the pillows, chastised but laughing. *Can't fool you, you smarty pants.*

She couldn't fool Dr. Stojanovic, either.

Can you tell me a little more about that?

And that was fairly satisfying, was it?

It sounds as if there's more there than what you've told me.

So, since Dr. Stojanovic passed the test—he heard every single ellipsis and insisted she backtrack, no fair to condense—she stopped editing and began to talk, really talk, about her life before jail. About reading and writing, how math had never been a mystery for her as it had for Sharon. About Professor Miller's honors seminar, the way Miller let her students speak through their arguments without interrupting. Watching Dr. Stojanovic's expressive face, hearing her own voice describing her classes at Cal, she recalled the walk from Wheeler Hall down to University Avenue, the swaths of shadows cast against the long lawns by the setting sun beyond the eucalyptus trees. She missed school. This awareness sturdied her, as if she'd been suddenly cinched by a seatbelt locked in the sharp stab of brakes. She'd liked school for its own pleasure and for nothing else. She'd been proud of her smartness; she'd deserved those grades because of her own hard work. She could tell Dr.

Chapter Fifteen

Stojanovic, the words tripping against each other in their eagerness, all about studying and grades and the rewards—yes, the blessings—of smartness.

When Dr. Stojanovic rose and extended his small hand to signal the end of the session, she'd wanted him to stay, to let the soft rise and fall of his questions walk her through her whole life. He'd be back, he said. They'd talk again. Pick up where they'd left off. Following the guard back to GP, the smell of the evening meal rising like the spoil of fallen fruit, she wondered where that place was, where she'd left off.

CHAPTER

16

Leah stopped at Clara's as she took Coffee out for his walk of the day. "Might you want to have dinner with me tonight?"

"That would be nice," Clara said, framed in her doorway. "I'm serving at the Shelter tonight, though. I don't usually get home until after seven."

"Seven thirty?" Leah said. "I don't mind waiting. I could get us some fish on the way home."

"Nice," Clara said again. "I could make up a batter before I leave this morning, if you want."

Often Clara already had plans; Leah was pleased she'd come. Hard as it was to talk, the silence of the nights was sometimes harder. "I've got salad stuff and I'll get some baguettes, too. That good French bakery is close to the fish market," she said.

"My, my," Clara chortled. "Just turning me into a yuppie, aren't you? My Eddie would surely turn over." She pointed at the dog with her chin because her hands were busy with a big spoon and a metal mixing bowl. "After he's done outside, come on back here. I've got bran muffins about to go in. I'll make us a pot of coffee."

"Great." Leah's forced burst of conversational energy faltered, and the dead air got too long, though it never seemed to bother Clara. "Hey, aren't muffins awfully yuppie? What happened to cornbread? And thank you for referring to me as young. But I've got to get set-up; I can't

Chapter Sixteen

lollygag all morning." Lollygag. She'd picked up the word from Clara, but it had been her mother's, too. When Clara first used it, Leah had felt a flush of recognition, as if Clara had been wearing Esther's polyester bright knit pants and white sneakers instead of black wool slacks and flats.

"I know. You've got to eat, though. You come have a bite, then I'll keep that monster so he doesn't unpack your paints faster n' you. I'm home this morning. He still likes to drag things out, doesn't he? I caught him chewing on my underwear the other day." She pointed with her thumb over her shoulder, toward the back of the apartment. "I forgot to shut the bathroom door and the little devil got into my laundry basket." Sometimes Coffee stayed at Clara's; she'd come to like the company, she said.

As if he'd recognized himself as the subject, the dog started off after a calico cat foolish enough to cross Coffee's parking lot. Leah was jerked back though the open door onto the landing.

"Drags all kinds of stuff, including me." Leah said. "Send a search party if I'm not back in four days." The Lab, glossy and sleek-muscled, panted hoarsely against the leash as he stretched Leah's arm by straining for the stairs.

Send a search party, Leah mused on her own words as Coffee settled into a steady pull on the sidewalk, eager for the park, for freedom. *Like you did for Allie. They're Search and Rescue parties, though.* Allie was found, but not rescued. The air felt like March, even like March in Philadelphia, breezy, a little wet, a little raw, but softening toward the first chartreuse fuzz on tree branches. Leah missed her life, but most of the time she was too distracted to identify the homesickness gnawing at her insides.

She was cycling into a diurnal rhythm now, thanks to predictable tasks: walking Coffee three or four times a day, morning work in the apartment and afternoon visits to Allie, a pattern emerging out of chaos like a quilt seen from a distance. Jeffrey Earle hadn't known exactly how long the psychiatric examinations would go on, but daily visiting hours didn't start until two o'clock anyway. Leah had asked Cory to box and send certain tools and brushes. The rest of what she needed to set up a basic studio—like the one she'd had for years in the rowhouse basement—she'd ordered out of the Italian Art Store catalog. Two boxes had arrived yesterday, and a crate that held the unfinished Bradshaw commission painting. Maybe work would anchor her again, along with the familiarity her days were taking on. She'd already spent nearly two weeks sparking Allie's apartment to life.

She kept everything Allie had in place, only added. A double mat, rich cream over blue, around the Mary Cassat mother and child print. She'd done it herself at a framing shop while she resolutely thought only of Allie and herself, not the dark-haired baby that swam into her dreams. Painted ceramic pots for Allie's plants. And she hadn't killed the jade yet. Scatter rugs in kitchen and bathroom and a fringed off-white rug over the dull apartment carpet in the living room. She'd found a moon and stars mobile for a dull corner, small green and cream pillows for corners of the couch. Hanging plants, one over the kitchen sink, cascading ivy in front of the window over the parking lot. Simple paisley curtains that included the blue of the couch and the neutral carpet tone but then startled and pleased the eye with ivy green and off white. New towels. Allie definitely needed new towels. *And no damn monograms on these*, she'd thought, and then was ashamed.

She didn't hurry through Clara's muffins, fragrant and crammed with raisins and walnuts and pineapple, but she didn't lollygag either. Another thing to feel bad about: how good it felt to slit open the boxes and set up a painting area by the smaller window. She used the pass-through to the kitchen as a shelf for her paints and the fresh bottle of Turpenoid she'd bought downtown. It was makeshift, but it would do. She'd had to buy an easel and palette, of course—they would have been too much for Cory to dismantle, but she'd donate them to Clara's shelter when this was over.

When this was over. How rarely she let the notion take on light. It was safer to leave it alone, like an undeveloped negative.

She used a knife to slit the professional crating on the Bradford piece. Cory had taken it to a professional packer. The commission was already overdue and she couldn't expect George to keep making excuses for her. Did everyone back home know? Had they seen her on the news, in the newspaper? The reporters weren't camped in the parking lot anymore. They'll be back, Jeffrey Earle warned her. They're just taking a break until the trial.

The trial. Leah had trouble wrapping her mind around the idea of a trial, around how adamant Allie was about keeping the public defender even though the verdict would be the fulcrum of her life now. Leah tried to make it small, the far distance, and kept her eyes on the foreground where details could distract and fuel her. Dennis had blamed Leah for Jeffrey Earle until he flew in for a weekend and ran into the same wall, Allie's will. "She likes him, Dennis," Leah said when they met for dinner at a quiet Chinese restaurant, "and I have to admit I see why. But I don't know what's best. I'm basically in agreement with you, but what can we do?"

"Look, I'm sorry. I'm glad you're here with her. This is a bad time for me to be away from home. It's pretty emotional for Missy, too, what with a newborn . . . it's unthinkable. . . ." Dennis kept the full heft and weight of his wife's reaction undefined. Leah could imagine, though; she'd read some of the hate mail delivered to Allie's box. She thought of the feel of a newborn, how her floppy shape molds to your chest, her skull fits in the shepherd's crook of your neck, her milky breathing.

"Yes." Leah had said. "It was good of you to come."

Now, the easel in place, she wrestled with the crate holding the painting. Large, awkward, heavier than she expected, Leah had to lay it flat and slit three edges. Then she understood why. Cory had taken it on herself to send the unfinished painting of Allie, too, along with the sketches off her bulletin board tucked into a big manila envelope. Leah pulled them out. Her pregnant daughter looked back at her, graceful, sad, unfinished.

The sessions with Dr. Stojanovic were broken by the span of weekends, breaks that had seemed to last forever for Alyssa. She'd tried to keep her meetings with the psychiatrist private, dodging the whispered epithets in GP. *Little rich bitch. Baby killer. Psychopath.* They hated her first because of what she'd done; now they hated her doubly because she was, by virtue of Dr. Stojanovic's attention, made special.

Curious and edgy, as if he thought she'd been unfaithful, Joey picked at what went on between her and the psychiatrist, but she found she could say little to him. What she spoke of with Dr. Stojanovic she just couldn't speak of with Joey, not in the same way. Joey wouldn't make fun, it wasn't that. With Dr. Stojanovic, their talks dipped back and forth from childhood in Philadelphia to the present in California with the lazy, reductive swing of a plumb bob. With Joey, where the hook of memory didn't reach the eye of meaning, her recollections came out spoiled, childish, begrudging. But he kept at her, nagging at it during their reading and writing time, pretending to see words like *psychiatry* and *therapy* when the printed page said *please* and *thank you* until she'd come close to losing patience. "I'm not *in* therapy," she snapped. "Let's play poker then, if you're not even going to try to remember the words."

Today Dr. Stojanovic was waiting for her when she entered the classroom, his hands folded on the tabletop. Like him, they were small and pudgy. His ring finger was banded by a thick circle of plain gold topped with a red stone. The ring reminded her of mood rocks, the tables on Telegraph whose goods remained faithful to the psychedelic sixties. Tie-dyed T-shirts. Ribbon-wrapped bundles of stick incense. Hand-

Chapter Sixteen

shaped silver hoop earrings. Moccasins. Feathers and baskets, Indian dreamcatchers.

"How are you sleeping?"

"Not so well." He watched her, attentive. She'd flawed the design, tripped him up with an unmatched thread. She'd always said *okay, okay, okay* to the questions he used like handshakes, his ritual inquiries about sleeping and eating and even bathroom habits that left her self-conscious, made her want to hide the body she was living in, to drape its emerging hip bones and ribs with flannel shirts and sweatpants.

"A change in pattern?"

Alyssa considered: true/false, which way to turn? If she said yes, she'd have to confess she hadn't yet described to him the sleeplessness plaguing her, the long nights she spent cornered on her mattress, her arms strapped around her bent knees. If she said no, if she refused the doctor's patient inquiry, her refusal would become one more part of herself left inexplicable, one more shadow coming sideways at her in the predawn turmoil. Dr. Stojanovic waited, unreadable. "Big change," she mumbled.

"Your inability to sleep now is a big change from before, from childhood?"

"Not childhood," she corrected him, then saw that was what he wanted, how he worked. She was to find her own mistakes and fix them, like changing *who* to *whom* in an error recognition test. "From college . . . before."

"You slept well in college."

"My freshman year . . . I slept . . . a lot."

"Ten hours a day? Fourteen? Can you tell me how much?"

She was good at math. "Sixteen, maybe . . . between classes I'd sleep. Long nights I'd sleep." She winced. "My roommate's boyfriend, he used to call me the goddess of nepenthe."

"Ah. Anything else?"

"Did he call me anything else?"

"That, or, anything else about your sleeping habits, their change."

"He called me fat." She twisted her hands, working the skin in a gesture that surprised her with unfamiliarity. "They all called me fat. And yes, I slept way too much. It was—"

"It was an escape?"

She shook her head. Not escape. Sleep was obstinance, denial, refusal. Passive aggression against Tricia and Marc Raymond, against Cindy's unceasing cheeriness. She let the silence lie for her.

Dr. Stojanovic had seen something, a shard, the glint of metal. He kept digging. "The names must have been hurtful. For you. How did that make you feel then?"

"I felt . . . abandoned."

"Oh." He didn't show surprise. She knew she'd given him a non sequitur, the wrong word landing in the blank space like a flat note.

"Abandonment . . . your roommate then, had abandoned you by letting her boyfriend criticize?" He would tie the frayed laces of this knot himself, eventually. Or she could tie them for him.

"Look. I know where you're going. My parents divorced. My dad was barely around. My mom had to work. My grandmother died and my mother didn't take me to school like everybody else's. So I ate too much, and they called me fat. He was an idiot, anyway. Is that enough?"

Dr. Stojanovich was watching her as though every word were a jewel, a bright and rare felicity of speech. "The boyfriend. He was the idiot?"

"Yes."

He pushed his chair back from the table and stood. He stretched his small hands as if he were a pianist or a surgeon preparing for duty, then rested them on the metal chairback. "Can't sit for too long at a time, anymore. Might not be able to rise again." His chuckle soothed her, distanced her from the muffled clang and bang of the jail beyond, what she'd grown to think of as the constant shaking of a giant cage.

Chapter Sixteen

Watching his hands on the rungs of his chair, her muscles tensed like the clamps of a vise against her shoulders, she imagined Dr. Stojanovic circling the table until he stood behind her. She imagined his hands light on her shoulders, his short, strong fingers working at the collarbones that poked through her skin, unfamiliar bones that she'd never known she had until jail had thawed her flesh like sorrow.

"Your analysis is both enough and not enough, Alyssa," he said.

Because his voice was like strong fingers finding her own bones, because he nodded without judgment no matter what she said, she lengthened the story, letting the low vowels of his murmurs massage the words from her throat, telling her when to steer straight, when to round a corner. She talked about Gran and she talked about Leah; she talked about Dennis and Cindy and Tony. She talked about Clara and the untaken photograph given to her by Clara's hands. She talked about Ostrom and Joey. She talked until her mouth grew dry and Dr. Stojanovic patted her on the hand and told her, as she was counting on him to do, "More the next time, Alyssa. More the next time."

Jeffrey Earle had asked to talk with Leah once she'd met with the defense psychiatrist, Dr. Stojanovic.

"So what did you think of him?" he asked. They were in Jeff's office. McGeorge Law School? Leah tried to read the city and year on the hanging diploma, but the print was too small. Undergraduate from Cal in 1973. At least she knew that one. He certainly seemed to know the law, but so much was riding on how he guided Allie. He toyed with an intricate model dinosaur on his desk, where files spewed in every direction.

Leah itched to straighten out Jeffrey's desk, the way she used to occasionally attack Cory's when she couldn't stand it any longer. "Dr. Stojanovic? I ... don't know. He looked sort of silly, I mean, his tie was tucked into his pants, and I first thought he was sort of a sweet teddy bear who wouldn't be too swift. ..."

"But then?" Jeff seemed to know where she was going. His coat was off, hung on a hook next to the door, one sleeve rolled higher than the other, and his tie loosened, though it wasn't tucked in his pants. Leah hoped she wasn't being tactless.

"Yes, well, right. Then somehow I found myself remembering things I hadn't thought of for years. I thought I'd dredged up every minute of our lives."

"Good."

"He said he might want to talk to me again."

"That okay?"

"Well, sure. I just wish he'd answer some questions instead of asking them. Not to be defensive, but I wonder if he thinks I was a bad mother. If he's going to say that." She met Jeff's eyes. "I know I made mistakes, I've tried and tried to think of. . . ." It was happening again, the same as when she met with the psychiatrist, the wild back and forth pendulum in her head swinging from defending to blaming herself.

Jeff interrupted her with an upraised palm. "Don't go there," he said. "It won't help either one of you, and kids don't come with an instruction manual. You make it up as you go along . . . you do the very best you can, right?"

"Yeah," Leah whispered, rummaging in her purse for a tissue. Jeff figured out what she was after and reached to the credenza behind him to pull one from a box.

"So just keep right on doing that," he said. "It'll be more than good enough."

"Okay," she said. "Okay."

He left a little silence as if to let a door close from its own weight. "How does she seem to you?"

"Better. I mean she looks a lot better, don't you think? She's thin—very thin for Allie—and, it's strange, it's like she's turned. . . ."

"Beautiful?"

"Yes. It sounds wrong to say, I don't know why."

266

Chapter Sixteen

"I've noticed that, too," Jeff said. "Has she said anything, though, about the other inmates? I've been concerned they might be giving her a bad time."

"No," Leah said. She reconsidered, then repeated, "No. I don't think so. She hadn't said anything, and she's not typically slow to speak up if she thinks she's being wronged."

"*If* she thinks she's being wronged . . ." Jeff said, letting it fade without a conclusion. "Well, I wanted to check if she's said anything to you. And there's one more thing." He looked uncomfortable as he re-rolled the longer sleeve of his blue shirt. Jeff's eyes looked the same heightened color. She calculated how to mix the shade, nearly cornflower just slightly grayed.

"What?"

Jeff took a breath. "The coroner has released the baby's body. If you want to claim it, you can. I'd talk this over with Alyssa, but since it would fall to you, I thought I should mention it."

Leah didn't answer, didn't have an answer. She felt herself stare at him as if to say *you're going to have to tell me what to do.* "It sounds like you don't think Allie is going to be . . . out."

"Not anytime soon."

"You can't budge her on the bail at all." It wasn't really a question. "Can you?"

Leah shook her head no. Jeff shrugged his shoulders and turned palms up to the ceiling.

"I just have to keep hoping that somehow the trial will . . . I don't know, go really well, and she'll get off . . . out." Leah felt naked. She'd always been one to act deeply rooted in whatever was logically predictable.

Jeff was already shaking his head, poking his tongue into the side of his cheek the way he did when he was frustrated, closing his eyes for much longer than a blink before he spoke. "Listen. I'd like you to be realistic. Remember the 'not guilty' plea has to do with not guilty of first degree murder. We need to focus on getting the charge down—to reduce the sentence."

"But you'll try for not guilty, right? You'll try? People are found not guilty all the time when everyone knows they did it. Like. . . ."

"This is different, Leah."

"How?" she demanded, the word sparking on the flint of her tongue. "Exactly how? Because even her father and I together can't afford The Dream Team?" She leaned forward in her chair to dare him.

"Because . . . we're not denying that she did it. We're denying that she did it deliberately, with malice, with intention. If they'd charged her with negligent homicide, we'd plead guilty. That's how it's different." Jeff took a breath, and seemed to cast for how to explain it. "Negligent homicide's the same thing as manslaughter, see, it doesn't carry a mandatory sentence. Franklin isn't one to think Alyssa is a threat to society, which she's not. My guess is that he'd give her a two-year sentence, count the time she's already served, and maybe five years probation. It's why we asked for sentencing by the judge. He'll want her to use her life for something worthwhile." Jeff's throat worked, his Adam's apple rising and falling as if marking tempo. "I don't want you to set yourself up, is all. The prosecution wants a murder conviction because then the judge is hamstringed on the sentence. Or should that be hamstrung?"

Leah wanted a drink. She wished the law books listing on cheap shelves that sagged in the middle were bottles lined up on the mirrored backdrop behind a bartender instead. She wanted some soft amber whiskey that burned its way down your chest and over your brain and lent you the fire to believe what you had to. Not guilty *could* happen. Nobody had to know what she hoped.

"What should I do about the baby?" Leah was hot, sweaty in the room where the air was too close, heated by the ripening spring sun. "Any chance you could crack that window?" she said, taking off her camel blazer and twisting to hang it over the back of her chair.

"Whatever you think is right. Whatever you'd feel best about. I don't

Chapter Sixteen

know that there's exactly a formula here. You can get a casket and a cemetery plot. Or you can just *not* claim it. You don't have to."

"My father and mother were cremated," Leah said.

"Well, that's simple enough to arrange if that's what you want," he said. "Do you want to talk to Alyssa about it?"

"No." A hesitation. "I don't feel . . . like I could."

"It's up to you."

"Who do I call?" Leah said finally.

CHAPTER

17

It had started with wanting to do the right thing. Most of the time, Leah tried to keep the images out of her mind, the pictures of a baby who would be six weeks old now, whose face might have amazed a family with a first crooked gassy smile. She'd kept her mind on Allie and slowly, carefully, picked her way through their visits. But when Jeffrey Earle put the question to her, she couldn't bear the thought of the baby girl: Allie's daughter, her granddaughter abandoned twice.

She regretted it when she picked up the cardboard box of ashes, marked in black ink and circled with cotton string, from the undertaker she'd called. She'd bought a cemetery plot, paid in advance to have a grave opened and closed, ordered a white marble headstone, then faltered when asked about the engraving. "I don't know," she'd said. "Can I leave it blank? Or, wait. Just a date?" The salesperson had looked up, but retreated to his pen and form when she met his eyes.

"Yes ma'am. What dates shall we put? And you need to choose the lettering."

"Not dates. Just February 4, 1998. That's all."

"You, um, don't want a name?"

"No. No name," she'd said staring him down again. The death certificate said Infant Girl Staton. The papers called her the BART Baby. Maybe that's what he thought she should do: name the baby Bart Staton. Barta, perhaps, since it was a girl. *Stop it, Leah*, she told herself.

Chapter Seventeen

"Yes, ma'am. You let us know the date and time you'll be having the interment. If it's a private ceremony, we'll have the site opened that morning, and close the grave quick as we can that day. You leave the box there, we'll take care of it. And ma'am, I'm sorry for your loss." He couldn't have been twenty-five, Leah thought. What did this boy know, with his big Hispanic eyes made to chase women, what did he know about loss? What did Allie know? She didn't tell her mother anything real.

Leah had thought to do it alone, but again, it didn't seem right, and all she could stand was to come as close to right as she could. At dinner, she asked Clara to help her bury the baby. "It doesn't seem enough of a ceremony if it's just me. Maybe we could read something or say a prayer. Would you?"

" 'Course I'll go with you. Alyssa know about this?"

"No. This is just something I'm doing." Leah cut her chicken carefully, not meeting Clara's eyes.

"You're angry." An observation. Clara had stopped eating and spoke kindly, but the words felt like a judgment.

"Clara, she's thrown our lives—both our lives—right down the toilet." Leah glanced at her hands and then hid her paint-rimmed fingers by curling them in. She uncurled them when she realized they'd balled into fists.

"I felt that way with my boy," Clara said. "You'll get past it. You're here." What she meant was that duty had won, and of course, it had, it did, it always would.

"Yes," Leah said. "I'm here."

Two days later, she was still there. She was still there to carry the white box in two hands and pick her way between graves in the cemetery's special section for children. Some of the headstones had helium balloons attached to them. Several Tonka trucks, teddy bears and a blonde doll had been left propped against inscriptions that promised never to

271

forget. The sky was mixed and swift-moving, three dimensional clouds crisply stacked on top of a near-turquoise clarity, so at any given time Leah and Clara might be in shadow or light. Water glittered on the horizon. Leah had chosen a plot with a slice of a bay view, a distinct line, at least sometimes visible, beyond which she could imagine hope. Neither she nor Clara had worn black. Clara, in fact, had on a joyous tunic, rich with blue and gold, and a handmade dreamcatcher pendant hanging from a black cord. Leah was her tailored self, white button-down blouse, and camel blazer. She felt old, older than Clara, and empty.

She and Clara took places facing the distant water where light played, although that moment the two of them were in the shade of a cloud. Leah closed her eyes, tried to forget Clara's presence. She raised the box and pressed her lips to it. *Forgive your mother,* she whispered. Then she opened her eyes and looked straight out. "Forgive my daughter," she whispered like a prayer. "Forgive me, forgive us. Dear God, Spirit, forgive us and take this soul. Amen."

She looked over to Clara. Clara looked back and nodded yes, almost imperceptibly. Then, surprising Leah, she sang very softly in a resonant alto, while Leah knelt and set the box in front of the waiting hole. The tempo was a yearning legato, with pauses between phrases long enough to set a spirit on the back of Clara's vibrato as it floated toward sky and water.

The water's wide . . . I cannot cross. And neither have . . . I wings to fly. Give me a boat . . . that will carry two . . . and both will cross . . . to the other side. . . . As she repeated the refrain, Clara took off the dreamcatcher pendant and set it on top of the box. *Give me a boat that will carry two, and we will cross . . . to the other side.*

The slow hills of the melody were familiar as home. From her pocket, Leah drew out a picture of herself with sixteen-year-old Allie, one Sharon had snapped at Papa Jack's Spaghetti when Leah took the girls out to celebrate the end of their sophomore year. Allie had spontaneously wrapped her arms around her mother's neck just before Sharon clicked the shutter; Leah had cherished the picture in her wallet since that summer. She slipped the picture face up beneath the dreamcatcher, and stroked the box. *You're not alone*, she whispered. When Leah stood up, Clara embraced her.

Thank you, Leah said into Clara's ear. Clara nodded and rubbed Leah's back before she released her.

"Have you had any visitors this week?" Dr. Stojanovic asked, his pudgy hands trading position, left over right now. Anymore when Alyssa entered the room, he picked up quickly as if their encounters were unbroken by the intervening days. He continued to monitor her sleep, her eating, asked her each time if she were crying, then kept pursuing in his kindly, courteous way something she sensed he wanted very badly.

"You know my mother comes. Usually. In the afternoons." Alyssa shifted her ponytail behind her shoulder. It seemed to be growing heavier, her proud headful of hair. Often, combing it out after the shower or tucking it into the elastic grown frayed with constant use, she wondered what it might be like to have cropped hair, as short as Joey's, or shorter. To match the rest of her diminished self, a distillation of matter and energy. "My friend Clara comes, too."

"I've noticed that gesture before . . . your hair over your shoulder . . . I'm wondering what it means."

"You're the shrink . . . you're really asking about my mother, aren't you?"

"I'm wondering what it is like for you . . . your relationship with your mother, here, under these circumstances."

She tugged at her hair now. It was too long, too thick, too healthy. Still growing, thriving, when the rest of her was shrinking. During uniform exchange, Ostrom had studied her, then handed her a laundered bag of mediums. She was beginning to look like a scarecrow, a match to the Jack-o-Lantern. Everyone could see it: Ostrom, Joey, Clara, Leah. "I know my mom is doing . . . everything for me. She's left her whole life in Philadelphia for me. I know that."

"It sounds as if that may be something for which you feel both gratitude and a sort of resentment?"

If she could, she would let herself wither, cut her hair and flush it down the toilet, melt her flesh into a stain on the floor. "She buried the baby."

"Your mother buried the baby . . . you gave birth to."

She hung her head. No cape of hair, no hiding.

"That must have been very hard, hearing of that."

Leah's face through the glass, the tears on her own face she could see but couldn't touch. "I didn't mean to do that . . . to her."

"You didn't mean to do that to . . . the baby?"

"My mother! I didn't mean to do that to my mother!"

He'd got it wrong. She hadn't done anything to the baby.

Dr. Stojanovic looked tidier somehow, as if he'd cleaned up to apologize for misunderstanding Alyssa, for bringing up what she'd done to the baby. Maybe the neatness of his too-long silver hair was a signal for forgiveness. That might be wishful thinking; perhaps it was simply that he was standing instead of sitting when she entered the classroom, or because she had just grown so weary of the orange suits of the inmates that any variation—even the doctor's teal sweater vest and his crooked bow tie—looked formal, festive. He was interested in visitors again and didn't even play the game of posing the questions to which he'd already been given the answers by the jail computer, the in-and-out log of who'd come to see her and when.

"I see you've visited with your father." A statement, not the slightest inflection of amazement that her handsome father, the accomplished painter, the proud progenitor of sons, had flown across the continent on her behalf.

Chapter Seventeen

She'd been glad, actually, when Ostrom had announced the visitor. Leah had told her, her wan face drawn at the end of their visit, that Dennis would be coming, but Alyssa wasn't sure she believed in his presence until she saw him for herself, windblown white hair, his rangy savior's body in jeans and a Levi jacket. Straight from the airport, he'd said. He hadn't seen Leah yet. Then, in tones hushed not by the telephone but by awe or disbelief or something worse, how thin she'd grown, he wouldn't have recognized her.

"The food's not so hot," she said, joking and realizing she was going to look flip when all she wanted was to say *Daddy, I'm sorry. You don't owe me this.*

"Alyssa, we need to get you a private lawyer." Speaking even before he'd pulled out the chair to sit, leaning into the glass, the handset clenched in his hand like a hammer. "I've got people I can call—"

"No, Daddy." Stern, schoolmarmish. She wouldn't let him invest in his own solutions, they'd be so misdirected, so off-target.

"It's foolish not to!" The tightened flex of his fingers around the telephone told her he would rather fight this issue than turn to the one he was trying to bury by keeping it unspoken, *what she'd done.* Different from Leah's tactics, the secretive, creeping questioning that drew closer and closer, circling her like a noose. Dennis pitched his efforts deliberately wide of the mark, an angler casting beyond the bass breaking the surface of a still pond. She thought of their fishing trips. She remembered the quick lift and snap of the wrist he'd taught her, his hand over her smaller one on the rod that became a wand bewitched by her father's skill. The silver hooks hidden in the rainbow of flies had seemed too cruel to her when she was a child; when she'd learned to cast by herself and could make the fishing line billow through the air like a spider's web, she used to pray that the fish wouldn't bite.

"Jeffrey Earle is a really good lawyer. I like him . . . better than anybody else . . . in all this." Her hand was sticky on the receiver, her breath hot against her fingers. *I love my father.*

"He's a public defender!"

"He's *good*. He comes by nearly every day. He believes in my . . . in the . . . in defending. . . ." She was barn blind, too close to what neither of them wanted unearthed, exposed where each could see it.

"Lyssa, money can buy the best. . . ."

"No, Daddy!"

And that was that. Dennis came twice more, to talk about Missy and Caleb, an upcoming show, the Montessori school where Caleb was a star student. He was silent on his secondborn son, like a still life's white space, the silence shouting louder than the shapes. She cried when he left—she'd tell Dr. Stojanovic that—in a hot spurt of shame and longing that made her nauseous. But it would be easier to think of her father, to imagine the babies that were his sons, when he was three thousand miles away.

Dr. Stojanovic brought her back. "Alyssa? Can you tell me about his visit?"

"He wanted to hire a private attorney."

"What were your feelings about that?"

"I was—" she stopped, uncertain. Mixed was the word she wanted, a choice Dr. Stojanovic would appreciate for both its accuracy and its ambiguity. "Mixed. I don't want another attorney, so he was mad with me, but he came all the way out, and he didn't seem. . . ."

"He didn't seem upset?"

"No, he was upset. He didn't seem . . . like he wanted to disown me or anything."

"So you feel as if you have your father's support?"

"I guess." Not so sure here. When he'd left, Dennis had messed up, mentioned something Missy had said about her three men, then covered himself with words, loving, yes, but easier to say when he was leaving.

"Have you felt earlier, recently, that you were without support? In other matters perhaps, school . . . or what brings us here?"

Chapter Seventeen

She shook her head, no, no, no, she'd been supported—she'd had more goddamn support than anybody she'd ever known, except maybe Cindy Cheung.

"I'm not speaking financially, or even academically." Here is where he'd been sighted the entire session. He leaned forward. *Pugnacious*, Alyssa thought, frantic for words she could use like tarps to shroud what was coming. "Emotionally. Could you describe whether you've felt emotionally supported in the course of this . . . event . . . why we're here."

Tenacious. Voracious. Loquacious. Like blankets smothering flames. Swaddling. Suffocating.

"Alyssa. Can you tell me why we're here?"

Even with the thermal undershirt she'd asked Leah to bring, even though Dr. Stojanovic's misplaced Santa face was ruddy with warmth, she was shivering, shaking with cold, her clenched fingers brittle as if they'd been set in ice.

"Alyssa?"

"A baby died. My baby. It's dead. I let it die."

Still, always, the glass between them when Leah visited Allie. Maybe Allie wanted it like that; she assiduously avoided talking about what she'd done. Instead, she'd sometimes pass on a legal tidbit from Jeffrey Earle, or she'd talk about what she was reading with Joey. (*I'm proud of you*, Leah had said about that, then caught herself. What a ridiculous thing to say. Allie had answered with a stare and silence.) Sometimes she talked about what she'd eaten—the pasty burgers bothered her and she thought she might become a vegetarian after all—or how the television was always droning, constant and grating as construction noise. Occasionally it was even what another inmate was in for; but when Leah pressed—when the bile of her discomfort rose and she tried to discover what was inside her daughter—Allie deflected the questions as if Leah had pushed on a bruise.

277

Baby's Breath

Leah had buried the ashes on a Friday. Two days later, she sat in the back of a Catholic church for the stained glass and candles, letting the liturgy wash over her as a spirit rather than for any of the words. Then, knowing Clara was at her daughter's for the day, she'd eaten by herself at a café, and gone on to the jail. She'd not said anything to Allie about the details of the burial. Allie hadn't asked, either.

"Hi," Alyssa said into the phone on her side. She had her hair loose today, which made her look like her high school self, only thinner, her facial structure more defined. She was too pale, though it was probably the cruel lighting and the terrible orange shirt warring with Allie's skin tone.

"How you doing today, honey?" Leah said from her side of the glass.

"Okay. Bored out of my mind. Joey's getting saved at the Apostolics." A weak smile. "He thinks I should go."

There it was again. Allie really hadn't said anything bad, not even insensitive, but it struck Leah wrong. Surely Allie shouldn't be joking about being *saved*. Later, Leah would think it wouldn't really have mattered what Allie said. She was raw from the cemetery, raw from the mosaic of worry-pieces of her broken life grouted together with pain.

"Maybe that's something you should be thinking about."

"What do you mean?"

A surge of irritation waved through Leah's chest, but she held it down and consciously kept her voice neutral. "I guess it means just what I said. The obvious."

"You couldn't understand."

They just pushed out, the words. Since she'd buried the baby, they'd been pushing up from her chest, out from the inside of her head.

"There's a lot I don't understand."

"Probably," Allie said. She tucked her hair behind one of her ears, just as she used to, an utterly familiar gesture to Leah.

"How can you say that?" Leah flared.

"It's true."

Chapter Seventeen

"My god, Allie—"

Allie interrupted. "You don't even understand that I want to be called by my real name. Let's not talk about this any more, okay?"

The glass, slightly opaqued by the frustrated touch of thousands of hands on each side, didn't keep Leah from noting Allie's eyelids getting red, the deep brown of her eyes too glittery beneath a skim of water. But rather than making her back off, it inflamed her further. "You cry about being called Allie? But you won't talk about what's really going on? Allie—*Alyssa!*—you're right, I don't understand. But do *you* understand? Do you understand that this is not the same old business of 'my mother doesn't understand me'? Do you understand that what you've done isn't something people are *going* to understand?"

"I get that," Allie said. Was there a swirl of bitterness in her tone? Leah heard another criticism right beneath the surface.

"Hold on. I've been here for you every bit of the way. What are you saying?"

"Mom. I know how you feel, you've made it clear."

It was Leah who pushed it. "What have I made clear? How? I've done nothing but support you."

Allie looked away. "Sure. You brought me to college like you said you would. You got me a great lawyer."

"You didn't want another lawyer! You wanted Jeffrey Earle!"

"No, I mean right at the beginning. I was completely out of it. They stuck me in here. I was all bloody. . . ." She waved her free hand toward her abdomen and legs as if to display the stains. "Jeff *is* who I want now. But at the beginning, I was completely out of it, and I needed—"

Dennis had accused Leah on negligence on the lawyer point, too.

Leah interrupted. "You wouldn't even see me! How was I supposed to know what you needed? How was I supposed to know you hadn't talked to a lawyer? For god's sake, Allie." The truth was Leah didn't know why she hadn't, though she'd created a reason list in her mind: thought it was all a mistake, thought Allie had one, didn't know if she really wanted Allie out of jail if she'd done this. Whose responsibility would she be? The last she'd not articulated even to Clara, whose son had been in prison and who understood breathtaking disappointment, unwordable sorrow, even the angry shame. "I'm here for you. I always have been, I always will. . . ."

"You were there for Gran. You're not there for me, not like that." Allie's face twisted as it had when she was little and didn't want to cry. "But it's okay, Mom."

It was like being forgiven for robbing a store when you were the security guard who'd risked her life. Leah shoved back abruptly, the metal-legged chair rocking back precariously, then banging back down. She grabbed the shoulder strap of her purse, intending to leave before the words got out, but then she couldn't restrain herself, or just didn't.

She pounded her free hand on the table. The phone was hard against her ear, straining the leash of its elastic cording, like Coffee. "I haven't been there for you? I lied to the *police* for you! I told them I didn't recognize the towel with my own mother's monogram! I buried your baby two days ago! Were *you* there for *her*? Am I here now? Even if I don't understand, I'm here. How much more can I be here, Alyssa?" Leah kept still, staring Allie down.

The face she watched lost a fight for control. Leah watched her child break like water against rock. "I'm sorry, Mom." Allie's voice was only a little over a whisper, tears walking their old angled path from the outer corners of her eyes in toward her mouth. "Where . . . did you bury her?"

Leah gathered herself, tried to think of words. "In a section for children, Peniel Point Cemetery . . . I had her cremated, Allie. I thought that was best. They'd done the . . . autopsy and so many tests . . . Clara went with me. She sang a song."

Allie closed her eyes. "Thank you for doing that. Thank you." Still a whisper, the words sounding as if they'd passed over gravel to get out. "What did Clara sing?"

"About the water being wide, needing a boat to cross to the other side . . . It was like a prayer. We were facing the water, the horizon. And she put a dreamcatcher in the . . . grave." Leah didn't mention the picture of herself and Allie, her own gift to the baby.

"I've heard her . . . Is there a . . . could I ever see a picture? Is there a marker?"

"Yes. I mean, there will be. White marble, very simple. The way you like things."

"What does it say?" Every question was preceded by a long hesitation, like Allie was struggling to breathe.

"February 4, 1998."

"Nothing else? No . . . name? Oh god, oh Mom, I'm so sorry. I'm so sorry."

Allie's shoulders were rising and falling, though there was no sound to the sobs. Leah put the palm of her left hand on the glass, fingers spread. "Touch me, honey. Come on, put your hand up. I'm here with you. I'm here. I can have more put on the headstone later. Do you want to name your child?"

Allie opened her eyes. After another hesitation, she put her hand on her side of the glass to match Leah's and nodded yes.

CHAPTER

18

The courtroom was completely empty when Leah and Clara arrived, an hour and a half early to avoid the press. They were nearly successful. Just one local, a pushy young Berkeley reporter Leah remembered from last winter, staked out the apartment building. Jeffrey Earle had warned Leah that even the nationals would cover the opening of the trial. Fayler had offered a plea bargain: murder in the second degree in exchange for a guilty plea, but wouldn't drop the charge down to manslaughter or negligent homicide going into the trial. "She thinks she's got this one wrapped up," Jeff said. "High profile, using the outrage, all that. She's sending a message to these terrible young women. As if anyone really planned to do this. Anyway, she thinks she can show malice and intent."

"Allie's still pleading not guilty, isn't she?" Leah asked, frightened.

"So far. If Marcelle comes down to negligent homicide ... well ... but second degree murder has mandatory sentencing of twenty-five years to life." Jeff's funny half-brows knit together when he worried out loud, so they formed a near V. "Leah, she's full of guilt, but I've told her, the point here isn't for her to use the court to work out her feelings about what she did, or to punish herself. We can agree to plead guilty to what she's guilty *of*, but not more. Let's keep this straight and right. You okay with that?"

Leah had nodded yes.

Baby's Breath

"And you remember . . . don't look for a not guilty verdict, right?"

Leah, pretending distraction by the bustling entrance of two reporters, acted as if she'd not heard him.

Jeffrey Earle shook his head then. "You know," he said softly. "She still can't talk about the birth itself."

"Is it that she *won't*? I've tried, too. . . ."

Again the head shake, no. "Dr. Stojanovic says no, just can't bear it yet." He looked over Leah's shoulder into an indeterminate distance. "As if anyone would *plan* it that way," he mused. "On the floor of a BART station. Alone. Absolutely alone on the floor of a dirty subway station. . . ."

She knew Jeffrey Earle was hoping the district attorney had overplayed her hand, that by pressing for first degree murder the prosecutor would lose the jury. "Juries are funny," he said, pushing against the bridge of his nose with thumb and forefinger. "They rightly see this as different. But I need Alyssa. . . ." Wrinkles webbed out from the corners of his eyes. "I need her to talk. They have to see her whole."

Already the earth had rolled around the solstice toward fall. Late summer, now, the gardens wild and high with overripe blossoms. All that time already in jail. Sometimes Leah picked dahlias from the strip of flower bed Clara had claimed next to the apartment's sidewalk. She brought them in for Allie to see through the glass, so she wouldn't lose the sight of another whole season. She wished she'd thought of daffodils during the spring, but she hadn't. At Allie's insistence, Leah had even brought in the finished Bradshaw commission painting and held it up to Allie's approving study. She'd done six more paintings, too, seascapes with dwarfed feminine figures on a foreground of coast. She'd shipped them to George in groups of three; all except one had sold almost immediately. Leah needed to get home, *wanted* to get home.

The prosecutor came into the wood-paneled courtroom, closely followed by a suited man. Another lawyer? A beaked one, this, whose

Chapter Eighteen

half-bald head emphasized a massive forehead. Marcelle Ward Fayler, the prosecutor, wore a power suit, navy blue, with a plain white silk shell underneath it. Her hair was subdued, the side wings lying obediently flat against her head. She looked like she could take anyone down, and like she was ready to.

Jeffrey Earle came in next, followed by Allie, transformed in the chocolate brown suit and creamy silk blouse Leah had bought and delivered to Jeff's office for Allie to change into before she was brought to the courtroom. Allie was slim—thin!—under the fitted suit jacket, and Leah saw how changed her daughter's body was.

But that was the smaller change.

At first it seemed Allie had her hair in a loose chignon because her neck was exposed, a stripped branch, pale and vulnerable. But then she turned and, with Allie's profile to her, Leah realized Allie had cut her hair. Chin length, wavy, the ends curving under and forming a set of parentheses around her face. Just then, Allie reached up and tucked one side behind an ear, but it promptly fell loose again. Leah was looking at a stranger, an adult woman with a reservoir of experience beneath the composed surface of her face.

"Her hair!" Leah said under her breath, as she nudged Clara with her shoulder.

Clara wrapped her hand over Leah's.

"All rise. The Superior Court of Alameda County is now in session. The People of the State of California versus Alyssa Pacey Staton. Judge Albion Franklin presiding." A tall, slender man, black robe flapping behind him like a crow, entered from a door behind the bench and mounted it. White hair was long on his collar, and the hollows beneath his cheeks gave him an austere look. He put on half glasses, looked at the contents of a file in front of him, then looked up.

"Counselors, are we ready to proceed?"

"Marcelle Ward Fayler for the prosecution, Your Honor."

"Your Honor, Jeffrey Earle for the defense." Leah was pleased to see

287

Jeff pressed and crisp as the prosecutor. No reptile hanging out of his pocket, either, but shouldn't he have another lawyer with him, the way the prosecutor did? Leah's mind darted around the room like a fly, banging against every detail.

"Bailiff, please escort the jury in," said the judge. His face was unreadable.

Those twelve men and women didn't look nearly wise or good enough as they and two alternates were led into the paneled courtroom by a bailiff who looked like the metal clasp on a motley string of beads. They looked as ordinary as they had during jury selection, when Leah sat in the back of the courtroom and watched Jeff use his peremptory challenges, every one. "I watch how they look at Alyssa," he'd told Leah. "Not as scientific as a jury consultant, but I get a feel from it."

Every prospective juror had been asked whether he or she would be able to impose the death penalty, although Leah noticed the prosecution let several through who said they had serious reservations about it but "might" be able to impose it.

"Don't worry about that," Jeffrey told Leah. "The issue is prison time. The prosecutor is trying to scare her into a plea bargain to murder two."

How could he be so sure?

As he'd told her that, Jeffrey Earle had been hanging something in his office that looked, for all the world, like a bat. Leah didn't ask. A sheaf of music lay on the visitor's chair; he'd had to collect it so she could sit down. As she often had, Leah worried about the odd, gentle man planning her daughter's defense while he fiddled with toy lizards. *Allie's choice, Allie's decision*, she told herself, and was heartened until she let herself think of how *not good* some of Allie's decisions had been.

But Allie struck her as stronger now. And Allie seemed to think Jeffrey Earle had hung the moon. Leah thought maybe Allie had a crush on him, and then thought *no, it's that he pays real attention*. For Dennis

Chapter Eighteen

to give Allie such close examination would have been playing against his hand, in which every card was a mirror. *That's not fair*, Leah chastised herself. *He's been better.*

"Ms. Fayler, are the people ready for opening statement?"

"We are, Your Honor."

"If it please the court," she said, squaring her shoulders and buttoning her suit jacket like a television lawyer as she came from behind the table and approached the jury. "Ladies and gentlemen of the jury. Alyssa Pacey Staton thought about it a long time before she decided to take a newborn child's life."

Jeffrey had warned Leah what hard words the prosecutor would have. How sure she'd sound, how convincing even. "Try not to react," he'd said. "I'll put it in a different context in the defense opening."

Leah couldn't listen. Phrases penetrated her consciousness here and there, but she focused on the wood paneling of the courtroom. The bench matched in color and grain, but she wasn't close enough to it to determine whether that was real or simulated veneer like the walls of the large oblong space. She studied the spectators, ticking off which of them she knew to be reporters and which were under-occupied citizens who thought this was the damn circus. It was an obscene violation that they would all watch and hear the baring of Allie's life. And Leah's. What would the psychiatrists say about her? A television camera was mounted above the jury box, trained on the bench and witness stand. Clara seemed to be absorbing every word, though Leah couldn't even sense her blinking or breathing. She'd come prepared, two small plastic bottles of water in her oversize purse. "Gets dry in there," she said without reference to how she knew. "Your throat gets to hurting."

Her eyes went back to Allie. The haircut was stunning, really, though Leah saw that the thickness could do with some long layering, softening around the face. How did a woman in jail get her hair cut? When Allie was eight, confused and sad as Leah had been when Allie hacked off her braids, the ragged edges were something Leah could fix as easily as putting Allie into the car, taking her to a salon and writing a check for a cut that redeemed the destruction.

* * *

The courtroom lighting wasn't intense, not like the jail's unforgiving fluorescence, but Alyssa imagined the whiteness of her neck shone, disturbing the eye like the white spots on a badly developed print. She couldn't keep her hand away from that newly exposed skin. With every turn of her head, the air grazed it like a blade.

Alyssa Pacey Staton thought about it a long time before she decided to take a newborn child's life.

Ostrom had done it for her—not the haircut itself—but scheduled the appointment with the jail barber, then watched the dark coils fall and curl on the cement floor like regret. "Must be three feet long," the barber said, nudging them out of his way with his small shoes. No styling because styling would have involved a shampoo and rinse with her head tipped backwards over the sink, exposing her bare throat and trapping her hands beneath the plastic barber's shawl. It had been all she could manage to hold herself still when the barber's scissors clipped across her shoulders, then cut again higher next to her cheek, the cold metal of the scissor handle touching her jaw, her ear. *The wrong side,* she'd thought, then recanted.

The district attorney was warming up. The words of her opening statement tumbled from her, gathering momentum like a wagon running downhill. She would have been a forensics champ in high school, Alyssa could tell. She was a speaker who relished the power of her own words, who worshipped what they could build from air. Jeff had greeted her when they entered the courtroom, addressing her, *Marcy,* as friendly as if she were his neighbor. Alyssa drew her hand across her neck, settled both fists into her lap. She heard Leah's expelled breath behind her and recognized the sound of her mother's refusal. Leah

Chapter Eighteen

wouldn't listen, but Alyssa would. She'd make herself pay attention. *Pay the piper.*

"Ladies and gentlemen of the jury, our case is very simple. On a Sunday evening in February, February 4 of this year when other coeds at Cal were studying for midterms or spellchecking their essay assignments, Alyssa Pacey Staton committed murder in the first degree. She...." Marcy stopped in front of Alyssa and Jeffrey, the deliberately synchronized pause in her movement and her speech calculated to mesmerize. Alyssa tried to visualize the calendar in her apartment kitchen, the Ansel Adams photograph calendar Howie had given her for a housewarming. Had she ever turned the calendar to February? Didn't it still hang at January, the blank, bald walls of Yosemite's Half Dome yielding hieroglyphics framed by Adams's fine eye?

Her back to Alyssa, facing the jury, the district attorney continued. "She delivered her own baby, a full-term baby girl who, in other circumstances, would have been a thriving six-month-old by now. Alyssa Staton delivered her own baby on a floor in a BART restroom in Berkeley." Marcy, no, *Marcelle Ward Fayler for the prosecution* let her voice drop to a whisper as though she were promising a secret to the jury, who listed into the softness of her voice like one body, its muscles trained by a single nervous system.

"She delivered a healthy baby girl and then, because it would have been just too much trouble for this straight-A student, this child prodigy from an entitled background, to offer it up for adoption or at least notify somebody of its existence, this young woman with every resource in the world available to her, she left her baby in a trash can, intending for it to die. More precisely, ladies and gentlemen, and I apologize for this, she left that female newborn, that perfect infant, to bleed to death from an untied umbilical cord. A cord Alyssa Pacey Staton severed with her own pocket knife."

Jeffrey stirred beside her. The tense line in his jaw, the stern profile of his face, made Alyssa look away. Not at the jurors, who watched

291

Baby's Breath

Marcelle Fayler's face as intently as if they were lip reading. Not at the judge, shifting in his high seat behind the bench, who held one arm of his half-glasses to his mouth like a pipestem. Down at her hands, at her lap and the dirt-brown skirt bearing the faint perpendicular wrinkle lines from the accidental pleats of its hangered position inside the Macy's garment bag. Leah had brought the suit to Jeff, so Alyssa could change into it in the high-ceilinged courthouse restroom, two guards posted outside the door. If Leah had been able to see her pull the skirt on, snap the loose waistband above the bony cage of her hips, she would have insisted on ironing it, on making it right for Alyssa. She traced the wrinkles, then stretched them with her pressed fingers, but as soon as she let go, there they were again, like railroad tracks. Or bars.

For the first time in years she wore stockings. The taupe pumps slipped from her feet when she shuffled them, one ankle over the other beneath the defense table. She was raising a blister on her heel, sliding her foot in and out of the too-large shoe. Leah had asked her for sizes, but Alyssa could neither remember her old body's sizes nor guess those of the new body she lived in, all lines and points like the figures of geometric planes. Not bra or underpants, not blouse or jacket. Even her shoe size seemed wrong, though Leah hadn't asked it, wouldn't have had to. She knew Alyssa's size, the same as her own, an even seven, but her feet had seemed to resculpt themselves into a slender, foreign knobbiness she didn't recognize unless she traced the angles of her own limbs from knee to calf to ankle. The suit and blouse she wore smelled like Gran's favorite sewing store, where the multiple rows of standing bolts of fresh fabric made a single choice impossible and Gran would say, every trip, *pick two then, baby. We'll make two dresses.*

"That Alyssa Pacey Staton did, on the evening of February 4, 1998, willfully and with malice aforethought kill one infant baby girl she delivered, and said victim died as a result of exsanguination thereafter." As easily as they'd been fused into a single unit by Marcelle Fayler's opening lines, the jury broke into pieces. Alyssa watched them, twelve

Chapter Eighteen

separate people being told a terrible story, a horrific story they were determined to hear through their own ears and nobody else's. An elderly woman's spotty hands flapped against her sweater coat, pulled out a Kleenex and brought it to her face to catch a sneeze turning to a cough that wore itself down behind the Kleenex mask. Two men in the back row of the jury box looked at each other, then away, as if they'd been caught conspiring. She felt Jeff pat the back of her fisted hand. He moved his head, the slightest shake. Stay with me, Alyssa, he'd repeated twice before they'd entered the courtroom. When Marcy lets loose, *you stay with me.*

"Ladies and gentlemen, on behalf of the State of California I want to thank you for being here and serving on this jury. I want to tell you we realize the imposition this duty makes on your lives, and it's not an imposition the court system takes lightly." Marcelle was smarter than smart, Alyssa could see. She knew when to back off, when to come in the side door.

"So we appreciate that you realize serving on this jury is something very important, especially important when you are called on to judge a crime against a human being who had no one else to speak up for her." Marcelle paused, glanced quickly at the table where Jeffrey and Alyssa sat, then went on, her voice lowered. "I'd like to go through a few definitions with you. The first one is murder itself, the unlawful killing of another human being with malice aforethought."

Marcelle brought her fingers to her chin, then raised both hands, drawing wide loops in the air. "Malice is a legal term. To have a murder in the first degree, you must have malice. It's been defined as a wickedness, an evilness of the heart, a heart devoid of social duty and human feeling. It comes down to a wrongfulness, an evilness, a wickedness... so you must have malice before the fatal act." Alyssa predicted her pause, anticipating how the attorney would let the heavy, bad words ride the froth of their own wake.

"Aforethought does not mean you have to plan it out weeks or

293

months in advance. You don't have to have some well laid-out plan premeditated for weeks in advance to have malice aforethought. If you've got malice, you've got that evilness at any time before the fatal act." She stopped, shook her pointed finger in time to her words. "Any time before the fatal act. That is malice, it is aforethought." She looked pleased. She'd gotten something established. Her premise, Jeffrey had explained to Alyssa, will be that you meant to do what happened.

Aforethought was just more syllables for *before*, Alyssa knew, yet when Marcelle defined the word it took on the connotation of witchcraft, voodoo, the casting of smoky spells over the entrails of baby birds. As Marcelle went on with her definitions, *presumption of innocence, reasonable doubt*, Alyssa heard her voice coaxing, coaching the jury. *You'll hear the state psychiatrist testify that this young woman knew what she was doing and understood the consequences of her actions.*

You can do this, Marcelle was telling them; you can remember these terms and distinctions, all the pieces of the story and the character description we gave you and still come up with the right verdict. Establishing expectation, Alyssa knew from Psych I. You established expectation and your population—kindergarten kids, a football team, a jury—would do their best to rise to it. Vote for me, Marcelle argued to the jury with her confident voice and her manicured hands, no color on the nails, not the hint of blood, just honest gloss, transparent. *See it my way. Go for murder one.*

"Ladies and gentlemen of the jury, we intend to prove this case, to show you malice aforethought, by starting at the very beginning of this sad and horrifying, unnatural story of inhuman behavior. By starting with Alyssa Staton's hidden pregnancy, her refusal of offers of help for medical intervention, by showing her deliberate planning before the birth of her baby, to her escape into the Tenderloin district of San Francisco where she hid for nearly a week, we intend to prove that this young woman had malice aforethought. The State bears the burden of proof, and we intend to meet that burden in this trial." Marcelle re-

Chapter Eighteen

turned to her table, her high heels clicking out the seconds of her intentional caesura like Gran's metronome. *Andante.*

Marcelle Fayler turned from her table to the jury and approached them with four long strides, her voice earnest, eager. "We will start by producing testimony from the police detectives who investigated the death of the baby girl left in the trash can of the Shattuck Avenue BART Station on the evening of February 4. We'll tell you about the extensive efforts made by the Berkeley Police to discover the identity of the infant girl's mother. You will see items of evidence found at the scene of the baby girl's birth and death."

Pause, Alyssa silently commanded, her eyes locked on the back of Marcelle's beautifully coiffed wings of hair. She bent her own head and felt again the unfamiliar cool on the back of her neck, the kiss of a pain almost as real as that she felt pressing her own bruises, the fit of her fingers against the shapes left by Jack-o-Lantern's heels and fists. Her hair fell forward against each cheek. Don't let it go to waste: *birth and death*, a murder conviction's damnation in one breath. On cue, Marcelle did pause. Alyssa straightened her head and fixed her hair, looping the shorn pieces behind each ear. Marcelle shifted her shoulders, swung her head around; for a moment their eyes met. Marcelle's fell away first, the quickened shift of glassy pupils in the face of somebody who hadn't really seen you at all, or can't see you, or won't.

"We will work through the investigation as it unfolded. You'll see the forensic evidence and the testimony of others regarding the circumstance of the victim's, the baby's, birth. You'll hear that Alyssa Staton agreed to the medical examination and the blood samples which identified the child as her own; you'll hear that early in the police investigation, she acknowledged that dead baby as her own."

Jeffrey left his hand on hers this time, took hers in his and pressed it against his thigh, beneath the table where the judge and the jury couldn't see. Blood she could remember. Not capped in a vial on a lab tray, though, not like what Marcelle was describing. On her hands, her pants, the tile floor, the walls of the bathroom stall. Running from between her legs, clots of it the size of fists. Alyssa shut her eyes. Jeff's thumb rubbed the ridge of her knuckles, back and forth, back and forth. Suddenly she wished she could sleep, cover herself completely and sleep. But the desire for sleep was dampened; she hadn't been able to sleep soundly in weeks. Even now, given a dark bed and a thick blanket with Coffee curled against her side, she'd not be able to sleep.

"... so it comes down to one thing, the conscious decision of this young woman to do away with the child that would inconvenience her, certainly tarnish her reputation, possibly interrupt the schooling at which she excelled. This was her motivation: that baby would have gotten in the way of the life she was used to living. She knew what she was doing, and she did it. She went ahead and did it. And, after abandoning the baby she delivered in the saddest of circumstances, she fled the scene, left the baby—her baby—to die, ladies and gentlemen."

The jury was squirming. Out of the corner of her eye, Alyssa could see them, could feel the discomfort that had them pulling at a tie or a lapel, crossing legs, pushing eyeglasses up the bridge of a nose, shifting feet. They weren't following Marcelle, they didn't believe anybody could be so selfish. Jeffrey had told her this was their best bet: that Marcelle would describe a girl nobody could understand. Then he'd step up and describe the real Alyssa. Here was his hope: the real Alyssa and her account of what happened. *I want you to take the stand.*

"How could somebody do this? This is not a case of insane behavior, of diminished capacity. This is a case of selfishness, of me, me, me all the way." Marcelle stopped, as if she too were noting the shifting angles inside the jury box, the elbows and shins giving up their resting positions. She changed strategies, cool and smooth like a stage actress.

"This is a very difficult situation for you all to be in, and we appreciate that. Nobody here asked to be on this jury and hear this sad, sad story, we know that. And you'd probably rather be anywhere else than here. You're going to have to see and hear things you'd rather not see and hear. But . . . " Again she leaned into them; once again she was going to win them back with her demonstration of faith. "But we picked you because we thought you would be fair and use your common sense, and we believe—we *know*—that you will be.

"Common sense—and here we'll reach the last phase of our case— common sense would tell almost anybody that an untended umbilical cord means a slow death for a newborn infant. We're going to end, and I apologize again, ladies and gentlemen, for what you're going to hear as you serve your duty in this courtroom, we're going to present the coroner's report, with the autopsy of that seven-pound infant that was, with malice aforethought, delivered and then abandoned to a certain death."

Marcelle breathed deeply, a sprinter taking in the oxygen that would see her through the hundred-yard dash. "Malice aforethought. You remember that definition? This whole case turns on the fact that Baby Staton's death was no accident. Now I want to thank you all for serving. We have every confidence that you will do a fair and good job." Graceful as a dancing partner, Marcelle turned to Jeffrey and gave him a modest smile. "The defense is going to speak to you now," she glanced at the judge, "or perhaps after lunch, and then the State will start putting up its evidence. Thank you very much."

The din in the courtroom rose after the judge left, his robes flapping around the tilt of his lean body like the wings of a prehistoric bird. Leah's hand on Alyssa's shoulder brought her back from the space where her mind had slipped during Marcelle Ward Fayler's closing. That space was small and dark and gummy. Her hands were palmed into the finger paint stickiness. For a moment, one breathless moment tinged by tenderness in that cloistered space in memory, she'd held something against her breast.

Then her mother's hand caught up her cropped hair and pulled

297

Baby's Breath

Alyssa's face against Leah's own breast where all she could hear before the bailiff pulled them apart was the sound of her mother's heartbeat, the oldest rhythm in the world.

Jeffrey Earle stood up. He buttoned the jacket of his navy suit. Did they teach that in law school? Stand up and button your jacket? "Your honor . . ." he said, with a hesitation and nod toward the bench before he walked around in front of the defense table and approached the jury. Leah's chest was so tight her breathing felt constricted. The air conditioning was set at too low a temperature, surely. Other people must feel it.

"Ladies and gentlemen of the jury," Jeffrey said quietly. "You are going to have what few people have in their lifetime; the opportunity to change your society for the better. You will have the opportunity to delve into what many of your peers—if we judge from the media—consider the act of a monster. Alyssa Staton's own mother would understand that characterization." Jeffrey turned and looked at Leah. "In fact, Alyssa Staton's own mother *does* understand that characterization," he added softly. Leah had an impulse to lower her head, but then set her chin and looked at the jury. A couple of jurors' eyes flicked toward her. Of course, they already knew who she was, would have even if Jeffrey Earle hadn't turned and as good as identified her with a finger.

Clara's hand snaked over and covered Leah's briefly as Jeffrey faced the jury and continued. "You *can,* of course, remain unchanged by an examination of what's undeniably happened. You *can* cling to the surface of life, and you can simply see this as a horrific, utterly alien act. You can say things like *I have children,* and imply that to achieve any understanding of Alyssa Staton or other women who have committed this terrible act would somehow diminish you as a loving parent." Jeffrey paused, giving the notion weight and time in the jurors' minds. His suit and shirt still looked crisp, a good sign for Leah. When Jeff was disheartened, he looked it. "Or you can require something higher and

Chapter Eighteen

finer of yourselves: you can go the distance and set an example of humanity for those same children, the ones I know you love more than life. You can be willing to listen and to think for yourselves."

A little shiver radiated out from Leah's center in ripples. Tomorrow she'd wear something warmer than the beige jersey dress she'd bought at Casual Corner. (Nothing either too gay or too dark, Jeffrey had warned her. And not rich looking, but not poor, either. Juries don't like the very rich or the very poor.) Leah hardly ever went out without a blazer. Why had she today? She could have stood up and buttoned it, which must be the courtroom version of a stadium wave.

She pulled her mind back to Jeffrey Earle. He was saying, "This is a journey for you just as it is for me, for Alyssa's mother, for her doctor, and most importantly, for Alyssa herself. It is a terribly difficult journey for us all. Sad, infinitely sad. Painful. The destination is understanding. We don't expect you to be there now; we only ask that you be willing to go."

"Ms. Fayler rightly told you that murder in the first degree requires malice. It requires that the act be planned and that there be deliberate intent to take life and that the intent be malicious." He left a space in the air and when he went on it was a slow commanding march. "You listen. You decide if a first-degree murder took place. Really look, really listen . . . and we'll trust your decision. If you can bear to really look, really listen—if you're willing to give your community that great a service, that great a sacrifice—then we have no doubt as to your verdict." Jeffrey shook his head no. *Not guilty, not guilty*, Leah intoned in her mind. "What happened in that BART station had nothing to do with malice. Nothing to do with murder." *Not guilty.*

But Allie was guilty and everyone knew it. But not with malice! Not with intent! Leah argued silently and lost some of what Jeffrey was saying. *Pay attention*, she admonished herself.

"We don't have a long list of witnesses, and we won't be making shallow excuses. What we have to offer is insight into the human condition.

299

Into a woman's psyche. Into our common soul. You *can* emerge from listening to Alyssa's mother, Alyssa's neighbor, the woman who befriended Alyssa after the birth, and to Alyssa's doctor, as deeper, wiser, better people. People who are not so personally threatened by this act that they are unable to be strong or unable to be compassionate. You *can* achieve understanding and by your understanding challenge your community—and your country—to grow. We trust you to do the right thing. To do what is right for Alyssa, and for society, in the name of society. You'll know what the right thing is. Have courage. Really look. Really listen. Follow carefully. Then lead."

CHAPTER
19

Alyssa wore a blue dress the next morning when Marcelle Ward Fayler opened the prosecution's case. The dress, a simple shirtwaist, was a deeper blue than the patches of sky lightened by the scrim of fog she had seen from the portals of the county van that brought her to and from the court. But it wasn't as dark as the bay, which she couldn't see but could smell, the salt taste riding the crisp morning air like a welcome. In the courthouse after she'd moulted the jailhouse orange and stepped into the blue dress, she sat for a moment studying her stockinged feet, her arms wrapped around her waist. When she stood and ironed the dress against her hips with her splayed hands, something inside the pocket, a stiffness beneath her fingers, stopped her from slipping her feet into the loose taupe shoes.

She pulled out a leaf of binder paper folded into sixths. A note from Leah tucked into the pocket of the dress that by law had to pass from Leah's hands to Jeffrey Earle's after submission to the metal detecting scanner in the courthouse lobby. *I love you*, it said in sloping handwriting, maybe shaken off course by the shiver of a car engine, maybe composed at a stop sign, laid against the steering wheel, written by a hand made doubly unsteady from shaking inside and out. Then, another line, midpage, another tone, insistent: *I love you, Alyssa. I'm with you. Mom.*

In the courtroom, with Jeff's hand on her shoulder guiding her to their table facing Judge Franklin and the witness box, she kept the note folded in her palm and remembered the necklace she'd bought for her mother and handcarried to Philadelphia as an early Christmas gift. She remembered it—hanging?—the shimmer of the silver chain as she'd lifted it from a hook and tucked it into her backpack. She remembered the inventory of her possessions during booking: Lazzie, her soiled pants, the tiny pocket, useless really, where she'd zippered the necklace so the booking officer—Hop, Hopkins—had forgotten to count it.

Was it stealing when you took something back that you'd given away? Was it good enough to make amends if you returned something to its owner after you'd stolen it? Give, take, give. . . . Could she make it balance somehow, the way Joey said the Apostolics promised? Jeff nudged her, pulling her backwards out of the wringer of thoughts. She slipped Leah's note back into its pocket and laid both of her hands on the table, cupping each other in the position Jeff said was best. *Nothing under the table.*

"If it please the court, Your Honor, the State would call Detective Barbara Halsumae to the stand," Marcelle announced, then stood back as the police detective in her svelte, dark suit matched to Marcelle's swore to tell the truth, the whole truth, nothing but the truth. Alyssa registered her face and found at once a comfort and a threat in its vague familiarity. As soon as the detective spoke, the context dropped into place: the hours in the police station after she'd been examined in the hospital, the courteous impatience the detective had shown over Alyssa's answers, the ropy veins on her strong hands, the spilled Pepsi. And the story the detective told was true, as true as Alyssa could remember, but it seemed to be heading in a direction that Marcelle Fayler controlled with her upraised hands, fingers pointing like pistols.

"So when you initially questioned the defendant, Ms. Staton, on the evening of February 8 after the preliminary medical exam, you say she did acknowledge having given birth?"

"Not in those words."

Chapter Nineteen

"What were her words, then, Detective?"

"She spoke repeatedly about a baby—"

"Her words, Detective?" Sharp and fast, Marcy jockeyed the detective, straightening her testimony, flat out for the home stretch.

"She said, it's written twice in my notes, that 'the dwarf was taking care of the baby.'"

"'The dwarf was taking care of the baby.' Is that correct?"

"Yes, that's it."

"Did you make sense of this? 'The dwarf?'"

"I understood her to refer to—"

"Objection!" Jeff was up and out of his chair. "Purely speculative, that question goes to interpretation, to state of mind, and this witness, your honor, is not qualified to testify as to state of mind."

Judge Franklin tipped his head so he could look eye-to-eye at Jeff across the panes of his half-glasses. "Sustained, Counselor."

Marcelle smiled at Jeffrey as he passed her on his return to his seat. Softly, in the same breathy whispers she'd used to woo the jury in her opening argument, "We're getting to state of mind."

"Ms. Fayler." Judge Franklin hooked her with his quick admonition. *Behave*, Alyssa guessed he might say next. But he didn't.

The forensic pathologist from the coroner's office was next, a mammoth red-haired man who would have looked like a lumberjack had he been wearing plaid flannel instead of a badly fitted suitcoat threatening to tear apart at the seams every time he moved his arms. Jeff kept his hand on Alyssa's as the doctor was sworn in, his educational background recited, the total number of completed autopsies reported. All Alyssa could hold in her mind as he talked, Marcelle priming him like a pump, was the immense size of the pathologist's fingers, the thick thumb and forefinger that seemed far too clumsy to ever handle anything as small as a baby's hand. Yet he'd performed them: twenty-six post-mortem examinations of babies less than two days old, a total which enabled Marcelle to get him to agree that yes, he considered himself experienced enough to determine that the Staton baby, the Baby Jane Doe he'd seen way back in February, had died not of birth trauma, or exposure, or inflicted injury, but had simply bled to death through the unclamped, rather raggedly cut four-inch long umbilical cord.

Marcelle stepped up to the jury box, a batter to the plate. "I want to get this clear for the jury, Dr. McConnell. This was a full-term baby?"

"Yes. Seven pounds, one ounce."

"Would you say this was a baby who, in a hospital setting, would have had any immediate postnatal difficulty?"

"There's always the possibility—"

"Let me rephrase the question. From the findings of your autopsy, could you conclude that this was a healthy baby at birth?"

"This was a healthy baby at birth."

"Was this a baby with heart, lung, any internal organ dysfunction?"

"No, it was not."

"So this was a baby who lived for some time before it . . . while she was bleeding to death, am I correct?"

"Some time, yes."

"How long, Doctor?"

"Objection!" Jeff was up, so suddenly fierce that his chair nearly tipped as he untangled himself. "Your honor, we have no quarrel with cause of death. This is unnecessary inflammation of emotion—"

"Overruled. I'll allow the question."

"How long," Marcelle paused, her face in mourning, "how long did the Baby Staton live before she bled to death, Dr. McConnell?"

"It's only an estimate . . . you can only fix a range in these things . . . somewhere between three and four hours."

Marcelle sighed, one drawn out breath expelled to exaggerate the silence of the courtroom, the frozen jurors. "Thank you, Dr. McConnell. Thank you for your expertise. That's all I have." Marcelle went back to

Chapter Nineteen

her seat, her head bowed. Alyssa read the drama of her gestures: this was a funeral parlor, a visitation, a memorial.

"Are you cross-examining, Mr. Earle? The witness is waiting." Judge Franklin said, unmoved.

"Yes, I do have one question, Dr. McConnell." As if he were shrugging off the strain of a heavy pack, Jeff's shoulders rose and fell while he approached the witness box. "You were the doctor who handled the baby initially, that is, from its arrival at the coroner's facility, is that correct?"

"Yes. I followed the autopsy process through, that was me."

"And could you describe the baby's body when you first saw it?"

"Yes, I could—"

"Excuse me, I don't mean in medical or biological terms, Doctor. We don't need to hear that again. I meant the condition, the position, what a layperson might notice?"

"Yes, I can. The baby was wrapped in a towel."

"Describe the towel, please, Doctor."

"A relatively clean towel . . . given the circumstances . . . a green bath towel, monogrammed, I think."

"When you say relatively clean, you mean what?"

"Not as bloody as one would expect. The expectation is that there would be a good deal of blood on something wrapped around a newborn, a neonate born outside of a hospital setting."

"You're talking about the mother's blood, not the baby's blood?"

"Yes. From the birth process. Unattended, it is a . . . bloody one."

"So you're telling us the baby was wrapped inside a towel which was not soaked through by the birthing blood."

"The towel was bloody, yes, but the blood stains centered on where the umbilical . . . the unclamped umbilical . . . would have drained."

"The towel was stained but not soaked, correct?"

"That's correct, yes."

Baby's Breath

Jeff took a plastic-wrapped parcel from the evidence table. He held it in front of Dr. McConnell like a poster, dangling it from the pinched fingers of each hand. "And this is the towel you've already identified as the one found swaddled around Baby Jane Doe on February 5?"

Alyssa caught just the colors—green and a swatch of something dark, darker than pain, before she turned her head away. A clutch of organs inside her—her lungs, her heart, her womb—pulled her into herself, turned down the outside volume. She thought she could feel her mother tensing behind her, as if Alyssa were riding a two-wheeler or diving into the deep end or boarding a school bus for the first time, her own childhood muscles distancing her from her mother's out-stretched arms. *I'm sending you Gran's towels, honey*, Leah had written. *The ones we haven't washed to threads.*

Dr. McConnell spoke, his eyes on the package. "That's the towel I identified for Ms. Fayler, yes."

Jeffrey held the package schoolbook-style against his chest as he continued. "Doctor, how much blood does a newborn have?"

"Eight, eight and a half ounces."

"A cup?"

"Give or take. Just about a cup."

"And the blood on the swaddling towel, was it the baby's blood?"

"Mostly the baby's blood, yes."

"How would you explain the absence of birth blood, the mother's blood there?"

"I'd guess the baby had been cleaned, wiped clean of the birth blood."

"Objection!" Dramatic, pronouncing her words with force, Marcelle argued. *Speculation.* Judge Franklin agreed.

"And the binding of this towel, the wrapping that you noted? Can you describe that to us?"

"Well, the word would be ... swaddled, I guess. The baby was placed in the towel, the towel wrapped around her so her face was free but her body was covered . . . the towel was tucked into itself, the way a woman would tuck the ends of a bath towel around her head, tur-banned, you know."

"Would you say this is similar to . . . to the way that a baby might be swaddled in a maternity ward?"

Marcelle jumped. "Objection. Irrelevant. Professional comparisons are hardly appropriate here—"

"Sit down, Ms Fayler. I'm allowing the question." Judge Franklin leaned forward, his half-glasses dangling from his hand. "Go ahead, Mr. Earle. Proceed with your cross."

"My question, Dr. McConnell, was whether the swaddling, this relatively blood-free green towel tucked around the baby, was done with consideration, with some care, some compassion, some—"

"Objection!"

"—some tenderness." Jeff finished, waited.

Judge Franklin slipped on his glasses, then nudged them down the bridge of his nose until he had both attorneys in his sights. "Objection sustained."

Sustained. Sustenance. All Alyssa heard as the bailiff announced that court would adjourn for lunch, twelve to two, was a word changing textures like a wren's feather under sunlight, turning itself from lustrous to dull and back again in the briefest twitch of a wing. What ricocheted inside her head, an echo rebounding against mountains of deaf bone, was Marcelle Ward Fayler's insistent questioning of the pathologist, the attorney's deliberately rephrased repetitions draped in the courtroom air. *What small effort would it have taken to sustain the life of this baby?*

For the long afternoon that followed, Alyssa listened to the description of herself to which she had contributed in the uneasy sessions with the state psychiatrist, Dr. Bulton, the rickety thin woman presenting her wordy answers like dissertations. Her long face stiff with purpose, the psychiatrist made simple conclusions complex with her contortions of syntax and vocabulary. Yes, she had ascertained that the defendant was an extremely intelligent young woman. Yes, her diagnosis, her professional opinion was that the defendant had probably suffered major depressive episodes as an adolescent, episodes gone unrecognized because the severity of depression in adolescents is often missed. Yes, she had declared Alyssa competent to stand trial. Yes, she could agree with Dr. Stojanovic's finding of major depression now. Yes, the defendant was aware of the difference between right and wrong. Yes, yes, yes, until the court was adjourned, and the weary, silent jurors followed each other in single file from the courtroom.

The next morning, an hour into her continued direct examination of Dr. Bulton, Marcelle ignored Judge Franklin, who had twice looked pointedly at his wristwatch. "Doctor, as to the mental illness of depression, you did a separate evaluation when you found that the defendant, regardless of any mental illness, diagnosed or undiagnosed, had the capacity to conform, to know right from wrong, is that correct?"

"Yes, that's right."

"And your evaluation shows that while the defendant may be more severely depressed now than in earlier episodes, she is also more in touch with reality than she was previously, do I understand correctly?"

"Yes. Depression—any episode of major depression—does not necessarily interfere with the ability of the person to have a rational and factual understanding of the situation."

"And you did a separate evaluation as to criminal responsibility, presented to the court—" Marcelle nodded to Jeffrey, "—in which you found the defendant expressed awareness as to her role in the abandonment of her infant?"

"Yes."

"Thank you, Doctor. Your honor, I'm through with this witness."

Alyssa kept her eyes on Jeff, the soothing pace of his easy movements across the floor. He faced Dr. Bulton, swiveled to the jury, and turned back to Dr. Bulton.

Chapter Nineteen

"Doctor, in your evaluation, you. . . ." Jeff thumbed through the packet of highlighted papers he held like a clipboard in his left hand. "In your evaluation, you note that the defendant didn't want to appear ill . . . that her depressed condition prior to February 4 would have been hard to detect because of her desire to tough it out on her own, to appear as if everything in her life was fine, correct?"

"That's right, yes."

"So it would have been easy for someone—a family member, a professional even, to make the mistake of thinking that she was in better condition that she actually was?"

"That's true. Unfortunate, but true."

"And you also found in your evaluation, this is dated March 7, now, that the defendant appeared to suffer from a lack of recall, you write that this may be the residual effects of a dissociative episode, is that correct?"

"That's correct."

"Could you explain those terms please, Doctor?"

"Dissociation?"

"Yes, that."

"Dissociation is a condition wherein the individual experiences a separation of related psychological activities into autonomously functioning units—"

"Thank you, Doctor. I'm sure we'd all appreciate. . . ." Jeff turned to the jury, "we'd all appreciate a translation, please." The jury's murmur, a ripple of appreciation punctuated by someone's cropped laugh disguised as a cough.

Dr. Bulton drew herself higher in the witness box, her long neck extended, cranelike. "Dissociation occurs when an individual feels as if she is, well, perhaps floating above the action, that she is not an agent in the action, observing but not initiating or participating in the action . . . but it occurs rarely in postpartum psychosis—"

Jeff cut her off. "And following episodes of dissociation, as you've described it, the sense of oneself as the actor can return in bits and pieces, so to speak?"

"Yes, that's right."

"And your evaluation concludes that those bits and pieces have been returning to the defendant, yes?"

"Yes."

"But that the boundaries of time are, well, sort of preventing us, preventing the defendant from reaching the point where she could render a full account."

"Yes."

"But that the defendant was neither evasive nor deceptive in her attempts to find, to *reclaim* those bits and pieces?"

"Neither evasive nor deceptive, that's right."

"Thank you. That's all for cross."

Marcelle was itching for a fight. Alyssa wanted it to be over, wanted instead the flat mattress of her cell, the nightlight glow of the computer screen at the housing officer's station filtered through the humming dark of the jail night. She deserved it all, the orange suit hanging from her shoulder bones like a shroud and the rubber-soled slippers and the pasty meat congealed on plastic plates and the constant television drone driving you to a madness even Dr. Bulton could diagnose. She deserved Jack-o-Lantern's threats, fulfilled more and more frequently. Even now, pulling her sleeves down with every movement, she couldn't completely cover the long bruised scrape running from her elbow to her wrist where her arm had caught the door of the restroom to break her fall but then, without her willing it, had let her go down. She deserved it.

Judge Franklin asked Marcelle Ward Fayler, was she going to redirect? Yes, she was, she answered, already positioned in front of Dr. Bulton. "Your findings state that the defendant does understand fully the proceedings and the nature of the charge against her?"

"Yes, that's correct."

Chapter Nineteen

"And she has insights now as to the nature of her depression, these episodes of major depression you've identified?"

"Yes."

"And that she's able to assist in her own defense?"

"Yes."

"But that she hasn't ..." Marcelle looked pointedly at the jury, "... that she hasn't yet fully remembered—'reclaimed' is Mr. Earle's word—the exact sequence of events from the night of February 4?"

"Yes."

Marcelle stopped then, smartly, before Judge Franklin could stop her. "We've been there before," he'd told her twice already. But when Alyssa looked at Jeff and saw the dark smudges under his eyes, she knew he was hearing Marcelle's unspoken words just as she was, just as everybody in the courtroom was. *How convenient for the defendant.*

When she got her wish that night, when the jail was as quiet as it would get, the lights lowered and the television shut off, she couldn't sleep. She should have known that she'd lie awake for hours, the reel of prosecution witnesses playing inside her head like a soundless movie. She should have learned by now that wishing could be as dangerous as doing because wishes cheated you, doubled back and betrayed what you thought you had wanted for yourself, and then what did you have: less than nothing.

She'd daydreamed of sleep while Marcelle Ward Fayler had grilled her mother, who'd lied about the towel, denying recognition of Gran's initials, EPR, monogrammed as clear as day. *Because you'd do anything to protect your child when you can't believe her guilty of what they said.* That's what Leah had said back to the district attorney, her face drawn but her words firm, loud even. And, when the attorney kept on and on about lying, obstructing an investigation, Leah had said, louder still: *You don't have children, do you, Miss Fayler?* And been admonished by Judge Franklin. *Please respond only to the questions put to you.*

Baby's Breath

The dark spillage, the stain that had turned the green fabric to brown just like a color wheel, she didn't recognize, couldn't remember. Why would she . . . with a towel stained brown? Marcelle had shown those blown-up pictures of a baby wrapped in a towel swaddled just how the coroner had described it, with the triangled ends tucked about each other in the envelope folds she and Sharon had used to wrap their baby dolls, the way Gran had taught them. *Babies like to be wrapped snug. It reminds them of before they were born.* Marcelle had shown pictures of a baby who was unwrapped, lying on a white table, baby eyes shut. Alyssa had shut her eyes, too, after the first picture. She'd shut her eyes and waited for the forward clicking of the projector to end and the coroner's voice to cease its flat captioning of the pictures, to conclude its terrible lesson.

She turned onto her side and pulled the thin blue blanket over her shoulders. The coroner was such a big man, big like a football player. She imagined his huge hands around the baby, one cupping its body, one bracing its head, those big hands whose fingers would spread like the strands of a hammock to hold its little cargo. She sat up, the blanket falling from her shoulders, and swung her legs off the mattress. Leaning forward with her shortened strands of hair brushing her cheeks, the missing length seemed like a misplaced memory threatening to return.

CHAPTER

20

"Is the defense ready?"

Judge Franklin was unfathomable, though several times Leah thought he'd been unnecessarily warm to the prosecutor. She'd tried to keep track of how many times the judge had sustained a defense objection and how many times he'd sustained one for the prosecution, until she realized the sums were useless unless she remembered the total number of objections each had made. Her mind tried to catalog instances, but sidetracked into distress when it was so much easier to count the prosecution's objections. Jeffrey Earle was letting too much by, too much in. Leah was alone, Clara babysitting grandchildren for her daughter. No shield for Leah, no one to talk with during recesses. She'd thought Dennis might show up after all, since the defense was beginning; she'd have welcomed even him. He'd been vague about if or when he would arrive during the trial, and Leah knew it was another wound for Allie.

"Ready, Your Honor. The defense calls Darlene Ridley."

A bleached woman, frowzy as an overblown rose, raccoon-eyed with drugs or excessive eyeliner, stood up and clicked toward the witness stand on high heels. So this was Dara, the prostitute or addict or both who'd helped Alyssa when Alyssa wouldn't turn to her own mother. She certainly wasn't a likely candidate for help now, either. A shiny purple shirt and tight black pants molded to her bony frame. How bad things really were if Allie needed this person to testify for her.

Dara paused as she passed between the prosecution and defense tables just long enough to smile over to Allie. Allie's teeth actually showed when she smiled back, a genuine response, and Leah was jealous then, a strip right underneath the overlay of gratitude. *Don't be petty.* Jeff buttoned his suit jacket, gray pinstripe today, a darker shade than his hair. His tie was a muted red, yet not maroon. Just a fingertip of blue would mix that shade. At least he was managing to look like an expensive lawyer, though the papers had made a big deal about him being a public defender. As if she and Dennis hadn't tried.

"Ms. Ridley. You've given your address as The Bay Breeze Hotel on Seventh Avenue. Is that located in what is known as the Tenderloin of San Francisco?"

"That's right." Dara sounded nervous, though she'd managed to walk with something between a sway and a swagger.

"Did you have occasion to meet the defendant Alyssa Staton there?"

"That's right."

"Would you explain to the jury how you came to know the defendant?" Jeffrey was patient-sounding. Leah checked the jury, most of whom seemed to be studying Dara as if she were some sort of lab specimen. Her hair *was* improbable, teased platinum curls like a mass of too pale seaweed, and those clothes . . . surely Jeffrey *had* told her how to dress. He'd told Leah, and he thought Dara was important enough to have scrubbed the Tenderloin daylight to find her.

"She was real sick. I saw her first in the hallway of our building, waiting for the bathroom."

"Did you have an opinion as to what might be wrong with her?"

Old Marcy just couldn't jump up fast enough. Didn't even button her jacket. "Objection, Your Honor. Calls for a conclusion; the witness is obviously . . . not an expert."

"Sustained."

Chapter Twenty

"I'll rephrase, Your Honor," Jeff said smoothly. Leah had to admit that sustained objections didn't seem to get to him. "Ms. Ridley, was there anything unusual about the defendant's appearance?"

Dara shifted in the witness seat. She licked her lips, hesitating. "Do you need to have the question repeated, Ms. Ridley?" Judge Franklin peered over his nose and half-glasses, a hawk on a perch.

"No, sir. Um . . . she was all bloody on her pants and up around her shirt some." Dara pointed to the area between her left shoulder and breast and then spread the gesture down toward her waist. "I thought it might be something female, real bad."

"Did Ms. Staton ask you for anything?"

"No, I asked her. I mean, anybody could see she needed help."

"And you helped her?"

"Yeah, I'd say. Hope I did anyway . . . she didn't belong there, she was. . . ."

"Just confine yourself to the questions," Franklin said to Dara, but there wasn't an edge to the admonition. Leah had heard him snap at the lawyers more than once.

"Can you please tell the jury specifically how you helped her?"

"I . . . helped her clean up. And I loaned her my coat. It's a leopard skin, not real, but . . . she was shivering."

"And what else did you do for the defendant?"

"I got her a couple sandwiches and water here and there, got some clean sheets to make up a bed for her . . . the place isn't . . . too clean unless you know how to get stuff from Lenny." Dara caught herself in the explication and stopped.

Jeff leaned a little toward Dara, and made it clear by the pace that he was choosing his words with precision, pieces of a mosaic. "Ms. Ridley, now I am not asking for an expert opinion, just your opinion as a lay person, an observer. . . . Did Ms. Staton appear to have her wits about her?"

Dara spoke immediately, earnestly. "She was out of it."

"Out of it? Could you explain that more?"

"She was weak, like she could hardly stand up. And she wasn't talking right."

"You mean like she was out of her mind?"

"Objection, Your Honor. Calls for a conclusion, and witness is not expert on state of mind." Marcelle was unruffled, smooth, her perky hair sprayed rigidly in the exact wave patterns every day.

"Asking what the witness thought about what she observed, Your Honor." Jeff faced the bench. He had square shoulders, medium-broad, very, very straight, though Leah would have bet he'd not been in the military. Where would he have kept his rubber lizards?

"I'll allow it, but proceed carefully, Mr. Earle."

Dara looked from Jeffrey to the judge and back. Leah watched her realize she was supposed to answer. Dara licked her lips.

"Not like she was crazy, but like she was hurting and couldn't string words into a line right."

"Did she ask you to hide her?"

"No."

"Did she seem—*to you*—to be hiding?"

Marcelle Ward Fayler stood quickly, but Judge Franklin anticipated her. "I'm going to allow that, Ms. Fayler."

"If she was trying to hide, she was doin' a pretty bad job," Dara said. "She went out on the street . . . to get stuff, I think."

"Stuff?"

Dara gave an embarrassed little cough. "Like personal . . . supplies. Um . . . pads. I'd of given her some but I had none to give. I don't have . . . all my parts."

"Was there anything else you gave her?"

"Um, well, she asked me for some Tylenol, but I didn't have any. I . . . used to have some Percocets from once when I was hurt, and I gave her them."

"Percocets. Is that some kind of medicine?"

Chapter Twenty

"It's a painkiller."

Marcelle was on her feet. "Objection, Your Honor. The witness isn't qualified...."

"I'll rephrase, Your Honor," Jeffrey said to the judge. "Ms. Ridley, can you please tell the court what you had used those drugs for?"

"Like I said, it's a painkiller."

"And how did Ms. Staton behave after she'd taken the painkiller you gave her?"

"She slept."

"Can you tell us how long?"

"Couple days, pretty much. She was knocked out. Had a fever, I knew that much."

"Ms. Ridley, we'll be calling a physician to testify as to how the prescription drug Percocet can affect a person, but would it be fair to say that Ms. Staton was in something like a stupor—as you observed her?"

"Like I said, she was completely out of it. She was, um ... indisposed ... She was completely indisposed." Pleased to have come up with the word she wanted.

"For several days."

"Yeah."

"Was she taking Percocet all that time?"

"... Yes." Head down.

"How many did you give her?"

"All I had. She was bad off, hurting, and sweating."

"To the best of your knowledge, Ms. Ridley, did Ms. Staton appear to be under the influence of alcohol or narcotics when you met her?"

"Objection."

"Asking as to witness's personal and contemporaneous observation, Your Honor, not history."

"I'll allow it. Ms. Ridley, you may testify only as to what you personally observed at the time you met the defendant."

"No. She'd of been better off if she was, wouldn't of been suffering like that."

"When did you last see Ms. Staton?"

"I'm not exactly sure."

"Could it have been the day of February 9?"

"Could have been, sure. I don't keep a day runner, myself."

"Was she better?"

"She could get up. I guess you could say she was some better."

"Did she say where she was going?"

"No. But she said she had to get back to something. That's all."

"Thank you Ms. Ridley. The defense is finished with this witness, Your Honor." Jeffrey nodded toward Marcelle as he headed back to the defense table. His eyes met Leah's, and she felt his acknowledgment, though she couldn't identify how she knew he was reassuring her.

"Do you wish to cross?" Judge Franklin spoke to Marcelle.

She buttoned her jacket as she unfolded. Leah imagined the button falling off, tried to will it to happen. Would that rattle Marcelle's cage?

"Good morning, Ms. Ridley. Would you please explain to the court when and why those Percocets—a controlled substance, a narcotic— were prescribed for you?"

"I . . . don't remember. It was a long time ago, when I was under a physician's care, of course. I had them a long time."

"And the name of the doctor?"

"I . . . don't remember."

"Is it true in your experience that Percocet are illegally obtainable as a street drug in the Tenderloin district?"

". . . I wouldn't know."

"I'm sure you wouldn't, Ms. Ridley. I'm sure. Nothing further, Your Honor."

A doctor testified about the effect of narcotics, and was allowed to speculate about the severity of the pain Alyssa might have had during and after an unattended birth, the tears in her perineum documented by the hospital, the blood loss. Leah imagined her daughter lying alone on the winter-cold, winter-hard ceramic underneath a public toilet bowl and then tried to block out the image.

Then, the next morning, Jeff called Clara to the stand to establish Alyssa's behavior just before the birth: that she sounded and appeared disoriented. *I'll do my best for her*, she'd told Leah. *I know you will*, Leah said. *I know the courtroom brings back memories. Thank you for doing this.*

"Ms. Edwards, would you please describe to the court your observation of Alyssa Staton in the several months and weeks immediately preceding February 4?" Jeff's slanty brows rose when his voice did at the end of his sentences, straightening them nearly into horizontal lines. Leah sat deliberately off-center today, behind the prosecution side so she could see more of Allie's face, and Jeff's as he questioned each witness.

Clara was imposing with her hair up in a simple twist, a low pompadour on the top, unfamiliar and formal. Her cheekbones were high and fine under fingers of light rouge. Lipstick, too, on her thin mouth. "Yes sir. I thought she was sick."

"Can you be more specific?"

"I saw she'd put on weight. She looked poorly. Tired a lot, and too pale."

"Did she ever mention that herself?" Jeff asked. One hand—on the small side for a man of his stature—gestured twice, palm up, as if to suggest this would have been an obvious conversation between Alyssa and Clara.

"No sir."

"Did she ever mention being pregnant?"

"No."

"Did you have the sort of relationship in which information of this sort would be shared?"

"Yes, we did—do—but I'm not sure she knew herself," Clara said.

Jeff paused, letting the jury absorb that one, then went on. "The morning of this past February 4, did you have occasion to see the defendant?"

"Yes, I did."

"Would you describe that encounter to the court?"

"Her dog had been barking and scratching on the door. It's not like Alyssa . . . she always takes care of her dog. I knocked quite a while before she came to the door. Then she wouldn't let me in because she was sick. I did notice the dog had . . . relieved himself on the floor. I asked her if she was all right."

"And how did the defendant respond?"

"She said she was sick," Clara repeated.

"What did you do then?"

"I told her I'd take the dog out, to walk him, and take care of him for her."

"Ms. Edwards, can you describe to the court if the defendant seemed like someone who just didn't feel well?"

". . . No sir. She was talking too slow, and I thought she was very sick. Maybe in pain."

"Were you concerned?"

"Yes. But she wouldn't let me help."

"Now, Ms. Edwards, at that time, did Alyssa Staton seem to you to be someone who had full presence of mind?"

"Objection, Your Honor. Witness is not expert as to. . . ." Marcelle made every objection as dramatically as if it were her last opportunity to object to anything in her life. Sickening.

"Asking the witness' personal opinion, Your Honor, her observation," Jeff said calmly.

"I'm going to allow that, Ms. Fayler. The witness may answer the question." Judge Franklin looked over the top of his glasses again. His brows made a bony ledge over his eyes when he tucked his chin chestward, and the habit wadded his neck into strata of shadows.

Chapter Twenty

"No, she wasn't right. I only saw her face because the door wasn't open all the way, but she looked like she was in a daze."

"In a daze? Can you be more specific?"

"She sounded, well, out of it, like she . . . couldn't get the right words together." Leah could see and hear that Clara's testimony was unrehearsed. Good. Let the jury hear an honest woman, not think that everything was just so simple, the way Marcelle Ward Fayler would have them see it.

"Thank you, Ms. Edwards." Jeff was gracious without fawning. Leah liked that. Last night she'd dreamed about him, dreamed he was examining her teeth. She'd been in a dentist chair, and he'd wiggled each one as if she were a child and he were checking for looseness. Gently. So gently. He'd found some old food wedged between two of them, debris that brushing should have cleaned, and he'd removed it without revealing her shame to some people clustered behind him. Thank you, she'd whispered in the dream. It's nothing, he'd answered with his characteristic dismissive gesture, never making much of himself or letting anyone else make much of him. Bob was like that, Leah thought. He'd called her four or five times, not excessively, to see how she was. Cory had, of course, given him the phone number, but Leah found she didn't mind.

"I have nothing further for this witness, Your Honor," Jeff said.

It was Marcelle's turn. She stood up but stayed at the prosecution table. She looked the same every day, a tailored suit with straight skirt to the knees, jacket on over a coordinating shell, some simple necklace. Earrings, often some variant on pearls. Everything always matched, always coordinated, which fascinated and repelled Leah. That someone was in such military control! Down to where the waves in her hair fell. Leah poked at her own less-than-organized waves and then pushed against her forehead with her fingertips, not quite the gesture that says headache, but nearly. She took a deliberate, deep breath. The defense didn't have many witnesses, especially when lined up after the prosecution's parade of police, detectives and doctors. So far they'd had Dara, whom Jeff had called before Clara only because he was afraid Dara would change her mind and disappear into the shadows of her city.

"Ms. Edwards," Marcelle began. "You have testified that you thought the defendant was sick for quite some time before February 4, is that correct?"

"Yes." Clara omitted the *ma'am*, which would have matched the *sir* she'd used to Jeffrey.

"And you testified that she never mentioned it?"

"That's right."

"But what about you, Ms. Edwards. All the times you thought she was 'sick,' as you say. Didn't you ever say anything to her?"

"Yes."

"What exactly did you say?"

"I said I thought she should go to the health center or a doctor somewhere else," Clara said.

"Did you think she was pregnant, Ms. Edwards?"

"I didn't know. The thought occurred to me, but I didn't know."

"I see. And when she was so 'sick,' as you say, on the morning of February 4, and seemed 'dazed,' again as you say, did you consider getting her medical attention?" The phrase *as you say* was powdered with irony.

Clara paused. "I thought she needed it, but . . . no."

"So, perhaps you knew what was happening—that she was in labor—and was likely to hide the birth. Even dispose of her baby."

"Objection." This time Jeffrey was on his feet quickly. "That's not a question."

"Sustained."

"Did you have an idea of what Ms. Staton intended? Is that why you took her dog, so she could slip away to have her baby and kill it?"

"No!" Strong face and voice, but calm, not outraged.

"Did you call for medical help, Ms. Edwards?"

322

Chapter Twenty

"No. I didn't."

"Then perhaps Ms. Staton didn't appear as sick and dazed as you've suggested?"

No quick answer.

"Which was it, Ms. Edwards?"

"It wasn't my place to do more than she asked," Clara said. She kept her voice strong, credible to Leah.

But Marcelle was right back at her. "Ms. Edwards, would you have this court believe that if you witnessed an accident, you wouldn't call for help unless a dazed, injured victim specifically asked you to? You wouldn't use your own judgment?"

Jeffrey's seat clattered behind him when the backs of his legs hit it. "Objection. Hypothetical."

"Withdrawn. Ms. Edwards, it was you who called the defendant's mother several days later and suggested she fly across the country, correct?"

"Yes."

"Had the defendant asked you to do this?"

"No."

"So sometimes you do something you're not asked to. . . ."

"Yes."

"And did you call the defendant's mother because you thought she was still sick?"

"I was worried."

"Worried that she might be in trouble?"

"Yes."

"Had it occurred to you that she might be the mother of the BART Baby, as the press was calling the newborn found dead in the trash at the Shattuck Avenue station?"

"Yes."

"And you thought she might need some high-powered help to get her out of this one?"

Baby's Breath

"Objection! The question is—"

"I'll withdraw the question, Your Honor. I'm finished with this witness."

The press couldn't, wouldn't, didn't leave her alone. Somehow it had leaked—for all Leah knew there were no secrets about her or Allie left anywhere in the universe, period—that Allie's attorney was calling her back to the stand. Leah's every coming and going was attended by cameras, microphones and microcassettes. "No comment," was how Leah exhaled now.

"Don't let the bastards grind you down," Jeffrey Earle told her in a conference room in the courthouse the night before she was to testify for the defense. His jacket was on the back of his chair, and he'd rolled up his light blue sleeves to different heights, which bothered Leah. Now she wanted him as organized and in control as the prosecutor. She knew he had a black toy snake in his pants pocket; he'd pulled it out accidentally with his wallet when he'd reached in for money to buy them sodas out of the machine. Every time she started feeling that he really was managing this trial every bit as well as any big-name famous lawyer possibly could, something brought her up short.

"Well they do," Leah snapped. "I'm sorry. I don't mean to take it out on you. I just want. . . ."

"I know," he said. "I do too. So let's get it done. I'm going to try to undo Marcy's work. . . ." He grinned. "She hates when I do that." The overhead light reflected on the bald front of his head and it looked like its own source of light. *If only*, Leah thought.

"She made me look terrible, but the real thing is how bad she made Allie look. I *did* lie, not that it helped, but I wish it had." Leah's eyes watered, but she recognized the first tingling in her nose that signaled tears and stopped them short.

"Listen. Don't give up. We've got a good judge. He's fair. And I *feel* the jury wanting us to explain this, to give them a way to understand. That'll be up to Alyssa. That's what'll make or break us. They've got to hear from her. You can't do that for her and neither can I. It's there in her, if she can just trust them enough to let them see."

"Okay. I'm all right." Leah said, lifting her shoulders as she consciously breathed in, letting them settle back in a straighter line with her spine.

"Let's go over your testimony now. Tomorrow is another day, but morning will come awfully quick," he said, taking a legal pad out of his briefcase and clicking a ballpoint pen to ready.

"The defense calls Leah Rhee Pacey back to the stand at this time, Your Honor."

Jeff took her through the Allie's Thanksgiving visit. No, she hadn't thought her daughter was pregnant. No, there were no signs or symptoms. Allie had always had a tendency—until now, eyes over on Allie at the defense table—to heaviness, especially when she was under stress which Leah had assumed was the case at a school like the University of California, especially on the Berkeley campus. No, she hadn't appeared to make any attempt to hide anything from her mother; in fact they had gone clothes shopping together. (Now Leah wore a plain black dress under a beige cotton and linen blazer, trying not to look as if she'd bought something new in which to appear, which she had. She'd clipped her hair up in a wide black and beige barrette. No jewelry except the medium black and gold square earrings. *Keep it simple; don't look like an artist*, Jeff had told her. *People think artists fool them all the time.* She protested. *"Well, we don't. A real artist is honest, or the work doesn't . . . work."* "I believe you," Jeff had said softly, then repeated. *"I believe you."* She did like the man. No artifice, no oil.)

And on to the towel. The damned monogrammed towel. Yes, she'd lied to the police. No, not because she thought her daughter had done this, not because it was in keeping with the daughter she knew, but exactly because it was inconceivable. She'd been afraid. She'd been convinced of a terrible mistake.

"But haven't you previously testified that you believed your daughter had been in her apartment in your absence that same day?" Marcelle pressed.

"Yes."

"Did you give that information to the police?"

"No." Leah tried to keep her posture from revealing her discomfort. Marcelle was too close, thickening the air with her presence. Leah felt like she needed to draw back to get a clean lungful of air, but refused to give way.

"Why not?"

"I . . . it was instinct."

"Instinct? I'm not sure what you mean, Ms. Pacey."

Leah hesitated, considering. "To protect her."

"I'm not clear why you'd think she needed protecting if you thought it was inconceivable that she'd give birth secretly and take the baby's life."

"It wasn't that. I didn't know *what* was going on, I was just trying to create some space around her . . . around myself. It was sort of like putting myself between her and . . . danger . . . until I could know she wasn't in danger. It's what mothers do," she finished lamely.

"It's what mothers do?" Marcelle repeated, lacing her voice with incredulity. "It's a shame your daughter didn't learn that. Nothing further, Your Honor."

Dr. Stojanovic would be the final witness for the defense before Allie herself, who was to be last. Jeff asked for an early lunch recess—a motion to which Marcelle, amazingly, didn't object—so the psychiatrist could begin after the jurors were refreshed. "It can backfire," he told Leah in the hallway. Jeff wore glasses today, fairly thick and set in gold wire that appeared too insubstantial for the job. He must usually wear contacts. "Jurors sometimes like to nap after lunch." The lenses made it hard to read his eyes, where Leah usually found some comfort.

"Literally?" Leah scanned the jury frequently and thought she'd have noticed. Sometimes she'd catch one studying his fingernails or digging in her pocket for a handkerchief, but—except when the prosecution showed pictures of the baby, towel-wrapped in its trash can bassinet, then unwrapped, then a close-up of the attached umbilical cord, ragged and drained—their faces had been impassive. There were a few, women, whose faces were soft when they looked at Allie, and Leah willed them in her mantra: *not guilty, not guilty, not guilty* even while she tried to get the tears off her face with a wadded-up Kleenex. (The baby was dark-capped, the image of Allie as a pale newborn, the same face unscrunched in placid sleep.)

"Well. No, not literally. Their minds wander or they sleep with their eyes open. But if you have lunch late and they're hungry, they get mad. And guess who they blame?" He lightened it with a smile. "Don't worry. If the judge thinks they're really not paying attention, he'll call a recess. Franklin's good."

Dr. Stojanovic looked better than he had the two times Leah had met with him, in a navy suit now, with a good-looking red paisley tie. A big plus: the tie wasn't tucked into his pants and his too-long wispy gray hair and beard were combed into order. Allie's theory was that the doctor's wife dressed him on days when his appearance might matter.

Like now, Leah supposed. The doctor's testimony and Alyssa's own were the shoulders that would bear the defense's world. *Be strong, be strong, be strong.*

"Dr. Stojanovic," Jeff said, after he'd ushered him through a recital of his training and experience. "Would you please describe the nature and extent of your contact with the defendant?"

The doctor cleared his throat and specified he'd spent twenty-one hours—an exceptional number—with the defendant. He'd also reviewed the psychological test results. Yes, his opinion was that she understood the nature of the accusations against her, knew the difference between right and wrong, and was able to cooperate in her own defense; therefore he agreed with the state's psychiatrist that she was competent to stand trial. "Which is not to say there are not significant psychiatric conditions that should be considered," Dr. Stojanovic tacked on.

"We'll go back to those," Jeff said.

Previous scholastic aptitude tests had indicated her IQ to be in the superior range, the doctor reported without consulting the file of notes he'd placed on the stand in front of him. Yes, he'd had access to the social history taken by a social worker and discussed significant aspects of it with her: her parents' relationship to each other and to Alyssa, her school experiences, her grandmother's strokes and subsequent residence with Alyssa and her mother. Esther Rhee Pacey's death. Alyssa's friends—no, she wasn't a gregarious sort, perhaps a little too easily hurt. Allie's response to her mother's recent professional success. Well, that, too, had displaced her somewhat in her own estimation.

Leah's eyes filled even as her mind rebelled, listing all she had postponed to raise her daughter.

"Overall, would you characterize Alyssa Staton as having been a happy child and young woman?" Jeff asked.

"No."

Despair had never been so real to Leah as now. Not when her father had died early and she'd not gone away to college after all; not as she'd changed diarrhea-reeking sheets and nightgown, or struggled with the feeding tube while her mother lay dying in the hospital bed that had assumed control of Leah's house. To have done all she could and still to have failed, completely failed.

"Doctor, did you find evidence of mental illness?"

"Not mental illness in the sense of a psychotic disorder that would render her unfit for trial."

Chapter Twenty

"Is there another sort of mental or emotional condition you noted?" Jeff looked taller than usual, straight and lean as a pole compared to the doctor, squatty and rotund in the witness box.

"The defendant was seriously depressed during the time I spent with her. In my opinion, the condition most likely existed prior to her giving birth and worsened afterward. I suspect it began as an adjustment disorder with depressed mood. Perhaps during her grandmother's terminal illness, or perhaps leaving for college. On the other hand, she may have had episodic bouts with major depression."

"Would you tell us the signs and symptoms which led you to this diagnosis?"

"Excessive sleeping, significant weight gain last year followed by excessive post-natal weight loss, social withdrawal, lethargy, persistent sad mood and affect, loss of interest in normal activities . . . ah, I suspect at least a passive suicidal ideation in that the patient indicated she thought things would be better if she were dead. And guilt." Dr. Stojanovic didn't seem to notice that a lock of gray hair had drifted down over one of his eyes. His glasses had slid down his nose a little, too, with the gestures that ticked off the catalog of symptoms.

"Would you characterize this as a mental illness?"

"The Diagnostic and Statistical Manual of the American Psychiatric Association doesn't refer to mental illness at all, but to disorders. Yes, clinical depression is a serious mental disorder."

"But the defendant is not insane?"

Marcelle was up. "Your Honor, the ruling on sanity was made a long time ago."

Jeff directed his response to the judge. "Your Honor, this goes to state of mind, not sanity. I'll show relevance."

"I'll allow it. Overruled."

Yes, Leah breathed. Clara, beside her today in case Allie was called, slid her hand from her lap across to Leah's hand and squeezed it briefly. Leah hadn't realized her exhalation had formed a word.

"Let me put it this way, Doctor. You are in agreement with the court's finding that the defendant is sane?"

"I am."

"But you also found evidence of a serious mental disorder."

"That's correct. As did, I believe, the state's psychiatrist."

"Here's what I want to get to. Would a mental disorder involving depression compromise a person's judgment?"

"Certainly." Emphatic.

"So is it accurate to say that although the defendant is sane in that she knows right from wrong, her judgment was affected by her depression? In other words, she may have made decisions that she wouldn't have made if she weren't depressed. Is that accurate?"

"In my opinion, yes."

"Would you explain specific ways in which her judgment might have been compromised?"

"People suffering from a depressive disorder, or clinical depression, often view situations as hopeless. Other people often see actions they might beneficially take, but the patient can't. Not won't. Can't. For Ms. Staton, an example might be that she could have sought help from her mother. Conceivably also from her father, but certainly her mother, a viable source of support and help." As Dr. Stojanovic spoke, Clara reached over and patted Leah's hand. "She was unable to discern, as a reasonable person would, a prudent course."

"Do you believe, Doctor, that Ms. Staton's behavior was premeditated?"

"I do not. I believe Ms. Staton was only intermittently and marginally aware of even being pregnant." He shook his head no. "She was so paralyzed by her small awareness, found it so hopeless and paralyzing, that she simply failed to plan at all. In any way. Denial probably describes it best."

"Now, on another issue, Doctor. If Alyssa Staton had been in treatment for her depression, would it likely have led to a different outcome?"

"Very likely. Medication would have probably been quite beneficial, as would have psychotherapy."

"Has medication been prescribed for Ms. Staton now?"

"Yes. She is taking 100 milligrams of Zoloft, which is an antidepressant medication, a selective serotonin reuptake inhibitor."

Jeff adjusted his glasses, which Leah could tell he wasn't used to wearing because they didn't sit evenly. "And Doctor, how would you describe Ms. Staton's personality, the depression notwithstanding? Can you make any determination?"

"I'd guess her to be sensitive to a fault. Tenderhearted. Wounded. Somewhat angry because of those wounds. Self-conscious. Shy. Wants to please others, but doesn't believe she can."

"Would you help us understand Ms. Staton's current emotional state?"

"She continues to be depressed."

"Would you characterize her as remorseful?"

The doctor hesitated. "I would characterize her as guilt-ridden and remorseful, in spite of the fact she has no affective memory of giving birth."

"No effective memory?" Jeff deliberately misunderstood for the jury's sake.

"No *affective* memory. That means no emotional memory, no memory of feeling. In other words, she believes it happened, even has vague intellectual memories of the scene, but it is like a dead zone inside her. I suspect it is the last vestige of the denial."

"So when you talked with her, the defendant didn't remember giving birth, or anything about the baby, but at the same time she didn't deny it?" Jeff wove the smallest thread of incredulity in his voice. It made Leah uneasy, but he'd told her he sometimes simply had to ask what the jury was probably thinking and approximate the reaction of any who might be skeptical.

"That's correct. I think it's simply so overwhelming to her that she has blocked a memory which at some level she believes she couldn't bear."

"But Doctor. . ." Jeff said, playing dumb again, "if she truly denied being pregnant to herself, and doesn't remember giving birth, why doesn't she deny that she did?"

"Because she believes us . . ." the doctor said. "The mechanisms are a little different. She didn't block out that she was pregnant. She was depressed and hopeless, felt utterly alone, and simply avoided dealing with it. Denied that she had to, if you will. But with regard to the birth, at that point, we can assume the pain, fear, well, the great trauma of an unattended birth was—is—so great that she simply blocked it from her conscious memory."

Leah looked at Allie who was looking down, studying her own hands, one cupped over the other. *Look up, Allie,* Leah willed. *Let them see you have some feelings.*

"Sort of like a robot?"

"Sort of like a robot. I believe during that time she dissociated, which is not an uncommon response."

"Dissociated?" Jeff pressed.

"Disconnected from what was happening around her. Didn't take it in or process it emotionally. It's actually a coping mechanism, though not one of the more functional ones." He shifted his weight and, by the way his body listed, seemed to cross his legs in the witness box.

"So . . . would you check me on this, Doctor? Your salient findings are that Alyssa Staton was and is still suffering from depression, a condition that seriously compromised her ability to assess her circumstances and to make good judgments." Jeff consulted his legal pad, then looked back up. "She is not insane, yet she dealt with her pregnancy primarily by denial and was too traumatized to remember the birth."

Chapter Twenty

"Yet," the doctor added. "Remember it yet. I think she will, as she is able. Perhaps a little at a time."

". . . Too traumatized to remember the birth *yet*. Am I correct in how I've summarized your testimony?"

"Yes."

"Is there anything else you'd like to add?"

"Well . . ." the doctor, "only that she's a . . . very nice young woman." He looked beyond Jeff, to the defense table, straight on at Alyssa. "There's a lot to her. She thinks she's a bad person and she's not."

"Move to strike, Your Honor. The doctor's personal reaction to the defendant is not relevant."

"Sustained."

"I have nothing further, Your Honor," Jeff said to the judge. Then, to Marcy, courteously, "Your witness."

Marcelle, fake-tall in her high heels, intimidating in her power suit and the highlighted, slightly-unfurled wings of her hair, drilled methodically, but Leah didn't see that she struck oil. The doctor was unflappable. "Doctor, how do you know the defendant is telling you the truth when she says she doesn't remember giving birth?"

"Because it was congruent with her psychological tests—she tends to withdraw from difficult, conflicted or unpleasant situations—and because her credibility is high."

"But she could be lying to you."

"Anything is possible, but I don't believe it occurred. Were Ms. Staton lying, she would have been most likely to give an answer which she thought would please me. That and withdrawal are her two preferred paths in a painful or conflicted situation."

"Are you saying it would have pleased you to have her remember?"

"Indeed. It is in Ms. Staton's best interest to remember and process what happened, not repress it." The doctor looked at Alyssa again.

"She's not sure—inside herself—that she can handle it, but she's strong and I know she will."

Marcy moved into the sight line between Dr. Stojanovic and Alyssa. "Along the same lines, Doctor, you also believed her when she told you she had not planned to actively OR passively cause the death of her infant?"

"That's true."

"And that she wasn't . . . ah, did you say conscious?" Marcelle took several steps back to the prosecution table to consult a yellow legal pad on which she'd steadily scrawled notes while Jeff questioned the doctor. "She wasn't conscious of her pregnancy? You believed that?"

"Yes. Although I think I talked about denial, which is somewhat different."

"Yes. But how would you explain the infant moccasins which have been introduced into evidence as People's Exhibit Number Six?"

"I can't specifically explain them. But. . . ."

"That's all," Marcelle said, cutting him off. "Thank you for your testimony, Dr. Stojanovic."

CHAPTER

21

Your decision, Alyssa," Jeff said to her after she'd traded her brown suit for the jailhouse orange. Standing in the quiet of the emptied courthouse, he'd waited for the transport officers with her, his habit of the past several days. *Decompression chamber*, he'd laughed once when she'd asked him why he didn't tear away as Marcelle did, as if a stroke of the clock threatened to transform them all into something less than human.

She silenced the chains on her wrists and waist by freezing her shoulders, locking her elbows. You could put yourself in prison, easy enough, she'd learned that much. Even without the shackles and the razor wire, a person could seal herself right up, pull the tomb's iron door over her brain and never be heard from again. Dr. Stojanovic had told the jury she hid from things she didn't want to know, hid herself from people she didn't want to face. She neither recognized nor controlled these denial mechanisms, he'd assured them when they'd shifted in their seats, unconvinced by the psychological mumbo jumbo the doctor had to conjure up to explain Alyssa Staton, what she'd done. Traumatized, he'd said. No affective memory.

She'd been in prison already, she'd told Joey the night before when he passed her cell and found her, crying herself dry-eyed, just before lights out. She'd put in time the jailhouse computer would never be able to tabulate, she who had despised the abuse excuse, the recovered mem-

335

ory movement, any hint of a suggestion a person could claim to be less than responsible for her own behavior. Had she been a juror, she would have squirmed, too, expressing her disbelief with averted eyes or the urgent need to find something hidden beneath the clutter at the bottom of a deep pocket.

"I'll testify," she said to Jeff, the lift of her shoulders jingling the chains tying her hands to waist. "But if I can't—"

"Whatever you can remember, the jury deserves to hear." He fit his hand around hers, the squeeze of his fingers pressing the metal cuffs against the ridges of bone, *carpals*, outlining her wrists. She was as skinny as the Jack-o-Lantern, all bone and bruise. Bone and bruise and the thickness of remembered images that skittered through her artificial sleep like upside-down images cast from a haywire slide projector. Dr. Stojanovic said the Restoril would bring her sleep, but the two pills she swallowed each evening after dinner under Ostrom's watchful eyes sucked her into something more like paralysis than sleep. In the mornings when the warming hum of the jail's lighting system awoke her before the light itself, she remembered visions—hallucinations?—that made her heavy in daylight, weighed her down like the pounds of flesh dissolving from her, still. Then, after a breakfast choked down only as prologue to the Zoloft Dr. Stojanovic had prescribed, the visions fell away, leaving her light, emptied.

"Alyssa?" Jeff called to her when she turned to follow the officer into the elevator. "I'm going to be with you every minute." She nodded; she knew he would, Jeffrey with his rubber dinosaurs and plastic snakes, the unfeigned sweetness charming nearly everybody in the courthouse halls, the bailiff and the court clerk, the court recorder, even Marcelle Ward Fayler when she turned into Marcy, racing the clock, sprinting for the stairs because the elevators were too slow.

"Your mom, too," he said through the sliding doors, abbreviating Jeff to six inches, then three, then gone.

Yes. Leah too. Every minute.

336

Chapter Twenty-One

*

"Just because," Leah said that night in the tube, nearly nine o'clock, when Alyssa asked her why she'd come out to the jail, she didn't have to do it, they'd see each other the next morning. "And to tell you that I gave Jeff another suit . . . for tomorrow, honey."

"Mom. It's not a debut."

"No, it's not . . . but I couldn't sit, and you're so thin, you're just lost in the other one, sweetheart, I just—"

"It's not a fashion show, either. You don't get points for haute couture."

"Oh, Allie . . . I did it for *me*."

A strand of Leah's thick, wild hair, longer than Alyssa's now and turned loose since she wasn't on the courtroom stage, had twined itself into the layered loops of a dangling silver earring, just like the pairs that lay tied together on the street vendors' velvet tabletops next to silver bracelets and necklaces. It would hurt if her mother, unknowing, were to pull the earring off or run a comb through her hair. If the glass weren't between them, Alyssa could reach over and untangle the dark strand from the silver hoops without breaking a single hair so the earring would swing free and her mother wouldn't feel even the slightest hint of loss.

"Mom?"

"What is it, honey?" Leah lifted her head from the hand she'd been bracing it with, a tired return to the posture of readiness, of support.

With her free hand, Alyssa touched her own bare lobe.

"Clara gave them to me," Leah said, bracing the receiver against her raised shoulder, both hands working her hair through the silver loops. "Pretty, huh? Very Berkeley, I thought."

"Get my backpack, Mom, okay?"

"What?"

"When I was booked . . . they took my backpack. They said I could sign a release for you to pick it up. I want you to get it."

"Of course I will. Was there something you—"

"Lazzie's in it."

"Oh."

"That's why."

"Okay."

The officer behind Leah pointed to the face of his wristwatch. *Time's up.*

"They're pulling up the drawbridge," Leah said, gathering herself. "Jeff will give you the suit—it's dark blue, the prosecution's favorite—"

"Mom," Alyssa said, holding her mother with her voice travelling through the thin cord like oxygen, like blood. After she'd returned the phone to its cradle, their connection cut, when her mother turned to go, *Mama.*

She used the two silver clips she'd found, still pinched onto their square of felted cardboard and tucked inside the skirt pocket of the navy suit, to pull her hair back behind her ears. Fully facing the changing room mirror in the courthouse, for a moment she'd thought of pulling them from her hair, returning the barrettes to the pocket and pretending she hadn't found them. Then Jeff's knock was on the heavy door, and it was time to go into court. She looked at herself once more, the fineness of the bone structure riding her own face, the deepness of the dark-browed eyes. She startled when, turning toward the door, the cant of her mirrored face darkened by half-shadow, she recognized her mother's bones, her mother's eyes.

"If it please the court, Your Honor, the defense would call its final witness, the defendant Alyssa Pacey Staton, to the stand."

One question at a time, Alyssa. That's all you answer. One question at a time, Jeff's last words to her before they entered the courthouse, single file, silent. She found her way to the witness box by following his directions, one foot at a time, one before the other, until she'd stepped up and been sworn in and then seated. Then it came to her, what she hadn't considered before, that she would be facing the entire courthouse: the jury to her right, the reporters in the back row with their press cards flashing codes into the courthouse lighting, her mother and Clara dead center behind the defense table. She'd be talking to them, all of them, as much as she'd be talking to Jeff. She pulled at her hair, then remembered and put her hands in her lap.

"Miss Staton," Jeff said, the lawyer-voice he was using assuring the jury that he wouldn't coddle his witness, not with a charge like murder. "Have you ever denied, either during interrogation by the Berkeley police or during subsequent questioning by your counsel and court-appointed psychiatrists, that you delivered a baby girl in the Shattuck Avenue BART station on the evening of February 4, 1998?"

"No." She was lifting a slab, a fallen gravestone that wouldn't give.

Judge Franklin leaned toward her, his half-glasses pushed to the tip of his long nose. "Miss Staton, you'll need to speak more clearly. The jury needs to hear you."

"No." Louder, but Judge Franklin raised his hand, a quick gesture, *louder*. "No. I never denied that." Loud enough. True enough.

"And you have never denied that you *left* the baby girl in the Shattuck Avenue Station on the evening of February 4, is that correct?"

"Yes." Judge Franklin wouldn't have to direct her again; she'd found a voice. If she talked to Leah and Clara as if they were across a room, or a street, the jury could hear her. She could hear herself.

"According to the psychiatric evaluations submitted to this court by both Doctors Bulton and Stojanovic, you were suffering from a 'serious mental disorder' at the time you gave birth." Jeff paused. "Miss Staton, do you understand the term 'clinical depression?'"

"I do . . . I think so. It means—"

"That's all right, Miss Staton, we've heard it, we've heard it already. I'm interested in something else. Would *you* have described yourself as severely depressed during your freshman year at the university?"

"Objection!" Marcelle was up, soldier-straight. "I don't see relevance

here . . . we're concerned with the defendant's account of the events including and subsequent to February 4, not her college history."

Jeff countered, "Relevant to premeditation, Your Honor, both expert
psychiatric witnesses indicated that previous—"

"Overruled," Judge Franklin said dryly, as much to Jeff as to Marcelle. "It goes to establishing state of mind at the time of the act, so I'm
allowing."

"Miss Staton, let me repeat the question. Did you, during your freshman year—ending in June of 1997—and the following summer and
fall, ever consider yourself severely depressed?"

"No . . . I never used those words, I didn't think of myself as depressed."

"Could you tell us what words, what words you *did* use, or would
have used?"

"I was . . . I felt sad a lot . . . I felt . . . homesick, and sad, and lonely."
This was true. She'd been lonely the whole year at Griffiths, even with
Cindy and Linnie, with Professor Miller and the pizza nights in the
lounge, she'd been homesick, mistaking her hunger for home as hunger for food, stuffing her yearning with cookies and candy bars.

"You felt *sad* and *homesick* and *lonely*, your words?"

"Yes."

"Did you tell anyone? A roommate, a counselor, your family?"

"No, I didn't."

"Can you tell us why you didn't try to convey these sad feelings to
someone else?"

Leah wiped something from her cheek, looked down, then back up.
Alyssa looked back to Jeffrey. "I didn't want to . . . use up anybody's
time with my own problems."

"Was there something more?"

"I didn't know, I wasn't sure if anyone I could have told would have
. . . cared enough to . . . listen . . . or do something . . . for me." No way
around it, the bluntness of truth, it hurt people, no matter what.

Chapter Twenty-One

"You were unsure if anyone you could have told would have cared enough to listen, to help?"

"Yes."

"So you hid those feelings, sort of counterfeiting your real sadness as being okay, getting along?"

"Objection! Counsel is feeding the witness! This isn't direct, it's scriptwriting!" Marcelle spoke so loud and fast spit flew from her mouth. That had happened once to Alyssa, in speech, and though she knew it happened to everybody, it had embarrassed her so much she'd had to leave class early, had to go home and go to bed. Marcelle didn't care, though, with her perfect hair and her power suits and her dangerously high heels, she didn't give one whit. And now, Alyssa could feel it like calcium inside the new bones that poked from her skin at every turn, if it were to happen to her, Alyssa wouldn't care either.

"Sit down, Ms. Fayler. Sustained, Mr. Earle. Stop the screenwriting."

"Miss Staton. Tell us, tell the court, whether you revealed those great feelings of sadness."

"No, I didn't reveal . . . or tell anybody. I pretended . . . when I went home—" eyes straight to Leah's, "—even when I went home, I pretended to my mom and my dad that school was great, that I wasn't homesick . . . I didn't stay very long. I hid it . . . from everyone who knew me . . ."

"And you hid, also, your pregnancy?"

"I didn't think about it . . . I didn't think about it as being pregnant. I was overweight, everybody used to talk about it, so it was easy . . . to just think that I was getting . . . heavier . . . since I had been, anyway."

"You deliberately disguised your pregnancy?"

"No, I just wore my regular clothes. When you're . . . heavy, you wear baggy clothes, you eat by yourself, you sort of . . . make yourself invisible. And I felt sick, I felt sick a lot and I thought that—I did tell the father—"

"Go on," Jeff said softly, just to her, but Judge Franklin didn't make him repeat it for the jury. "You told the father of this baby about the pregnancy?"

"Yes . . . I . . . told him, I thought it was too late, though."

"Too late for?"

"Too late for . . . what he said I should do . . . an abortion. He said he'd go with me . . . but he didn't really . . . I couldn't really . . . I didn't think it was his responsibility."

"You told the father and you felt it was too late for the help he offered?"

"I knew it was too late, but I didn't tell him so . . . and it wasn't his fault because . . . because I told him I'd taken care of it."

"You told the father you'd taken care of the pregnancy, meaning had an abortion?"

"Yes."

"You led the father to believe you'd resolved the problem that he was indeed responsible for?"

"I didn't think it was his responsibility . . . because I'd lied to him . . . and I didn't talk to him again because . . . because I just didn't want to think about it. I didn't think about it. I went to class and I stayed by myself and I didn't think about it."

"Miss Staton, would you name the father for the court?"

"No, I told you already I wouldn't."

"You will not name the father of this child?"

"No. He didn't do it. I did it. He isn't responsible. I am."

Jeff let the silence be. It was Judge Franklin who broke it, adjourning them. A respite for the jury, he said, looking at Alyssa.

"Miss Staton, would you describe for me the first week of February, what you were feeling, what you were doing."

"I was going to class until I got sick."

"You got sick?"

Chapter Twenty-One

"I started feeling sick at the end of January. I thought I had the flu . . . I'd already had it twice before, and I didn't feel like seeing anybody or doing anything." She hadn't opened the door to Clara, she remembered, she'd stood with her wretched, sagging, soaked body blocked by the door and spoken to Clara through the chain.

"Were you sick, as you say, on February 4?"

"Yes."

"Miss Staton, I'd like you to go over for us, the best you can remember, what you did on that evening. Can you do that? Just start at the beginning?"

Alyssa caught her breath. She felt Judge Franklin watching. Marcelle, Clara, and Leah. Women's eyes, mothers' sight. "Yes."

"Just start at the beginning," Jeff coached.

"I was sleeping on the couch of my apartment. I'd been sleeping, sort of sick with a fever, for two days." Behind Jeff, Clara reached for Leah's hand, pulled it into her own lap.

"This was your apartment on Dwight Way?"

"Yes. I couldn't get out to walk my dog. I knew I should, my apartment was a mess, but I kept having to go to the bathroom, and I didn't want to be too far to, you know—"

"To reach the bathroom?"

"Yes."

"When did you go into labor?"

"I don't know what time. Late, after dark. Clara had come and taken my dog, and my . . . my water broke . . . I know now."

"You know now?"

"I didn't know what it was then . . . when it was happening. I thought I'd . . . had an accident."

"Then what did you do?"

"I took my backpack . . . with some towels because I'd . . . wet myself . . . and I walked."

Baby's Breath

"You walked. Where were you going?"

"I didn't know. I walked downhill, toward the bay. It was like I couldn't stay still . . . the pains . . . I had to move . . . so I kept walking."

"Where did you stop?"

"I stopped at Shattuck, at the BART station. I had to sit down, get out of the wind."

"And what did you do?"

"I went down the stairs . . . into the restroom."

"What were you feeling?"

"I couldn't stand. My stomach was turning inside out. My pants were wet. I went into a stall and closed the door. I thought I was going to faint if I didn't sit down. It . . . hurt." She caught her breath, heard the dwarf's screeches, her scrabbling hands against the closed stall door. *Don't mess my kitchen.*

"And then?"

"Then I, I didn't think of it as labor, but I was in labor. I put a towel on the floor, the floor was so dirty . . . and I sat on it . . . and I pushed. Not very long . . . maybe I fell asleep, I don't know."

"And?" Jeff's voice was there with every pain, a midwife's coaxing, gentle hands now, nursing, stroking.

Her throat contracted, her voice stumbled, she rode through the wave of pain. "I felt the . . . the baby pushing through and I shifted, I lay further back on the towel so the baby, the baby wouldn't touch anything but the towel. I pushed as hard as I could. . . ." She faltered, reached her hands to her eyes.

"It's okay," Jeff whispered. "Stay with me now." Judge Franklin lifted his tufty white eyebrows, but he didn't admonish. "You positioned yourself on the towel so that, you say so that the baby wouldn't be born onto the dirty floor, correct?"

"Yes, I had . . . I had the towels in my backpack."

"And after the baby was born . . . delivered?"

Chapter Twenty-One

"I think I—I mean they told me I—cut the umbilical cord . . . with my knife."

"You cut the umbilical cord with your knife."

"I knew if a, if a doctor were there, that's what he would do, so I did it."

"And then?"

"I pressed on the cord . . . on the baby's stomach . . . because it was bleeding and I wanted it to stop. I pressed on it with the towel and then with toilet paper, trying to make it stop." She *had* done that—she could see it now, her white hands against the baby's red belly, the blood trickling from the umbilical, mixing with the smears of blood from her own womb, her bare, bloodied legs. The baby's lips, moving. Her own terror.

"You tried to stop the bleeding through the umbilical?"

"Yes. I wiped the baby, I cleaned it with toilet paper, too, because of all the . . . you know . . . I wiped around its—her—mouth and I wiped her body—" The perfect body, the tiny hands that had flexed when she'd wiped them, the miniature palms coming clean like petals. Did she imagine it now, or had she held the hand, felt the curled fingers attached to her thumb? The pictures were tumbling into focus, freeze-frames and moving sequences layering themselves like falling petals, the little hands, the thrust of a tiny foot against her wrist, the mat of dark hair striking her now, a surprise.

Jeff's eyes flicked to the evidence table and back. He nodded at her, go on. You're almost there.

"I wrapped her in the green towel, tight, because I thought it would . . . would stop the . . . the bleeding. I thought it had, the towel was clean, and she was, she was sleeping, I thought. Her eyes were closed." Another contraction of the throat now, so sharp and tight that she thought she'd faint this time. Her cheeks were wet, her hands wet from wiping them. Judge Franklin handed her a box of Kleenex.

Baby's Breath

Inside her, growing, was a chrysalis of horror and remorse and regret, yet, her hand brushing the Judge's fingers when she accepted the Kleenex, conviction, too, because she knew now she'd swabbed her baby girl's body, held that tiny hand. *Handled with care*, she thought, and buried her face in the scented Kleenex, soft as a baby's bunting.

Judge Franklin motioned Jeffrey to the bench. "Mr. Earle, do you want to recess for your witness to pull herself together?"

Jeff looked at her. *Your call*, he was saying without a word.

"No," she said. She swallowed her tears, the taste of her waxing penitence. A substance like sorrow fused itself to her cells, changing her into another person, one already dead and newly delivered. They all watched her, Jeffrey and the jury, Marcelle and the judge, her mother and Clara. They were watching her as if she were an amputee, a leper, a mooncalf. That didn't matter, though, what they thought, or what they thought they were seeing. What mattered was what was growing inside her, the gift of cognizance, the knowledge that shame could be its own blessing.

She told them she'd held the baby, her baby, in her own hands with their nubby nails and their childhood scars from the car door and the bread knife marking her, making her who she was. She'd fit the baby against her heart, one moment against her breast, and breathed her damp, just-born smell, her lips pressed against the red skin of the baby's face, the faintest tickle of the dark hair. She'd wiped her baby clean and wrapped her in a clean towel and found her a safe place—soft, safe—where someone was close and would hear her crying and would be able to take care when she couldn't, wasn't able to. And the moccasins, the moccasins were for when she would be able, when she'd figured out—

"Miss Staton, what was your expectation after you put the baby into the trash receptacle?"

"I thought . . . someone would find her . . . there was a woman who was there, I'd seen her before, and I thought she'd be back."

Chapter Twenty-One

"Your expectation was that the baby would be cared for?"

"Objection!" Marcelle was fighting mad. "Your Honor, with all due respect, that question is absurd. What bearing—"

Judge Franklin touched his temple with two fingers. "State of mind, Ms. Fayler. State of mind. Overruled." He picked up his glasses. *Tired,* Alyssa thought, *as tired as I am.*

"Look, I know it sounds wrong. I didn't imagine her—" She was talking to Marcelle, looking her straight in the eye, making sure she could hear, would know Alyssa was talking to her. "I didn't think that she would die—" She caught the sob, stuffed it down. She had no right to be a crybaby now, not ever again. "I never, ever would have run away if I thought that. . . ." No use, tears coming now, but her voice strong, not breaking. "I would never have left her if I thought she'd die. I would have died first, I could die now, I never meant it, I'm sorry. I'm sorry. I'm sorry."

She hadn't killed her own newborn baby, not like Marcelle had been saying she had, with malice aforethought and premeditation. She hadn't *killed* her, but she had died, the perfect baby girl she'd held against her heart, whose head she'd kissed, whose body she'd wrapped snug *because babies liked it that way.* First grief descended on her, lowering itself into a deathbed, like old flesh too tired to refuse the last lying-down.

"I know I deserve . . . punishment. I'm not trying to change that. I know I'm guilty of her death, like they've been . . . what I'm saying, all I'm trying to say is . . . I didn't mean for her to die."

Alyssa looked at Judge Franklin, Jeffrey, finally to Leah. She spoke to her mother's shining face, stripped to nakedness.

"I meant for her to be found."

CHAPTER

22

Waiting. It was worse, now the jury had been instructed and sent to their deliberations. Waiting wasn't something that led to good outcomes. During Esther's various hospitalizations, Leah had waited in airless, lightless boxy places where walls were painted to match old, bitter coffee left all day in the pot. Rooms claustrophobic as coffins, spaces shared with other waiting people when all she wanted was privacy, a cool cloth and an open window so she could breathe in some sky. Rooms in which she'd had to impose such rigid control on herself that she felt she was reining wild mustangs as their hoofs beat through her chest.

When the horses were quiet, though, they laid themselves down in beds of despair. Marcelle's cross-examination of Allie had been predictably brutal. Jeff explained to Leah that he'd not been able to help much on redirect because Marcy hadn't segued into new terrain, and there weren't apparent contradictions he could let Allie correct. What there were, instead, were innuendoes, raised eyebrows, expressions that translated to *this is not credible, nobody can believe what you are saying.*

For the first time, Leah thought about what she'd do if Allie were found guilty. "It's bad, isn't it?" she'd said to Clara, who'd come with her again today to hear the closing arguments.

"Alyssa's lawyer was good, though," Clara said thoughtfully as she gathered her purse and water bottle. "And he had the last word. That's what they'll remember. That business about being wise leaders."

"I know. And it's not that I think someone else would have done it better. Ready to do the press dodge dance?"

"You bet, honey. I'm sorta hoping one of 'em will try to mess with us. I'm about due to knock someone outta our way again."

Leah grinned. Clara's purse strap had become tangled with a reporter's camera strap quite by accident, but Clara didn't let go and the camera had clattered to the ground which had dispatched one of the throng completely and made the others back up some in response to the photographer's angry yelp. Leah had noticed that they left a little more space around her and Clara now, as if a force field were in place.

"They took Allie back to the jail, you know."

"Yeah. They do that." The voice of experience again. Clara touched Leah's shoulder lightly. "Her lawyer'll call you when the jury's in. They probably won't even start 'til tomorrow morning. Do you want to get something to eat on the way home?"

"You don't think there's any way they'll come back tonight?" Leah said as they headed out the side door, although she knew it would be staked out just as the main courthouse entrance was. Tonight there would probably be some nationals there too, since the case had gone to the jury.

"You've got a little time. They'll eat, they might meet and elect a foreman and take their first poll tonight to see where they stand, but I'm not thinking they'll get to unanimous tonight, are you?"

"No." Leah admitted. "I'm not. About dinner—thanks so much for asking. But Allie asked me to come out to the jail and sign to pick up her things. Not that I couldn't have done that months ago. But it seemed urgent to her that I get them now." She made a wry face. "And before that, I need to call Dennis. I promised." She clutched the strap of her purse as she pushed the door open. A camera flash ignited. "Here we go."

Baby's Breath

*

Leah tossed her purse on the couch, ran cold water into her palms cupped over the kitchen sink, and leashed Coffee for Clara's walk. When she took the panting Lab across the landing, Clara opened the door immediately. "Here," she said. "You eat, all right?" A microwave container of vegetable stew was in her hand. "Just heat it up."

Leah put her arms around Clara, lingering an extra few seconds as Clara returned the hug. "Thank you," she whispered. "You've been such a friend to me. And to Allie." As if it were all over. As if there'd be no more need, Leah heard herself put it in the past tense. How tenacious hope is, how randomly shaded with despair.

"You and Alyssa are good people," Clara said. "It's simple enough. You go call Alyssa's father—I've got the critter." She patted Coffee's head as he frisked around the women's legs insisting on their attention.

It was easier and easier to call Dennis, though Leah couldn't put her finger on why. She knew he was fighting Missy some on the issue of how supportive he should be to Allie, though even that was diminishing as Missy's baby progressed well out of the newborn stage. He was more subdued, like a softer hue, when she talked to him. Less bossy. More deferential even.

He answered the phone on the fourth ring. The baby was crying, too close to the phone for Dennis not to be holding him. Once, in a different lifetime, it was Allie over his diaper-covered shoulder while he patted her back with a painty hand.

"Dennis? It's me. Sounds like a bad time. I can call back, or you can call me."

"No! It's okay. Hang on a second." Leah heard the phone being set down and Dennis calling Missy to take Justin.

"Is it over?" he said when he came back to the phone.

"The jury's out. Oh Dennis, hearing her on the stand—god, it broke my heart. She didn't know what she was doing, you could tell, listening to her, if you didn't already think that."

350

Chapter Twenty-Two

"But no deal for lesser charges?"

"Not really. I guess they talked about second degree, but they wouldn't drop it to negligent homicide, which Jeff said would be right. That's manslaughter. The prosecutor's trying to make a name for herself, I guess. Anyway, Jeff wanted Allie to turn down second degree because he says the sentencing guidelines would still give her a life sentence."

"He thinks the jury will give her a lighter sentence?"

Leah shifted the phone to her other ear to free her right hand. She stuck Clara's stew in the microwave as she spoke. "It's not the jury, remember? The pretrial motions they agreed on? Sentencing by the judge?"

"Oh yeah. Well, listen," Dennis said. "I'm going to get on a plane out there tomorrow. I think I should be there to support her, one way or the other. Do you have a problem with that?"

"No, Dennis. You have a right. And anyway, I appreciate it. She'll be glad to see you. I'm going out there when I get off the phone."

"Good," he said, and for a moment in the silence that followed, they were just Alyssa's parents, together.

What came back and back to Leah as she drove to the jail beneath clouds as flat as old quilts was Allie's testimony. She'd seen her daughter's soul. Like the glints of light on the bay, pure and unfiltered each time the sun was briefly uncovered.

Leah signed in and went up to see Allie before even asking about the procedure for her to claim the bag of Allie's things. Maybe tonight would be the last night there would be glass between them. She wasn't allowed to touch Allie in the courtroom, though the first time Leah had approached she'd gotten both hands on her daughter's shoulders just before the guard intervened and made her step back. Now it had become a physical yearning real as a nursing mother's for her infant, Leah's need to take Allie in her arms. The analogy had occurred to

351

Leah when she was trying to remember if her body had ever hurt with wanting before.

"You must be tired, Mom. I'm sorry to get you out here tonight."

"It's okay, honey. I'm fine. Clara brought over some vegetable stew; I called your Dad to let him know the jury's out, and here I am. I didn't get your things yet . . . I thought I'd do it on the way out."

"Look in the smallest zipper compartment, okay? It's for you. Again. For keeps this time."

Leah questioned her with a tilt of her head, but Allie only said, "Just get it."

Allie looked tired beyond the way the orange jail clothes jaundiced her skin. She hooked a short curl that had bobbed into her sight line back behind her ear. It was still startling to Leah that her daughter could look so transformed, as if all that hair were a coat she'd just, finally, taken off. "I feel like we need to talk about it," Allie said, "but I don't know what I want to say."

"That's okay, honey," Leah said. "I feel the same way. Like we could analyze every word of the trial and still not know where we've come out. But you handled yourself so . . . honestly, on the stand. Some of them have to have heard you." The phone receiver felt sticky in her hand tonight, sweaty, as if too many people had used it.

"That's not exactly what I mean. I'm talking about what I've done. To you. And to my daughter. How sorry I am."

Leah couldn't answer. The words were all in her chest, but none would line up in the right order, into forgiveness and asking forgiveness in turn. How ordinary, how trite her complaints about Allie had been back then. All the times she and Cory had commiserated about daughters, all she'd really wanted was this sense of connection, even communion, with Allie. Alyssa. Well, she had it now. At unfathomable price. How large an ingredient had her needs, her expectations, been in this dish of pain?

Chapter Twenty-Two

Leah put her hand up, fingers spread, on the glass between them. Allie matched it with her own on her side. Both of them had tears glazing their eyes and cheeks.

"I'm so sorry I hurt you," Leah whispered. Then she put the receiver down, let the tears find their course, and put the other hand up against the glass. Allie matched that, too.

Allie just shook her head no, and Leah read her lips. "It's all right."

"I love you," Allie mouthed.

"And I love you."

It happened at night. It would.

Returning from the courthouse to the jail every evening, wearing her orange suit and appearing like any other white woman in the General Population unit, she'd felt it, the menacing shift in the currents when the transport officers walked her through the parted steel doors and unchained her. Sometimes, waiting at the computer station for the housing officers to record her return, the officers laughed, teased even, while she dangled like bait from a line about to break. The officers didn't sense the molecules unsettling themselves, lowering semaphores in the wake of the deliberate passes made by Jack-o-Lantern and her gang, but Alyssa did.

Head down, she rubbed the imprint of chains from her wrists and climbed the stairs to her cell, waiting. After Leah's visit, with two hours left to lockdown, she gathered her towel and her shrinking bar of soap and the small bottle of shampoo that lasted twice as long now that her hair was cut short. She walked the balcony skirting the open floor of the pod and looked down at the table where Joey was arm wrestling with Serafina, new to GP last week. Serafina had done something to her husband with a razor blade which Alyssa hadn't wanted to hear about, not after the first few details, but Joey did. Grown lonely with Alyssa gone, he'd become Serafina's mentor. Alyssa had graduated, anyway. *She* was going on to prison. If she'd wanted, if her tenure in jail weren't about to end, she could have taken Serafina under her own wing, shown her the ropes, set her up for a survival she didn't ask for herself.

Since the long string of days in court, her daily absences lengthened by strip searches and transport to and from at either end, Alyssa was thankful that Joey had withdrawn, transferred allegiances. It would make it easier when she went to wherever she was going to go. Joey wasn't headed for prison; he'd do two months at the honor farm and be back on the streets. Maybe he'd keep up with his reading practice; maybe he wouldn't. He'd said he would, anyway, and she'd made him a list of books he could find at the library. Just ask, she'd told him, his face falling when she described the electronic card catalogue, see how easy it would be to find whatever he wanted. *Just ask for help.*

She could have asked for help, she thought when she reached the shower room. She pulled the barrettes from her hair, studying her face while she rubbed her scalp where the clips had pinched it sore. At six or seven years old, with her hair in braids, she'd felt the same release at the end of each day, as if her loosened hair were a costume she was donning like pajamas, a garment that allowed her to say whatever it was she needed to say. Sometimes Gran, usually Leah, would pull off the elastic baubles and comb the plaits out, first with her fingers, then with the soft brush Gran ordered special from Avon just for her. *Don't stop*, she'd tell her mother when the stroking bristles slowed and the mesmerizing rhythm of touch warmed her to her toes, *don't stop brushing.*

She could have asked for help. If she'd asked for help—

The door to the shower room whispered open, shut.

"Little Miss Rich Bitch," Jack-o-Lantern hissed, sliding to one side of her while her ally, the pair of pocked arms, thready muscles flexing, slipped to the other. Jack-o-Lantern picked up the clips Alyssa had rested on the shallow counter of the sink. "All prissied up, gonna get out of here." She clipped the barrettes into her own hair, scraping her bangs back from her forehead.

Chapter Twenty-Two

The voice above the arms chuckled, crossed the chest of their matron. "You look like shit, you wear your hair like that."

"Somebody looks like shit ... thinks she's gonna walk outa here without a goodbye." Jack-o-Lantern stroked the back of Alyssa's head, took up a thick handful of hair and tightened it, rolling it into her fist. "Say you look like shit, girl."

Alyssa let her head roll back against the pull of hair, kept her eyes open, her mouth shut.

"Say it! Say it, baby killer." A quick jerk. Alyssa tripped backward, stumbled against the arms, which pushed her into Jack-o-Lantern.

"No."

"Say it!" This time it was faster, the back forth pass between the hard hands. Jack-o-Lantern tore her hand from Alyssa's hair. "Say what I told you!"

"No."

Then she was down on her knees, Jack-o-Lantern's gap-toothed grin so close to her face Alyssa could smell the bad teeth, the raw, roiling scent of vengeance. "One more chance ... you're gonna say it."

"No."

Ostrom stopped it. Ostrom who'd never before batted an eye when she'd monitored Alyssa's strip searches and seen the fist-sized bruises on her belly, the scabby welts on her arms without once opening her mouth. Ostrom pulled off Jack-o-Lantern and passed her to the young officer, the new one. She knelt by Alyssa and told her not to move, to wait on her back until the nurse arrived and pushed the gurney into the crowded shower room. Together they rolled Alyssa onto it and trollied her toward the elevator.

It was Ostrom who said to her, after picking up Alyssa's slippers from the floor and nestling them against her side with her jailhouse comb and her used-up sliver of soap, "I'll be sure you get your other things, Staton. I'll be sure it's written up right in the incident report

355

how they did you." She felt Ostrom tap her shoulder, twice. "We're gonna keep you in sheltered, now. You done your time here."

Even with the taping on her ribs, the skirt to the brown suit hung on her waist when, for the last time, she changed her clothes in preparation for the courtroom. She could have taken the Darvon the jailhouse nurse had given her; she had the envelope of white capsules in her pocket. But she chose instead the pain of every breath, the anguished intake reminding her of the flesh and bone and blood joining her until her own death to the nameless baby lying beneath a single line, a day marking birth and death, in the Peniel Point Cemetery. Leah had told her: at the burial, Clara had given the baby a dreamcatcher, Leah, her prayer. Alyssa had given nothing, less than nothing.

The hills holding the cemetery would be brown now, but greening in the coming fall, lush through winter and spring. She would go there when she could, after today, if she ever got out. She would fill her arms with flowers—blooms whose names would fall like kisses, like caresses—sweet pea, daisy, bluebell, iris, marigold, lily, dahlia, *alyssum*. She would carpet the grave with blossoms whose petals would fall against the soil like a mother's touch at the end of day. And she would carry a name to her baby, a single word to invoke the words of a prayer for mercy for her daughter and mother, for herself. She and Leah would stand at the grave where Leah said the floating sky and the solid earth and the distant bay made a holy place, and together they would name her baby. Above the date, chiseled in white marble, in memory. *Grace.*

She slipped on the cream-colored blouse, considered the jacket and decided, no. She pulled her hair high into Leah's clip, a black and beige barrette her mother had worn once to testify and would never want to wear again. She straightened her shoulders, draped the jacket across her arm. With her belt of pain bracing her, girding her, she opened the door.

Chapter Twenty-Two

As she followed Jeffrey across the courtroom to their table, Dennis called to her. "Alyssa!"

The bailiff stepped forward, motioned to Dennis to back off, pipe down. Dennis bridled and kept moving, stepped up to the gate separating the bench from the spectator seats. "Lyssa, honey!" Alyssa turned to him. He caught her in his long reach, pulled her against him. "What?" he said as the bailiff pulled her back. "Lyssa, I—"

Her jacket dropped to the floor. Jeff bent to pick it up, then turned her around to face the bench. She heard the bailiff's loud warning, Dennis's retort: "She's my daughter, goddammit! Get your hands off!" Then Leah's voice, low and full, "Don't, Dennis please, not now."

Jeff stroked her back, his fingers hesitating on the thick tape, her too-small penance. "Sit down, Alyssa," he told her, watching her face. He sat down too, finally, and templed his fingers. Waiting.

Judge Franklin, robes flapping, strode to his bench. The jury last, solemn and weary-looking, their duty nearly over. She'd violated them, too, made them listen to a story they, thinking of their own children and grandchildren, would never have chosen to hear. There were no words she could invent to use in apology to them, no way to tell them to forget the story forced on them, to resume their lives and keep living as though their civic duty hadn't transformed them, every face masked by an alteration she had caused. Jeff had told her, *they're wiser than you think, those twelve people.* Alyssa believed it possible that wisdom, confounded, had recused itself from the courtroom.

Jeffrey opened his briefcase. Unnecessary, Alyssa knew. Nothing inside any briefcase on earth could change what was coming. But the rubber alligator was there, coiled into the corner. Jeff made sure she saw it, then closed the lid, latching the briefcase, resting it beneath their table, its glossy surface uncluttered by tablets or folders. "Whatever they say," Jeff said, "whatever you feel right now, there are still things worth doing in this world." He hesitated. His face colored. It was *him*, Alyssa thought. *He liked me all along.* In orange or brown, beyond the psychiatrists and the testimony, in the tube or in the courthouse, *he liked me.* "I'm counting on you to find those things, Alyssa. You find them, the alligator's yours."

He took her hand when the court was called to order. When Judge Franklin asked the defendant to rise, Jeff kept her hand in his until they stood and squared themselves to the bench. They waited.

"Ladies and Gentlemen of the jury, have you reached a verdict?"

A young woman stood. Brown hair cropped short like a boy's, dark, long dress, flowing to the floor. A priestess. "We have, your honor."

"Will you read the verdict for the court, please."

"Yes, sir." She held a short sheet of paper, looked to the jurors on her right and left, sighed, and began to read in a girl's voice, lilting and pure.

"On the count of murder in the first degree, we find the defendant . . . not guilty." Leah's gasp, Clara's soft murmur. Jeff's shoulder brushing hers.

"On the count of murder in the second degree, we find the defendant . . . not guilty." The reporters' grumbles now, spreading discontent. They'd lost their headlines. There was no more front-page story.

"On the count of manslaughter, we find the defendant, Alyssa Pacey Staton . . . guilty."

Jeff hugged her, briefly. Not a celebration, an affirmation. She felt a hand, Leah's, on her shoulder, a quick squeeze. Dennis' *thank god.*

The jury looked at Alyssa's face now, signaling to her they believed her when she'd said she'd lost her soul one night in a BART station. They had not found the premeditating, maliciously selfish woman Marcelle had urged them to find, and they wanted Alyssa to know. Judge Franklin was explaining to the court he would recess to chambers to determine the penalty as agreed upon by pretrial motion, but Alyssa wasn't listening. She watched the jurors, joined eyes with every one of them.

Wisdom. Jeff had counted on it.

Chapter Twenty-Two

She turned to Leah. Her mother waited, silent amidst the growing white noise of the courtroom, her head bowed, one hand raised to her breast.

"Mama?" Alyssa whispered, ignoring the bailiff who stood on guard, ready to part them if they were to commit the crime of touching, as if love were against the law. "Mom?"

Leah looked up, tears tracking her cheeks. She dropped the chain of the necklace she'd held like a rosary—the silver chain, the jade pendant—and it fell against her breast.

"Alyssa."

"Mom."

"We'll make it, Allie. We'll make it."

ACKNOWLEDGMENTS

Alan de Courcy provided inestimable research support, technological help through computer and fax glitches, and insightful early comments on the manuscript. Any writer knows the unquantifiable but indispensable value of true spousal support, and Alan's to Lynne Hugo has been unwavering. Both of us thank him from our hearts.

We have relied on the kindness of strangers, family, and friends. Of special significance:

Scott Jackson, a painter in Philadelphia, gave with great generosity of his time and expertise, providing detailed information about myriad aspects of painting, as well as photographs of his studio and surroundings.

Jeff Tuttle and Gerald Osmer, Attorneys at Law and Defenders of the Public, gave us transcripts, opinions, and advice regarding legal matters, as did Evan Fogelman, an attorney in Dallas, Texas.

Brooke Hugo de Courcy served as consultant regarding contemporary college life and located instances of neonaticide media coverage. Adria Tuttle Villegas assisted us with specific details about teen music, clothing, and language.

Librarians Paul Jenkins at The College of Mount St. Joseph in Cincinnati, Ohio, and Jan Mullen and Jun Wang of Goleman Library at San Joaquin Delta College in Stockton, California, identified precious research sources for us.

Doris Scanlon, Inmate Programs and Services Director, gave an afternoon of her time and wisdom at the San Joaquin County Jail in Stockton, California. Dr. Sally A. Fitterer, Pathologist, answered specific questions regarding

Acknowledgments

unattended births. James P. Simcoe, M.D., of Fairfield, Ohio, provided medical information regarding newborn infants.

Professor Andrea Tuttle Kornbluh, Raymond Walters College, Cincinnati, Ohio, provided us with research and trial transcripts.

Quotes from Radiohead's "I'm a Creep" are used permission of Warner Bros. Publications, Inc. All rights reserved.

"The Water is Wide" is an American folk song.

Rhonda Rupel of Oxford, Ohio, contributed a meticulous proofreading of the final manuscript.

J. C. Rupel and the staff of the Oxford Copy Shop in Oxford, Ohio, gave clerical support.

Finally, Bud Johns, the Senior Editor of Synergistic Press in San Francisco, California, saw an important story where no other publisher dared, and then did what a real editor does: helped us to tell our story better.

WORKS CONSULTED

Bonnet, Catherine. "Adoption at Birth: Prevention Against Abandonment or Neonaticide." *Child Abuse and Neglect* 1991 : 301–311.

Begley, Sharon. "The Nursery's Littlest Victims." *Newsweek* 22 Sept. 1997: 72–73.

Binswanger, C. K. "A Secret Birth, A Baby's Death." *Glamour* Sept. 1997: 302.

Carlson, Margaret. "Prom Nightmare." *Time* 23 June 1997: 20.

Eggington, Joyce. *From Cradle to Grave: The Short Lives and Strange Deaths of MaryBeth Tinning's Nine Children.* New York: William Morrow & Company, 1989.

Diagnostic and Statistical Manual of Mental Disorders. Washington, DC: American Psychiatric Association, 1994.

Fields-Meyer, Thomas, Ron Arias, Cynthia Wang, and Maria Eftimiades. "Dance Macabre." *People* 10 November 1997: 147–150.

Grigg, William Norman. "License to Kill." *The New American* 19 Jan. 1998: 3–11.

Howard, James. "New Explanation of Postpartum Depression & Psychosis." Posted by James Howard on August 15, 1997.

Kantrowitz, Barbara. "Cradles to Coffins." *Newsweek* 7 July 1997: 42–44.

Kerwin, Barbara. *The Mad, the Bad, and the Innocent.* New York: Little Brown & Company, 1997.

Marks, Philip A. and William Seeman. *The Actuarial Description of Abnormal Personality.* Baltimore: The Williams and Williams Co., 1963.

Moore, Kelly. *Deadly Medicine.* New York: St. Martin's Press, 1988.

Works Consulted

Oberman, Michelle. "Mothers Who Kill: Coming to Terms with Modern American Infanticide." *American Criminal Law Review* 34 (1996) : 1–100.

Opinion on the Appeal of People and C., Respondent, v. Stephanie Wernick, Appellant. November 21, 1996.

Opinion on the Appeal of People, Plaintiff and Appellant, v. Scott Eric Flores, Defendant and Respondent. June 12, 1970.

Opinion on the Appeal of Robert Harrison Keeler, Petitioner, v. the Superior Court of Amador County. June 12, 1970.

Opinion on the Appeal of the United States of America, Appellee, v. Martha L. Woods, Appellant. May 9, 1973.

Pawling, G. Patrick. "The Prom Mom: 'Seems Pretty Normal to Me'." *Time* 29 December 1997: 128.

Pinker, Steven. "Why They Kill Their Newborns." *The New York Times Magazine* 2 November 1997: 52–54.

Piers, Maria. *Infanticide*. New York: Norton: 1978.

Reece, Laura E. "Mothers Who Kill: Postpartum Disorders and Criminal Infanticide." *UCLA Law Review* 38 (1996) : 699–757.

"Susan Smith, A Modern Mother: Reflections on the Destiny of Children at the End of Childhood." *Critical Quarterly* 39 1997 : 28–42.

The Susan Smith Trial Transcripts, July, 1995.

Welsh, George Schlager and W. Grant Dahlstrom. *Basic Readings on the MMPI in Psychology and Medicine*. Minneapolis: University of Minnesota, 1956.